Praise for *Hello, Transcriber*

"As poetic as it is suspenseful." —Megan Collins

"Hannah Morrissey's precise, lyrical prose; chilling sense of atmosphere; and talent for crafting sexual tension just as twisted as the central crime make her haunting debut a unique and exciting new entry in the contemporary crime genre." —Layne Fargo

"A dark, highly atmospheric, somber edge-of-your-seat thriller."

—*Mystery and Suspense Magazine*

"*Hello, Transcriber* is a dark, atmospheric, and compelling debut by a unique talent. I was sucked in immediately and could think of little else until the last page."

—C. J. Box, #1 *New York Times* bestselling author

"Former police transcriber Morrissey brings her expertise to this suspenseful debut. . . . Will appeal to fans of Jess Lourey's atmospheric books." —*Library Journal* (starred review)

"A moody, unsettling debut novel." —*The Washington Post*

(Best Thrillers and Mysteries of November 2021)

"*Hello, Transcriber* is a shudder-inducing series kickoff." —*BookPage*

"Morrissey is a psychologically attentive writer who captures the bristly tension between longtime locals and newcomers."

—*Shelf Awareness*

"An atmospheric suspense debut [with an] intriguing premise."

—*Kirkus Reviews*

"*Hello, Transcriber* is a perfect bridge between more traditional procedural-focused crime fiction and psychological suspense, all wrapped up in a dark, gritty atmosphere." —*Crime by the Book*

"A solid debut . . . This mystery largely succeeds thanks to its strong sense of place and realistically flawed heroine. Morrissey is off to a promising start." —*Publishers Weekly*

HELLO, TRANSCRIBER

HANNAH MORRISSEY

MINOTAUR BOOKS
NEW YORK

This is a work of fiction. All of the characters, organizations, and events portrayed in this novel are either products of the author's imagination or are used fictitiously.

Published in the United States by Minotaur Books, an imprint of St. Martin's Publishing Group

HELLO, TRANSCRIBER. Copyright © 2021 by Hannah Morrissey. All rights reserved.
Printed in the United States of America. For information, address St. Martin's Publishing Group, 120 Broadway, New York, NY 10271.

www.minotaurbooks.com

Designed by Omar Chapa

The Library of Congress has cataloged the hardcover edition as follows:

Names: Morrissey, Hannah, author.
Title: Hello, Transcriber / Hannah Morrissey.
Description: First edition. | New York : Minotaur Books, 2021.
Identifiers: LCCN 2021021935 | ISBN 9781250795953 (hardcover) |
ISBN 9781250795960 (ebook)
Subjects: GSAFD: Mystery fiction. | Suspense fiction. | LCGFT: Detective and
mystery fiction. | Thrillers (Fiction) | Novels.
Classification: LCC PS3613.O777928 H45 2021 | DDC 813/.6—dc23
LC record available at https://lccn.loc.gov/2021021935

ISBN 978-1-250-84741-6 (trade paperback)

Our books may be purchased in bulk for promotional, educational, or business use. Please contact your local bookseller or the Macmillan Corporate and Premium Sales Department at 1-800-221-7945, extension 5442, or by email at MacmillanSpecialMarkets@macmillan.com.

First Minotaur Books Trade Paperback Edition: 2022

10 9 8 7 6 5 4 3 2 1

To Hanns. You had me at "Hello, Transcriber."

HELLO, TRANSCRIBER

1.

FRIDAY

I shouldn't be here.

It's stark daylight. The evergreens cut sharp silhouettes, arrowheads piercing a pearl sky. Someone will see the woman standing on Forge Bridge and they'll call the police or try to save me themselves.

No, they won't. This is Black Harbor, a purgatory where people mind their own. I could scream bloody murder, and it's not that no one would hear me—someone probably would—but they would write me off, convince themselves that I'm just a rabbit being eaten by a hawk or something.

My heel catches in a knot in a railroad tie. My hands slam on the corroded iron tracks. The skin on my palms tears, the metal like dry ice. Standing back up, I slip off my pumps and set them aside. In my gossamer-thin nylons, I edge toward the middle. It's the first time I've been here in almost ten months. It feels wrong and yet a little bit like coming home. I know this place. The trees with their wet, charred-looking trunks; the smell of fish scales and soil; the coal-blackened bridge that looks like the exoskeleton from some prehistoric beetle, stretching from bank to bank.

Coldness pricks the soles of my feet. I'm still wearing the clothes from my interview earlier this morning.

You'll have problems here, they told me.

They were a trio that operated as one: a man whose mustache resembled a wire brush my dad would use to scrape coagulated oil off his workbench, and two women; one was fox-faced and squashy, the other wore her black hair pulled into a tight bun and teal, bullet-shaped earrings.

Barely an hour ago, I sat at a large pine table in a nondescript room, wearing the only blazer I own. The lake effect punched through the cement walls, slithered through the seal of the lone window. I wondered if the room was ever used as an office, or reserved solely for interviews, because what would anyone do in there besides slowly go crazy?

When the door opened, I watched them filter in like smoke. My chair screeched as I stood to shake each of their hands. I smoothed my skirt as I sat back down, brushing off a sliver of chewed fingernail.

They stared at me, their clinical smiles simultaneously out of place and yet perfectly in consensus. The man spoke on behalf of all three of them as though they were a modern-day Greek chorus. They asked where I'm from.

"Not here," I said.

The vulpine lady's smile deepened, a pair of parentheses framing her lurid red lips.

"Where is home?" the man asked.

H-O-M-E. I typed the word on my lap, beneath the table where they couldn't see. It's a habit I picked up somewhere along the way of wanting to be a writer, this compulsion of secretly transcribing conversations. I found liberation in letting my fingertips dance, unbridled by the fear of anyone ever reading the words they spelled.

The man gave me a measured look over the rims of his glasses and I wondered if he could see my fingers moving after all, the tendons in my forearms faintly twitching. Perhaps this was the behavior people noticed when they diagnosed me as strange.

Home. That was a thought. Home was a dirt road that wended its way through a field of oats and barley to a house at the edge of the woods. Home was my dad's rusted pickup truck, the bed of which I would lie in and stare up at the stars on warm summer nights. Home was the apple orchard behind the house and a maze of Dad's wood carvings—trees and railroad ties whose armor had been sculpted away to reveal the spirits within: wolves, owls, wise men. Home was the spruce tree tattooed on the back of my arm, just above my elbow, the one I always kept covered when visiting Tommy's parents.

Home was, "Three hours north."

They looked impressed, as though I'd walked the 160 miles to get here. "What brings you to Black Harbor?"

"The lake," I said, and explained that my husband is an aquatic ecologist. He was hired by the City two years ago because the lake was, and still is, devouring the shoreline. Every other day, the news chronicles people's yards precariously disappearing. All those sediments and landscaping chemicals can't be doing the aquatic ecosystem any favors.

The two ladies shared a smile, and I reminded myself that they had no idea what it was like up north, where jobs are scarcer than striking oil.

The man spoke again. "If you choose to accept this position, Mrs. Greenlee, everything you type must be treated with the utmost confidentiality. You can't tell your best friends, your family, even your husband."

"I'm good at keeping secrets," I said.

"Your social life will suffer." Another warning.

"What social life?"

They laughed like I was being ironic. The man leaned back in his chair, arms crossed over his stomach. His tie scrunched to the side, revealing a coffee stain he'd no doubt tried to hide.

"This job is violent and graphic in nature. You'll have to listen to accounts of things that are . . . traumatic . . . to say the least. It's not for everyone."

"Is anything?" It was the first time I'd asked a question instead of answering them.

He grinned, his lips peeling away from his teeth. "You're a clever one, Mrs. Greenlee."

There it was again. I'd seen it in print like on junk mail and bills, but it wasn't often that I heard it spoken aloud: *Mrs.* How it makes one sound hideously domesticated, an unforgivable slaughtering of its better, more scandalous-sounding honorific, *Mistress*. Now, that was something I could get on board with.

I tried to smile back while I kneaded my hands in my lap, twisting my wedding band. The cold made it so loose.

I needed this job. And I actually wanted it, too. At least it was interesting, and it paid better than any of the others I'd interviewed for. As it turned out, jobs weren't exactly plentiful in these parts, either. A hard truth I learned pretty quick after quitting the bookstore with nothing else lined up. Not my finest moment.

"It's a shame putting you on nights." The man chuckled. "Young kid like you. You'll never see the light of day again."

The ladies laughed, too.

"Irregardless, we could always check with the other transcriber and see if she wants to stay on the night shift. Some people like it."

My insides wilted at his use of *irregardless*. "No, I'll take it."

He leaned toward me, and I got the feeling that the confidentiality agreement had already started. "Forgive me for saying this, Mrs. Greenlee, but you're very pretty."

I looked at the women. They just stared like they had since the second they'd walked in.

"You'll have problems here," he promised, and then slid me the pen to sign the contract.

It's too fresh to even have been filed away, and yet the memory seems from another lifetime. The reality, though, is that I've just been hired as the new police transcriber and have two days to put myself together, a task that shouldn't involve edging my way toward the middle of Forge Bridge.

Ever since Forge Fuels closed nearly fifteen years ago, resulting in practically everyone within a fifty-mile radius of Black Harbor losing their jobs, there's been a localized epidemic of people jumping from the bridge—including the fuel company's former CEO. That's when Black Harbor really took a shit, as our neighbor, Old Will, put it. A former maintenance man for the coal giant, his hands are all jacked up from thirty years of turning wrenches. Now, he eats pain pills with his bacon every morning.

My discovery of the bridge had been an accident. Shortly after we moved to Black Harbor, I took to the running trail in the woods across from the duplex Tommy and I split with Old Will and his son. The path stretches and winds through the entire city, but I keep to a five-mile strip that spits me out at Forge Bridge. It called to me like a siren that day, and has every day since. I was already halfway across when I suddenly felt its railroad ties beneath my feet, and I stared for the first time into the cruel black below. Everything went silent, then, as the river demanded something of me. Just one piece. A tribute in exchange for it letting me remain above its obsidian surface.

I'd given it the only thing I could spare from my person, a corded bracelet with my name spelled in yellow and emerald beads. A gift from our honeymoon from a man who walked the shore selling conch shells. Untying it had felt ceremonious. My skin burned where the hemp cord had begun to chafe. I tossed it and watched it twist and writhe like a worm falling from a hook. Then it hit the water and disappeared into the pitch-black water.

I'd smiled afterward. I did. I remember I stood there with the mist soaking my hair, my red long-sleeve clinging to my body. Anyone else might have cried, but the euphoria that flooded my veins was almost too much. It was a rush of accomplishment similar to typing a period at the end of a perfect string of words, a unique thought that existed in print because of me. There is truth, I think, in writers desiring immortality—not for ourselves, necessarily, but for our words, our thoughts, our ideas to live on long after we're gone. We are addicts, forever chasing the impossible dream, and walking off the bridge—away from its pull—offers a glimpse of it, this ability to cheat death.

The next time I visited, I surrendered a glass shamrock my mother had given to me before she left. Taking it from my book crate had felt like stealing from myself. When I stood on the weather-soaked ties preparing to toss it, I touched it to my lips, not to kiss it but to feel the warmth left by my own hand, perhaps to prove that I am alive and that the items I relinquish to the water never were.

Sometimes I wonder what's become of the things I've given. I like to imagine they're rinsed clean and moving on to a better place, but a small part of me knows that they're probably wedged between slick, slimy river rocks, stuck in Black Harbor forever. I wonder about the other things they must encounter—fishing lures and beer cans, muskellunge and minnows, bodies before they pop up to the surface.

My scarf rips free of my jacket as though volunteering to be the next tribute, but the thought of the chill biting at my neck dissuades me. Mylar crinkles in the same wind that rocks me backward, deflated foil balloons tugging at rain-washed, curling ribbon, their length stripped of pigment by the elements and punctuated with broken ends, like an em dash at the end of an unfinished sentence. Below them, a teddy bear leans against a pole, its lavender fur matted and raindrops glistening on its button eyes. Minding my steps, I pick it up and press it to my chest, my chin resting on its plush, wet head. It smells like rain and noxious air and a little bit sweet like maple.

I take a breath and listen as the air whistles through my nose. I can hear the river beckoning me to come closer. Looking down, I watch the river lap against large, snow-encrusted rocks—a monster sucking clean the bones of its prey.

It isn't fair that the bear is here, in Black Harbor. It could have been anywhere, belonged to anyone who wouldn't have abandoned it to the wind and the rain and the toxicity that flees the rails of the bridge, fine black spores like gunpowder infecting the air we all breathe, filling all the cracks and fissures of the city. It coalesces to create a gritty film over the place that not only keeps decent people just racing past on the highway but attracts criminals and seedy characters who need somewhere to hide.

I look at my pumps leaning cockeyed against the track. Do they say that here, *cockeyed*? Or is that another *up north* word I brought with me? Raindrops glisten and slide down their plastic sides. I'll need them for work. I start Monday.

Jump, whispers the river. Its voice is a chorus all smashed together; but unlike the three people I met earlier, I can discern each individual fighting to be heard. Voices climb on top of one another, like bodies grappling, trying to claw their way out of the water. They're lost forever, all those people who jumped. They'll never leave Black Harbor. Instead, their voices will lace the river, calling to souls like mine to join them in their misery.

My imagination puts me there, next to him, the body I saw one cold April morning. His face was bloated beyond recognition, eyes milky like roe. Dark hair clung to his skull like kelp on the side of a boat's hull. In my mind, I am floating, staring up at the underbelly of

Forge Bridge, at the woman who stands barefoot on the railroad ties, wondering what it would feel like to jump. The corpse and I bump gently against each other like buoys whose anchors are sunk too close in the muck.

I shake the dark fantasy from my head. I'm still up here. Not down there. There's no dead body in the water, either. Not today. A shiver trickles down my spine. The hair on the back of my neck stands on end. My fingertips are too frozen to feel the bitter bite of the air as I surrender the teddy bear and watch as it falls end over end, finally splashing facedown. I will it to go on and be free. To ride the current out of Black Harbor and wash up anywhere but here. But it just spins in a lazy circle, caught in a relentless whirlpool, and the truth hits me as cold and hard as though I am the one who hit the water. One of these days, I'll have nothing left to give but myself.

2.

ONE WEEK LATER

There's a row of blue apartments across the street. They're almost lost to a beryl-colored sky; their peaks, trimmed with white, are all that separate them. They look like the whitecaps on Lake Michigan, the kind that slam into the half-sunk pier and pull children and drunks under. The top left window is empty. A trash bag is duct-taped over the hole, sucking in and out like a diaphragm. Even from where I sit, inside a narrow office easily thirty yards away, I can see the glass ground to powder on the sidewalk below, mixed with snow and salt and cocaine. Probably fentanyl, too. Nobody cuts anything without it these days.

Good job security for me.

There are four front entrances, each marked with a crimson door. On the far left beneath the broken window, someone wearing a gold hoodie sits slumped on the crumbling concrete steps. Drunk or stoned or dead, maybe. He doesn't seem to notice the black plastic bag that rolls by like a tumbleweed, the one I recognize as the kind my husband brings home after a visit to the corner store. It skips languidly over the salt-encrusted asphalt, wandering past black-and-white police SUVs that are parked while their windshields defrost. Finally, it floats out of view, probably to catch on a branch or a chain-link fence or the grille of an old Crown Vic.

That was the first thing I noticed about Black Harbor after we moved here: the bags.

The scene outside my window is a still life I could get lost in all morning: the diaphanous plastic bag tumbling past in the foreground, a row of apartments like dilapidated dollhouses in the middle, and in the background Forge Bridge half-obscured by haze and lying like a predator in wait. But, the reports won't type themselves, as Mona says. Pressing down on the foot pedal, I listen to the soft static that precedes a man's voice.

"Hello, Transcriber, this is Investigator Rowe of the Black Harbor Police Department, payroll number 7122, phoning in a supplemental report for a death investigation. Summary's been completed, and names have already been added to the form. What follows is the, uh, narrative.

"On January 15, comma, at approximately 0536 hours, comma, I received a phone call from Lieutenant Mobeck of the Black Harbor Police Department advising me to respond to the area of Fulton Street and Forge Avenue for a report of a possible suicide, period."

My fingertips fly over the keyboard like raindrops pattering against a windshield. As I type, I envision Investigator Rowe—tall, dark-haired, five o'clock shadow, Benjamin Bratt–type character—in a black wool coat, his breath a cloud in front of him and his polished Dockers crunching on old snow as he walks down the slope of the riverbank to meet the corpse that's been pulled ashore.

"Based on Medical Examiner Winthorp's examinations, comma, the victim had been deceased for approximately three days, comma, due to the color of the skin and the buoyancy of the body . . ."

The color of the skin is something upon which I ruminate. Here, tucked away in the little terrarium-like office, I stare at the frost on the window. I examine it with intention, analyzing how I would write about it: thousands, if not millions, of crystals blooming and fracturing to give the glass the illusion of being shattered; the pearlish hairs of a dandelion seed having blossomed into tiny, ethereal umbrellas, frozen in mid-float; dendrites beneath a cold corpse's skin. Every fractal fits so perfectly together to create one single sheet of frost so delicate a whisper could obliterate it.

I've seen skin like that before. The memory is enough to make me rip my hands away from the keyboard. I curl my fingers. My knuckles glow white as the peaks of the apartment building as I will myself to stop remembering the way the wet, half-frozen soil felt pushed beneath my nails when I scrambled up the hillside all those months ago.

The window is thinly coated with aluminum. We can see out. But no one can see in. Mona compared it to a two-way mirror. "It protects us from the public eye—you might have noticed we're not exactly in Mayberry here—and stops us from baking in the sun, the two times a year it comes around."

I take a breath, my gaze sliding over my shoulder at Mona, now, who appears enmeshed in her querying at the portal behind me. Scooting my chair a few inches backward, I open the bottom tray of the industrial printer and remove a sheet of paper. Mona turns, catches my eye, and smiles. I wish we could be more than temporary office mates. I've been given only a week to train with her, which means that after today, I'm on my own. Ten-hour shifts Sunday night through Thursday morning. Sink or swim. Mona's officially moving to days, Wednesday through Saturday. We'll see each other in passing on Wednesday and Thursday mornings, but other than that, we fly solo.

I smile back. Turning around again, I fold the paper in half so it could easily fit betwixt the pages of a book, and write: *frost on the window—crystals blooming and fracturing . . . dendrites.*

I resume typing, listening to Rowe describe the deceased party as a white male possibly in his forties; approximately 6'0", 250 pounds. Blurred, bluish tattoos are visible on his forearms as he was just wearing jeans and a soiled white T-shirt. A pilled Forge Fuels embroidered pullover was discarded on the bridge as well as the contents of his pockets—a wallet containing his identification and credit cards, a scratch-off ticket, and a suicide note.

"I didn't think it was high enough to kill yourself," I said the other day when Mona finished typing up a report similar to the one I'm working on now.

"The water's only six feet deep underneath, Fargo. Hitting the bottom is like hitting a fuckin' slab of cement."

She's been calling me Fargo since Monday, when on my guided tour, Liv, the pretty redhead from the Records Department, suggested I sound like the characters from the eponymous movie. She'd even thrown in a few *yahs*, *heys*, and *youbetchas* for her impression of me, though for the record, I've never, in all of my twenty-six years, uttered a *youbetcha*.

"It's how you say your 'o's'," Liv explained matter-of-factly. "Say boat."

"Boat," I said, and she and Mona both laughed at an accent I couldn't—and still can't—detect. It didn't help matters when I told them I come from a small town three hours north of here—and by small, I mean population less than two hundred.

Now, staring at my reflection in the portal to my right, I mouth the word *boat*.

I type everything Rowe says verbatim, only adding in punctuation where he forgets it and taking the liberty to separate blocks of text into paragraphs. It's interesting work, and certainly beats my previous—and thankless—job as the assistant manager of the community college bookstore, but it's not overtly creative. My fingertips twitch as I quell the urge to type my own words into the document instead of regurgitating his. The fact that I signed an oath never to compromise the authenticity of these reports always wins out. In writing, rules are meant to be broken. But this isn't writing, I remind myself. This is transcribing.

"The suicide note reads as follows. Transcriber, can you type this next part in italics? *The only way out is down*, period."

Rowe has some closing comments after the note, and forty-five minutes after I'd opened the job in my queue, I punch in my initials "HG" and the date under, "This concludes the investigation at this time."

I copy and paste his finished narrative into Onyx, the shared database, click *submit*, and send him a memo via the in-house messenger system.

"Damn, you really do have the fastest fingers in the Midwest." Mona spins around, mug of hot lemon water in hand. Her eyes look enlarged behind her spherical lenses, like someone who has spent a great deal of time in the dark, which she has. She had been the night-shift transcriber for eleven years when Beverly "up and died," as Mona so eloquently put it, and for the past six weeks, it's been just Mona taking on the world . . . until I came along.

I blush and stare at the foam earbuds I just set on the desk.

"Let me guess," she says as she pulls her knees up into her chest, proceeding to sit pretzel-legged in her office chair. The mandala-printed palazzo pants suit her. All she needs is a fuchsia crop top and she'd look like a genie. It hadn't surprised me when I learned she collects crystals in her free time. A spiral of hair—messy like a child's scribble—falls in front of her eyes. "Suicide."

"How'd you know?"

She takes a sip. Her glasses fog. "Morbid intuition. You develop a keen sense of it when you've been here as long as I have. Plus, we've had a few jumpers lately." The way she looks up when she says it suggests that "a few" means more than a few. "As you can see, I've fallen behind on my housekeeping."

I look over her shoulder at the open E-scribe queue with twelve hours' worth of dictation waiting to be typed. Suddenly, my phone buzzes beside my mouse pad. Tommy. He always texts when he leaves for work. I shoot him a quick response and give Mona my full attention again. "So, what are you working on?"

"Meh. Heroin overdose."

"Fatal?"

Mona scrunches her nose, shakes her head. "We used to have a lot more fatalities, but they've been pretty liberal with Narcan the past couple years."

"That's good . . ."

Mona scoffs. "Don't tell that to the Drug Unit guys."

There's a knock at the door. It's always open, but people knock on the door frame anyway to announce their presence. Must be a cop thing.

"Hey Andy!" Mona says with such excitement you'd think he came bearing a gift. "Perfect timing, Hazel just finished typing—"

"—my report. Damn, that's incredible. I just finish calling it in, head out to the Vine for a cup of coffee, and it's already done. Hey, I'm Andy Rowe, I work upstairs. Don't worry, I'm not a Drug Unit guy." He reaches over to shake my hand.

I try to be discreet as I look him up and down, comparing this bald, barrel-chested investigator to the one I'd envisioned walking down the riverbank at the crack of dawn. He looks more like an accountant than a cop, wearing a slate button-down and a tie whose pattern was inspired by a slide under a microscope. His badge is clipped to a walnut-colored belt that matches his loafers. No resemblance to Benjamin Bratt whatsoever.

"Hazel Greenlee," I offer. "Um . . . I work down here."

"Hazel's the new me, heyhowfastdoyoutypeagain?" Mona plucks the introduction right from my lips so abruptly that I begin to wonder if she's earning commission on them.

I shrink a little in embarrassment, yet obediently mumble the score that had displayed on my printout at the employment center. "111 words per minute."

"Shit," says Rowe. "And I thought I was pretty speedy with my hunt 'n' peck method." He mimes one-finger typing.

"All these jumpers," Mona says as nonchalantly as though talking about weather patterns, "it's starting to feel like 2010 again."

"Déjà vu," Rowe agrees. "Honestly, I think I should just pitch a tent on the riverbank so I can save my wife the agony of getting woken up at 3 a.m. every other night."

"Or you could just sit underneath the bridge in a kayak," Mona suggests. "I have one if you want to borrow it. We could limit people to jumping only on certain days, too. It'll be like the DMV: you can jump from the bridge only on the first and third Wednesday of every month."

"I take it he didn't have the winning ticket." Apparently, I'm so desperate to be included in the conversation that my tongue gets tangled in the rush to spit out the words. I clamp my mouth shut to prevent any more discommodious spillage.

"Lottery?" Mona asks.

"Oh." Rowe laughs. "The guy from this morning left his shit on the bridge and we found a scratch-off in his wallet."

"Was it scratched off?" I ask.

Rowe frowns. "No, it wasn't. Why?"

I shrug. "Who jumps off a bridge before checking to see if they won?"

"Da da dummmmm!" Mona sings in an ominous tone. "No wonder she's a writer."

My cheeks get hot and I wince. "Well . . . I write," I correct, because there is a difference. I wish now—and not for the first time—that I hadn't mentioned my aspirations of becoming a traditionally published writer to Mona. I'm normally much more closed off to people, and especially considering what happened with Elle just a few months ago, you'd think I'd learn. But then, humans are contradictions, and writers—or those of us who strive to be—are no different.

I let my gaze drift out the window again and see that the man in the gold hoodie is no longer sitting outside of the blue apartments. Well, we can eliminate him being dead, then.

"I told her she'll find no shortage of material here," Mona says to Rowe. "Speaking of, what's going on with that whole Dylan-Kole investigation? Is he coming back? Well, I know Dylan's *done-zo*, but—"

"You know how news works around here," Rowe says. "I swear, someone's out there actually shooting the messenger, 'cause we never know what the hell's going on."

Mona laughs, and as supporting evidence, she holds up the newspaper that's been sitting next to the printer and shows Rowe the headline: *Small City, Big City Crime*. "With how many shootings we type up, I don't doubt it. That's why you couldn't pay me to live anywhere near this hellhole." She takes a drink of her lemon water in a *that settles that* manner. From previous conversations, I know that Mona lives in a rural area forty minutes outside city limits. And to be honest, I wish I could say the same. Before moving here, my only exposure to Black Harbor was that it was once featured on an episode of *Gangs in America*.

I look at the sworn personnel roster on the wall near my computer. Earlier this week and per Mona's recommendation, I'd familiarized myself with all 216 names. There are some, now, that I can look at and know the voice that goes with. I can't say the same for faces. I think Rowe rounds out the handful of people I know by all three: name, voice, and appearance.

I don't remember ever seeing anyone named Dylan on the list. But Kole is familiar. I find him about two-thirds of the way down in the second column: #6186 INV KOLE, NIKOLAI.

"How long you think Kole will be suspended for?" Mona asks.

Rowe shrugs. "What's it been, six months? Who knows, Kole may not come back at all. Damn shame about Dylan."

Mona and Rowe both fall quiet, then, observing a moment of silence for Investigator Dylan, who, by the sounds of it, was fired. I'm about to ask what for, when Mona scoots my way and hands me a blue pen. "Here, Fargo. Cross out Kole's name, would you? So I remember to print a new list. Gotta add some newbies, anyway, too."

"You're sure he won't be back?" I pause with the pen hovering over his name.

Mona tilts her head to regard me quizzically. "Listen, Fargo. No one gets suspended for shit around here. You could literally throw someone in a woodchipper and get a week's paid vacation. Whatever Kole did to warrant a suspension this long . . . Trust me, he's as good as gone."

I look at the fresh pen strike I've just drawn. If there's a way to forget about someone, this isn't it.

Rowe's phone rings. He answers it. "Hello. Yep. Mm. OK. I'll be right there. You want Riley, too? OK, see you then." The conversation is over in four seconds. He slides the phone back into his jacket pocket and after welcoming me to the BHPD, bids us both farewell and walks out the side exit of the building.

Now that Rowe's not standing in front of it, I read the clock on the wall above Mona's desk. 7:48 a.m.

All that excitement and it isn't even eight o'clock, yet. The counter won't open for another twelve minutes, and then the parking lot will become congested with cars pulling in and out, their tires crunching on old snow as the citizens of Black Harbor hurry inside to argue their parking tickets and file everything from restraining orders to shots-fired complaints.

I turn back to my computer to click on the next report in the queue, and a figure in the parking lot startles me. I jump, slamming my hand against my chest.

"What the—" Mona sees him, too.

The man in the gold hoodie stands just three feet from our window. He looks about my age, with eyes that resemble a pair of waxing gibbous moons tilted on their sides and sunken into the shadows of his sockets. His cheeks are blistered, though when I look more closely, I can see that the blisters are actually tears frozen to his skin.

The blood in my veins slows, and I feel the color draining from my face to match Rowe's description of the corpse pulled ashore. I know him. I've sat in a dark living room with him watching documentaries while Tommy and Old Will talked about guns and politics and cracked bottle caps off the edge of the kitchen table. He lives next door. Sam.

His jaw hangs so slack I'm convinced something is going to crawl out of his mouth. I squint and lean toward the window, trying to hear the words his lips are forming. He's so close now, his breath fogs the glass.

"Dude, he's fucked up or something." Mona fumbles with the phone next to her portal. She dials the extension to the sergeants' office, but I'm concentrating too hard on what he's saying to listen to her conversation.

I shake my head and point to my ear. "I can't hear you."

"He can't see us," Mona reminds me, and I hope to God she's right.

He steps forward, unsteady like the bottom half of his body is petrified with rigor mortis. Shivering violently, he reaches toward me, points. I'm frozen. My throat is so tight, I couldn't move even if I wanted to. All I can do is watch as Sam drags his finger down and over and up and down. But it isn't his own finger. It's small and broken off below the first knuckle.

"Holy fucking shit," Mona breathes.

I shift my focus from him to the message he's just written in the frost. The letters look like meaningless symbols at first, until I read them backward. *I hid a body.*

3.

SUNDAY

The table is set for dinner and a game of Russian roulette. Our plates boast the spoils of Tommy's latest kill: mourning doves and halves of baked sweet potato with a side of asparagus. His newest handgun lies in the middle of the cheap card table we salvaged from his parents' garage, and his bug-out bag—a tactical backpack filled with seventy-two hours' worth of survival supplies, such as ammo, knives, a med kit, and nonperishable snacks—sits heavily in the third chair like an uninvited houseguest.

He and his coworker, Cameron, shot the birds this past weekend. Since we moved to Black Harbor, it's like Tommy and him have reverted back to their Boy Scout days, gallivanting around in the woods and shooting anything that dares skitter up a tree. They sleep out there some nights, in little thin-skinned tents, prepping for the moment all government infrastructure fails and neighborhoods are reduced to lean-tos and lakeside caverns. "You'll thank me someday," Tommy whispered in my ear, the one time he'd convinced me to sleep outside with him. A root had wedged between my vertebrae, and my toes were so painfully cold they felt like they'd been cut down to the knuckles with garden shears.

Living next to Old Will doesn't help, either. The man is as paranoid as a teenager smoking weed in his parents' basement. And he's always watching documentaries on conspiracy theories.

I stare at the handgun on the table. The dining room light reflects in its blued surface. It's a 9mm Smith & Wesson. Tommy bought it two weeks ago for $400. One quick Google search told me he overpaid for it.

He wears his hat at the dinner table, a black one with *Greenlee Fields* embroidered on the front. It's his parents' pheasant farm: 220 acres of long grass, hunting fields, and flight pens. Thor, a bird that Tommy raised and later shot, sits stuffed in the corner of the living room, frozen in mid-flight. I don't know how a person could do that—raise something and set it free, just to kill it. It seems heartless to me, but the way Tommy tells it, Thor popping up between his sights was a quintessential snapshot of the circle of life.

The house is filled with dead things: the squirrel he stuffed for a high school taxidermy course, a ten-point buck mounted to the wall by the TV, rabbit pelt pillows on the couch. As for the guns that killed them, we have more of them than we do fingers for their triggers. There's a .22 pistol jammed between the cushion and the armrest of the dusty green recliner I dragged in from off the street, a semiautomatic rifle in the upstairs closet standing guard behind Tommy's work shirts, a Glock in each of our nightstands, and a .38 Special under the mattress. The 12-gauge he used to kill the doves leans against the wall in the corner directly across from me. He keeps a Ruger in his glove box, too, because he would honestly love nothing more than to pull into the driveway one day after work and see someone breaking into the house. He'd rush in, draw his weapon, and shoot the perp on grounds of home defense, protecting little ol' me. Then, we'd go upstairs and make babies!

I roll my eyes at the thought of it, and Tommy asks what's wrong.

I dig out a BB with the tine of my fork. It rolls along the inner curve of my plate, nudging up against the sweet potato. The bite of asparagus I just swallowed leaves an acrid aftertaste. "That weekend is Elle's engagement party." I know I've lost the argument before it even begins.

I wait while he chews and think back to every pertinent conversation I've had with my husband in the past month and a half, and there hasn't been any talk of a boys' trip. I feel my insides folding in on themselves, deflating. I don't want to be left in Black Harbor, alone.

I clench the handle of my fork so hard I imagine it turning to liquid metal. I don't meet his eyes, because as Elle has told me for going on two decades now, I'd be a terrible poker player. *It's that eyebrow*, she says. *It never stays . . . put*. Everyone has a tell. Some people have a vein that pops out in their forehead when they're nervous or upset. Others stutter. My right eyebrow shoots into my hairline.

"Cam and I are fishing the Boundary Waters. We just got our vacation days approved." He shrugs like he has no control in the matter.

I sigh and use my fork to create lateral lines in my mushed sweet potato. It looks like the fields the highways slice through on the way up north. It's been only a few weeks since we made that drive, to visit for Christmas, but it feels like much longer. Perhaps because before that I hadn't been home for three months. And three months the time before that. It feels like I'm caught in a relentless current, and whenever I manage to come up for air, Black Harbor pulls me down again.

"His wife just left him for an accountant, Hazel. I'm not gonna make him go alone." He says *accountant* the way one might say *cockroach*, or something equivalent.

I grit my teeth and concentrate on the sound of him scraping his fork across his plate. It's not the way he eats that I can't stand; it's the way he scrapes. He scrapes his plate clean every night at dinner; he scrapes the milk off the side of his cereal bowl with his spoon, the inside of his yogurt container. *It's sweet potato, Tommy, not cocaine*, I want to scream at him.

He gets it from his mother, I tell myself. It's become my mantra whenever I discover a habit of his I can't stand, as though those six words excuse him.

"I went to the first one." It's his way of chastising Elle when she's not here to defend herself—an eye for an eye to retaliate against her for constantly pointing out my failures over the air. I don't know whether to feel sorry or a little appreciative.

"Hey." He cups my chin lightly, turns my face up to look at him. I search his blue eyes. Twin halos encircle the deep, dark wells of his pupils. Ocean eyes. That's how I'd described them, once, in a note we passed back and forth in high school. *Gazing into them beautifies the thought of drowning.* His friends found the note, of course, and teased me endlessly, batting their eyelashes at me like pageant queens, until Tommy, in a very diplomatic manner, made them stop. I fell in love with him that day—a boy who used words instead of throwing punches. He's still that boy, I think, observing how his ears will probably always stick out just a centimeter too far, how his face will always light up with a subcutaneous curiosity that comes with the belief that the world is one great big backyard to explore.

He's aged, though, in the two years we've been here. We both have. Thin creases cut across his forehead and flecks of silver glint prematurely in his almost-black hair and beard that is long enough, now, to tuck into the collar of his shirt. He smiles at me with lips that are fuller than mine, and lowers his hand to rest on my wrist. I can't tell if he's trying to be sweet or tactfully avoiding being stabbed. "No one will even care if I'm not there."

"I'll care." The words spill out as quickly as the ones that started this conversation. I wish I could pull them back in when Tommy's face crumples even the slightest bit. I hate making him feel guilty. His mother does enough of that.

I look at the window. The air from the register causes the beige vinyl blind to waver like someone's breathing behind it, and suddenly the image of Sam behind the frost materializes. But he isn't there. Is he in jail? Or is he on the other side of the wall with Old Will?

We watched the search warrant from our window, afterward. Within a couple of hours, police vehicles blocked the roundabout, but we couldn't tell what happened. I would find out later tonight, once I listened to a report or two.

"What's wrong?" Tommy starts. He sets his hand on the gun that's become as customary on the dinner table as the butter dish.

I swallow, thinking of the confidentiality agreement I signed. "Nothing," I say, and force a smile. "You're shooting tonight?"

He reaches for a resealable bag on the chair and suddenly, there's an avalanche of brass as he dumps hundreds of reloaded casings into the open mouth of his backpack. The sound is like nails on a chalkboard, now, but I remember a time when I found his world exciting, when I enjoyed the smoky scent of gunpowder on my hands and stitched into my clothes, the exertion after hiking for six miles through the woods to hunt quail. Dating Tommy was always an adventure; being married to him is a game of survival.

That's why I can't tell him about Sam. We can't afford to move even if Tommy agreed to it. Rather, he'd welcome the possibility of danger and leap into high alert, probably booby-trapping the place in case Sam tries anything. He's already installed double dead bolts on the front door. It's counterintuitive, I think. All it does is give the impression we have something worth stealing. Never mind the fact that Will's place next door is about as secure as a pizza box. One kick and you're in—if it's even locked at all. I don't think about the fact that we share a basement. It only invites unnecessary paranoia of an intruder breaking into Will's and popping up on our side.

Besides, in all likelihood, Sam had nothing to do with the death of the individual. He'd simply found her, panicked, and dragged her somewhere, and soon after his conscience got the best of him. Where he would have hidden her remains a mystery. The ground is too frozen to dig a grave.

"Cam's letting me use his pass for Ryder's again," he says. I recognize the name, having been to the indoor shooting range more times than I care to count. I'd planned on buying him a membership there, until we spent our Christmas budget on international plane tickets for his sister Bea and her baby to visit from Sweden. Instead, I bought him a hunting knife, its stainless-steel spine curved into a gut hook, and a box of 30-caliber bullets. He got me a hot cocoa kit.

"Nice of him," I acknowledge.

"Yeah. What are your plans?" His chair scrapes across the floor as he stands. "Writing?"

I shrug and proceed to stare at the mess I've made on my plate. It's barely 6 p.m. I have almost four hours until I need to leave for work—my first night alone. I could definitely squeeze out a thousand words or so. "I should," I say finally, too softly for him to hear over the noise of putting on his battered Carhartt jacket. A tuft of his dark hair pokes me in the forehead when he leans in to close his mouth over mine. His kiss tastes like warm milk. "I love you," he says.

"I love you, too. Text me when you get there."

"Will do." There's a clicking sound as he locks the 9mm into his side holster and then slings his tactical pack over his shoulder.

The door slams and he's gone. I sit at the table, my ears tightening at the *brap!* sound of his muffler. Listening to his tires crunching over the snow-covered driveway, I can envision his green Oldsmobile turning left onto the road.

It's so quiet that I can hear the clock on the wall ticking away the seconds, then the hum of a microwave as Old Will makes his evening Jimmy Dean breakfast platter. There's a ticking like raindrops against the window. Or someone tapping. The curtains move again. Indents and shadows ripple through them so humanlike that

I catch my gaze traveling down the length of them, looking for feet. There aren't any.

I stand to clear our plates. Then pause. He didn't fasten the dead bolts.

The closer I get to the window, the colder it gets. Yet despite the chill, a thin film of sweat beads on my upper lip. I press my left hand to the door as though to stop anyone opening it from outside, and yank the bolts to the right. I exhale slowly, then dare to peer behind the curtain. I startle immediately, but calm when I realize the shadow I see is just a support post. "Get a grip," I mutter to myself, but when I squint, I can see a small orange ember glowing like a firefly in one of the clay flowerpots, like someone just stubbed out a cigarette.

4.

LATER

When I arrive at the municipal parking lot across from the Black Harbor Police Department, it feels as though I've driven into a crime scene. Police SUVs are parked, engines running and lights flashing as officers move duffel bags from their personal vehicles into their duty vehicles. A strange juxtaposition of urgency and routine. I walk through a cloud of exhaust, coughing, my heels punching into the snow.

Made it, I text Tommy as I hurry across the street. My heels clicking across the salted asphalt sound deafening, amplified by the night. My key fob lets me in. I stomp off clumps of snow on the already soaked industrial rug and make a beeline for the time clock terminal. 9:49.

"Check the drawer." I repeat Mona's order of operations under my breath. "Check the drawer. Fresh arrests. Criminal warrants. Dictation. PO Holds. CIB Hits."

I go left toward the sergeants' office and face the wooden and brass fixture that's probably been here since the building's inception in the 1970s. Each drawer has a black printed label: *Records, 1st Shift GIU, Lt. Wojciewicz, Marjorie DePalma*, ah, *Transcribing*.

I pull open the drawer. The stack of paperwork is staggering. There have got to be more than twenty arrests in here.

You have ten hours, I tell myself as I walk the way I came, past the time clock and into the dark, empty office space. *Ten hours to complete all the arrest paperwork and whatever urgent dictation is in the queue.*

The Records Department is thick with a postapocalyptic vibe. The only light is a faint glow coming from the sergeants' double doors and a lone streetlamp in the parking lot, shining through the drive-up window. Mesh-backed office chairs are turned away from their monitors as though whoever had been sitting in them just got up and disappeared. It's moments like this, when, wandering through a police department alone and in the dark, I regret every scary movie I've ever watched.

I exhale a breath of relief when I key my way into the Transcribing office. It's isolated down its own hall except for Lieutenant Wojciewicz's office—"Wick" for short. I drop my tote bag onto the countertop and freeze. The blinds are open.

Biting my lip, I force myself to look at the space where Sam had stood just two days ago. There's no one and nothing, just police vehicles crawling through the parking lot. The window was cleaned, but if I squint, I can see ghost strokes of the letters he scratched into the frost. Beyond that, I see the apartments, their robin's-egg-blue siding washed out in the lone streetlight, where he'd been sitting before walking up to us. I exhale slowly, willing my nerves to calm, and, gathering my courage, I reach toward the window to pull the blinds down.

There.

If anyone else wants to confess to some heinous crime tonight, they can call Dispatch.

I turn my computer on and get settled. Log in. Then, begin prioritizing the arrest paperwork, shuffling PO Holds and CIB Hits to the bottom of the stack. Out of the twenty-two forms, there are only twelve arrests that need to be done before 8 a.m. I hear Mona's voice as an echo: *If you get stuck, you can always ask the sergeants. They should be able to help you out.*

Should being the operative word, right?

I open E-Scribe. There are almost two hours' worth of new reports since Mona and I clocked out at 4:00 on Friday. I won't have time to get it all done, because by the time I set up each report with appropriate names, affiliations, and charges, I'll have monopolized my entire shift, 111 wpm or not.

My eyes land on an entry about halfway down the list, and I pause for the second time since coming in. Not because of the red exclamation point in the left-hand column marking the report as urgent, but because of who called it in.

Kole, Nikolai.

With one hand hovering over the keyboard and the other on the mouse, my fingertips, still frozen from my walk in, begin to tingle.

Trust me, kid, he's as good as gone. That's what Mona had said, and yet here he is. The time on the report is Friday, 4:02 p.m.

I feel a rush, like I'm about to do something I shouldn't. Putting on my headset and pressing down on the foot pedal, I hold my breath as a light static starts. And then his voice.

"Hello, Transcriber, this is Investigator Nikolai Kole, payroll number 6186, calling in a supplemental report pursuant to a search warrant that occurred on Friday regarding a suspicious death at 3704 Fulton Street."

Pursuant. I swirl the word like a fine wine, appreciating the way the "s" coaxes my tongue to lightly touch the roof of my mouth and my lips to curve into an "o" shape, the abrupt "t" at the end. I first encountered it Tuesday morning in a dictation by Investigator Whitmore, and I've been thinking about it ever since—this lovely word I will incorporate into my own writing.

I hear Investigator Kole through the foam earbuds as clearly as though he is sitting next to me, speaking quietly in my ear. His voice is pleasantly unexpected: calm, commanding, and slightly serrated. It's a change I've noticed in myself since starting here not even a week ago. My sense of hearing seems heightened. I am starting to read voices like braille, the smoothness or roughness of them, the pauses.

Exhilaration courses through me as I listen to him name the suspects and victim like he's reciting the cast list in a play: "William Samson, Jr.; Transcriber, can you add 'Sam' as an alias for him, he's a suspect; Tyler Krejarek, that's K-R-E-J-A-R-E-K, suspect, known alias 'Candy Man,' two words. You can list the victim, Jordan McAllister, as deceased . . ."

I scroll down and check the box for *deceased*. My eyes follow the line to the right of the name, landing on a "M" in the gender column. So it was a man, not a woman as I'd initially assumed. But then, my breath catches in my throat when I see the age.

Nine.

The victim was a little boy.

Revulsion curdles in my stomach. Although I didn't know the victim, I feel awful for whatever terrors befell him in that apartment across the street. I wonder about his parents and think about how destroyed they must be. Where would Sam have hidden him, and why?

Gently, I step on the pedal and listen as Investigator Kole tells me every morbid, confidential detail.

"On Friday, comma, January 15, comma, at approximately 1042 hours, comma, I arrived at 3704 Fulton Street regarding a suspicious death investigation, period. Upon my and Investigator Crue's arrival, comma, I observed Sergeant Hammersley, comma, Officer Ahles, comma, Officer Leibowitz, comma, and Investigator Riley on-scene, period. Sergeant Hammersley and Officer Ahles were maintaining security outside the residence, comma, while Investigator Riley met with Medical Examiner Winthorp, period. Officer Liebowitz was Evidence Technician, period. New paragraph.

"It should be noted that at approximately 0750 hours, comma, William Samson, comma, Junior, comma, alias, quote-unquote 'Sam,' comma, approached the Black Harbor Police Department and confessed to hiding a body, period. For more information regarding that incident, comma, see Sergeant Hayes's report, period. Next paragraph.

"The victim was identified as Jordan McAllister, comma, who lived in the lower level of Tyler Krejarek's building, period. I made my way behind the apartment structure, comma, to a parking lot where I observed a dumpster, period. Investigator Riley and Officer Liebowitz were present, comma, along with ME Winthorp, period. I peered inside the bin, comma, and observed, comma, lying on top of the trash, comma, a male who appeared to be approximately eight to ten years old, period. The victim was clothed in pajamas, comma, and from the waist down, comma, the body was encased in a Spider-Man sleeping bag, period. There was a white foam around his mouth, comma, which is often seen in drug overdoses, period. However, the victim's left pinky finger had been snapped off, period. It should be noted, comma, that the ME determined this to have occurred post mortem, comma, as there was no blood surrounding the wound, period. Next paragraph."

I feel my mouth fall open as Investigator Kole walks me through the scene. My insides twist at the mention of the Spider-Man sleeping bag; of all the details, that's the one that makes me catch my breath, even as he goes on to describe the stiffness of the body. Eyes like a doll's. Frost on his lips. A dark red-rimmed cavity where a finger was no longer attached.

"For more details regarding the body, comma, please see both Investigator Riley's report and Officer Liebowitz's photo log, period. Next paragraph.

"I, along with Investigators Riley and Crue, comma, then responded to the upper unit at 3704 Fulton Street, period. Outside the unit, comma, I knocked and announced police presence three times, comma, and upon receiving no response from within, comma, Investigator Crue breached the door with a one-man ram, period. The apartment was a one-bedroom unit, comma, and can be described as squalid at best, period."

Squalid, good word. Also, is it wrong to be turned on by the fact that his commas are in all the right places? I conjure up Kole in my mind, watching him step over the carnage of game pieces and jugs filled with urine and little foil wrappers that have been crumpled like wilted flower petals; raking a hand through his hair as he looks around; squinting as he deciphers the "ALG 265" markings on the little blue pills tucked inside a Newport cigarette box. He identifies the pills as oxycodone hydrochloride, a Schedule II narcotic.

There's something about his voice that makes me hang on every word. He sounds a bit like a young Kevin Costner, and I imagine him to look somewhat like him, too: blond and gray-eyed with a square, stubbled jaw. Although, look how wrong I was about Investigator Rowe.

He describes the living conditions of the place as *deplorable*; with garbage and clothes strewn about the floor; a black trash bag covering the bedroom window. Mail on the countertop denotes the apartment as belonging to a party named Tyler Krejarek, who is nowhere to be found.

"At approximately 1216 hours, comma, I returned to the BHPD to interview Sam, period. I interviewed Sam upstairs in the Detective Bureau in Interview Room #1, period. I read him his rights, comma, and he agreed to speak to me without a lawyer present, period. Next paragraph.

"I asked Sam what he'd been doing over at 3704 Fulton Street, comma, Apt. 11, period. Sam stated that he had gone to the address the night before, comma, to play Dungeons & Dragons, period. I asked Sam whose residence it was, comma, to which he stated, in quotes,

'Tyler's,' period. Transcriber please note, that I know, quote, 'Tyler,' quote, to be Tyler Krejarek from his involvement in the drug community and the mail inside the residence, period. Next paragraph.

"I asked Sam where Tyler was now, comma, and he stated he didn't know, period. I asked him when he last saw Tyler, comma, and he said he thought three or four in the morning, period. I asked if that was when the two of them threw Jordan McAllister in the dumpster, comma, and he started to cry, period. I gave Sam a minute to compose himself, comma, and asked him again if he and Tyler threw Jordan McAllister's dead body in the dumpster at three or four in the morning, comma, to which he replied, quotation marks, 'Yes,' period. Next paragraph.

"I informed Sam that I'm aware of Tyler Krejarek's history of sharing his prescription medications, comma, and asked him if Tyler had ever given him any of his pills, period. Sam stated he knows Tyler has multiple prescriptions, semicolon; however, comma, Krejarek has never shared any of his pills with him, period. I told Sam it was stupid of him to lie to me, comma, because right now he's on the hook for homicide and hiding a body, period. He started to cry again, comma, and I informed him that a download of his cell phone revealed a conversation of Krejarek telling Sam that he, quote, 'got new pills,' quote, to which Sam replied that he quote-unquote 'loves' Krejarek's pills, period. New paragraph.

"I then asked Sam if Tyler ever shared his pills with Jordan, comma, and he said he didn't know, period. I asked why Jordan had been over there in the first place, comma, seeing as how he was only nine years old and I know Krejarek to be twenty-six, period. Sam stated Jordan was often at Krejarek's residence, comma, because he lives downstairs, period. He stated that Jordan and Tyler were already playing video games that night when he arrived, period."

Kole sighs. It sounds like a gust of wind hitting the microphone. He slips into a more conversational tone, forgetting to include punctuation. I type on autopilot, adding commas and periods where he omits them, clinging to his every word as though he's reading a book to me. "I told Sam, listen. You're not in trouble for this kid overdosing. What you *are* in trouble for, at the moment, is hiding a body. I told him I know he didn't act on his own and that Tyler probably helped him, to which Sam nodded his head yes. I suggested Sam was likely scared and emotional, and when Tyler asked him to help throw the body in the dumpster, he just went along with it. Sam stated he thought he was having a nightmare, and began to sob into his hands. After about a minute or so, he said, 'I went back later to take him out. But then I saw him and he was frozen stiff. I lifted him up and he got caught, and then—' The rest of the sentence was unintelligible, period. Have I been forgetting punctuation throughout this whole thing? Ah, hell. OK. Sorry, Mona. You can just type it as is and I'll go in and fix it later. Next paragraph."

Despite the graveness of the report, I can't help but smile at Kole's mess-up. There's something thrilling, too, about the fact that he thinks he's telling this story to Mona. He has no idea who I am or that I'm listening.

"I told Sam I knew he was telling the truth, comma, because of the finger, period. Sam stated that as he tried to heave Jordan's body over the lip of the dumpster, comma, his finger got pinched and snapped off, period. He said that was when he decided to tell the police what had happened, period. I asked Sam why he used Jordan's finger to write the message in the window, comma, to which he stated, quote, 'I wanted you to believe me,' quote, period. Next paragraph.

"I informed Sam that we conducted a search of Tyler Krejarek's apartment, comma, and that the only pills we recovered were oxycodone in a Newport cigarette box, period. I asked if he knew anything about that box and where it came from, comma, and he said he didn't, period. I told Sam that he would be one step closer to clearing his name, comma, if he told us where Tyler keeps his pills, semicolon; however, comma, it seemed Sam was done talking, period. Next paragraph.

"At this time, comma, after consulting with the District Attorney's office, comma, William Samson, Jr. will be released pending his cooperation, period. Although Tyler Krejarek has not been convicted of selling drugs, comma, I know based on past experiences and quote-unquote 'word on the street' that Krejarek often sells prescription pills to minors, comma, earning himself the nickname, quote-unquote, 'Candy Man,' period. It is my strong belief that Krejarek could be responsible for distributing the oxycodone to Jordan McAllister, comma, resulting in his death, period. However, at this time, comma, we are unable to conduct inventory of his prescribed medications, comma, and Tyler Krejarek remains to be found, period. Investigation to continue, period.

"Transcriber, this will actually wrap up my report for now. Ah . . . thanks, and . . . have a great day, period." I can see him close his eyes in frustration. "Sorry, no period. It's been a while."

There's a click as he turns off his headset.

Silence.

I type a message in BHPD messenger.

From: Greenlee, Hazel
To: Kole, Nikolai
Sent: 11:14 p.m.

Investigator Kole, your report is ready for review.
Thank you,
Hazel

Send.

Half in a trance, I tap the letters on the keyboard, "C-A-N-D-Y

M-A-N," over and over as the weight of being dreadfully alone begins to set in. The terrible sensation that someone is watching me makes me shiver. Without turning my head, I sigh with relief when I see that the blinds are closed. I sit, utterly still, and then I feel it. The cold from outside seeps in through the hairline gaps in the windowsill, grips me like a pair of invisible arms like when I feel pulled to the bridge. Creeping closer to the window and leaning over the countertop, I use my thumb and forefinger to separate the dusty, vinyl blinds and look out across the parking lot to the blue apartments. The trash bag remains in the window, like a patch over an eye socket. And then suddenly, the frame illuminates with the pallid glow of a flashlight.

5.

MONDAY

"Hazel, hello?"

I come to with Elle waving her hand in front of my face. Edison bulbs surround us like stalactites and a pair of silver espresso machines emit rich, roasted aromas that fill every molecule of the café. "Sorry, I was just . . . Never mind."

Setting her phone down after having just snapped an Insta-perfect photo of her green tea latte surrounded by bridal magazines and wedding planner (#gettingmarried #forthegram #engagedaf #160days) Elle finally takes a sip. "Jeez, one night on duty and you're already spacey."

Spacey. That's an understatement. I feel anxious and overtired. The computer's blue light pulsed behind my eyes even as I slept, and when I woke at one in the afternoon, I felt as though I'd been hit by a bus. This new, offbeat circadian rhythm feels like coming up for air after a long time underwater. My mind is a mess. Everything, even my bones, hurts. "I'm always spacey," I yawned.

"This is true." Elle's wedding planner with laminated pastel tabs is spread open between us on the reclaimed wood table, as though I have any interest in reading upside down and learning how to match flatware with centerpieces. She could do all of this online like everyone else, but it's obvious she enjoys the way women's gazes seem to be magnetically attracted to the magazines and checklists, and how their eyes automatically rest on her princess engagement ring. Three people have already interrupted our conversation to congratulate her. I don't understand what's to congratulate. Anyone can get married. It's not really an accomplishment.

Not like typing 111 wpm with 98 percent accuracy.

Since she announced her engagement over the air barely two weeks ago (she and Garrett got engaged on New Year's Eve), she's been flooded with wedding vendors begging to give her free shit: bakers, macaron makers, florists . . . Because everyone knows that if Elle loves something, she'll promote the hell out of it.

No one seems to care that this is the second wedding she's planned. Apparently, her last almost-marriage had been too perfect for her taste. "Cookie-cutter" was her exact terminology when she publicly announced she'd broken off the engagement just days before the nuptials. I saw her ex about six months later when I'd driven back from her apartment. He was outside mowing his yard. I didn't stop. What would we have talked about? *Hey Max, did you see Elle's banging her kickboxing coach? Oh, by the way, your peonies look nice.*

The other bridesmaids will be here soon. Or soon-to-be-bridesmaids, I should say. She hasn't formally asked anyone yet, but the goodie bags are kind of a dead giveaway. I rehearsed what I might say on the drive up here, the dreaded small talk I will inevitably need to make. *How's your job? How are your kids? What's your go-to Instant Pot recipe?*

Kinney is among them, of course. Elle could never fathom shopping for bridesmaid dresses without his brutally honest and unfiltered opinions. He's always the voice in her ear telling her when her ta-tas are either saying a perky "hello" or giving a passive-aggressive nod, or, like a few years ago, when her haircut made her look like a poor imitation of 1997 Jennifer Aniston.

"So, tell me the 4-1-1," Elle says. "That's cop-speak for information, right?" She leans slightly forward, fingers pressing into the edge of the table. A piece of honey-colored hair falls across her forehead. Her blue eyes sparkle like a stained-glass mosaic, lips slightly ajar so I can see a hint of her bottom teeth in a neat row. Is it weird that I can see why Garrett fell in love with her? She makes me feel as though I have the power to captivate her entire world. It's what I love most about Elle, and what I miss most about her when we're not near each other.

I pick up my caramel macchiato, reveling in the warmth that spreads through my fingertips. "I think it's telephone-speak, actually. Like, for the operator. Back in the olden days before we had cell phones."

"Watch it, sis. I've talked to the operator before."

I'm not surprised; Elle loves to talk. More than that, she loves to *hear* herself talk. Her raspy voice is literally the talk of the town—a result of her being a collicky baby. Thank God I came along seven years after she'd screamed her vocal cords to shreds. At least all her screaming paid off. Thousands of people tune in to 95.9 every morning to hear her and Kinney's banter.

I prefer one-sided conversations, the ones where investigators tell me the gruesome goings-on of the city. I fell asleep this morning to Investigator Kole's voice playing softly in my memory, like a new favorite record.

"I really can't." There's a certain allure, I have to admit, with keeping such a big part of my life now from Elle, whom I've always confided everything to, until a few months ago. I can still hear what she said as clearly as though she's repeating it to my face at this moment, when on her show, she shared with the greater metropolitan area that her sister is a failure and a sellout: "She just seems so . . . lost. Ever since what happened with that editor, I don't know, it's like she's given up. Now she sells textbooks at a community college."

"Not that there's anything wrong with a community college," Kinney had chimed in for the save.

"No, no, of course not." And as it must, the show went on.

But it didn't for me. I drove back to the duplex, ignoring the missed calls and texts from my boss. A week later, I deleted the messages without having listened to or read them, because what would have been the point. Even today, I don't know what it was that bothered me so much about that conversation, whether it was the fact that Elle told everyone I was an abysmal failure or the fact that she was right.

What happened with that editor. Nothing had happened and that was just it. *I can make things happen for you, kid.* It had been out of character for me to believe him. But I was naive then, even more so than now. The simple truth of the matter was that I wasted a colossal amount of time, doing free work for someone who never intended to carry out his promise of reading my manuscript.

"Well, if nothing else, this job should yield some good material for your next book." Elle sets her latte down and I stare at the light-green foam that's gathered on the inside of the mug. "Write what you know, isn't that what you always say?"

"I don't know anything yet."

It's quiet for a blessed moment. I watch the baristas on the other side of the coffee bar steam milk and pour espresso.

"So, Mom's coming to visit in a few weeks." The end of the sentence hangs there, an open invitation, but I'm not biting.

I take a sip of my macchiato and swish it around in my mouth. It's suddenly bitter. "You mean she's realized the spa will survive for a few days without her?"

Elle sighs. We can go weeks—months, even—without bringing

up Mom, and things are harmonious. Or as harmonious as they can be, now, with Elle newly in the throes of wedding planning. But Elle is always, inevitably, the one to crack. I wonder if she's on a weird schedule I can begin tracking and strategically avoid contact with her on certain days. Perhaps I should start researching moon phases.

"When was the last time you talked to her?" she asks.

"Phone works both ways, Elle. I don't know. Last year?"

"I don't even know what you two are feuding about this time."

"We're not feuding." The word *we*, as in *Mom and I*, tastes like vinegar. The last time we spoke on the phone was November. We fought about Christmas ornaments. She claimed she had a container of ornaments I'd made as a kid—puffy felt snowmen with toothpick noses, toilet paper tube reindeer, salt dough Santas—and asked for my address so she could send them. I told her I didn't want them, and that was it. I was a monster. I didn't tell her what I knew: that her purging my childhood homemade baubles from her storage locker was just another step to my total erasure from her life. She accused me of not loving her, and I've tried off and on to convince myself that's true. But we're programmed to love our mothers, aren't we? Even when they leave us to start a business grooming bougie peoples' dogs in Phoenix.

"Well, I hope this *non-feud* fizzles out soon, because I'm tired of being in the middle of it." Elle shuffles her magazines as though she might actually look at one.

"No one put you in the middle of it."

"Mom always asks what you're up to. How am I not in the middle of it?"

"That's her putting you in the middle of it, not me. So, what's important enough for her to fly on over to these fly-over states?"

"I don't know, Hazel, why don't you ask her yourself. Because she misses us, obviously. That's typically why people visit each other."

Misses Elle, more like. Aside from looks—dark hair, blue eyes, a dusting of freckles on slightly scooped-up noses—Mom and I have very little in common. But she and Elle—total opposites in the looks department—are partners in crime. Elle visits her two or three times a year and Mom vice versa; they get cocktails and manicures together, talk about men and life and careers—and me, apparently.

"Just think about it," Elle says, and I can tell she's ready to conclude the conversation.

"When is she coming?" I ask, already knowing I won't think about it.

"The week of the second. She's flying in Tuesday, staying 'til Saturday."

"She's not going to make it to your party Friday?" Suddenly, I'm dreading Elle's engagement party a lot less.

"No, she's got a high-profile wedding this weekend in Phoenix. Six bichons all need bridesmaid dresses or something like that."

I snort. "You think there's a correlation between people having too much money and being absolutely insane?"

"Must be why you and I are so levelheaded. Hey, how is Angela these days, by the way?" She asks as though the levelheaded comment didn't trigger the antithesis of such: my mother-in-law.

"Still inhumanly bitchy," I reply. The last time I saw Angela was three days after Christmas when she screamed Tommy and me out of the house, accusing him of stealing his dad's ice-fishing boots. She refused to consider the fact that they might be buried under the mountains of stuff that inhabited the garage, instead wailing and threatening to call the police until Tommy gave her a crisp one-hundred-dollar bill to pay for the missing boots. There went our grocery money.

"I mean, how's her health?" Elle asks.

"I'm still waiting on the house to fall on her, so . . ."

Elle purses her lips, failing at fighting back a smile. She knows my mother-in-law is what nightmares are made of. No, she's what nightmares *aspire* toward. She's familiar with Angela's stage 4 emphysema when, during the setup of my own wedding, Angela had screamed herself into a coughing fit when she discovered I hadn't purchased any tulle for the gift table. She was so frustrated, in fact, that she'd gone outside for a smoke break. Last I heard she was down to four cigarettes a day, but she'll never *quit* quit. I try to cut Angela some slack, sometimes; I suppose I'd be irritable too if my lungs were constantly treading water, and my only daughter had ditched me for a life overseas. Her senior year of college, Tommy's younger sister, Bea, traveled to Sweden to study abroad, and stayed. Now, she has a boyfriend, a toddler, and a 150-square-foot apartment. I couldn't blame her. I always thought of Bea as a lily trying to sprout up in a snowdrift; a delicate thing meant for the minimalist charm of Scandinavia, not a pheasant farm.

Nevertheless, Bea's absence and the emphysema are both conditions Angela brought upon herself.

"On a positive note," says Elle, "did everyone love the spread?"

"The . . . oh." The memory of humiliation unfurls within me. Monday, my first day, Elle had a smorgasbord of coffee and donuts sent to the PD on my oblivious behalf. There had been bagels of every variety, too: cinnamon, onion, wheat, chocolate chip, blueberry, sesame; cream cheese spreads and jam and peanut butter; donuts with nuts on top and without, custard-filled and glazed. It was a complete spread made even more complete by an ample supply of *Elle & Kinney Live on 95.9 The Rush* napkins. It had felt like I was throwing a welcome party for myself, or like being the new kid in a new school and your mom shows up with treats bribing everyone to like you. *Look everyone, I bring bagels. Love me.* "Yes. Loved it. Thank you," I say.

Elle beams. "Glad I could help out. You're making friends?"

Making friends. What am I, a kindergartner? Nevertheless, I nod, because I'm happy to report that yes, the introvert of all introverts is actually making friends. Mona invited me out for brandy old-fashioneds after work last week with her and Liv from Records. Although I don't have a taste for them like the rest of Wisconsin seems to have, I sipped on one for two hours while Liv filled us in on years' worth of PD gossip and entertained herself with imitating the way I talk.

All in all, the old-fashioned outing had been a success. The brandy blanketed my mind like a peaceful fog and I found myself actually enjoying the company of someone besides my computer for the evening. I summarize the outing to Elle, who seems just as impressed as Tommy had been. I can see her eyes visibly light up as she mentally adds to my résumé: Excellent Written Communication Skills, Advanced Typist, Demonstrated Capabilities of Human Interaction.

"It sounds like you're off to a good start."

"Yeah."

"What's wrong?" Elle looks concerned. She leans over, sets her hand over mine. The rays that shine off her diamond engagement ring are blinding.

I draw in a rattling breath. What's wrong? What isn't. I could tell Elle that my neighbor confessed to hiding a body, that it haunts me like the dead man I saw floating faceup in the river when I stood on the suicide bridge. I could tell her about the light I saw in the child killer's apartment late last night, when Candy Man himself is supposedly MIA. I could make her promise not to say anything. But Elle, for all her good intentions, would never not say anything. In just ten seconds on the air, she could destroy me as well as the ongoing investigation.

Instead, I tell her about something so trivial, it didn't even make the list. "I got . . . written up. Friday."

"Wait, what?"

On Friday after the incident with Sam, Marjorie stopped me in the Records area as I was making my way to the time clock. She gave me a pink slip of paper, denoting a reprimand for *inappropriate attire*, and motioned to the black pencil skirt I was wearing.

"Wait, the one that you got with me at Sylvia's?" Elle asks, mentioning our favorite thrift store.

"The one and the same."

She shakes her head. "There's nothing wrong with that skirt. It *exudes* professionalism."

"The reprimand called it *distracting*."

Elle guffaws. In my peripheral vision, I see people turn their heads in our direction. "*Distracting*?" she mocks. "Oh Hazel, women are brutal."

"Really? You think it was a woman?" In all honesty, I have no idea who made the complaint that triggered Marjorie to write me up. I had several suspects, of course: Ravina, a red-haired pixie of a woman who processes warrants, newly divorced; June from Records, who wears clogs with white socks and seemed to take personal offense on Wednesday when I passed on trying her homemade jelly tarts; and finally, Lieutenant Sullivan, who stood from sitting on the corner of Liv's desk Friday morning to introduce himself. He sported a military crew cut, and although he was friendly enough in the moment, he could be the rigid type.

"No man complains about a woman's outfit being distracting. It was a woman." She crunches down on a biscotti, punctuating her point.

Her candidness actually makes me feel a little better. I'm glad I told her. It's a stupid thing to be upset about, especially considering what happened earlier that day. The realization must bring a shadow over me, because Elle asks, "Are you sure that's what's bothering you?"

I look up. Her eyes are slanted, the outer edges turned down so they look like a pair of sparkling quotation marks. She can't do anything to help me. Telling her would only make matters worse.

Suddenly, I hear Kinney shouting from the entrance. “Who’s a guy gotta flirt with to get a triple skinny mocha with half the pumps and a shot of peppermint around here? Oh, my adoring fans.” Unraveling himself from his cashmere scarf, he makes his way toward us.

“Tell me later.” Elle pats my hand.

“I will.” The lie tastes bitter, like an ash pretending to be a snowflake.

6.

THAT NIGHT

Tommy went ice fishing with Cam. I ate cereal for dinner and contemplated a blank document on my computer screen. It didn't stay blank, however, and I consider that a victory. I wrote what I remembered from Friday when Sam walked up to our window. The snowflakes that melted into the matted mess of his hair. The gold hoodie I should have recognized even from across the street. I've seen him wear it on multiple occasions before. I'm sure it's in Evidence now, concealed in a plastic pouch after hanging in a drying locker. And then, as though my fingers had retained muscle memory from the night before, I retyped Kole's entire report: the boy in the Spider-Man sleeping bag lying stiff and dead on a bed of trash, Sam sobbing in the interview room, the rough and smooth edges of Kole's voice as he coaxed information from him about Candy Man.

The alias still prickled my skin. As I wrote, I envisioned a seedy character stalking children outside the school grounds, giving them poisonous pills in exchange for their lunch money. Kole mentioned oxycodone in a Newport cigarette box. I wondered how Jordan McAllister would have come by them if not by Candy Man luring him to his apartment.

After an hour, I'd accomplished a 1,200-word stream-of-consciousness narrative. It was nothing really, and yet, it was something. Perhaps I was finally breaking out of my slump.

Now it's after 10 p.m. and there are thirteen arrests in the drawer, only seven of them fresh. The rest are CIB Hits and PO Holds. Not terrible. The true test will be how much dictation is waiting in the queue. One two-hour report could eat up my whole shift.

Though I've passed through it many times since this hour yesterday, the empty, dark Records area is no less frightening. I still think something is going to grab my ankles from underneath a desk.

When I log in to E-scribe, there are no reports from Kole or Crue, meaning there are no updates on the investigation at Fulton Street. After processing the arrests I'd collected, I dive into a forty-five minute report by Investigator Riley. She is well-spoken and articulate; more so than her partner, Investigator Rowe, at least, who's developed a love of the word "however." Her thoughts are organized and concise as though she's reading from a paper. My fingers tap an arrhythmic and hurried song as she takes me through the scene. Another jumper.

I can practically hear for myself Investigator Riley's dress shoes crunching as she carefully descends the snow-covered hill toward the river. I imagine I can see her breath as cloud in front of her each time she exhales. Finished, I punch my initials at the bottom of the document and send Investigator Riley a message that her report is ready for her review.

There's a curt knock at the door. I swivel around to see a man in a patrol uniform, sergeant stripes on his sleeves. He's built like a retired pro wrestler, aeruginous tattoos blurred on both of his forearms. I read his name tag: Hammersley.

"Hi," he says.

"Hi." I move to stand, but my heels wobble and I fall back to my butt. I brush it off as though I'd only been shifting in my chair.

"Hammersley." His grip crushes my hand, even though I've always been conscientious of presenting a firm handshake.

"Hazel."

"There's pizza in the back. Come on."

I look over my shoulder for a second, like there could possibly be someone else he's talking to. He's already ten steps ahead of me when I heed his directives, following him back through the dark Records area and into the fluorescent glow of the sergeants' office. There are seven of them all in uniform, six males and one female who looks barely twenty-one. They wave hello as they continue eating their pizza.

"Hey there," says a second sergeant. He wipes his greasy fingers on a napkin. "You're the new, uh, the new Beverly, eh?" His voice is friendly. I like him instantly. The name stitched into his uniform reads: Rourke.

"Hazel," I say.

He nods like that's an acceptable answer. A string of mozzarella clings to his mustache. "So, where you come from?" he asks.

Should I say something about the mozzarella? It's just hanging there like a loose thread, bouncing as he chews. Thankfully, the female officer catches his eye and signals by tapping at her lip. He wipes it away with a clean napkin and I take the opportunity to distract myself by grabbing a square of pizza.

"Up north," I say. "About three hours from here." It's become my catchall reply to that question. No one's ever heard of my hometown. It's not even on the map.

"What the hell are you doing all the way down here?" asks Hammersley.

"There's no work up there." I can feel the pizza cooling in my hand, the melty cheese dripping onto my palm. I wince.

"Married?" asks Hammersley. "You got kids?"

"No," I say, an automatic riposte. "I mean, I'm married, but no kids." Where are the plates?

"Just as well," says Rourke. "These days you've got to drive across county lines for a decent school."

I'm surveying the rows of desks and cubicles when one of the younger officers offers me a white paper plate. I smile a silent, polite thanks, and set my pizza onto it.

They ask what my husband does. I tell him he's an aquatic ecologist.

"A what?" asks Hammersley. The "t" is sharp, like I've just insulted his grandmother.

"He studies the lake," I say. "Or rather, the impact the environment's having on it, now that we're—"

"Sinking," Rourke finishes for me.

"Yes." I remember an article I recently read online, where a woman returned home from a weekend in Chicago to find her entire front yard collapsed, the lighthouse statue she kept as a fixture in her flower garden floating on its side thirty feet past the pier. *Black Harbor is sinking, and we're all going down with it*, the reporter wrote.

Hammersley is shaking his head like he's had enough of a science lesson for today.

"Bet those coal tankers are just dandy for it," says Rourke. "Corroding into our drinking water and all that."

"Dandy?" repeats Hammersley. "Who are you, Yankee Doodle?" He reaches to plop three more squares onto his plate.

I take a bite, finally remembering that pizza is indeed for eating. The cheese burns the roof of my mouth, but it's so good. The crust is thin and crispy and sprinkled with Parmesan. I don't remember the last time I had pizza or something Tommy didn't shoot or yank out of the lake.

The dispatcher's voice comes over the radio. My ears perk up at the name. "Krejarek, Tyler. White male . . . Area 6."

The young female officer and one of the male officers each grab one last slice and head out.

"Knew he'd turn up," says Hammersley.

"Is that the suspect from Fulton Street?" I ask. "With the dead kid—"

"—in the dumpster? Sure is," Rourke answers as Hammersley crosses in front of me to walk over to a phone. He dials a number, the receiver wedged between his ear and shoulder as he holds his pizza. "Wake up, Sleeping Beauty. Your Prince Charming is here. No, it ain't me. Patrol's got your guy. They're bringin' him in. OK. Yep." He hangs up and takes a bite.

• • •

Twenty minutes later, I've just filled the coffee decanter from the faucet in the women's bathroom when, in the hall, Hammersley catches me by the fixture of drawers. "Hot off the press. Jesus, every time it snows, it's like people forget how to fucking drive."

I look down at the arrest header he's just handed me for a hit-and-run. "Welcome to Wisconsin," I say.

"Ain't that the truth." He goes his way, then, and I mine. I'm halfway down the hall when the exterior door swings open in the alcove behind me. A blast of winter air hits me like a ghost train, and a voice I'd know from anywhere echoes in the stairwell. "Put him in Interview Room #1, please. I'm headed upstairs, now."

I turn to see a man in a dark jacket take a sharp left and ascend the stairs to the bureau. I pause, frozen between the time clock and the stairwell, and listen as his footsteps fade. Thinking of the 1,200 words

I'd written this evening that, as of yet, have no conclusion, and checking to make sure Hammersley has returned to the sergeants' office, I follow Investigator Kole's snowy footprints up the stairs.

I push open the door at the top of the landing. The main hall light is on, bathing everything in a harsh, fluorescent glow. Like in the rest of the building, the walls are thick cement block painted bone white. A short walk to my right, a pair of heavy oak doors. The nameplate reads COMMAND STAFF.

I turn left, wincing as my heels click on the linoleum. So much for being inconspicuous. I walk on my tiptoes to minimize it, but it isn't enough. The sound echoes in the empty hall. I take my shoes off then, resigned to carrying them at my side.

When I pass a door labeled Identification Bureau, I recall Mona taking me there my first day to get fingerprinted. I sat in a pea-green leather chair with a rip in the seat as a lady with a weathered face and smoker's voice pressed the pads of my fingers in ink.

The hall cuts to the right. I pass a stainless-steel bench with three sets of shackles bolted to the wall. Across from it, another set of double doors denotes General Investigations Unit. It's dark; there's not even light from a computer monitor or desk lamp. On the far side of the room, a streetlamp peers through the window like something from a Lovecraft story. Clutching my shoes and the arrest header to my chest as though for protection, I walk inside.

As I wander down a column of desks, my thigh catches the corner of a folder. It makes a loud slap as it hits the floor. I freeze, my eyes wide as I slowly survey the empty bureau. Taking a deep breath, I pick it up and return it to Investigator Riley's desk. Her papers are all neatly stacked, unlike her neighbor's. Everything has a place: a mug full of pens, a clear desk organizer filled with paperclips, scissors, Post-its, a mini stapler. My eyes have adapted enough by now to notice the photo of a woman with braids and glasses who might be her, hugging a golden retriever. She looks close to how I imagined her. Perhaps I'm getting better at this.

Adjusting my path to the center aisle so as not to disturb any more paperwork, I hear the low murmur of voices, getting louder as I near a recess on the left side of the room. A line of muted light glows beneath the door. My heart pounds as I stand outside, listening, and then notice the door next to it that's slightly ajar. It might be a closet, but it seems the closer I approach, the better I can make out what they're saying. Gathering my courage, I slip inside.

It takes a second to register that I'm on the other side of a two-way mirror; like the window in my office, they can't see me. This must be how the storied fly on the wall feels. But I don't feel like a fly. I am more or less than that. I am bodiless. A crepuscular creature free to observe and listen as I please. I am a shadow.

The interview room is a shoebox, even smaller and more depressing than the room I was interviewed in across the street at City Hall. There are no windows at all.

I've witnessed interviews like this on TV. Sometimes it's two detectives performing the good cop/bad cop routine for the suspect. Other times it's just one detective, haggard after so many hours into the investigation, wearing a dress shirt with the top buttons undone, tie loosened like a noose around his neck. But in this case, it's only Investigator Kole dressed in a black pullover and jeans. My eyes take their sweet time studying him. Albeit younger, he looks more or less like the image I conjured up: sand-colored hair pushed to one side, square jaw sporting a five o'clock shadow, a faint dimple in his chin. He's criminally attractive, and I despise myself for even thinking of the pun.

Tyler Krejarek looks like an invertebrate. He shifts in his chair and I watch as his neck moves first, and then the rest of his body with it. He's scrawny, swallowed up by a grungy maroon sweatshirt. His mustache is a sad dusting over his top lip and his hair is an oily mullet, or what Tommy would call a Wisconsin waterfall. The fluorescent light doesn't do his pallid, pockmarked skin any favors. Next to him, there's a plastic water bottle and an unopened bag of chips.

I feel like I've scored front-row tickets to a performance. A chill crawls up my spine, though, and oddly enough, I'm more unnerved by Investigator Kole than the supposed Candy Man. I know beyond a reasonable doubt that I've seen the investigator before; I just can't place where.

"Jordan McAllister is dead," Kole says. "But you know that."

Krejarek keeps silent, a tactic to which Kole seems accustomed.

"You know what I couldn't get out of my head as I was walking through your place the other day, Tyler, is what the hell was a nine-year-old doing over there? You're . . . twenty-six, twenty-seven? I mean . . . this kid still went to recess, for Christ's sake."

"He lives downstairs. His mom ain't never home." There's an edge of defense to Krejarek's response. His words jam together; he sounds like someone with a mouth crammed full of teeth.

I watch Kole watch Krejarek. He commands the room as though he's conducted a thousand interviews by now—some with characters a lot grislier than the one presently sitting in front of him. "Would you say he was like a kid brother to you?"

Krejarek says nothing. He looks down at the floor.

Kole sits in the chair across from Krejarek. His forearms slide across the stainless-steel surface of the table as he leans forward. He crosses his arms, his hands resting on his biceps. "You have any friends your own age, Tyler? Any guys you can call up and grab a beer with?"

Silence.

"What about Sam? He comes over sometimes, doesn't he?"

Krejarek moves, finally. He brings his right arm across his torso to scratch at a patch above his elbow. It's a slow, thoughtful scratch. I feel like I can hear it all the way over here.

"You probably can't drink with all those meds you're on." Kole's needling.

"They're all prescribed to me."

"I know. Trust me, we checked. You've got a laundry list of problems, Tyler. Once I read your medical records, I began to think that a dead kid with your name written all over him might just be the least of your worries. What've you got, manic depressive disorder, epilepsy, insomnia . . ."

Krejarek continues to scratch with his sleeve pushed up. I can see his skin reddening.

"That game board looked pretty intense." Kole changes tracks. "Looks like you guys might've been up all night, playing. I'm sure it's not a problem for you—staying awake, with your insomnia—but what about your friends? How do they stay up? Energy drinks?"

"Yeah." Krejarek catches the easy underhand pitch. He knows he didn't clean up the energy drink cans.

"What about pills? You ever share any of yours with them to help them stay awake?"

Krejarek falls silent again. He shoves his hand in his jeans pocket. The denim ripples from his fingers fidgeting. The skin on his arm is irritated now.

"Oxys will do the trick," says Kole. "You know that. The oxys keep you up at night, and that's why you've got the amitriptyline and Lyrica to balance it out. Jesus, I don't even know how you can think straight. Maybe you can't, I don't know."

Amitriptyline. He makes an antidepressant sound beautiful.

"Was that Dungeons & Dragons you were playing?"

Krejarek says nothing, but Kole proceeds as though he'd answered. "Man, I commend you. That game's too complicated for me. Too many dice with too many sides. Don't they all have like eight sides or ten, or something like that?"

Krejarek shrugs. “Depends.”

“Depends on what?”

“On what they do.” He answers with clenched teeth, as though he can’t help himself. “Like, if you want to attack or determine your damage or whatever.”

“Well, look at that. You learn something new every day. What about the turquoise one? What does that do?”

“The D20,” Krejarek says. “It determines initiative and damage. Stuff like that. It’s how you figure out your next move.” He sighs, though I can’t tell if he’s annoyed with Kole, or at himself for talking to him.

Kole rolls his head to one shoulder, then the other. When he turns my way, I swear he’s staring through the glass at me. I freeze, like a deer caught in headlights. Enduring the full weight of his stare, I’m positive he can see me. The edge of his mouth quirks, a subtle smile, and I’m dead. Every muscle in my body tenses. I squeeze my shoes and the arrest header tighter, wincing as the paper crinkles.

Kole’s chair screeches across the floor, and I’m terrified he’s heard me. But he begins to pace the room, walking a slow half circle around the table. I swallow my trepidation and sigh with relief when he passes by the door. I watch Krejarek, then, whose eyes follow Kole’s every step. His head moves in small jerks, like a robot malfunctioning at the end of its battery life.

“You did a pretty good job cleaning up the place, Tyler. Personally, I think you could have hit the windows with some Windex, but you were working under a tight time frame. You had to clean up and get the hell out before Sam grew a conscience. Which, inevitably, he did. You’d have to be pretty heartless to toss a kid in a dumpster and not feel something.” His eyes narrow, zeroing in on his target. “You were never popular in school. You were bullied. Ignored. People your age just never understood you. You felt like you were born just ten, even five years too early. But it changed as you got older, didn't it? Once you graduated, kids started looking up to you. The same types of kids that would have thrown you down at the bus stop or stolen your books or given you a swirly at lunch had come to revere you."

Revere. Good word.

"Maybe some of them even fear you—the ones who aren't interested in what you're selling. They see you across the street or they catch a glimpse of you standing at the edge of the soccer field—this figure in an oversize sweatshirt. With your hood up, you probably resemble the grim reaper." His voice dips. "Candy Man, right? That's what they call you because you've got a stash filled with anything a kid could want."

Kole pauses, and I watch Krejarek, my fingers mime-typing C-A-N-D-Y M-A-N over and over. His mouth twitches, the middle of his lips pursing ever so slightly and the ends pulling into a secret smile. He pulls his hand out of his pocket and wraps his arms across himself like a straitjacket. His knee bounces. "I never sold Jordan any pills."

"Never said you did. For all I know, he might've stolen them from you."

Krejarek cocks his head as though he's not entirely opposed to this new theory.

Kole leans forward with his palms flat on the table so he's eye to eye with Krejarek. "Look. You and I both know you hid your prescription medications. I would, too, if I had that kind of inventory. People will do some pretty insane shit for pills, and especially if the little neighbor boy was coming over . . . I get it. In fact, it was the responsible thing to do. But, you know, you missed a spot when you cleaned up. Actually, you missed a lot of spots. It's funny. After all the search warrants I've done—even the ones where people clean up—I'm always amazed at what you can find under the couch cushions." Kole walks over to a black backpack in the corner of the room and withdraws a plastic resealable bag that he proceeds to dump on the table. Coins bounce and roll off the edge. Crumbs of pretzels and chips sprinkle the surface. A crunchy sock falls limp like a deflated balloon. "Two questions, Tyler. One: you ever heard of a vacuum?" Without waiting for Krejarek to answer, he flips down a photograph of what looks to be a teal-colored box on top of the trash. "And two: you smoke Newports?"

Krejarek stares at the photo like he's working a Jedi mind trick on it.

"As you can see," says Kole, "there aren't any cigarettes in it, just oxys. So, what happened, Tyler? Why'd you package them up like that? As a to-go box?"

"He brought those himself," Krejarek defends. "I never seen 'em."

"Why would he bring oxys when he knows you've got 'em?"

Krejarek shrugs. He turns his chin up toward the ceiling. He looks frustrated. I wonder how much more Kole can pull out of him.

"I don't think you're a bad guy, Tyler. I think you're lonely. Maybe a little misunderstood. You gotta get ahead of this, and I want to help you. The moment you show me your oxycodone prescription with every pill accounted for, this is over."

Extracting his hand from his pocket, Kole tosses a turquoise twenty-sided die on the table. "Time to figure out your next move."

Krejarek stares at it for a long time without saying anything.

I hear the click of the door unlocking as Kole exits the interview room. I suck in a breath and press my back against the wall, melting into the shadows. He moves swiftly past. My shoulders fall. I can hear my heart drumming in my ears. Rapid, at first, then gradually ebbing back to normal. Before slipping out of the room, I steal one last glance at Krejarek. From the side, partially obscured by his tangled hair, I watch, as his mouth curls into a slow, almost imperceptible smile.

7.

TUESDAY

Fat flakes fall from the sky. I turn to admire the wintry scene across the street from the duplex. The boughs of the evergreens sag, weighed down by snow. It's almost pretty. They curtain where the ground drops off—a ledge that leads to an empty basin where a web of running and biking trails cut through the earth like shallow valleys. Empty, that is, except for discarded clothes and tinfoil. Crushed cans. Condoms. Mona was surprised when I told her I run down there, and insisted I find a new route—on the lakeshore, perhaps, where there are paved asphalt trails and affluent people walking their dogs. But it's five miles to the lake from here. I'd run there and back, and that would be the end of my exercise. Or I'd drive, which presents its own inconveniences. Besides I like the trail. That small wooded pocket reminds me of home, and for an hour a day, I forget I'm here and not there.

"Nothing good happens down there," Mona had warned, and she's probably validated in that statement. After all, Old Will swears he saw a man dragging a body on a sled a few winters ago. "It was bizarre," he recalled, his eyes bugging out of his head. "I look up from takin' a piss around 6 'er 7 in ter mornin' or so and 'ere he was. Had it all wrapped up in a garbage bag, trailin' blood through the snow. Prob'ly some young woman he raped and killed."

Instead of agreeing to adopt a new route for Mona's sake, I'd only shrugged, because I don't plan on it, and besides, it's Black Harbor; nothing good happens anywhere. Perhaps I'll remember to ask the sergeants about it tonight. Just to see if the trail is, indeed, any more dangerous than the rest of the city.

Dropping my tote bag and my purse on the sidewalk, I grab the plastic shovel that's leaning against the porch and start hacking at the snow and ice that encapsulates the stairs. I hear a car drive past and wonder what its driver must think of me, shoveling snow in heels. A dozen clay flowerpots line the porch railing, but I've never seen any plant matter in them. They're more like ashtrays, each one probably holding a carton's worth of cigarette butts.

I trek up the newly cleared stairs and pause, staring at the newspaper lying between our door and Will's. It's the same one that's been there since this spring with no one to either claim it or have the wherewithal to recycle it. The ink is all but gone from the front page; letters and photographs have bled into one another like a watercolor. I look at the blue recycling bin to my left, half-buried in snow on the strip of yard that separates this residence from the next one over. The lid is just as snow-laden as the steps. *Not today.*

The door creaks, announcing my presence to absolutely no one. On the other side, Old Will is assuredly still asleep, and there's no hideous brown pickup truck along the street anywhere to denote Sam is home. There are new drip stains on the counter next to the coffeepot, a ring around Tommy's cup with nothing but the dregs left in it. Next to the sink are two empty beer bottles. I throw them in the recycling, too tired to wince at the sharp sound of them shattering.

As I wash my face and brush my teeth at the pedestal sink in the upstairs bathroom, I glance at my reflection in the medicine cabinet. My eyes look larger than usual, wilder. A result of me adapting to the dark, I suppose, or also a side effect of drinking coffee at 2 a.m. Falling asleep is easier than I thought it would be. It's waking up that feels like struggling against a rushing tide.

I wake in the middle of a troubled dream and just lie for a while, all twisted in the sheets, fighting to catch my breath. My heart pounds as though I've just run a marathon and my eyes scan the room. The closet door is slightly ajar from when I'd changed into my pajamas. My work clothes lie on the floor. Tommy's dresser is bare except for our wedding photo and the handgun set on its top. I hear a car on the road below, cringe as I hear it pull into the drive.

He's home.

A few months ago, in the *in-between* time of me leaving the bookstore and landing this new job, I would have greeted him at the door with a cold beer. I would have done a project throughout the day, too—cleaning the duplex from top to bottom, painting all the rooms within it, making a gallery wall of photos along the stairs. A few months ago, I would have tried.

We'd had sex almost every day, then, too. It became something I owed him, the least I could do for not bringing in a paycheck. He didn't seem to care that it hurt me. He's always been good at *compartmentalizing*—a term the therapist later used. All he saw was a consenting body on the bed. Never mind the way my muscles twitched when he touched me or the blood I drew from my own lip.

You know the rules, Hazel. He says that whenever I exhibit reluctance or a point of view that doesn't match his. He'd said it when he drove me to the Social Security office the day after our wedding to change my last name, and he says it at least every three days as he marches me up the stairs so he can fuck me. Living with Tommy is the equivalent of playing a board game with someone who makes up the rules as we play. I don't remember where they all came from, though I believe the three-day sex rule started as a joke in college. Then, sex had felt . . . fine. Maybe it was even *good*—or I'd been content with it, at least. But over the years, it started to hurt, like he was shoving a hot poker inside of me. I couldn't have intercourse without crying out. It always left me wrecked, and after uncurling myself from the fetal position, I'd shower, sometimes watching the water run pink; then dress, and walk gingerly about. Sitting hurt. Wearing underwear hurt. Looking at myself in the mirror hurt.

I saw four different doctors who prescribed everything from topical ointments to pain pills that made my head foggy. I tried numbing myself with alcohol, getting drunk with him beforehand to see if it hurt less. It made the act more bearable, but I paid dearly afterward. I tried home remedies, too, standing naked in the shower with my feet shoulders'-width apart, a diffuser erupting a mist of eucalyptus and lavender between my legs.

Nothing fixed me.

When we moved here, I stopped looking for a cure. I stopped believing there is one. I am broken, like a doll missing an eye. A car with a busted wheel. A computer that won't turn on. Pick anything out of that dumpster that Jordan McAllister was in, and that's me. Used-up garbage.

The door whines to announce his presence. I hear him take off his polo and unzip his jeans where they puddle at his feet. He smells like lab chemicals and pH test strips, and the gunpowder that's pushed beneath his fingernails.

I lie still, because on the third day, resistance is futile. He doesn't hit me or anything, but the guilt trip that ensues is so insufferable, I'd rather he just smack me and get it over with. He'll accuse me of being a bad wife. Of being asexual. Of being just like my mother, who is never happy, no matter what. And perhaps these things are true.

But, at least my mother is not a screaming lunatic. It's true she's never happy, but neither is she angry like Angela. She just left, and maybe that wasn't the worst thing in the world. Maybe it just hurts me more than it should. And maybe that's why I'm too afraid to have children of my own: because I know I would eventually leave them. I feel it in my bones. Mom and I, we are made of the same stuff.

I'd be lying if I said I don't think of it from time to time: having one. I imagine there's something almost magical about it, coming home to little boots drying by the register, a rosy cheek pressed against yours, still cold from playing outside, a kiss planted on your lips like a snowflake. But at this point, having a child would feel like a concession, like giving in after having accepted the fact that I will never win the argument. And Tommy says you can't have just one, anyway.

The covers slide to the floor as he pulls my leggings down to expose me. The frigid air slaps my skin and goosebumps erupt on the backs of my legs. He mistakes it for excitement. I don't scream at the sensation of being burned alive from the inside out.

After, I lie on a sliver of mattress, gripping the edge. Mucus drips from my nose, some of it sliding down my knuckles. My tears fall and disappear in the fibers of cheap carpet. A silver corner of my laptop peeks out from underneath the bed. The Word document I started the other night is like a hand reaching for me. But I don't want it right now.

My body aches. Moving against the sheets feels like a thousand razor blades slicing into my skin. I feel his presence, and I know he's turned away from me, too. I hear his breath steadying as his heart rate slows to normal. I keep my eyes closed as he gets up and goes to the bathroom. Upon his return, he tosses a wet, crunchy washcloth on me. "You could make some noise once in a while," he says.

He walks out of the room again and I hold my breath until I count fourteen footsteps down the stairs. I hug the sheets tighter, imagining I'm pulling a wave over myself. I want to be submerged, to let my mind be taken by the darkness. I read an article, once, about people who survive drownings and plane crashes. They say there's no panic but a strange serenity that takes hold of you in the moments before death.

Downstairs, the door shuts.

A slam would hurt less.

A slam would give me reason to confront him when he comes back. It could ignite a screaming match between us—the one we've never had but maybe should. A simple closing of the door speaks of disappointment. It means that when he eventually returns after picking up a new twelve-pack, everything will be the same. I will say nothing and he will say nothing, and I will be in this same position three days from now. And he will leave and shut the door again.

I close my eyes. The silence rushes at me like a whitecap.

8.
WEDNESDAY

From: Kole, Nikolai

To: Greenlee, Hazel

Sent: 7:48 a.m.

You don't have to call me Investigator Kole. Nik will do.

P.S. Welcome to the underworld.

I've read his response four or five times, racking my brain for what to say, if anything at all. I still have time to think about it, when at 2 a.m., I finally get around to typing his latest report. I recognize the cross-referenced case number as the one from Friday morning, and I know it's got to be the interview I watched less than twenty-four hours ago.

A pot of coffee brews. Its roasted aroma fills my narrow terrarium. With my foam earbuds in place, I press down on the foot pedal.

"Hello, Transcriber, this is Investigator Kole, payroll number 6186, calling in a supplemental report regarding the death investigation at 3704 Fulton Street. You can list the victim, Jordan McAllister, as deceased, and the suspect as Tyler Krejarek, alias 'Candy Man.'"

"Narrative: On Tuesday, comma, January 19, comma, at approximately 0126 hours, comma, I interviewed Tyler Krejarek at the Black

Harbor Police Department Detective Bureau in Interview Room #1, comma, after receiving a phone call at home from Sergeant Hammersley of the Patrol Division, period. Upon my arrival, comma, I learned from patrol officers that Krejarek had been located in his neighborhood, comma, not far from his residence, period. New paragraph.

"I informed Krejarek that he was being interviewed as a result of a dead body found outside his apartment Friday morning, period. . . ."

I listen to the recap. He reports everything as I remember it, in addition to details that I'd missed from my vantage point, such as: "It should be noted that although I'd turned the heat down in the interview room to a cool sixty-five degrees, comma, I could see Krejarek visibly sweating, comma, which, comma, from my training and experience, comma, I know to be a common reaction of people who have something to hide, period."

He mentions showing Krejarek the photo of the Newport box containing the oxycodone pills. He leaves out the dice. The next part is what happened after I skedaddled.

"I exited the interview room for approximately ten minutes, comma, giving Krejarek some time to mull things over, period. When I returned, comma, he was still unwilling to cooperate, period. He denied knowing about the death of Jordan McAllister, comma, stating that Jordan was alive the last time he saw him, period. I provided Krejarek with evidence from Sam's cell phone that had been confiscated and downloaded on Friday, comma, with language indicating Krejarek had been sharing his medications with his friends, period. At this time, comma, Krejarek is being held at the Black Harbor County Jail on a PO Hold, period. Investigation to continue, period. New paragraph.

"For more information regarding Tyler Krejarek's arrest, comma, please see all reports under the cross-referenced case number.

"Transcriber, that will complete my report. Thanks and have a good night."

I enter my initials at the bottom of the document and sit, still. My fingers are poised over the keyboard, waiting for my command. What do I write back?

Nothing brilliant coming to mind, I resign to checking the drawer for fresh arrests. When I return, I startle at the presence of someone sitting in my chair. "Um, hey," I say, holding the papers up as if to shield myself from some unclear danger.

"Damn, you make me sound halfway intelligent."

I know that voice. Smooth with a quiet edge, it's the soft undertone of thunder rolling over hills. I let it carry me away for just a moment, home, to where I would sit on the porch swing and listen to the serenade of a summer storm. But I'm not home. Here in Black Harbor, his is the voice that took me through scenes of crunching on game pieces and peering into a dumpster to examine the sticky foam at the edges of a dead boy's mouth.

"Nik," he says. He turns my own chair around to face me and offers his hand. I grasp it, feeling the cold air still clinging to his skin like a memory. His eyes are frosted blue, the color of the window at dawn, when it's just light enough for the streetlamps to wink out. I study the way he studies me. He seems to regard me as some ethereal thing that's suddenly appeared in his world, and yet, it's my office into which he's wandered.

Our hands release. I open my mouth to introduce myself, but no sound comes out. I dig deep into the recesses of my mind, searching for the moment we've met before. But I can't find it. Perhaps he just has one of those faces. There's a subtle charm about him so easy it's unnerving. He seems the type of guy who looks best in a plain white T-shirt, with tousled hair and a slow, lopsided smile that always wins you over. There it is, that smile.

"You're the new transcriber."

I nod.

"You have a name?"

Transcriber is my name. It's what he's called me all week, without knowing it's me who's been listening. And yet, I wonder what it would be like to hear the hard whisper of the "H" from his throat, to know his tongue is pressed to the roof of his mouth as though lingering in thought as he enunciates the melodic 'l.'

"Wait, don't tell me. Hazel." He must recall it from the message I'd sent him last night.

"Yes."

Silence hangs between us. My stomach twists into knots. I wonder if he knows I was upstairs, watching him last night. Imagining another pink write-up slip waiting for me in the drawer makes me feel sick. But, knowing Kole's history of suspension and seeing a roguish glint in his eyes, now, I think he's more apt to break the rules than enforce them. Within reason.

I wonder what he wants. Is it rude to say, *Can I help you?* "Can I—" I start.

"Oh!" Mistaking my stammer for me wanting my chair back, he jumps up and crosses to the other side of the room.

I sit, now feeling inclined.

"Sorry." He rakes a hand through his hair. He wears his longer than most of the other investigators I've seen. But then, SIU, or rather the Drug Unit guys, don't have to play nice with the usual policies. They can have beards, for one, and they always wear casual clothes unless they're testifying in court. "I just saw my report up, and, well, I wanted to see if it was true."

My eyes dart to my monitor, where the report I'd just typed for him is displayed. *Shit, he knows.* Should I make up an excuse for being up there or just be forthright? I was curious, so sue me. "If what was true?" I ask, buying some time to invent a reason for why I'd been upstairs in the viewing room.

He leans casually on the back of Mona's empty chair. A black chain peeks from beneath the collar of his cobalt thermal. "If you're as good as they say you are."

I quirk my brow, eyeing him suspiciously. "What do you mean?"

He laughs. "What do you mean what do I mean? Everyone's talking about the new transcriber. How she types at the speed of light and doesn't make a mistake. That you even correct our punctuation. The DA's not gonna know what's come over us. She'll think we're all taking English classes."

"Or that you've figured out how to use spellcheck?"

He smiles and I feel as if I've won something. "Maybe, but it's too logical. In fact, I have a theory that this place is in its own invisible bubble that acts like a force field against logic."

"This place meaning the police department or all of Black Harbor?"

"Is both an option?"

I shrug. "It's your theory."

"We'll go with both, then. A bubble inside of a bubble."

"Like *Inception*."

"Great movie."

Out by the drive-up window, I hear Dispatch call out coordinates over the radio. I want him to stay, but I don't know where to go from here. It's been so long since I've had a one-on-one conversation with anyone besides Elle or Mona or Tommy. I imagine possible topics like low-hanging fruit between us. All I have to do is pick one and see what he does with it.

"Well . . . what do you think?" I ask. "Whether or not I'm as good as everyone says." I chew my lip. It's an uncharacteristically bold question.

"I think I'm gonna tell guys to start calling in their reports again."

I consider the hours' worth of dictation that were in the queue when I first started. It's caught up, now, but for a few dormant cases that have yet to be typed. "They haven't been?"

"Most still do, especially the older guys who can't type to save their lives. Others who could actually type a bit felt sorry for Mona, drowning in all that work after Bev died, and started doing their own reports. But you caught the place up in a week. That's impressive."

I blush and see that he's turned toward the window. He separates the blinds with his thumb and index finger, and I know he's peering out at the blue apartments. I glance at the clock, then back to him. It's 4:38. "Are you always in so early?" I wonder.

"When I can't sleep."

I think back to him asking Krejarek about using pills and energy drinks to stay awake. "So, you didn't find his stash?" It's rhetorical, of course. I know from typing the rest of his interview and reading the arrest header noting only a PO Hold that Krejarek hadn't given up any incriminating information. Yet.

"Not yet," Kole admits, echoing my thoughts. "But someone will crack soon enough and then it's go time."

"Go time?"

"Something funny?"

"It sounds like something a cop would say—"

"Well . . ."

"—in a bad action movie."

He rolls his eyes. "I see. Here, everyone's been telling me how sweet you are, and now I see the real Hazel comes out at night."

I don't really believe him. I've never been called *sweet* in my life. Not to my knowledge, anyway. It just doesn't suit me. "No one's said that."

"You wanna bet? I'll call Ox right now. You talked to him on the phone last week. Or Match; he called about a license plate. Said you were *pleasant*."

"Match?"

"Whitmore."

"Why do you call him Match?"

"Because he looks like a matchstick."

I've never seen Investigator Whitmore, but I now imagine him to be bald and thin. I do remember him calling on Thursday, though. I, of course, handed the phone to Mona since it concerned use of the NCIC portal, which I'm not allowed to touch. "And Ox is . . ."

"Mattox."

Right. He throws the flash-bangs and occasionally acts as breacher, whenever Crue is either leading the warrant or not present. "Because his name is Mattox or because he resembles an ox?" I ask.

"Both. Hmm . . . Ox, Match, who else? Oh yeah, Sully said he liked you. I've got him right here." He swipes his thumb across his cell phone and I jump out of my chair.

"OK, I believe you! Please. Don't call anyone." *Especially a lieutenant, my God.*

He raises his hands. "OK, OK. Don't shoot."

I settle back down. "Dang, you guys really gossip around this joint." *This joint? Who even says that?*

"Like you wouldn't believe," he acknowledges. "Worse than a sixties beauty parlor. I heard all these fanciful things about the new transcriber and I wanted to meet you in person before you had a chance to make up your mind about me, based on, you know, gossip."

He's not dumb, that's for sure. Interacting with him for this short while, one could almost forget he's the owner of the crossed-out name. My gaze slides over toward the sworn personnel roster.

"So what's a girl from the middle of nowhere doing in Black Harbor?"

I quirk my brow. "How do you know I'm from the middle of nowhere? You look me up?"

"Irrelevant." He smiles again, his eyes conducting a quick cursory search of me."People talk, Hazel. Everyone knows you're like this prodigy from a podunk town up north who can type freakishly fast."

"Everyone knows?"

"I told you, word travels around here."

"Apparently not much happens around here, either, if I'm news."

"Not much that isn't crime-related."

I wonder what else everyone knows. With Elle's stunt she pulled concerning the bagels and station-branded napkins, there's no doubt the entire PD knows of my relationship to the local celebrity. I'll have to be exceptionally careful with what I tell her from now on.

He shifts and for a second I'm afraid he's got somewhere else to be. *Don't leave.* But, instead, he lowers himself into Mona's chair. We sit across from each other, like he did with Krejarek in the interview room yesterday, and I find myself frantically preoccupied with the question of what to do with my hands. I resolve to interlacing my fingers to prevent any weird mime-typing while my mind returns to the possible conversation topics. There are a lot of things I want to ask him: about the investigation, and his suspension, and I can't deny the fact that I'm curious to learn more about the conversations that occur about me when I'm out of earshot—the ones that don't funnel through my earbuds and flow through my fingertips.

"There was something else," he begins, as though my questions are written all over my forehead. The ball of nerves in my stomach rises like a balloon, expanding in my throat. "Oh yeah. 'Can you believe what Liv did to the new girl already?'

"Huh?"

"That's what everyone was talking about on Friday. I'm walking through the bureau to interview some junkie who just threw a nine-year-old in the trash and that's what they're concerned about." He shakes his head, laughs. "Apparently she doesn't like the way you dress."

"Liv? From Records?"

"Know any others?"

My shoulders sag. Elle was right. It had been a woman who complained, but Liv?

"What's wrong? You look like I just told you your dog died."

"I—" My words catch. "I don't understand." Call me naive, but I thought with all her poking fun at my accent and going out for old-fashioneds, we were becoming friends.

His eyes illuminate with realization. "Oh, you didn't know? Yeah, don't worry about it. She's just jealous because, back in the day, she used to be who everyone talked about around here."

My fingernails press into my palms as I try to recount all the interactions I've had with Liv. She clearly isn't to be trusted. I feel like an idiot. I wonder if Mona was in on it.

Maybe to take my mind off the betrayal, Kole asks where I'm from.

Forcing myself out of my trance, I lift my gaze to stare at him and notice a tiny, chevron-shaped scar directly below the center of his left pupil. It's a circumflex, given to words that don't naturally belong in the English language, like crème brûlée and château. "You wouldn't know it," I say.

"One of those if-you-blink-you'll-miss-it towns?"

I nod. That's what everyone who's familiar with it says. Located about five miles off the main highway that runs north to south through the state. On rare occasions, people stop at the cheese curd shop on their way up to their cabins. Surrounded by farm fields and woods, it isn't a destination for anyone but the people who live there . . . and those of us trying to get home. I tell him its name.

"You're right. I don't know it." He smiles, and I find myself pleasantly contemplating his dimples, a pair of singular quotes on either side of his mouth. "That accounts for the tattoo, then?"

I blush, subconsciously drawing my arm inward. I'm wearing short sleeves tonight. "My husband hates it." The information tumbles out. I wish I could pick the words up off the floor and stuff them back in. Five-second rule.

Someone appears in the doorway, then, and I startle. Kole, on the other hand, seems used to being snuck up on.

Hammersley looks more surprised than either of us. "Oh, hey Nik! Didn't expect to run into you. What're you doin' here at this hour?" He glances up at the clock.

"Couldn't sleep," says Kole.

"You always let these investigations drive you crazy. How'd that interview go last night, with the Candy Man?"

Just hearing the alias again sends a shiver up my spine.

Kole shrugs. "We got 'em. He's being held on a PO Hold, but . . . I gotta find those pills."

"You think they're all in one place?" I ask. It seems I'm getting over my fear of inserting myself into conversations; that, or it's simply overridden by the determination to rid Liv from my palate.

"The way that place was cleaned up," says Kole. "They're in that apartment yet, I know it. No way he'd just dump all those."

"You don't think he had 'em on him when he ran?" asks Hammersley.

Kole shakes his head. "Having a buffet of Schedule II narcotics on you sure shoots a guy's chances at making up an alibi if he gets stopped. Plus, every dealer worth his salt has a trap. Ceiling rafters, toilet tank, buried in the backyard. It's never far."

Hammersley frowns. "Yeah, you're probably right. You deal with a lot more druggies and dope dealers than I ever have, that's for damn sure. By the way, I was just coming by to tell you about my retirement party."

"How many years?"

"Too many. That divorce really set me back. Oh, Hazel, bring your husband."

"OK, thanks." My face feels hot. I'm glad when the conversation moves along.

"What else you gonna do with all your free time?" Kole asks. "Don't tell me you're gonna get a security guard job like everyone else does."

Hammersley stretches. His arms and shoulders are too bulky to raise far above his head. "Vacation. Gonna take a drive down to Florida to spend some time with my granddaughters." He flips through some photos on his phone, landing on one of two dark-haired girls wearing goggles and neon swimsuits. They look about four and five.

"They're cute," I say.

"So you're gonna visit the munchkins. What else?"

Hammersley slides his phone back into his pocket. "I don't know. Maybe I'll just take it easy for a bit. Sleep for more than four hours at a time. And I'll write a book, too, about all the shit I've seen."

I fight the urge to smile. It's what everyone here says, and the funny thing is, I don't think any of them are aware they all say it. Or how hard it actually is.

"You better thank me in the acknowledgments for all those good times when I was in patrol. Remember when we convinced Bright to stick his tongue to the flagpole?"

"We gotta remind him of that at my party," says Hammersley.

"Oh, I'm invited?" Kole points to his chest, and I can't help but stare beneath lowered eyelids at the subtle outline of his pecs.

"Of course, dumbass."

"This isn't just by default 'cause you wanted to invite Hazel, and I happened to just be in here?"

Hazel. I love the way my name sounds on his lips.

Hammersley looks like he's ready to call Kole a dumbass again. "Look, I know you don't drink, but you should really think about it. It'd be good for you to get out."

"I need a desert island, Hammer, not a cramped room full of PD employees. I see you yahoos enough as it is."

"Just think about it." He drops his voice, then, and I don't know if it's to prevent me from hearing or if he's worried about someone stalking the hall. "Hey, how's Dylan doing?"

"Keepin' busy," Kole answers, somber.

"If you see him . . . tell him Hammer says, 'Hello.'"

"I will."

"OK." Hammersley raises his voice back to normal volume and slaps the door frame twice. "I'll see you both at my party. Last Friday of the month."

He exits and it's quiet. A few seconds later, I hear the swinging of the sergeants' doors, and I'm positive that's what Kole was listening for, too.

"Are you gonna go?" I ask. I've already decided that if he goes, I'll go. It's less than two weeks from now. Maybe Tommy will already have plans. Or maybe I just won't mention it.

"I don't do parties." He stands and pushes Mona's chair back in.

The statement stings like a paper cut. I get up and grab a stack of commitments I have no intention of processing at the moment, hoping my feigned nonchalance will be enough to disguise my disappointment. "So, you think Krejarek's stash is in his apartment?"

"It's there. We just didn't look hard enough the first time."

"I think someone was in there the other night," I say. "There was a glow like from a flashlight. I could see it light up the rim of the window."

"Guilty."

"That was you?"

Kole nods, then takes his cell phone out of his pocket and turns on the flashlight. "Apparently I'm not very good at covert operations on my own. The neighbors saw me and started raising hell. So if I want to get back in there without getting shot, I'll need another search warrant."

"Can you get one?"

"If I get Sam to squeal some more, yeah. The problem is I don't know how long I can keep Krejarek on this PO Hold. I might have only a couple of days."

"Is that why you didn't arrest Sam? To keep him cooperative?"

"That's exactly why."

"But he hid a body. Shouldn't he be locked up for that?"

Kole shrugs, holds his hand out like a blade, and teeters it back and forth. "It's a gray area. He dragged a kid to the dumpster—"

"—and snapped his finger off."

"And snapped his finger off. But he confessed. And his story adds up. And he's much more useful to me as a cooperative source than he is if he goes to jail and lawyers up."

"What if he runs?"

He looks at me quizzically as though daring me to come up with my most creative answer. "Where's he gonna go? He has no money. No means to get anywhere. Black Harbor is conveniently close to nowhere."

Oh, don't I know that. "You said you consulted with the DA's office. In your report."

He nods. "More like struck a deal. An ass for an ass. If he does anything messed up—"

"—like tossing kids in the dumpster and snapping their fingers off?"

"Yes, for example—it's my ass on the line."

A line Kole's pretty comfortable crossing, I think, considering his willingness to plunge right into the murky depths of the Candy Man investigation so soon after returning from a hush-hush suspension. "What about Krejarek?" I ask. "What happens if you don't have enough to put him away and he gets out?"

Kole rubs the back of his neck like there's a knot there he can't dissolve. "He goes free," he says finally. "Keeps killing kids. There'll be another one after this, I'll tell you that right now. Because if he evades charges on this case, he'll know he can get away with it. He's *been* getting away with it."

"You mean there were others?"

"Yeah, well. What I know and what I can prove are two different things. Just off the top of my head, I can think of three overdoses with Krejarek's stink all over them. No one died, though. And none of them were as young as Jordan McAllister."

"Do you think Krejarek really did it?" I ask. "Dealt Jordan McAllister the drugs and helped hide the body and all that?"

"Without a doubt. I just have to prove it."

I shuffle my papers on the countertop like I'm going to do something with them. "So, you don't think it's possible at all that Sam acted on his own . . . saw that little kid dead, freaked out, and threw him in the dumpster?" Frisson flows through my veins. I feel effervescent and investigative like a reporter gathering intel. I am, essentially. For the first time since Tommy and I moved here, I'm looking forward to returning to the duplex and regurgitating everything I heard tonight into my Word document. But talking with Nikolai Kole right now, face-to-face, is even better. As long as I don't do or say anything stupid.

"Not for a second," he answers. "Have you seen Sam?"

I feel my cheeks get hot again and I pray he doesn't notice. It feels like a trick question. He can't know I live next to Sam, that we essentially walk the same floors, that my husband breathes in his and his old man's secondhand marijuana smoke on a nightly basis. I'll be labeled a conflict of interest and thrown off the case. And a transcriber who can't transcribe the single biggest investigation that's going on right now is a jobless one. My throat's dry when I answer: "Yes."

Kole seems momentarily shocked at my statement, and then, "Oh, right. He came up to your window. OK, so you've seen Sam. He's what, 5'9" or 5'10", not terribly tall for a guy. Jordan McAllister probably weighed close to seventy pounds. Plus his sleeping bag. Plus, he's literally deadweight. There weren't any drag marks and the fresh snowfall wasn't enough to cover up any that could have been there. No way Sam could have carried him down the stairs and across the lot. And then hoisting him into the dumpster is another level of exertion." He pauses. "An in-shape person could probably do it, yeah, but not Sam."

I remember the way Tyler Krejarek had presented himself in the interview yesterday—a sack of bones drowning in a grimy sweatshirt. Him carrying the corpse out on his own is out of the question, too. Also, Sam already confessed.

"What do you need to charge Krejarek with reckless homicide?" I ask.

"A motive." He pulls up his phone and appears to be scrolling through messages. His eyes dart to the doorway where Hammersley stood less than a minute ago. "Can you keep a secret between you and me?"

Between you and me. My breath catches at the sound of it. I'm good at keeping secrets. "Yes."

I take a step toward him and lean in. He smells like sandalwood and sage, a hint of leather. My mind swims. His scent is so intoxicating I dare to wonder what it would taste like, if I pressed my lips to his neck. My eyes wander to the definition beneath his shirt again.

I catch a glimpse of the name "Pearl" among his messages, and feel deflated. Of course he has someone. Nikolai Kole: confident, commanding, charismatic; there's no way he sleeps alone.

And neither do I, I remind myself. Except that I do, technically, sleep alone. Most mornings, I crawl into bed when it's still warm from Tommy having left it. The scent he leaves behind on his pillowcase and sheets is less enticing, though: alcohol and gunpowder.

Kole touches a message from a sender labeled "Unknown" and shows it to me. *He keeps his shit in the walls*, it reads.

Who is this? Kole had replied.

There was no answer after that.

A tendril of my hair falls loose and grazes his wrist. I hadn't realized just how close we were until now. I inhale again just to breathe him in once more and sneak a glance at his lips, his mouth a gateway to all the secrets of Black Harbor. I wonder what it would feel like to kiss him, a stranger—someone who isn't Tommy. Just to see if I actually like kissing. I think I do.

"And you have no idea who that is?"

Kole shakes his head.

"Could it be Sam?"

"It could be." The way he answers makes me believe he's already considered the possibility. "I really don't know. It could be someone else entirely who got my number from a confidential informant or something and they're using an app to hide their info."

"Damn. Technology these days." I mentally slap myself. What am I, eighty?

"Tell me about it. But, assuming this tip is legit and I find Krejarek's pills in his walls . . ." He extends his arm and drops his phone, then catches it with his other hand. Mic drop. "That's enough to charge him with reckless homicide. Especially when we can validate those oxys weren't part of his med kit." He sighs heavily, having just made up his mind. "I gotta go back in, warrant or not. Like I said, they know me, but I'll just have to hope and pray no one sees me."

The world falls silent. It feels as though a weighted blanket has descended on the entire police department. The hum of the computers recedes; the dispatcher radio by the drive-up window goes quiet. The only sound I hear is my heartbeat, as I consider the possibility of this case wrapping up with Krejarek's arrest before anyone finds out I am a conflict of interest.

Boom. Boom. Boom. Boom.

I see myself staring into the pitch-dark cavity of Krejarek's apartment, the trash bag over the window blocking out all light, all hope. I feel myself being tugged, pulled toward the abyss as the shadows ask, *Are you in or are you out?*

Boom. Boom. Boom.

I remember the way the turquoise die cartwheeled over the stainless-steel surface of the table. *Time to decide.*

Boom. Boom.

I think about the Word document I had started, the cursor blinking on a stark white page. *Write what you know.* Here is my chance to know it.

"But they don't know me," I offer.

Boom.

9.

LATER

I stand in front of Old Will's door, fist poised to knock. I've been standing out here for what feels like ten minutes, petrified. If I'm out here any longer, I'll be as frozen to the porch as the newspaper everyone refuses to pick up. Sam will be inside, probably. He has nowhere else to go, as Kole pointed out to me in the twilight hours of this morning.

Just when I am about to turn around and forget the whole operation, Tommy's laughter rings over the noise of the TV. He has such a warm laugh; just hearing it is enough to convince myself that the other side of the duplex is safe.

I knock twice. The door opens. Old Will appears, a bristly silhouette backlit by the glow of the kitchen. He looks like a rock star past his prime, emerging through a haze of smoke effects. The skunky smell of weed hits me in the face. I hope it doesn't cling to my clothes.

"Hazel! Come in, come in." His goatee, strewn with strands of fiber-optic white, bounces as he talks. He smiles and even in this dark, I can see his eyes are glassy. I follow him in. Ever dressed in his old army fatigues, Old Will reminds me of a twentieth-century Rip Van Winkle who fell asleep at the end of the Vietnam War only to wake up two decades later in a mosh pit at a Metallica concert. He's only in his early sixties, though his arthritis causes him to move like someone much older. His hair sits on his head like an oil-stained mop.

Will and Sam's side of the duplex is like a college house. Pizza crusts litter the table like steak bones picked clean. Empty beer cans and bottles congregate next to the kitchen sink. There's a framed *Fear and Loathing in Las Vegas* poster on the shared wall of the kitchen and living room. My husband rounds the corner, smiling, his teeth clamped down on a cigar to hold it in place. He opens his arms wide, as if I would jump into them.

Perhaps it's the new distance the confidential nature of my job has inserted between me and everyone else, but I am beginning to see people more objectively. For instance, if I didn't know better, I would think that Tommy and Old Will are father and son—both with their dark hair, eyes watery and red-veined from drinking. I've even heard Tommy utter the word "bizarre" on more than one recent occasion.

Meanwhile, Sam sits in the other room, watching TV and smoking a blunt. "Hey Sam," I say, careful not to stutter. And then to Tommy, who wraps me up into a bear hug: "I just got called into work."

His breath is pungent when he goes to kiss me. I turn my head so he plants one on my cheek. "Gotta earn that bread," he says in his naturally projecting voice. I wince because he doesn't seem to realize how close his mouth is to my ear.

"Yer old man says you work for the cops." It's the most words I've ever heard Sam string along in one sentence. His verbal communication usually tops out at monosyllabic grunts.

So he really hadn't seen me on the other side of the frosted window. Tommy sets me down, and I feel my shoulders fall with relief. "Just in the office," I reply. "Typing reports."

"You get all the good dirt on everyone." It sounds like it should be a joke, but he doesn't smile. Smoke vents out of his mouth.

"I guess so." I watch him raise his blunt. His thumb pokes through the tattered material of his dark sweatshirt cuff, and I can just barely make out the sliver of a tattoo. His middle and index fingers press lightly to his lips as he sucks on the filter, like he's telling me to *Sshhhh*. His eyes fix to the TV screen again.

"So, what's going on tonight?" Tommy asks, now. "Someone jump from the bridge?" His face is over-animated. He gets like this when he drinks: eyes excited, mouth half smiling, ready to break into laughter at any second. At least he's not an angry drunk, a simple fact I've used to excuse a lot of his behavior. And I'm not worried about him smoking any weed. For one, I don't think Will or Sam would share, and second, Tommy's terrified of being randomly piss-tested at work. He would never do anything to jeopardize his right to own firearms.

"Isn't that bizarre?" Old Will says, shaking his head. "People still jump from that damn thing. Hey Tommy gun, grab me another beer, will ya?"

I brace myself for the two-minute monologue of him reciting all the people he knows who've jumped from Forge Bridge. It always reminds me of Bubba naming all the ways to serve shrimp. Thankfully, he refrains. "No jumpers," I say. "Just . . . there's a couple of lengthy arrest reports Mona didn't get to. They want to make sure they're done for tomorrow."

"Get that OT," Tommy says on his way to the fridge. "I've been eyeing up a new 9mm at Ryder's." He winks, but I know he isn't kidding.

"Hey man, what'd'ya know about that kid? Little boy found in ter dumpster. That's pretty gnarly, eh?"

My cheeks get hot as both Will and Tommy turn to me. Tommy's blue inquiring eyes and Will's black ones. That was the first thing I ever noticed about Old Will—how black his eyes are, like a bird's. And Sam's are even darker. To say the boy in the dumpster has plagued my thoughts for six days now would be an understatement. Them asking feels like an intrusion into my mind, but I imagine fragments of the story made it onto the local news. I shrug. "That's pretty much all I know . . ."

"Hazel signed a confidentiality agreement." There's a note of pride in Tommy's voice when he tells Will. "Even if she knows whodunit, she can't tell us."

I exhale, feeling relieved.

Will raises his crippled right hand, his left claw pressing his beer against his chest. He's wearing a faded AC/DC T-shirt, and I'd wager it isn't worn thin from washing, but wearing for decades on end. "Scout's honor, Hazel. I woon't say nothin'." He laughs, a broken, crackling sound, like the static of the dispatch radio. "No one listens to Ol' Will anyway."

He and Tommy clink beer bottles and drink to that. I watch as Tommy guzzles his down, the last of the foam sliding down the neck of the clear glass bottle and into his throat.

"They're still investigating it," I say as Tommy goes to the fridge to crack another. "It's been under pretty tight wraps."

"Secrets, secrets," Sam says, and takes another drag from his blunt.

I watch him from the corner of my eye. Obviously, he hasn't mentioned anything to Will or Tommy about his involvement. I wonder if Will even knows his son runs with a dealer named Candy Man. Judging by Will's usually catatonic state, probably not.

Will is shaking his head. "Just sick. What this world's coming to. Sometimes I wonder if the rest of 'em were on ter somethin' with jumping off that bridge."

• • •

Here. I send the text to a number I've never contacted before. Getting his info had been almost too easy. In a nondescript white binder in the cabinet above Mona's computer, there's a record of all BHPD investigators' and command personnel's phone numbers. He'll recognize my area code as belonging to up north, just like I recognized his as belonging to Black Harbor.

I turn off my lights and leave the engine running. His last correspondence over the BHPD messenger system said to meet in the municipal lot at 7 p.m. It's 6:58.

A lone police SUV cruises down the perpendicular street, past a row of slanted houses with crumbling porches. It's so quiet, I can hear the crackling of frozen icicle lights in the subtle wind. Directly behind me, a pair of headlights flash once, twice.

I turn the key out of the ignition, get out, shut the door, and press the fob twice to lock it. No one ever locks their vehicles up at home, but here, there's less fear of it being stolen than fear of who might be living in it upon your return.

I pause before tugging on the handle of the black SUV with tinted windows to count approximately how many times I've been warned to never get into cars with strangers. Oh well, if he's going to murder me tonight, I've had a good run. Or haven't I? He is a cop, I justify, as though that negates the fact that he's still technically a stranger. But in a city like Black Harbor, can you even trust the police?

I open the door to see Nikolai Kole sitting behind the wheel, wearing a dark jacket and jeans as always, the chain around his neck glimmering in the faint light of the streetlamp. The brim of his hat shadows his face, but his smile is bright. One might think he's picking me up to go ice skating, not sneak into a crime scene. "Hey."

"Hey," I say, and I'm embarrassed by my own breathlessness. There's something about his voice that draws me in, a winch that pulls me to him, and I'm powerless to stop it. I drop my purse on the floor between my feet and look around. All leather interior, vinyl floor mats that, unlike mine, are free of salt and pebbles. The dials on the radio glow blue.

"Either you encountered a skunk or you fell down in a weed patch." He waves his hand in the air between us.

"My neighbor," I tell him, and immediately sink in my seat when I realize my neighbor is indeed one of his persons of interest.

"Relax. If we spent our time tracking down pot, the City would go broke on OT. You and I got bigger fish to fry tonight anyway. I turned your seat warmer on." He points to a button with two out of three dashes illuminated. "You can adjust it here."

"Thank you. So, is this the chariot you cart your CIs around in?"

"God, no. I'd have to get this thing detailed twice a week."

"You mean you don't already?" The interior of the vehicle is immaculate and lemon-scented. There's not so much as loose change in the cupholder and the dashboard holds the telltale matte sheen of Armor All.

"Excuse me for not being a slob," he says as I fasten my seat belt. He pulls out of the lot just as a police SUV is entering. "What'd you drive here, a tractor?" He nods at my Blazer.

"It's an '02," I say, as though that earns me some sort of credit.

"I can see that." His eyes roam the rust around the wheel wells, the dimples in the teal paint. We pull onto the street and coast past the police department on our left. I can see the picture window of the Transcribing office. I'll be there soon enough, pressing down on the foot pedal and listening to half a dozen narratives before daybreak. Kole guides the vehicle around the curve of the roundabout, past the red door to Tyler Krejarek's apartment. He turns right down a dead end. The road is a steep slope, and from the vantage point of the windshield, it looks like we could crest off the edge of the earth as we begin our descent, especially when he shuts off the headlights. I don't know that I've ever experienced such darkness before. Even at home, where the spires of evergreens shoot into the night sky, the moon and stars light the way. I've never seen a star in Black Harbor.

"You never told me what you're doing here by the way. Why you left home."

He's right, I realized. He'd asked but then Liv had come up instead. I give him my default answer. "There's no work up north."

"Nothing?"

"Not unless I wanna work in my dad's woodshop."

"He's a carpenter?"

"A carver."

"That's pretty cool. What about your mom?"

"She doesn't live up there anymore. She moved to Arizona, where she has a pet-grooming business."

"Oh. I'm sorry."

I shrug. There's nothing to say about it. One night, I'd gone to sleep with her being home, and woken up the next morning to her being gone. I'd been seventeen, and yet, in that moment of realizing my mother was gone for good, I'd felt like a little kid being left at a store. To this day, I wonder if Elle had known anything about it. It wouldn't matter, so I've never asked. What would Elle have done anyway? Told me so that I'd have stayed awake, listening to the sounds of her zipping her suitcase and backing out of the driveway?

The path ends so abruptly that I think it might not be a road at all but an outlet for plows to push mountains of snow. Kole veers right to pull into the lot behind the blue building. Although it hasn't been plowed for a few days, the snow is packed down enough to drive on. He parks and shuts off the vehicle. "You ready?"

"Yes."

"All right. Come on."

I slam the car door, leaving my purse tucked under the seat. My breath is a cloud in front of me as we trek up the steep hill toward the looming structure. The lot being at a slant gives a disorienting feel, like we're in a topsy-turvy world where old theaters are opium dens and barbershops sell cocaine out the back door.

Crunching on ice and salt sounds deafening, but there isn't a soul around to hear us. A few of the windows are aglow. I'm glad for having bundled up. The cold bites at my nose and any patch of exposed skin. I steal a glance at Kole, whose baseball cap isn't doing anything to protect his ears. The light from a lone lamp illuminates the sharp edges of his face like a knife.

"You don't have to do this, you know."

The timing of his statement startles me. "Are you trying to talk me out of it, now?"

"No, I just don't want you to feel forced."

We slow our pace, eyes locked on each other's, until we finally stop walking altogether. "I want to help you," I say, and I mean it.

The look he gives me is serious. He nods, then his eyes dart up ahead to a dumpster about ten feet from the main back entrance. "That's where we found him."

I turn my head slowly as though I'm about to encounter a ghost instead of a waste bin. The thing is inconspicuous, just a run-of-the-mill container you'd find in any parking lot. A piece of yellow caution tape is stuck on the corner, the only hint that a corpse had been there less than a week ago. Tears instantaneously freeze to my lashes, and I can't articulate why I feel this sudden surge of grief, if it's because Jordan McAllister was probably terrified when he choked to death on his own tongue, or because I live in a place where children are found dead in dumpsters. And there's foreseeably no way out, except—

The only way out is down.

—to write a book that takes me far away from here.

Kole stands rigid, staring at it.

"You OK?" If I knew him better, I'd nudge his elbow. But I hardly know him. And yet, I can't deny the gravitational pull I feel toward him.

"You know, there's always a moment where you have this wire-thin sliver of hope that you're wrong about what's in there." He sighs. His shoulders fall and I wonder how many corpses he's examined from aboveground graves.

I don't know what to say. Again, if I knew him better, I might touch his arm or run my hand along the tense muscles in his back. But I know only his voice. The dips and depths of it, the way his "s's" slice like piano wire. He locks eyes with me one last time as though giving me a final opportunity to change my mind.

I look up at our target, a Vonnegutesque structure that blocks the illumination of the streetlamps. There's something arachnid and alien about it, with all its windows and ramps shooting out. The chipped paint looks like molting skin.

I notice four doors at the first level, another four along the top. "Upper left?" I ask, picturing the location of Krejarek's window on the other side.

"Correct."

"OK. What's the game plan?"

"When you get inside, just . . . act natural."

I gather a deep inhale . . . exhale. "Blend in."

"You're too pretty to blend in."

"*You're* too pretty to blend in."

He laughs and the air feels less ominous around us. "I know! That's why I'm staying out here!"

I roll my eyes. Smiling out here feels wrong. I bite my lip.

"Just pay attention to the walls," he says. "Loose panels, posters, pictures."

"OK."

He takes his phone out of his pocket. I watch as his thumb slides across the screen, and suddenly, my phone vibrates. His number shows up as requesting a FaceTime. Quirking my brow at him, I press "Accept."

"Hello?" he says.

"I'm two feet away from you." Not even.

"I'm just making sure you know how to answer the phone."

"I know how to answer the phone."

"You never know with you millennials. Always texting."

I narrow my eyes at his image on my phone screen. "Aren't you—?"

"OK, Podunk, here's the plan." When I wrinkle my nose, he adds, "Hey, don't give me that. It's better than some of the CIs we run. Crue's got a guy named Butterball."

"Oh." I frown.

"Don't feel sorry for him; he's a skimmer."

"A skimmer?"

"He skims some off the top whenever he does buys. 'An ounce of coke for them, one for me. An ounce for them . . . and one more for me.' Anyway, you and I will be connected the entire time. I can help guide you through the apartment, and, if anyone shows up, I'll be there as quick as I can run up those stairs, OK?"

In the minimized self-portrait screen, I see the stairs that cut across the back of the building like scars. "If anyone shows up?"

He winces as though regretting having mentioned it. "Krejarek's place is empty. But it's an apartment complex. I just mean if someone hears activity and goes to see what it's about. That's all."

"Ah."

"You OK?"

"Are *you* OK?"

He squeezes my arm. I feel warm, a capsule of fire having just blossomed inside me. The sensation surges up and down through my limbs, coloring my cheeks, and stopping short of my fingertips that remain ice cold. "You're something else," and the way he looks at me when he says it makes it almost easy to forget we're in a dangerous setting.

The zigzag ramp is a stairway to my greatest nightmares: dark places, dead bodies. Ticket for one, please. Climbing one stair at a time, I take note of the snaggletoothed nails in the wooden railing that remind me of Krejarek's mouth, the bullet holes that pockmark the corpse-blue siding, and I consider again the possibility that there is another way out of Black Harbor: *Up*. I may never have anything to do with Nikolai Kole ever again, but at least after tonight, I'll have fodder for my new story.

I'm high off the ground but not nearly as high as when I stand on Forge Bridge. Looking out over the shadowy expanse, I can see it from here, a black-on-black silhouette. The river blends into the night, though. It's the real killer, with its atramentous tongue dragging jumpers down into its belly.

When I reach the top, I throw a glance down at Kole waiting in the lot. He hasn't taken his eyes from me. Feeling somewhat reassured, I wrap my hand over the cold brass doorknob and twist. I cringe, expecting something ungodly to lunge at me. Nothing does. Nevertheless, my knees shake.

I take a deep breath and force myself to dream of all the words I'll be able to add to my document after this. Squeezing my hands into fists, I enter into the building's gaping mouth. At the end of the hall, a lone light bulb hangs from a wire like a uvula. The walls seem to narrow with each step.

Krejarek's door is crooked and clings to the frame like a stubborn hangnail. It's marred with a series of crescent-shaped dents from the one-man ram, compliments of Investigator Crue. It creaks as I push it in, the sound filling my world.

I gasp.

"You OK?"

I'd momentarily forgotten that Kole's with me on my phone screen. "Yeah, just . . . it's so dark." A feeling of déjà vu invades me. As my eyes adjust, I see the game board on the coffee table, the plastic jugs filled with urine along the wall, the empty energy drink cans strewn about the floor. The couches are cockeyed like they've been moved, the cushions torn off. On the floor in front of the trash bag-covered window, there's a spot cleared. That must have been where Jordan McAllister's body had lain.

Who can take tomorrow . . . Dip it in a dream . . . Separate the sorrow and collect up all the cream . . .

I stand frozen, too afraid to turn around. They're in the walls. The children's voices.

Candy Man . . . Oh, the Candy Man can . . .

The muscles in my back tense as I imagine a gray hand raking its nails down my spine.

'Cause he mixes it with love and makes the world taste good.

Where his sleeping bag would have been, Jordan McAllister sits up and licks the dust from his lips.

I shriek.

"Psst . . . Podunk?"

"Jesus Christ!" I hiss, jumping out of my skin. The corpse is gone. It's just me and the debris of that night.

"Hazel?"

I can't speak. My stomach clenches and unclenches. I feel sick. I have to get out of here. The shadows take hold of me. It feels like hands are squeezing my temples. My feet are shackled to the floor.

Something grabs me from behind. My scream is cut short by a cold hand over my mouth. Tears stream from my eyes and I sink down, down, down. I'm going to die here. I should have jumped all those times I had the chance.

"Hazel." His voice is the calming shush of white noise or waves. Holding my face in his hands, he wipes my tears away with his thumbs.

I'm malleable in his arms.

"Shh . . ." He rocks me back and forth like a child. "Are you hurt? Did you see something?"

I take in two deep breaths. "Just . . . my imagination." I know it's true as soon as I say it. The room rights itself. I have a sense of gravity again.

"We can go," he offers. "I shouldn't have made you come up here—"

"No." I surprise myself. Two seconds ago, if not for being paralyzed with fear, I would have sprinted out the door and thrown myself from the scaffolding. "Just stay with me, please."

"I'm not going anywhere. I promise."

We rise together. I grip his hand tightly. He turns on the flashlight on his phone. "You check any of the walls yet?"

"This is as far as I got." I gesture to the spot where my mind had conjured a sleeping bag and a dead kid just a moment ago.

I can hear the smile in his voice. "It's all good. I'm actually impressed you made it this far. I know guys on the SWAT team, even, who would've pissed their tactical pants."

"I'm not so sure I didn't," I admit.

We move along the perimeter of the room. I hold the light while he knocks on the walls taking pictures down and tossing them on the floor.

"Talk to me," I tell him. He must hear the edge of fear in my voice, yet, because he obliges.

"Talk about anything?"

"Anything."

"How do you like the PD so far?"

"Really? That's what you're going to ask me?"

"You know what's funny is that even in the dark, I can see that eyebrow shooting up. Wait." He turns the flashlight to throw some light on my face. "Yep, there it is."

"You're so dumb."

He laughs as though I've just flattered him. "Let's play a game, then."

"I spy?"

"We're always playing that one. As soon as you spy with your little eye a satchel full of pills, we can get out of here." He looks around as though saying the word might have summoned the object in question. " How about two truths and a lie. I'll tell you three things about myself. Two of them are true, and one's a lie. You have to guess which one."

"All right." A Cheeto crunches under my foot. I look down to see orange crumbs pulverized into the carpet.

Our hands separate as Kole moves to rip a poster off the wall. The sound tears through the silence and I brace myself for someone to come through the door. But no one does. He slides his hands over the wall, feeling for creases or holes that shouldn't be there. "One," he begins. "I'm originally from Pittsburgh; my family moved to Black Harbor when I was nine, my brother was twelve. Two: I initially went to college to become a veterinarian, but then realized I suck at anatomy. And three: I don't like pickles."

He moves along the wall, and I follow. "Two is a lie," I guess.

"False; two is true."

"Dammit. How about one is a lie?"

"Ding ding ding. Ladies and gentlemen, we have a winner. Come on up, young lady, and see what you've won."

I step toward him. He hands me a busted TV remote like it's a bouquet of flowers. The back plate is missing and it's cross-hatched with electrical tape. I grasp my prize, and pretend to wipe away a tear from my face. "There are so many people I'd like to thank for this award. First off, to our esteemed host, Mr. Tyler Krejarek, for lending us your atrocious abode . . ."

Kole laughs. The sound is enough to make almost me forget where we are. He keeps moving, though, progressing around the perimeter, searching the walls. "Are you from Black Harbor, then?" I ask. The countertop to the little inlet kitchen is so full of papers and mail, you can't see its surface. I set the remote on top of it.

"Born and raised, unfortunately."

"And you have a brother who's three years older than you?"

"I did."

We complete our search of the main living space and enter what must be Krejarek's bedroom. There's a mattress on the floor. Clothes lie like deflated bodies, sprawled near his closet as though they'd crawled out of it. Kole checks this room in the same manner, knocking on the walls, swearing when nothing turns up.

"There's still the bathroom," I suggest.

"Let's hope the third room's a charm. It's your turn, by the way."

"Two truths and a lie, let's see . . ." I follow him as he pivots around the corner into the bathroom. The shower curtain is clear with an aquarium scene on the bottom half, and water stained. Strangely, I feel braver in this tiny space. There isn't enough real estate for anyone but the two of us. "Well, I ran cross-country in high school, I pierced my own ears when I was fourteen, and I've never had a pizza delivered."

Kole laughs at the last one. "I hope number three is a lie."

"Is that your guess?"

"Hold on, hold on." He repeats the options to himself. "Ran cross-country, that's probably true. Pierced ears when you were fourteen . . ." He looks at me, his eyes searching my earlobes for jewelry, but my hair covers them. "Eh, probably true. Never had a pizza delivered. Yeah, that's my guess. Everyone's had a pizza delivered."

"Not me," I say, almost triumphantly.

"Are you for real? Goddamn, you really are a Podunk. Not even during college?"

I shake my head. "There was a pizza place right across the street. If we wanted one, we'd just go and get it. I wasn't about to pay a two-dollar delivery fee."

He laughs. "What did you just say? How much was the delivery fee?"

"Two dollars," I say again.

He's still laughing. "Oh, wow, you are something else. Two *doh-lars*." He emphasizes a long "o" sound. I feel my cheeks get hot, like when Liv teases me at work, but this is different. He's laughing with me, not at me. He doesn't have an audience to chastise me in front of.

"That's the most *up north* thing I've heard you say, yet."

"Well, there's plenty more where that came from."

"Good."

I smile. "What's your second guess? Ran cross-country in high school. Pierced my ears when I was fourteen."

He lingers in the shower for a second—thinking or searching, I can't tell—and when he steps out, there's barely an inch of space between us. He reaches upward. I tense when I feel his fingertips graze my neck, but the effect is so calming, tempting me to close my eyes. I stare into his instead, though. He's right about always playing I spy. He's doing it right now. I wonder what he sees. *I spy with my little eye . . . a failure.*

He lightly pinches my ear between his thumb and index finger. We're so close our noses are almost touching. The scent of his cologne is so intoxicating I could get high on it. Euphoria shuts out everything but the sensation of his skin against mine, the feel of his warm breath against my lips, when he says, "You don't have pierced ears."

"Cheater," I whisper. I flick the brim of his hat, knocking it onto the floor.

He touches the back of my head, then. I dare to close my eyes and give myself to the slow circles he's creating with his fingertips. This must be what ecstasy feels like. I turn to liquid at his touch, reveling in those languid circles like ripples in the black matter that is me.

The zipper of his jacket makes a groaning noise as I drag it down. I press my hand on his chest, the taut muscles warm and hard against my palm. It's wrong, but I want to feel more of him.

Reading my mind, he leans in, his other hand pressed to the small of my back. I turn my head and dodge his kiss, losing my balance and knocking into the sink.

He looks stunned and instantly apologetic. "Hazel, I'm sorry. I thought . . . "

My stomach churns. I feel like such an idiot. I want him. I might need him right now. And dammit, I didn't come this far to only come this far.

You're damned if you do, and damned if you don't. For once in your life, have some moxie.

Stepping toward him again, I grab hold of his shirt and pull him to me. I press my mouth to his, breathing him in like a shot of life. Endorphins rush through my brain. If this is what junkies feel every time they shoot up or snort powder, I understand why they do it. I feel outside of my body, brought back by his electrified touch.

His hand moves up my jacket, underneath the back of my shirt. I kiss him harder. He lifts me up, then, hoisting me onto the sink. My foot catches on the side of the door. He pushes it closed with the arm that isn't encircling my waist. I let my head fall back, exposing the soft curve of my neck to him. The mirror protests as the crown of my head pushes into it.

He stands between my knees and pulls me closer to him. I slide my hands down the valley of his chest, tugging at the bottom of his thermal shirt to reveal the tops of a V-cut, the rest of which disappears into his jeans. He scoops his hands under my bottom and lifts me up, kissing my neck as I fight my way out of my jacket, when suddenly, I notice a fissure in the wall behind him. I squint, trying to make out what it is. He sets me down and leans slightly away, trying to read my face. "What's wrong?" And then his eyes widen as in the mirror, he sees it, too.

Turning around, he issues one solid knock to the wall. The cheap panel crashes down, revealing a cache, like a wild animal's home in a tree. Without hesitation, Kole shoves his arm in the hole and retrieves a black satchel. On the flap, metal studs glint under his phone light.

"Holy shit," he says.

I hop off my perch and meet him on the floor, hovering over him as he dumps the contents of the bag into the sink. Dozens of pill bottles spill into a pile, the capsules rattling inside. A glass pipe clanks against the faucet. There are razors and tobacco papers, too; plastic baggies containing pills and powder.

"Good eye, Podunk," he commends. He sounds out of breath. I watch, then, open-mouthed, as he scoops everything back into the satchel and returns it to the wall.

"Wait, what are you—"

"I'll come back in the morning with a warrant," he explains. "I can't take it without—"

Suddenly, the *Star Wars* theme song blares.

I jump.

"Fuck." Kole hurries to answer his phone. I read "Unknown" on the screen before he accepts the call.

"Hey . . . Oh hey, Sully. Yeah, I'm around . . . Yeah, I'll come in . . . What?" His eyes dart to me, a feral glint in them. "Jesus. Yeah, he's at the jail, now . . . OK, see you then . . . Yeah." He hangs up.

"What is it?" I ask.

He stares blankly at the sink, where the drugs were just a moment ago. "Another dead kid," he says, finally. "Overdose."

My stomach clenches. I grip the edge of the cold countertop. The voices bleed out of the wall, another added to their ghastly chorus. *The Candy Man can . . . Oh, he mixes it with love and makes the world—*

A small scream escapes me as Kole drills his fist into the mirror.

10.

THURSDAY

Standing with my back to the doorway, I hear Mona before I see her faint reflection in the window. She shuffles tie-dyed tote bags and sets her metal water bottle on the countertop. "Ooh, what's going on across the street?" she asks. In my peripheral vision, I can see her loose spirals of hair falling from her headband. She smells like lemon and patchouli.

"Three of our guys just went into Krejarek's place," I say, though I know them to be Kole, Riley, and Sergeant Lewison from the bureau. A police SUV with lights flashing is parked at the entrance to the roundabout, and Kole's black Impala is parked in front of the crimson door.

"Hmm . . . wonder what for," says Mona. "Maybe they left something."

"Or went back for something," I offer, and I decide that I've said enough. About a half hour ago, I received a text from Kole: *Look out your window.* I opened the blinds, then, to see the three of them exit the undercover vehicle and ascend the crumbling cement stoop. If I'm being honest, I was a little envious, especially of Investigator Riley, who didn't have to wait for the cover of darkness to walk beside Kole.

Kole and I texted on and off throughout the night, too. I know that the kid who overdosed had been a fourteen-year-old girl named Anya Brown, and that her parents had discovered her blue on her bedroom floor when she didn't come down for dinner. Investigations had confiscated her cell phone and would be interviewing her friends. As far as I know, she's alive but not coherent.

Are you going to press Kejarek some more? I texted.

Yes, he responded. *As soon as I get that satchel out of his place.*

I used texting him as a reward for getting my work done. Complete an arrest, respond. Complete an arrest, respond. It made quick work of it all.

When can I see you again? he asked.

I set my phone down on the countertop and pushed it away, as though FaceTime would suddenly turn on and he'd see me blushing. It was 3:15 a.m. He had to be home, by now, I thought. And then I thought some more about my schedule. It was technically Thursday morning. Tommy was leaving after work for his parents' house, where Cam would meet him and they'd leave for the Boundary Waters in Minnesota Friday morning. I spent sixty dollars on snacks for them: granola bars, apples, Oreos, etc. I even picked up a six-pack of Tommy's favorite craft beer and set it by his tactical bag. Such a good wife.

Tonight, I sent, hoping not to sound eager.

I saw him respond immediately, but processed two arrests before reading it: *7 p.m. Beck's. I owe you a drink.*

"Well, one of them's gotta call in a report, at least," says Mona. "We'll know for sure soon enough." She wiggles her mouse to wake up her computer and turns on the portal.

I should invite her to Elle's party tomorrow. If it isn't too late, already. "Do you have plans for this weekend?" I ask. Not only do I genuinely believe that her company would enhance time spent socializing with Elle's friends but her having to work in the morning would provide a welcome excuse to leave at a reasonable hour.

"I'm hoppin' on a Greyhound to visit my cousin in Minneapolis," Mona starts, and I'm simultaneously disappointed and relieved. On one hand, I don't have to anticipate her rejection of my invitation, and on the other, it means I'll definitely be going alone. A dumbfounded look appears on her face as she scans the CFS board and sees Anya Brown's case. "Well, fuck me twelve ways to Christmas, another overdose?"

Liv materializes as though summoned by the word "fuck." She comes this way most mornings to "borrow" a cup of coffee from Wick, despite the fact that Records has their own coffee maker. Wearing a white fitted button-up tucked into gray dress pants, she could be a magazine model for business casual. She would probably light a match and flick it at me if she knew my clothes were all bought from thrift shops. "Who's fucking who what way?" she asks, immediately laughing at her own wit. I've noticed, too, that she stops to talk only on mornings when Mona is here. Monday and Tuesday, she'd been at her desk, stamping papers or whatever she does, and hardly looked up when I said goodbye.

I turn away, busying myself with packing my things into my tote bag. *Can you believe what Liv did to the new girl already?* I can't look at her.

"Search warrant," Mona says, nodding toward the window.

"Ooh." I can tell by the unnecessary high pitch that candy coats her voice that Liv's face is over-animated. I glance at her. She clutches her coveted cup of coffee with both hands, holding it with the rim just below her lips, her mouth forming a frivolously seductive "o."

"That's gotta be Kole's, yeah?" says Mona. "That guy hasn't taken a breather since he got back."

Kole. Hearing his name is like an ember that starts in the pit of my stomach and funnels warmth throughout my entire body. I am electrified by the sensory memory of how he felt last night: his hardness and heat; how I'd melted into him, shaping my body around his. Afterward, my face felt as though I'd abraded it with sandpaper, and I'd catch myself throughout the night soothing it with my cool fingertips, reveling in the tingling sensation of it and remembering his rough cheek against mine as we kissed. The only thing soft about him had been his lips and the way he'd shushed me when I'd been afraid.

A momentary lapse in judgment, most likely, for both of us. And yet, in that moment, it had felt so good to say yes to myself. I want to kiss him again. I want him to kiss me again. I want to hear him growl my name in the dark and touch me all the ways he didn't last night.

"You know he's fucking his CI, right?" Liv says it matter-of-factly, bored, almost, that we're so out of the loop when it comes to gossip, and yet the suddenness of it is more jarring than Kole shattering the mirror.

Both Mona and I furrow our brows—a reaction Liv takes, and accurately so, to mean she should expound on the rumor.

"Some junkie he caught selling heroin," she says. "I guess Kole slapped her boyfriend with all the charges, sent him off to jail, and he's been fucking her ever since. I mean, it's kind of prostitution if you think of it, since SIU pays their CIs."

"That's disgusting if it's true," says Mona, and I'm disappointed in her quickness to judge. But then, I don't know where she stands with someone like Nikolai Kole. She'd been happy enough to have me cross out his name.

"Right?" Liv rolls her eyes. "No wonder that dickhead got suspended."

"But you don't really know that." I'd meant it as a question, but it comes out as a statement. Sharper than intended, too. I straighten abruptly, already wishing I hadn't spoken when Liv's gaze zeroes in on me. I draw a breath. "I mean, it's not really fair . . ."

A grin slowly pulls Liv's mouth taut and she looks like a wolf wearing a wig. "Someone's got a crush."

"I don't." My cheeks redden.

Liv cackles, which prompts Mona to laugh.

"Hey, speaking of dickheads," segues Mona, "you ever find out who narked about your skirt, Hazel?"

"Oh." I shove my arms through my jacket sleeves. "No. I think I'm just gonna forget about it."

"A-boot," Liv mocks. Cackling again, she tosses her head back as an officer passes through the hall to Wick's office.

• • •

My ring lies in the cupholder, like a coin at the bottom of a well. More fitting, though, might be an eye, staring up at me from the mouth of a shadow. I drag a stray glove over the cupholder and step out onto the asphalt. Walking past an old vacuum repair shop with my hands shoved into my pockets, I caress my thumb against the smooth underside of my ring finger. The anticipation of taking it off and leaving it behind had felt more sacrilegious than actually doing it.

I stare at the dusty models on the other side of the window. It's more of a vacuum museum, really. Some of them I don't even recognize as vacuums, like the Electrolux that looks like a CO_2 tank and an old Hoover with a red hose that looks like it came from the set of one of the old *Star Wars* movies. Reflected in the dirty glass, superimposed over the antique vacuums, is me, dressed rather unassumingly, I like to think, wearing tights under my jeans to accommodate for the holes, sneakers, and a leather jacket. Makeup done smoky. It's odd to look oneself up and down, almost more so than when someone else does it. How will Kole see me, I wonder. Will he take the bait and view me as carelessly casual, or will he read on my face the mess of tried-on T-shirts strewn about my closet floor?

The neon letters that spell out BECK's glow like a beacon in the night. I feel suddenly queasy, my knees weak. I've never met a man out for a drink before who isn't Tommy. I should turn back. Pretend I never came here. Slip my ring back on my finger and return to the duplex like a good wife.

But, it isn't that I just don't want to turn around. I can't. Whether it's the fact that I know Kole is inside or the sheer reluctance to double my time exposed to the bitter elements that have already sucked all the moisture from my skin, I feel summoned to the door, like a moth to a porch light, or the way Forge Bridge lures me to it with its siren song.

Besides, nothing will happen. As painful a thought that is, it's also reassuring, because I know I will not have to push the self-destruct button on my life. The conversation will be easy at first, I'm sure, as we say hello and sit down. A few minutes will be taken up ordering drinks. I'll have one, then drink a water or two and be on my way to work. And in that time, I have no doubt that Nikolai Kole's apparent fascination with me will erode as dramatically as the shoreline being devoured by the lake.

I draw in one last breath that freezes the inside of my nose, grab the door handle, and push. As I enter, the warmth pulls me in like two invisible open arms.

The place is near empty. A bearded man in flannel and with gauges in his ears sits at the bar watching wrestling on one of the flat-screen TVs. Two other guys who look to be my age or a little older sit at a pub table near the air hockey machine. They regard me as I walk in, continuing their conversation. The bartender—a woman with icy blond hair and violet tips—blows a pink bubble with her gum.

I wend my way through the pub tables, toward the far corner, and find Kole near an old-school Pac-Man machine. He smiles when he sees me, and I smile back, feeling sick with excitement as he closes the distance between us, pulling me into an embrace as though we haven't seen each other for a very long time.

"How are you?" he asks.

"Good," I say, and it's one of the few times I actually mean it. I am good, now, next to him. Nervous, but good. I wonder if I should kiss him, or if he will kiss me, and I have to admit I'm relieved when he doesn't make a move. Perhaps what happened in the apartment was simply catalyzed by a heightened sense of danger. Danger or not, though, it doesn't change the fact that I want to feel his lips pressed to mine again, breathe the same oxygen. "This is a cool place." I shrug out of my jacket and hang it on the back of my chair.

"Yeah, here. Let me get you a drink."

I follow Kole up to the bar, where the bartender regards both of us with utter disinterest.

"What are you having?" I ask him.

"Diet Pepsi, on the rocks."

I order the same with a cherry on top.

Kole lays five singles on the counter as the bartender fills a pint glass. It's been years since I drank soda, but I seem to be living on the edge these days.

We make our way back to our table. I feel grateful to be sitting here with him rather than with Mona and Liv, or Tommy—situations wherein I pretend to enjoy myself and drink too much alcohol to pass the time. I feel buzzed enough to the point that if I didn't know better, I'd swear there was some rum mixed in. I wait for him to pull out a flask from his waistband and add the alcohol—whiskey or vodka, whatever you'd drink with a Diet Pepsi. That's what Tommy would do. But Kole does no such thing. Instead, he takes a sip.

I drum my fingertips on the table to keep from touching him.

His phone buzzes. The name "Pearl" appears on the lock screen. He ignores it for a moment, sparing it only a glance, until another message comes in quick succession. He texts a short response, then sets his device facedown.

I pretend not to notice. The knuckles on his right hand are split from punching the mirror. "That OD the other night," I say. "She died?"

He sets his drink down after taking a sip. "Oh yeah. They declared her brain-dead sometime yesterday and she passed this morning."

"Jesus."

"Yeah. Sad. Her parents went upstairs and found her blue with the foam cone."

"Foam cone?"

"It's what happens when someone overdoses on opiates. All their saliva bubbles up and makes this oddly perfect little mound of . . . foam."

"Like sugar." I realize I've made the connection out loud.

"Yeah. Fitting for Candy Man, right? That's how the others were, too. Except Jordan, because he'd been moved, but you could see the residue of it around his mouth."

The others. I've since conducted my own research. Last night, I typed the alias "Candy Man" into Onyx, and discovered three other overdose cases concerning children ages thirteen to seventeen naming him as a suspect. Jordan McAllister and Anya Brown made up cases four and five, with Jordan being the youngest of Candy Man's victims.

My spine tingles as I recall the image of Jordan McAllister sitting up and licking his lips when I wandered into Krejarek's gross apartment. "They think it was oxys? That killed Anya Brown?"

"It's looking that way. One of her friends mentioned seeing her with blue pills once, but that's pretty much it. No paraphernalia."

"You confiscated her phone, right?" Listen to me, it's like I actually, kind of, know what I'm talking about.

"It's locked. Can't download it. Hansen's looking into some

code-breaking software. Regardless, we'll know when toxicology results come back."

"Which takes a while?"

"Eight to ten weeks."

"Eight to ten weeks?" The time line seems ridiculous.

"I might be able to get them to expedite it, especially if this gets any more serious. But there are only two state crime labs. And there's a lot of crime."

"Damn."

"Sing it, sister." He raises his glass and taps it to mine. "In related news, Krejarek's being released."

I nearly spit out my drink. "Wait, what? But, the satchel."

He nods, like he's already covered everything that's racing through my mind right now. "He was definitely sharing pills. He'd just gotten them all refilled on the Wednesday before and the fluoxetine and amitriptyline were already half-gone. But—" He shrugs. "Every pill in that bag is validated with a prescription."

"Except the oxycodone," I point out.

"Except the oxycodone. But I can't prove it belonged to Krejarek."

"But you know it's his. He's Candy Man, for fuck's sake." I slide down in my chair, suddenly realizing how loud my voice has gotten.

"But I can't prove it," he says again, and I begin to read the harsh reality of what he's saying. "I talked with the DA's office this afternoon. It's final. He's being released."

"So he can sell or share his pills with some other kid now?"

"Probably will."

Anger tinged with disgust rises within me. "You don't seem to care."

"I do care. I care a whole hell of a lot, actually. Which means I'll have to double down if I'm going to bust his ass again."

The conversation pauses. I listen to the white noise of three different televisions, a chair sliding across the floor, cars crawling by on wet, salted roads. Lines of text scroll behind my eyes as I think back to typing Kole's interview of Sam. My heart flutters. I shouldn't, but—

"There was a text," I offer. "Remember, from . . . who was the other guy?"

"Sam, his buddy?"

"Yeah. Didn't he text Krejarek saying he *loves* his meds or something like that?"

"Good memory. Yeah, he did."

"But that text and the fact that so many of Krejarek's pills were missing don't hold any weight?"

"Not enough. It's still circumstantial. Krejarek claimed he ingested the missing pills himself. He's an addict. Which is why he's been court-ordered to go to rehab, which means I know where I can find him."

"Dang . . ." I lament, as if I'm the one who has to track down Candy Man all over again.

Kole smiles, clearly having accepted his temporary defeat before coming here. "Welcome to police work."

"It just doesn't add up," I say after a moment of quiet.

"Walk me through it."

"I mean . . . you'd think Candy Man would have everything, wouldn't you? If he wasn't prescribed oxycodone . . ."

"You would," Kole agrees with the first part. His eyes travel, then, from my hand lightly clutching my glass to my T-shirt. I hold my breath, perhaps imagining that his gaze seems to pause there, for just a second before he gives me eye contact. "Hazel, let me ask you a question. What's something you buy? Something you can't live without?"

"Books."

"Books, OK. So, you go to your favorite bookstore and you ask for a particular book. They don't have it . . . but they don't want you to go elsewhere because A) they don't want to lose the sale and B) they don't want to lose you as a customer. What do they do?"

"Order it from somewhere else. Like, either the warehouse or another bookstore." Light bulb moment. "You think he bought them off another dealer?"

"Possibly. Or someone even bigger than him. There are drug lords scattered every square mile from north of here to Chicago. As soon as you bust one, another one takes his place. Trust me, Candy Man is small change in the grand scheme of things. We're only in Black Harbor." He straightens up, pushing his drink just a few inches forward, and as he does so, his knuckles lightly touch mine.

My skin feels charged. I touch him back and don't meet his gaze. Instead, I scan our surroundings. The two men who were seated by the air hockey table are gone. It's just us and the guy with the gauges, who seems to be unsuccessfully hitting on the bartender. "I've never been in here before," I say, nervously. Stupidly. "Have you?"

Kole looks around but doesn't move his hand. Though to be fair, I don't move mine away, either. "Just for the occasional off-probation party. I don't go to those anymore, though."

"Why not?" I ask, remembering what Hammersley had said about it being good for Kole to get out.

"Ever since I went over to SIU three and a half years ago, I don't know any of the new guys in patrol. We're pretty isolated over there."

"Where is SIU?" I ask, knowing what his answer will be. It's an off-site location, and no one, not even Mona, claims to know its whereabouts.

"Nice try."

I shrug. "I could get it out of you if I wanted."

"Oh, you think?"

"Sure." I nod to the Pac-Man machine behind him. "Play you for it."

"Hold on," he says. "You think that you beating me in a game of Pac-Man—which would never happen, by the way—would warrant me telling you the secret location of SIU?"

"Yes."

"What if I win?"

"What do you want to know?"

"I want you to say 'dollar' again."

"Do—"

"Ah ah ah, not until I win." He approaches the bar to exchange a bill for four quarters. Judging by the bartender's expression, you'd think he asked her to skin a cat. "Ladies first." He gestures to the machine upon his return, and I step aside. He rolls his eyes. "All right, Podunk, let me show you how it's done."

I've actually never played Pac-Man before. I know the gist of it, though, and having to say the word *dollar* again isn't exactly capital punishment if I lose. I try to watch Kole's gameplay, but my attention keeps drifting down his back, lingering on the muscles tensed beneath his shirt, the subtle ridge of his spine running right down the middle. If I slipped my hand into his back pocket, would he turn around and kiss me? Hard like last night, or soft this time?

Who knows how long I've been standing here, entranced and fantasizing, when he turns to drop a quarter in my palm. "150,000. Beat it."

"I've never played before." I say it like a confession. I don't know why. Sometimes I feel like speaking to him is an involuntary action. I'll say anything to get him to look my way.

He smiles slowly. "Are you for real, Podunk? Where were you born again? Neptune?"

"The nineties."

He looks at me deadpan. "You're sure it isn't because you didn't have electricity in your little house on the prairie?"

I punch his arm. Just to touch him.

"Come here." He presses his hand to the small of my back and guides me to stand in front of him. "The name of the game is to eat the dots, don't get eaten."

"Simple enough," I remark. My voice is breathy. I sound a little like Elle. I can feel the heat emanating from his body, like I'm sitting too close to a fire.

"Let's see what you got, Podunk." He steps back.

I lean over the machine more than necessary, painfully aware of his gaze on me as mine was on him. I pop one knee to accentuate the curve of my butt. Closing my eyes, I imagine him coming up behind me, sliding his hands over my hips and down the front of my jeans. I would let him.

The game seems to last forever. Finally, the red ghost backs Pac-Man into a corner and he dives down into the abyss. My heart pounds. Now what?

There's something magnetic about the way Kole approaches. He's so close, I can feel the charge of his body as he comes up behind me. "Say it," he whispers into my ear.

I turn to face him, and suddenly there isn't an inch between us. My head feels fuzzy, like I've slammed two or three shots of vodka. Is this what *punch-drunk* means? I make a mental note to look it up later. I lay my up north accent on thick. "Doh-lar." I laugh.

He laughs, too.

Looking at him and the way he's looking at me, his eyes inquisitive, searching—I don't want this to end. Any of it.

"Best two out of three," I offer, a way to prolong the night.

"You're on. I'll crush you again."

Oh, please do. I smile innocently enough.

A new game powers up. I don't watch any of it. I lean slightly on the side of the machine, my fingertips pressed to the edges. I feel the cool air against a sliver of bare midriff. I may have inched my T-shirt up, just to see if he notices.

"That's not fair," he says, answering my question.

"What?"

I watch his arms work as he plays. The lean, striated muscles working and the faint blue veins pulsing as he pulls the black-knobbed lever down and over and down again. I stare at his hands, imagining where else I'd like him to demonstrate their dexterity.

Suddenly, he growls as if in pain and takes his hands off the game to reach into his pocket for his phone. He puts it to his ear. "Hey. Look, I'm in the middle of something right—You're fine. . . . Well, where did you see him? . . . That was hours ago. . . . You're fine."

I concentrate hard to listen to the distorted noise on the other end. The woman's voice is hysterical. My heart plummets. His wife. She knows.

Still on the phone, he shakes his head. "OK, just . . . don't go anywhere. I'll be right there." He ends the call and shoves the phone back in his pocket. "I'm sorry."

"It's OK." My voice is overly cheerful to mask my disappointment. I cringe.

"We can pick this up tomorrow?"

"I can't. I have my sister's engagement party."

"Damn." He runs both hands through his hair, his knuckles meeting at the top of his head. "I'm really sorry. If this wasn't an emergency—"

"It's OK," I assure him. Because it is OK. It has to be. Kole will leave right now whether I'm disappointed or not. I heard the woman's voice on the phone. She needs him. I don't need anybody.

Kole throws his jacket on. "Did you park close?"

I nod. *Close* is a relative term.

"OK." He steps toward me, and I am sick again with the hope that he will cradle the back of my head and kiss me. But he doesn't. Instead, he presses a quarter into my hand. "For next time."

Next time. I repeat the words to myself like a promise, and ten minutes later inside my frigid vehicle, I find myself drumming my fingertips on the dashboard: right index finger sweeping diagonally downward for the "N," left middle finger reaching up for the "E," ring finger reaching back for the "X," and so forth.

11.

FRIDAY

My fists punch through the wintry air. I wear a thin pair of gloves, crushing the coin so tightly in my left hand that my knuckles are sharpened to bone-white points. It's warm for January, forty-two degrees. I run past a man out getting his mail in shorts and flip-flops.

Glacial water splashes my ankles as I leap over dips in the sidewalks. The wooded trail across from the duplex is submerged under snowmelt, forcing me to adopt a new running path through the city. With six miles behind me, I'll be guilt-free as I indulge in cupcakes and wine tonight at Elle's party. Repentance in advance.

I pass the old vacuum shop where I'd parked last night. Krejarek's apartment is on my left, now. I stare at the vacant window in the corner. That's the room where I crumpled like a can thrown into a fire and Kole had to scoop me up, playing hero. Looking back, my behavior had been embarrassing: me latching on to him like he was a torch in the dark, kissing him in that grungy bathroom as though I'd needed resuscitation. And in the end, what? He pretended it hadn't happened and he'd gone home to someone else.

Krejarek is a free man again. He's probably at home, now. I shiver as I imagine him watching me from one of the windows, and when I look up at his apartment again, I startle to see a silhouette, but it's only a floor lamp. As I put the building's Frankensteined back behind me, though, I swear from the corner of my eye I see someone at the top of the zigzag stairs, smoking a cigarette and watching my descent.

I accelerate, increasing the distance between me and my watcher. Steam appears in front of my face in punctuated bursts. I lean back slightly, braking with my heels as I descend the sleek asphalt hill of Forge Avenue. The bridge lies in wait for me, its rusted, coal-black arms outstretched. Like a child coming home, I run to it, slowing only when I cross the threshold.

Deflated foil balloons crinkle in the breeze. Faded ribbon strands waver as though beckoning me forth. I look at the blackness peeking through the slats beneath me. Every cell in my body, from my toes to my fingertips, tingles. It isn't an excited tingle, though. It's more like the prickly feeling you get before something bad happens. When I reach the farthest point I've visited up until now, I take one more step and plant my feet firmly on the ties. I abandon the railing for a moment to remove my gloves, and feel as though the wind could carry me off.

I've pressed the quarter so hard to my palm that George Washington's portrait has been impressed on my skin. Shakily, I raise my right arm straight out in front of me, my fist suspended over the water.

Drop it in, says the river. *Give me the coin.*

There will be no more night escapades. No more laughs shared over Diet Pepsi and Pac-Man. Kissing Nikolai Kole the other night was a mistake. I'll send the coin into the river with a wish, like I used to do as a child when we'd visit the fountain in the mall. Then, I'd hope for material things like toys and books. Now, I'd simply wish to be a better person. One who doesn't lie.

I take a breath as I resolve to pry my fingers apart and let the coin fall. But I can't do it. Drawing my arm back in, I look at the quarter in my palm. My heart drums a blood-rushing cadence. The edges of my vision darken as I stare at the token Kole gave to me, and I realize I don't want to give him up just yet.

The siren call of the river grips me, immobilizes me. *Give me the coin.*

I shake my head, robotic.

Silence.

The world stops.

I feel as I did in Krejarek's apartment, when I'd given in to fear and let my imagination get the best of me. Light-headed. I could faint. I close my eyes for a second, and when I reopen them, I find that I've already slipped my glove back on with the coin tucked safely away. As I pull on my left glove, though, I pause. My wedding ring turns, my fingers shrunken from the cold. I study the ring's design as I have multiple times: twin bands of silver that intertwine and intersect at the point of a tiny diamond. I don't hate it. But I don't love it anymore, either.

He hadn't chosen it because he thought the size would be just small enough so as not to bother me when I write. Or because I might like the design. He'd chosen it because it was the cheapest one in the store. He and Cameron laughed about it once while playing darts, and then Tommy had planted a wet kiss on my cheek as though that made it all better. "I love you with all my heart, Hazel." And then he lifted my hand to his bristly lips and kissed the ring, too.

He texted me the same sentiment late last night, while I lay in bed, alone in the duplex. It had been riddled with spelling errors. *I loofah u with all my heat hazek my.*

Loofah. Drunk Tommy and autocorrect never get along.

It was a little funny if you read it out of context. But knowing Tommy as I do—as I did—it just made me sad. I remember the moment I fell in love with him. I was sixteen and had just finished running the mile, the last event on a flooded track. Everyone else had returned to the bus to wait out the torrential storm, except Tommy. He stood by the gate, his jersey soaked to his body, raindrops dripping from his ears, and holding a Styrofoam cup of hot chocolate. It was only half full by the time the wind had lapped from it, but it was warm sliding down my throat as we splashed our way to the bus. Whenever I fantasize about leaving him, I think back to that day, to that moment ten years ago, now, when he was the only person in the world who weathered a storm for me. And how could I leave him?

But lately, I've begun to question whether or not he stood out in that storm for me, or because the rules stated the meet wasn't over until the last person crossed the finish line. He wasn't waiting for me at all. I was just the last person to collect so everyone could go home.

A sudden gust of lake-effect wind rocks me back on my heels. Crushing my glove in my right fist, I slip my wedding ring off and watch as it falls like a raindrop into the water.

• • •

There isn't much to help Elle with. I think she invited me so I can witness her boss people around.

She texted me on my way with an address to pick up the cupcakes. *You're the only one with a big enough vehicle*, she justified. How many cupcakes did she order, I wondered.

I hate driving in Milwaukee. All the bridges and left-side exits. The fact that it's snowing out and everyone's forgotten how to operate a vehicle doesn't help.

I park at a slant, front right wheel wedged into a snowbank across the street from the bakery. "Gluten-free, vegan, delicious" is painted on the exterior brick wall. I frown, not too sure about that last promise, considering the first two. Of course Elle would order her cupcakes here. They were probably free. My hypothesis is confirmed when the lady behind the counter hands me a stack of cards asking if I'd be so kind as to set them out on the dessert table.

It's almost three o'clock when I arrive at the Olive. Nothing like being four hours early. Silver lining: good parking spot. I grab two boxes of cupcakes, resigning myself to the fact that I'll have to make two more return trips to my vehicle, and walk across the street, my boots slipping on patches of smooth snow.

My cousin Liza opens the door for me. Her red hair, curled in ringlets, bounces as she leads me to what I presume to be the cupcake table.

"Thank you so much for picking these up," she says. "Nell had a friend sleep over last night, and . . ." She shakes her head as though that incomplete sentence explains why she couldn't stop by the cupcakery today.

"S'no problem," I say.

"How are you?" she asks, smiling bright. "We didn't get to talk much last week." She puts her hand on my shoulder.

Quite the contrary, she talked plenty last week. About her daughter, Nell, and how she's into making bracelets for her little friends on the playground. How Nell had strep throat over Christmas. How Liza and her husband are going to the Bahamas for a week in March and how it will be the first time they've been away from Nell.

"Good." I smile to convince her it's true.

"That's great! You still love your new job?"

"Yeah. I have cupcakes in the car, yet. I'll be right back." I excuse myself and run out the door. When I've made the final trip, Liza has most of the desserts placed on a three-tiered structure, sorted by flavor.

"These are amazing," she says, I assume to me. "It was so thoughtful of Elle to get such a variety of hypoallergenic cupcakes. People these days have so many allergies. Nell's allergic to tree nuts and strawberries . . ."

. . . and there's my cue to stop listening. I look around to see who else is here. A few people I don't know are laying gold linens on high-top tables while a florist follows behind them, adding a vase and a tealight candle. The place is shaping up to be a mini wedding reception. All the area's best vendors coming together to celebrate Elle's engagement and show off their portfolios—pro bono. I'm sure Elle will have a table reserved solely for business cards.

"I heard she's getting an ice sculpture, too," says Liza.

"I hope it's one with a vodka luge." I fish the business cards from the cupcake lady out of my purse and plop them on the table. My other cousin, Madeline, is leaning over the bar, talking on her phone. She glances over at me and waves.

Suddenly, the door swings inward, forcefully as though kicked open. A flash of bright daylight shoots into the room, silhouetted in front of which are Elle and Kinney. Kinney balances a tray of lattes on each forearm, his right hand gripping a gallon of coffee; and Elle totes a paper bag full of what I assume to be bagels with every variety of cream cheese. Glad I got that run in.

"Ah, Hazel, my lovely sister!" Elle exclaims upon setting the bag on an empty table. Scooting toward me in her faux-fur and suede booties, she pulls me into a hug. She smells like winter and coffee. "I got you a caramel macchiato! Almond milk, right? Extra shot?"

I've never loved my sister so much. "Thank you," I say as I accept it.

"Guys, there's bagels and coffee! Check the cups for your names, please!" Elle yells, too close to my ear. And then no longer yelling, "Oh, thank you so much for picking up the cupcakes. Liza was going to, but Nell—"

"—had a sleepover," I finish.

"Right."

"Where's, um . . . ?" I half spin to my left, then right, stepping back as people swarm the carbs and coffee.

"Oh, Rose is allegedly on her way; she had a hair appointment this morning, and Kim has to work until five."

I nod. I could be miffed that only three of the five bridesmaids are here, performing their bridesmaid duties, but after a sip of this caramel macchiato, everything is OK with the world. "Cheers," I say to both Elle and Kinney as I raise my cup in a sudden atypical surge of euphoria. They touch theirs to mine.

I watch their eyes to see if they're at all drawn to my naked finger, and they're not. I smirk, feeling as though I've gotten away with something.

"Mm, Elle look how pleasant your sis is," says Kinney. "Glad we paid the barista to slip in that little somethin' somethin'."

Elle nudges him. "He's kidding."

Kinney makes a face that says otherwise. "Where's your man?"

Todd Kinney is everything my husband isn't. And consequently, everything my husband hates. Loud, proud, and flamboyantly gay, Kinney hasn't spoken to Tommy since the two realized they have abrasively different political views upon their first meeting, six or so years ago. Tommy being a self-admitted homophobe doesn't help matters, either.

"He's at his parents' house."

Kinney purses his lips in that way he does.

Elle asks, "How's his mom?" But it's clear the conversation is over by the way she's unboxing her small cake that will sit at the top of the cupcake tower.

I shrug. "Same ol'." I try to think back to the last time I heard from Angela. She was going on some new meds after the other ones caused bald patches. "She got her hair cut."

"Oh, like how?" Elle asks as she carefully turns the cake on its cardboard plate.

"Pixie. Sort of."

"I bet that looks nice."

"Yeah."

Kinney's eyes smile. "You hate her, don't you?"

"Kinney!" Elle bumps him with her hip.

He shrugs. "What? I'm just callin' Hazel out on her own bullshit. You should hear the two of you. Gabbin' these fake niceties about someone you can't stand. A modern-day Bracknell and Fairfax, the pair of you are."

"Nice Oscar Wilde reference," I commend, suddenly remembering Kinney was a theater major.

"Knew you'd appreciate that, pumpkin. Now, can we all agree we hate this witch and her shit haircut and where are the mimosas?"

Elle and I share a glance as he marches away on a mission. Even if my husband doesn't, I do love Todd Kinney.

• • •

Minutes after seven, the place is packed. The line to get in started an hour before. You'd think it was a club with a VIP list. Actually, there probably is a VIP list. I wouldn't put it past Elle.

I've changed into a short navy dress with gray booties. I was pleased with the look of it when I first saw my reflection in the bathroom mirror, as it's the first time I've tried it on. I picked it up some weeks ago while thrifting with Elle. She's wearing a thrift store find tonight, too—a burgundy calf-length dress with cold-shoulder sleeves. She looks so feminine and dainty standing next to Garrett, dark-haired and towering beside her in a slate suit coat, as they chat warmly with their guests. They do make a beautiful couple.

I stand next to a chair I don't intend to sit in, holding a martini I don't intend to drink. Kinney ordered it for me about forty minutes ago. What I'd really like is a Diet Pepsi with a cherry in it. If only there were a place to discreetly set down my unwanted drink, but there are people seated at every table and at the bar talking, listening, laughing. Everyone looks as though they belong together.

Over the crowd, I can see Elle's friends, Kim and Rose, and I think I might try to include myself in their conversation when Kinney sidles up to me.

"No ball and chain tonight?" he asks for the second time, obviously pleased by the fact that my homophobic husband will not quash our good time. His southern Des Moines drawl is out in full force, and he's got that dreamy look he gets when he's tipsy from too much gin. The man on his arm is out of his league, but as Kinney says, *Honey, this face could charm the pants off a nun.*

"Just me." I offer my most dazzling smile and take a tiny sip of my drink, resigned to the fact that I'll have to finish it.

"So, you're on the prowl, huh?" His eyes simper with delight over the rim of his glass.

I raise my brow. "I don't think I've ever been on the prowl, Kinney."

He looks at my hands, one resting on the back of a chair and one holding my martini, and meets my gaze. "Where's that little bread tie you call a wedding ring?"

Suddenly, I feel a bubble of dread in my stomach. "It's . . . getting fixed."

"Getting fixed?" His repeating of the excuse makes it sound even dumber. "Can't you just dig around in the bottom of a cereal box for another one?"

I shake my head. "You're such a dick."

"That's why all the assholes love me."

"Kinney!" I hit his arm as he's mid-sip, and he almost snorts gin out of his nose.

Suddenly, Elle's voice is amplified overhead. She laughs first, as though someone's just told a joke. "Hey, everyone! Before I drink too many of these lemon-drop martinis, Garrett and I just wanted to thank you all for coming out to celebrate our engagement!"

Cue the applause and exclamations of "We love you, Elle!"

"It's been such an adventure, to say the least, from the first day we met until tonight. In case anyone doesn't know, Garrett was my, um, instructor for a kickboxing course I took last summer."

Laughter, and there's always that anonymous person to shout, "Ow-ow!"

I can't say what prompts my eye roll, whether it's her use of "adventure" to describe their relationship or the fact that I'm about to hear the Elle-Garrett origin story for the nth time. I'm saved, however, by my phone vibrating in my hand.

A drunk call from Tommy, I think with near certainty. But the text on the screen reads: "Marjorie—BHPD."

Mumbling "Excuse me" repeatedly as I wade toward the door, I answer the phone as I plunge into the freezing cold. A car whizzes by, spraying me with slush.

"Hi, Marjorie." I sound breathless. "What's—is everything OK?"

"Hazel, thank you for answering. Can you come in to work tonight?"

"Um—"

"It's urgent."

I turn back to the glowing windows of the Olive, blurred silhouettes of people talking and toasting. Elle will kill me. What kind of maid of honor ditches her sister's engagement party? "I can be there in about an hour if that's all right. Maybe less, but—"

"As soon as you can get there. The sergeants are on my case to get a transcriber in and Mona's out of town."

"OK, I'll have to stop home and change."

"Don't worry about it. Just get there and don't talk to anyone. This is gonna hit the news fast enough as it is. We want all our ends tied up."

"OK."

The line goes dead.

I stand frozen for a moment, trying to make sense of the

conversation. Something bad has happened, that's obvious. Someone's been shot, I bet. My heart drops when I consider the possibility of it being Kole.

My hands are shaking, and I can't tell if it's because of the cold or because of the potential gravity of the situation I'm about to drive into. Fumbling with my phone, I text Kole: *Hey. Are you OK?*

I hadn't realized until now that I'm still holding my martini. I run back inside, the warmth hitting me like a feather pillow to the face. I set my drink on the corner of the bar and hurry over to the alcove to find my coat.

"We are just so grateful, and truly blessed to have so many friends . . ."

With one arm shoved into my sleeve, I glance up at Elle standing with the microphone on the opposite end of the room. Kinney's up there, too, leaning against a cocktail table with a group of similarly dressed guys. I wave, trying to catch his eye, but he doesn't see. He's focused on Elle, as he should be.

I'll make it up to her, I promise, and slip out the door.

12.

LATER

When I arrive at the police department, I feel as I did on my first night, like I've driven into the scene of a movie or one of those cop drama shows—one that my grandma might watch starring Tom Selleck. But he's too polished for Black Harbor. Clint Eastwood would be better; he's grittier.

Red and blue lights flash, reflecting off the road's wet surface. They distort prism-like through icy stalagmites that shoot up from the snowbanks. I climb over them, gingerly, nevertheless feeling their crystalline pebbles sliding into my shoe. Cresting the bank, I see a reporter spotlighted in front of the Black Harbor Police Department sign, brandishing a microphone and dressed like a drop of blood in a red parka. News vans are parked from here to the roundabout, swarming the annex and City Hall, too. The night is alive with the buzz of conversation and camera clicks.

A teeming mass of reporters and civilians block the side entrance as I approach. I can just barely make out Rourke's head. He's clearing a path with his grizzly bear arms, waving me toward him. "Get inside!" he yells. "Don't talk to anyone!"

"What's—"

"Get inside!"

A tumult of voices crashes against me, like waves colliding into the pier and swallowing it up. Microphones descend upon me like flies on roadkill.

Do you know the detective who's involved, Miss?

Conspiracy—

Murder—

"Hazel! Get in!"

Rourke waves his arms, keeping the crowd at bay. I break free and run toward him. He shields me as I press my fob to the electronic pad, warning me, "Keep the blinds closed. Don't answer to anyone."

It's the most authoritative I've ever heard him be. That fact alone, never mind the cacophony that surrounds us, is enough to frighten me. Opening the door just a sliver, I force myself through to the other side. It clicks shut. I turn, feeling guilty as I watch Rourke take on the horde by himself.

Quiet.

I punch in at the time clock, and look right and left down the hall. There's no one. I check the drawer to find a handful of arrests: disorderly conducts, PO Holds, shoplifting. Nothing out of the ordinary. In fact, judging by the paperwork in the drawer, it's a pretty slow Friday night in Black Harbor.

I peek in the window of the sergeants' office. Patrolmen walk swiftly as if on a mission, in and out of the roll call room. Lt. Wick is inside, staring up at the TV screen showing a grid of exterior surveillance footage. The doors burst open and I'm almost knocked on my ass by Hammersley.

"Oh, Jesus," he says. "Hazel, sorry. I didn't see you."

"It's OK. Hey, what's—"

"Vultures," he grumbles, and I notice he's tending to a series of scratches on his forearm. Blood runs in rivulets to the underside of his wrist. "Last fucking night of my career. I should have expected it. This place never fucking quits."

"What's going on?" I finally manage to ask.

If Hammersley gives a shit about the fact that I'm dressed for a party and not for work, he doesn't show it. "Homicide," he says. "It's bad. Worst one I've seen in thirty years."

"Sarge!" A patrol officer jogs up to Hammersley, waving multicolored papers, and I take that as my cue to leave.

I unlock the door to Transcribing. It's the first time I haven't been trepidatious about walking through the dark Records office, and I realize it's because I either don't have time to be scared, or because I know that the real danger lurks outside of these walls.

The door unlocks with a definitive click. I push it open and suddenly scream, throwing myself back into the file cabinets. The reporters are waiting for me on the other side of the glass. Their eyes are bright and hungry, squinting to see inside. Their breath fogs the window as they bare their teeth to shout. They can't see me, I remind myself. And yet, their searching stares are almost more unnerving than if they'd latched on to me. Frantically, I reach to close the blinds. Safe, now, from public spectacle, I collapse into my chair. It takes the last bit of my energy to power up my computer and flick on the desk light.

On the CFS board, I find the DOA code attached to an address I've never heard of before. The time stamp is 2012 hours, which would have been about an hour before Marjorie called me. I call her, now, to see what I need to do. She doesn't answer.

I send a text. *Hi Marjorie. I'm here at the PD. What needs to get done?*

Next to the mouse pad, my phone vibrates with her response: *Just get ahead on reports. We'll need to be prepared for the news tomoro.*

I really hope she doesn't believe that's the correct spelling of *tomorrow.*

Checking the dictation queue, I see there aren't any reports marked urgent, yet. I put on my headset and get to work.

Three completed reports later, I take the coffee decanter with me when I get up to check the drawer, though it's all an excuse to peek out the side entrance. The swarm is gone or at least moved. I wonder where Rourke is. I fill up the decanter from the bathroom sink, and, taking two new fresh arrests from the Transcribing drawer, and when I return to my office, Kole is sitting there in the dark. The glow of the computer screen makes him look like a cadaver.

I jump back, clutching the papers to my chest. "You scared me."

He doesn't move or say anything. He's dressed more casually than usual, wearing a hoodie only partially zipped over a plain white tee, I finally see what's attached to the black chain: an anchor. It floats against the backdrop of his stark T-shirt like a crow in flight or a letter punched on a page. He looks disheveled and alert, on edge like he's expecting a bullet in the back.

"Are you OK?" I ask quietly. "Nik?" I check discreetly over my shoulder, confirming an empty hall before I kneel next to him. I rest my hand on his knee. "What happened? Why were all those reporters outside?"

I watch the slow rise and fall of his chest. If it wasn't for that, he'd look like he'd just froze to death.

I get up to sit in Mona's chair and roll it next to him. "Are you OK?"

He opens his mouth like he wants to talk. His eyes dart to mine. "I fucked up, Hazel." The words are a struggle. He sounds jagged, unsure about everything except that one simple fact.

I look him over. No blood. No scratches. No bullet holes. His clothes look clean. "Well . . . you're alive, at least."

"For now." He leans forward with his elbows digging into his knees and rakes his hands through his hair.

"What happened? Did you shoot someone? Like, in self-defense, or—"

With his face in his hands, he says, "I didn't shoot anyone."

"But someone's dead," I say, thinking of the DOA code on the CFS board. Dead on arrival. Homicide, that's what Hammersley had said. The worst he'd seen in thirty years.

Dread courses through me as I remember the frantic call Kole gotten last night. Pearl. His wife. Who else would she be?

"Nik, just tell me what happened. You know I won't tell anyone. Confidentiality agreement, remember?" I hold out my hand, pinky extended for a promise. To my surprise, he links his littlest finger with mine and they stay connected like that—linked.

Please let it not be her, I pray. Pearl. His wife. Whoever the mystery woman is.

As if reading my thoughts, Kole unlocks his phone with his thumbprint and hands it to me. There's a string of missed calls, all from Pearl. I scroll down as bile rises from the back of my throat. There must be a dozen of them, if not more. They're all from last night into the early morning hours.

"Pearl." Her name already sounds like a ghost, evaporating from my lips. "She was the one who called, when we were—"

"Yeah."

That one syllable makes my stomach drop. "She was your—"

"CI."

The response catches me off guard. The tremors that run through my body calm as I take a deep breath . . . and then I remember what Liv had said: *You know he's fucking his CI, right?*

"There was so much blood, Hazel. Jesus Christ." He mashes the heels of his hands into his eye sockets.

"What happened?"

"Stabbed. Thirteen fucking times. And then splayed open like a goddamn fish."

"Holy shit."

"Yeah. I told her to get out of here. To move. She wouldn't listen. She never fucking listened." His voice is stronger, now.

"If she was your CI, do you think she could have been murdered for retaliation? For selling someone out?"

"It's possible, but who knows? She wasn't quiet about the fact that she worked with cops, that's for sure. She threw a house party when she sold out the Koken brothers."

It's a household surname here at BHPD. I recognize it from cross-referenced reports. Darryl and Dante Koken. Up until late last year, they'd run a pretty decent-size cocaine operation out of their uncle's barbershop. Between the two of them, their rap sheets could be bound into a book as thick as a dictionary. Guys like that would have connections everywhere.

"Did she snitch on anyone recently?" I ask.

"The better question is who didn't she. It was like she had a vendetta against every dealer within city limits. But this is my fault." He swallows, sets his jaw. "I should've quit with her a long time ago."

Vendetta, good word. I sit quietly for a moment, thinking. The knowledge that there is a killer loose in the city sends shivers up my spine. This isn't an overdose. This is cold-blooded intentional homicide. Judging by Kole's reaction and the manic activity outside, I take it this genre of crime is unusual even for a place like Black Harbor.

"Why didn't you?" I ask, fearing the answer. He was in love with her.

He looks away, his eyes scanning the horizontal slivers between the blinds, and turns back to me. "She said she could get buys on Candy Man. I was dumb enough to believe her."

"Did she?"

"Never had a chance to. Krejarek screwed himself over with that whole overdose. As soon as that went down, she started getting really paranoid. Like, more than usual. She thought he was gonna come after her."

"You think he did?" I summon my memory of Krejarek, sitting slumped and virtually boneless in Interview Room #1. His rows upon rows of teeth, his shifty eyes. I remember how he'd watched me earlier today as I ran to Forge Bridge and back. He might have just come from murdering Pearl. I hate myself for not turning around, now, and getting a good look at him, to see what he was wearing or what he looked like, or if he had even been there at all.

Kole shrugs. "I just thought he was a loser who enticed kids with drugs. He's not the type to murder someone in cold blood like that, and yet . . . worse people have been underestimated." He touches his forehead, smoothing the creases with his fingertips. "Christ. Pearl was a junkie, straight up. Always looking for one more dollar or one more fix . . . I guess I'm no better."

"Don't say that. You were trying to do your job."

"I used her."

"She used you. Nik, you didn't know—"

"That she would die? It's always a possibility. The ME estimates her time of death to have been just before midnight, on Thursday." That was a few hours after he'd left me at Beck's, when he'd gone to see what had Pearl so agitated that night.

"Who found her?"

"Her neighbor, some old guy. She helped him clean his place every Friday morning, he said, like dishes and laundry, odds and ends. After she didn't show up, and he didn't hear from her all day, he went to see if she was OK. Which . . . you know the rest."

"That was when? This evening?"

"Yeah, 8, maybe 8:15."

And I'd gotten a call from Marjorie to come in around 9. So far, the pieces fit. "You already searched her apartment?"

"I did a walk-through." He slips into a stream of consciousness as he describes the scene: clothes strewn about the floor, pockets turned inside out; the bathroom cabinets gone through, the medicine cabinet emptied into the sink, the lid off the toilet tank; in her bedroom, her pillows had been shook from their cases and her dresser had been turned over with every drawer pulled out. That was where the struggle had begun. Picture frames had been ripped from their nails and lay broken on the floor. Blood spattered the walls and soaked a corner of her comforter. He mentions, too, the overturned chairs in the kitchenette, and blood-soaked towels on the living room carpet that she'd pressed to her neck to stop the bleeding. Crumpled in the wreckage was a faded men's black sweatshirt, well-worn, with thumb holes torn in the cuffs.

"She wouldn't wear that," he says, and I'm bothered by the fact that he knew her well enough to know what she would and wouldn't have worn. "Whoever it belonged to had been over there for a while."

"How do you know that?" I ask.

"Because of the ashtray."

"The ashtray?"

"Two kinds of cigarette butts: Newport and Marlboro Red. She smoked Reds."

Another fun fact.

Kole shakes his head as though to clear images from his mind. "The way she was filleted . . . he was looking for something."

"He?"

"It's harder than it looks to strangle someone." His gaze is mildly apologetic. "No offense, but it's unlikely a woman could do that much damage."

"None taken," I mutter, and then, "But what would she have had?"

From what little I know of confidential informants, their primary income is what investigators pay them to snitch on their peers. Pearl was different, though; I can tell by the way he talks about her.

"What do CIs always have or want, Hazel?"

"Drugs?"

He raises one eyebrow, and I know I've answered correctly.

"You think someone splayed her open over drugs?"

"People have done it for less. Patrol's out looking for her phone now. It pinged about a mile from her place. So, either they'll find the suspect with it or just the phone. Either one will be helpful."

My stomach churns. "Didn't you go over there last night? After she called?"

"I did."

"What . . . what did she want?"

"She thought someone was stalking her. She was afraid to take her garbage out across the parking lot. So, I took her garbage out for her and that was pretty much that. I wasn't over there for more than ten minutes."

Do I believe him? I've no reason not to, so far. He seems appropriately agitated, to quote a phrase I've heard investigators use.

Investigator Crue suddenly shows up at the door. If he's surprised to find Kole here with me, his face doesn't show it. His eyes scan me from my disheveled updo to my navy party dress and booties, the dainty silver bracelet that I would normally never wear for typing. It's the first time either of us have seen each other up close. He's a weathered fifties with silver bristles on the side of his head and a nose that looks like someone took a triangular chunk from the top of it. "Dylan's upstairs," he says in the voice I recognize from his dictation, and then he offers a belated "Hi" to me.

"Hi," I return.

He nods toward the way he came, beckoning for Kole to follow him. Kole looks like he's going to be sick, but stands. "You'll be here?" he asks when Crue is out of sight.

"I don't know," I say.

When he leaves, I look at the sworn personnel roster to the left of my desk, remembering the day Mona had me cross out Kole's name. She hasn't printed a new one, yet. The pen strike is still there. *No one gets suspended for shit around here*, she'd said.

And yet, this Dylan character had been fired, probably in connection to Kole's suspension. He was back, now. Upstairs. I feel my breath slow and percolate in my chest, stirring up nerves that only come alive when being left alone at night, in a place like Black Harbor, where killers slink and stalk at the edge of the shadows and where exiled detectives are allowed back in the building.

My gaze slides toward the window, and I focus on the slivers of darkness between the blinds, as Kole had only a few moments ago. I scan from left to right as though reading a book, searching for the answer to a question that raises the hair on my arms: *What have I gotten myself into?*

• • •

Two hours later, Kole is still gone. Whether he's upstairs in the bureau or back at the scene, I have no idea. I haven't heard from him.

I work my way through arrest paperwork. The funny business about crime is that it isn't like motion with an equal and opposite reaction. Rather, the fact that a gruesome homicide investigation is underway has no effect at all on the disorderly conduct incidents, the domestic abuse cases, theft, and otherwise. The everyday crime carries on as usual, and in a warped way, a person could almost take some comfort from that.

At the moment, there isn't much to be told about this investigation. I've typed in the case number probably a dozen times, checking for updates. I've read the few reports by second-shift patrolmen, most of them only a few paragraphs long, stating they arrived at the location and watched the perimeter until relieved by third shift. The ones who went into the apartment detailed the scene: the body lying crumpled on the living room floor, the carpet soaked with her blood, a blood-soaked towel around her neck, smears of blood on the walls, a bloody footprint, and so on and on and on.

The name of the victim is what stands out on all of them, like a crimson thumbprint on crisp white pages: Dylan, Sarah. I should have figured "Pearl" was an alias. No one in this city is who they say they are; a truth that becomes more and more apparent every day. Her birth date indicates she's only a few years younger than me. Sarah Dylan. I'd bet any money she's related to Investigator Dylan.

I tried apologizing to Elle. I explained that I'd gotten called into work for an emergency. She was silent for a long time before replying: *Whatever.*

It's a response I've used before, when I've been too hurt or defeated to employ other words or start an argument. It might very well be the last thing I texted Mom before we decided to stop texting altogether.

Whatever.

I stare at it, still, the letters blurring on the screen as dark, mascara-dyed tears collect in the corners of my eyes. My imagination plays the scene: flashes of Elle laughing with Garrett, touching him on the shoulder and nonchalantly looking back at the bar, quickly scanning every corner; the crestfallen look on her face when she realizes I've disappeared from her party.

Surely, she would have done the same to me, wouldn't she have? If work had called and demanded her presence at a gathering or a concert, she would have left wherever she was and gone, because she's Elle and she needs to be the center of attention. And all the world loves her for it. But our worlds are different. If Shakespeare's right that all the world's a stage, then Elle is the leading lady and I am the stagehand who maneuvers the levers for the trapdoors and curtain, a master of smoke and mirrors who ensures each act runs so seamlessly that no one even notices me.

Kole reappears without warning, and I jump up as though to hug him. I lean casually back, though, against the countertop, crossing my arms over my chest and observing the fact that he's wearing latex gloves and has what looks like someone's lunch in his fist. He sits down in Mona's chair and extracts a red flip-style phone from the crumpled paper bag. I haven't seen one like it since high school. The phone powers up. I draw in a breath.

"Let's see how much juice this thing has."

A bar in the corner containing a hair-thin red line reveals our answer: 6 percent.

"Christ." He taps a messaging app icon and starts searching. I return to my chair and pull it so close to him our knees touch. Tearing my attention from the phone screen, I watch him, his eyes flickering as he scans through the messages, looking for names and numbers.

"You have your phone?" he asks.

It's lying faceup by the keyboard. I go to hand it to him, when he says, "Take photos of these messages, please. Who knows if it willl download."

"No charging cable?" I ask.

"They couldn't find one. And this thing looks ancient. I don't know if we'll have a match for it upstairs."

"What happens if the phone dies?"

"You can't download a dead phone. So, if it dies and we don't have a charging cable for it . . . we're—"

"Fucked."

"Correct."

Five percent.

A quick cursory search of her message library reveals that almost all of her contacts are listed by emojis. Hat emojis, flower emojis. I can bet the cop emoji is for Kole. A preview of her last outgoing message reads: *Im sorry Nik, ok just plz come get me.* She sent it last night at 11:37 p.m. I glance at him as he reads it. From the corner of my eye, I see the muscles in his jaw work as he swallows back something like guilt.

He clicks into various conversations, taking note of contacts to interview later: friends throughout the apartment complex; a few texts from her neighbor asking what time she'd be by and then asking if she was all right.

"She seems paranoid," I say, having lost count of all the instances she'd ask people to check her apartment or accompany her for menial tasks like doing laundry or taking out the garbage.

"That's putting it lightly."

"Did she really have a stalker?"

He shrugs. "To be honest, I don't know. 'Cause one night, it's the guy down the hall who's stalking her, and the next, she's asking him to go with her to take the trash out 'cause she's afraid of the woman two doors down. She thought people were climbing trees and peeping into her bedroom window. Full disclosure: there aren't any trees anywhere near her bedroom window."

A rock sinks in the pit of my stomach. I don't like the fact that he knows what her bedroom looks like.

He keeps scrolling. The battery flashes in the upper right corner: 3 percent. His brows knit when we arrive at the next conversation. I check the date. About two weeks ago, just before the overdose on Fulton Street. The contact's name is a hieroglyph of a blue sugar candy and skull emojis.

Pearl: *Got any blues?*

[candy + skull emoji]: *Nah I cant*

Pearl: *Plz . . . just enuf to get by. Last time promise*

[candy + skull emoji]: *How many?*

Pearl: *As many as you can give me. It'll be our secret.*

[candy + skull emoji]: *Secrets secrets . . .*

Pearl: *I luv uuuuuuu*

I take a photo just as the screen fades to black.

"Son of a bitch." He tosses the dead cell phone onto the paper bag.

"What are blues?" I ask.

"Oxycodone."

"Shit."

"Yeah."

Silence falls. I hear the electric hum of the computers, the static of the dispatch radio down the hall. "Does that mean Pearl was buying pills from Candy Man? Krejarek?"

"What gave it away, the candy emoji? I mean, I knew she wasn't clean, but fuck. I told her to stay away from pills."

"You also said she never listened."

"I did. And it's true; she didn't."

"But Krejark isn't prescribed oxycodone. He said they weren't his."

Kole's mouth twists into a roguish smile.

"What?" I ask, fearful I've said something stupid.

"You ready for a crash course in investigations?"

"Yes."

"Rule number one: everybody lies. I mean, he also claimed he didn't have a stash of pills in the wall and look what we found."

"You think he bought them off someone else, then? So he didn't lose business?" I ask, thinking back to last night's conversation about books and warehouses and such.

"All arrows seem to be pointing in that direction, yes."

I sigh and retrieve from memory his description of Pearl's apartment. "You said there were Newport cigarettes at the scene."

"And Marlboro Reds."

"The oxys that Jordan McAllister probably OD'd on at Krejarek's were in a Newport box."

"Yep." He picks up his phone and scrolls for a contact. He presses it to his ear, and I listen to his breathing as he waits for someone to answer on the other end. "Hey Josh, it's Nik. Are you in Area 6 right now? OK, can you pick up a William Samson, Jr. for me? He goes by Sam, twenty-six years old, male, white." I hold my breath as he rattles off my address, suddenly running a mental scan for anything on the exterior of the duplex that might point to me living on the other side.

"Great, thanks, buddy. I'll be upstairs in Interview Room #1." He ends the call.

"Why are you bringing Sam in?" I ask. My tone sounds defensive.

"Because if anyone knows what Krejarek's up to, it's him. I think I can get him to break."

I watch the seconds tick by on the clock, knowing that right about now, a squad car could be pulling up and knocking on Old Will's door. Thank God Tommy isn't home. He would want to be helpful in the investigation, perhaps volunteer to venture out on a manhunt himself, and I can't have my two worlds colliding.

I turn to Kole. I can see the gears turning in his head, the way his eyes move rapidly back and forth as though he's reading the backs of his own retinas. "Two weeks ago, Pearl texted Krejarek, aka Candy Man, for oxys. Now, she's dead. Last week, a boy in Krejarek's, aka Candy Man's apartment OD'd on oxys. He's dead, too, followed by a fourteen-year-old girl who looks to have OD'd on oxys as well. We found a Newport box at two of the three locations. If I were a betting man—and I am—I'd bet that whoever killed Pearl was the same person who distributed oxys to Krejarek for Jordan McAllister to get ahold of them, and maybe to Anya Brown."

Dashes of red and blue slice through the blinds as someone in the lot tests their lights. Kole slumps in his chair, his head lightly hitting against the back of it. "Fuck."

"What?"

"If this interview leads to an arrest, the DA will want to review the report first thing tomorrow morning. I'll be typing all night. If I can even get it done."

"How long until you think he's here?" I ask.

"Half hour."

I look at the easel where I keep the arrest headers. There's only a CIB Hit that can wait and no urgent dictation sitting in the E-scribe queue. My heart starts to pound like it did when I offered to go into the blue apartments. "You talk. I'll type."

Kole slowly leans forward. He regards me quizzically, thalassic eyes challenging me. "You think you can keep up?"

13.

SATURDAY

He doesn't know I've been up here before, I think as I follow him up the staircase to the one door at the top. Right goes to the command offices, left takes you to the Investigations Bureau.

"He's in the wagon," Kole says. "That gives us about ten minutes to get you settled." With a laptop tucked under one arm, he pushes open the double doors to the bureau, leaving the lights off as we wind our way through the aisles of desks. I don't know how he can be comfortable in just his T-shirt. It feels like a fridge up here.

"On your left, you'll notice May's fortress." He speaks like a tour guide, calm and collected considering that's just happened. He reminds me of Elle, a bit, using humor to defuse tense situations, and I feel racked with guilt all over again for leaving her party. Surely it's over by now. They're probably stripping the tables and dismantling what's left of the cupcake tower. Picking up half-drank sodas and cocktails. Turning down the lights.

But I don't have time for guilt. I squeeze my hands into fists as I keep close to Kole.

On my left, two heavy desks are arranged in an L-shape, each corner marked with plastic towers for various documents. An empty chair sits behind them, in front of a wall of filing cabinets, looking out over the entire bureau. My eyes adjusting to the darkness, I can read *May Peters, Secretary* engraved on the nameplate. Framed pictures of who I presume to be grandchildren sit atop her desk.

"She's been here since the eighties," Kole says. "She's an angel."

"You used to work up here?"

"For six months before I transferred to SIU. I did twelve years on patrol before that."

Twelve years. I've never been at any job that long. I do the math in my head. If he was on patrol for twelve years, even if he was hired at twenty-one, that would make him thirty-three years old. Plus six months in the bureau and however long he's been in SIU . . . "How old are you?" I ask.

"Thirty-six."

I laugh. "You are not."

"OK, I'm not. That's why I remember watching *Jurassic Park* in the theater."

I pause. There's something even more alluring to him, now, this fact that he is older and more experienced. "Twelve years ago, I was taking my driver's test." I smirk, unable to help myself.

I can't see him, but I bet he's rolling his eyes. I hope he's smiling, too.

He's so close to me, within arm's reach. I focus on the crease down the middle of his back. I want to drag my fingertips down it, softly, and see if I can't get his knees to buckle. I slip into a fantasy of me sitting on a desk with my legs wrapped around him, his hands traveling up beneath my dress. I wonder if he wants it as much as I do. Aside from the pinky promise earlier, we've hardly touched since the night in Krejarek's apartment.

"That's where Riley the Reaper sits."

It feels like déjà vu as my eyes light on the stack of blue folders on Riley's desk—the ones I'd knocked over the other night.

"Who?"

"Riley the Reaper." He shakes his head. "It became a joke when she was on patrol. Every call she went to, someone was dead or dying. Things didn't change much when she came up here, with all the jumper calls."

I remember what Mona had told me, too, about Investigators Rowe and Riley responding to most of the jumper incidents. I wonder how many corpses they've seen dragged onto the banks by now.

Kole sighs. "She's a damn good detective. I keep telling her she should put in for SIU once Match is out."

"Once he's out?"

"It's a four-year position. Oh hey, this is cool." He stops so short I almost run into him. If it's only a four-year position, that means in a couple of years, Kole will be . . . where?

"Can you go back in once you come out?" I ask while he reaches for something. "Like, come back here for a year or two and then put in for SIU again when someone else leaves?"

"In theory, but no one's ever been given a second shot."

I feel it like a punch, the gravity of the realization that everything is transient. There will come a time when Nikolai Kole will not be an SIU detective, commanding interview rooms and conducting secret operations. And perhaps I won't even know him anymore when that happens. *This will end, too,* I think. All good and bad things do.

From a mess of spread-out papers, plastic energy drink vials, and other office-related debris that litters the desk next to Riley's, Kole extracts a pair of dust-covered glasses. He holds them up to me, and I can see a thin silver wire sticking out of one of the hinges.

"It looks like an antenna," I say.

"Close. It's a probe. Rumele got his Taser wrestled away from him and this was how close the guy came to shooting his eye out."

"Damn."

"Yeah." Kole places the glasses back where he found them. "What a slob." Judging by his reaction, I half expect him to pull out a travel-size bottle of hand sanitizer, but he's got other matters on his mind. He leads me to the alcove with the coffeepot where I know is Interview Room #1. He turns the knob of the door next to it.

"You stowing me away in the broom closet?" I ask, even though I know what it is.

He laughs. "It's not much bigger than one."

The light switch is three or four steps in on the right. Setting the laptop on a nearby table, he reaches to flip it on, but I stop him by lightly touching his arm. I pull the door shut behind us. It's pitch-black. He draws in a breath when my fingertips travel down toward his wrist, gliding along his palm, and fitting into the spaces between his knuckles.

It's so dark. Without being able to see him, my other senses are heightened. I hear his slow, measured breathing and the beating of my heart as it thrums against my rib cage; I smell a hint of his sandalwood and sage cologne masking his sweat; I feel his warmth as our hands join together, our bodies aligning, and excitement as I tell myself that doing something in here would be very wrong.

He brings my hand up to his mouth and presses his lips softly to the back of it. He kisses each of the birdlike bones, then turns it over to kiss the inside of my wrist, where thin blue veins run like rivulets beneath the skin.

I press my other hand to his chest, feeling the shape of his badge, the curves of his muscles, and the slats of his ribs. I feel invincible and strong, because I have the ability to bend a man like Nikolai Kole to my will with just my fingertips. We kiss and he tastes like unadulterated freedom.

He unlocks his fingers from mine, then, and grips my waist with both hands. Our foreheads touch. I close my eyes, allowing myself to dip my toe just beneath the surface of a blissful oblivion.

Suddenly, I hear footsteps and static from a radio. I jump, immediately creating distance between the two of us.

"You're sure you're all right in here?" Kole is at the door.

I open the laptop. The screen bathes the room in a bluish glow. Pressing my finger to my lips, I promise not to make a sound. He smiles, a faint dimple appearing in his cheek, and then walks out to greet Sam and the patrol officers.

"Hey, thanks for bringing him in. We'll be over there in Interview Room #1 . . ."

I sit at the small table poised to type as Sam enters the room first. He's dressed in flannel pajama bottoms that are shredded at the hem, black salt-stained sneakers, and a faded black hoodie. He looks thinner than he did last night, even, more disheveled. His eyes are vacant and red rimmed, and his hair is flat against the back of his head like he was pulled off of his pillow to come here.

From the doorway, I can see Kole's arm, hand open to gesture to the chair on the other side of the stainless-steel table. Sam takes a seat, slumping down with his hands shoved between his knees. Carrying a bottle of water, Kole closes the door behind him. He sets the water on the table in front of Sam and sits across from him. "That's for you."

Sam looks up at him but says nothing.

"Thanks for coming."

"Didn't think I had a choice."

Kole ignores him. "You want coffee?"

Sam doesn't answer.

"Before we begin, I want you to know that you're not under arrest. I'm just . . . hoping you can help me with something."

Sam looks up at him as though telling him to get on with it.

"A woman was found brutally murdered in her apartment," says Kole. "She was a friend of Tyler Krejarek's, Sarah Dylan. You know her?"

I watch Sam from the other side of the glass. He clenches his jaw, swallows, then frowns as he shakes his head. He crosses his arms over his stomach and bounces his right foot.

Meanwhile, my fingers fly over the keyboard, capturing everything from the moment Kole entered the room: *I provided him with a water and informed him he was not under arrest. I told him I hoped he could help me with something, and proceeded to inform him of the murder of Sarah Dylan—*

"Why am I bringing this up, you're wondering? Well, in light of certain events, I have reason to believe that Jordan McAllister's and Sarah Dylan's deaths might be connected. Remember the last time you and I talked, Sam? You told me you didn't know where those oxys came from, the ones that poisoned little Jordan McAllister. I've got some more questions for you and I'll tell you right now, I already know the answers to most of 'em. I just want to see what you've got to say this time around."

I can see the Adam's apple bob in Sam's throat. His mouth is slack as though he's poised to speak; he isn't as tight-lipped as Krejarek.

"You said I'm not under arrest," Sam reminds him. His voice trembles.

"You're not at the moment. Let's see what you've got to say, though. You cooperate, you'll go home. You don't, well . . . I can keep you here all night. So let's get to it, eh?" He doesn't wait for a response when he asks, "You smoke, Sam?"

Sam's eyes flick to Kole, then to various corners of the room.

"Listen, I'm not talking about weed. If you think there isn't a skunky haze spanning a five-mile radius around your place, you'd be sorely mistaken. But I've got bigger fish to fry. What brand of cigarettes do you smoke?"

A cold, unnerving sensation hits me. It feels like ice melting in the pit of my stomach. He's familiar with Sam's residence. Which means he's familiar with mine. I race through a mental inventory of anything that could give me away as living there. Aside from my Blazer being registered to me, there's nothing. No monogram on the mailbox, no tacky signs with our last name on them. For the past two years, I have treated the duplex as nothing more than temporary.

I know he's asking because of the Newport cigarette box found in Krejarek's place and the crushed filters in Pearl's ashtray.

"I smoke weed," says Sam. "Me and my old man. That's it."

That's a lie, I think, and immediately question myself. Is it? I've seen Sam smoke cigarettes before; I'm sure of it. And yet, I can't recall ever noticing a box left lying on the table atop stained pizza boxes and porno magazines, nor have I noticed a rectangular patch worn thin in his jeans pocket. Not that I spend much time in his company, but still, after two years you'd think I would know.

"No one else?" Kole asks.

I pause, long enough to be able to cross my fingers over the keyboard. The tendons in my neck pull tight. *Please don't mention Tommy*, I pray.

Thankfully, he doesn't. His head wobbles back and forth on his neck like it's on a spring.

I let out the breath I'm holding. Tommy doesn't smoke. I know that for a fact. But he's over there almost every night.

"What about Krejarek? What does he smoke?"

Sam shrugs.

Kole leans in. "You mean to tell me you've been friends with this guy since middle school and you don't know what the fuck kind of cigarettes he smokes? Some friend you are."

"We used to pick up butts off the sidewalk when we were younger," Sam says. His words are a little slurred, they're coming out so fast. "Relight 'em. Just . . . kid stuff. It wasn't no particular kind."

"But you're not kids anymore. I know Krejarek gets a check every month from the government. He can afford a pack of new cigarettes. And like I told you a few minutes ago, Sam, I already know the answers. I just want to see if yours match up."

Sam sighs. He sinks in his chair. I notice how deep his hands are shoved into his sweatshirt pocket. His arms shake as though his fists are magnets he's trying to keep apart. "Newports," he says, finally.

Newports, I type. My focus blurs. The ink on the screen seems to bleed, like that one word is going to take up the entire screen.

Kole pauses. "You're sure?"

Sam sits, grinding the ball of his foot into the floor. "Can I go now?"

"Not yet."

A suffocating quiet settles. It's one of those silences that is so, so deep, it's loud. I fix my gaze on Kole. I wonder what he's waiting for. Five minutes pass. I watch them tick away at the bottom of my screen and notice the cadence of my breathing becoming more clipped, as though I'm the one in the interview room.

At last, Sam breaks. "Look, I didn't have anything to do with Pearl. I don't know—"

The slightest smile tugs at the corner of Kole's mouth. "Who's Pearl?"

Sam looks at him like he's crazy. "The chick who was murdered. You said—"

"—I said Sarah Dylan was murdered. I never mentioned the name

Pearl. But since you do seem to know her, let's talk. Man-to-man. You ever fuck her?"

The abrupt crudeness seems as startling to me as it is to Sam. "What?" he spats.

I asked Sam if he'd ever had sexual intercourse with Sarah Dylan, to which he seemed perplexed, I type, all the while wondering whether Kole's going somewhere with this, or if he's curious for personal reasons. Liv's voice plays in my head again: *You know he's fucking his CI, right?*

"Sex." He gets up as he says it and begins to pace the room, like a lion circling a rat, and I can't help but feel a little bit sorry for Sam. "You know. Your old man ever talk to you about the birds and the bees?"

"I didn't know her," Sam says. Some of the edge has faded from his voice.

"Don't lie to me, Sam," Kole cautions.

Sam swallows, stares at the wall behind Kole as he chews on a piece of thumbnail. I check the clock in the bottom right corner of my screen. A minute passes before he speaks again. "Tyler liked her. A lot. But I don't think she was into him the same way. I think she might'a been using him."

Kole nods. "That actually sounds pretty in character for her," he says. "Pretty girl, right?"

"I only saw pictures, but yeah."

I can't tell whether or not Kole believes him, but he doesn't miss a beat. "And you're saying that a girl like that wouldn't be interested in someone who looks like Krejarek?"

Sam shrugs. "Probably not. What does this have to do with her getting murdered? I thought Tyler was in custody—"

"He was released yesterday."

Sam seems stunned, like he's hearing this news for the first time.

"But you already knew that," says Kole.

"I swear I didn't." He slouches toward the table, his elbows sliding across its surface, and buries his hands in his hair. He shakes his head and keeps on shaking it, like he's short-circuiting.

"What are you thinking?" Kole asks.

Sam's still shaking his head when he answers: "That he can give drugs to a fucking nine-year-old and make me drag his dead body out to the dumpster, then the second he gets released, he's gotta go kill someone else."

"You think Krejarek killed Pearl?" Kole says, for the record.

Sam slowly sits up. His face is wet with tears. "Who else would've?"

"You said you think Pearl was using him, but were they friends? Or did he think they were, at least?"

"Yeah, kinda." His voice is thick. He sniffles.

"How do you know?"

"'Cause, they'd, like, help each other out and shit."

"Explain."

I watch Sam wring his hands nervously under the table, picking at calluses. He cursorily scans the room, as though to make sure neither party he's going to talk about is standing by. "He got stuff from her sometimes."

"Drugs?"

"Yeah."

"Pills?"

"I don't know. I never seen any needles or anything else."

"You don't necessarily need needles to do other stuff. You can smoke it, ingest it—"

"I'm just sayin' I never seen that stuff, OK?" Sam huffs, clearly angry at how much he's divulged. Clearly angry at Krejarek for getting him into this mess, and clearly angry at Kole for dragging him out of his bed at 1 a.m.

"I know you're angry," Kole says. "But you wouldn't be angry if you didn't have something to hide. If you don't want to help me, then help yourself for Christ's sake. If you lie to me, I'll slap you with obstructing a homicide investigation, and I'll add some weed charges to your tab while I'm at it. Now, you said Krejarek would get stuff from Pearl sometimes, too? Not just the other way around?"

I recall the Candy Man conversation in the red flip-style phone. *You got any blues?* she'd asked.

Sam stares hard at the stainless-steel surface of the table. "Yeah. He bought from her sometimes. Like I said, I think they'd help each other out. Sometimes she'd buy from him and sometimes he'd buy from her. Or they'd just trade, I don't know."

"And then she'd resell it?"

Sam shrugs and goes back to grinding his foot into the floor. I listen to his breath rattling in his chest. He raises his arm to wipe his nose on his sleeve.

Although Kole remains calm on the exterior, I know the information probably hit him like a kick to the chest. He turns toward me, slightly, and I can see the shock he keeps at bay, lingering just beneath the surface. The gears behind his eyes start to dial. His brows knit, twin creases appearing in the middle of his forehead, and I know he's blaming himself for not detecting the fact that his CI was dealing drugs right under his nose.

"Who did Pearl get her drugs from to sell to Krejarek?" he asks.

Sam shakes his head. "I don't know." And the falling pitch of his voice makes me believe him. I'm not sure I can say the same for Kole, though.

"The funny thing about the drug world, Sam, is that everybody knows everybody. You never ran into any of these characters?"

Sam just stares at the table. He isn't part of the drug world, I think, just like I'm not really part of Black Harbor. He barely stepped his toe over the threshold and this is where it landed him. He's just a loser who lives with his old man—a wall away from me.

Kole takes a moment for himself, then. With his eyes closed, he tilts his head from side to side, working out the kinks in his neck, and walks to the corner of the room where a blue folder lies on the floor. I remember him walking upstairs with it, but he's kept it so discreet this whole time, I forgot about it. He picks up the folder, sets it on the table, and slides out three letter-size photographs. From where I sit, I see a pale hand against a Styrofoam takeout container. A gash of red identified as the Spider-Man sleeping bag. A pair of eyes like doll eyes.

"You blame Krejarek for this, don't you?"

If there was any color remaining in Sam's face, it's drained now. He looks like he's about to throw up. Anguish twists his features. Silence.

"Sam, yes or fucking no."

He's frowning so severely, his mouth resembles a lowercase "n." His lip quivers. "Yes."

"You wanted him put away for it. You wanted some justice for Jordan."

"Yes."

"That's why you went up to the police department window and confessed."

"Yes."

"That's why you sent that text. *He keeps his shit in the walls.* What'd you use, a burner phone? Or an app to hide your number?"

Sam looks up at Kole, meeting his gaze for the first time in a while. His watery eyes scan rapidly back and forth, and a worrying crease cuts into his forehead. "I never sent you a text," he says.

All the air escapes the room. Kole takes his phone out of his back pocket, and shows something—a screenshot of the message, I bet—to Sam.

Sam squints, shaking his head. "I didn't send that."

"Then who did?"

"I don't know."

"Krejarek have any enemies. Besides you, I mean."

"I'm not his enemy."

"He made you drag a dead boy into the dumpster, Sam. He made a monster out of you. He *should* be your enemy."

Sam's nostrils flare. He looks like he's going to cry again.

"Where's Tyler Krejarek?" Kole asks, leaning over and setting his hands on top of the photographs.

"I don't know."

"You're lying." Kole's voice is as quiet as it's been throughout this entire interview, but it's cutting.

"I don't know!" Sam yells, punctuating each word. His face is red and blotchy. Cradling his head in his hands, he begins to sob. His shoulders shake. "Can I go home now?"

Disgust darkens Kole's features. He narrows his eyes at the pathetic creature in the chair. "Yeah, we're done." In two long strides, he's got Sam by the arm and he's pulling him toward the door. They disappear from my view as they exit the interview room and walk through the bureau. I close the laptop and tuck it under my arm to follow a safe distance behind them down the stairs.

"Can I have a ride?" I hear Sam ask.

"Where's Tyler Krejarek?" Kole ripostes.

"I told you, I don't know."

"Then I don't know where your ride is."

They make it to the bottom of the stairs, in the narrow hallway where the bathrooms are. I watch from the second landing as Kole pushes open the door, grabs Sam by the scruff of his sweatshirt, and throws him out. "Stop!" I cry, and immediately clap my hand over my mouth.

There's a thud as Sam hits the salted cement.

Kole yanks the door shut, and when he looks up, his eyes burn into me. I shrink, clutching the laptop like a shield. "You can leave that part out of the report," he says.

14.

WEDNESDAY

Snowflakes dense as rain sting my face. For the first time since receiving it as a gift last Monday, I stare at my reflection in the compact mirror. My eyes are pink with plumes of red diffused at the edges, my cheeks scarlet and blotchy, melting any snowflakes that dare to light on my skin. The kraft-paper tag is still attached, on which the question *Will you be my maid of honor?* is stamped in gold foil.

A script is engraved around the mirror: *Forever sisters, forever best friends—E+H.*

Forever has an expiration date, apparently.

It's been four days since I've heard from Elle.

I can't believe you left last nite. That really hurts, Hazel. I read her text late Saturday morning, when I finally crawled out of bed after my grueling shift speed-typing Kole's interview with Sam.

I closed my eyes. A screw twisted in my gut. *I said I was sorry, Elle. But you know what? The only thing I'm sorry about is having to break the news to you that the world doesn't revolve around you.*

My phone buzzed in my hand with her retort. *You are so selfish.*

"Ha." I actually said it out loud. *Fuck off*, I punched. *That will shut her up,* I thought. And it did. Until this morning, at least, when *The Elle & Kinney Show* came on and she posed the question to all of her listeners: "What would you do if your maid of honor just up and ditched your engagement party? OK, get this. What if that maid of honor was your *sister*? Can you fire a bridesmaid? Seriously, I wanna know what y'all think 'cause, whew, I've got some d-r-a-m-a comin' your way at the hour."

I cringed. Since when is it appropriate for a midwesterner to say *y'all*?

Mona turned toward me, pausing from logging in to her portal. It's Wednesday, one of two days that Mona's and my shifts overlap for two hours. "Sounds like that OT got you in hot water with your sister."

I shrugged. I'd just finished filling Mona in about being called in Friday night. She'd heard about it on the news, of course: Twenty-three-year-old Sarah Dylan was a loving daughter, a former celebrated high school athlete who was slaughtered in her apartment in the early hours of Friday morning. I wondered if the first part of that story had any truth to it.

"It is what it is," I said. "She'll get over it." Or she won't. Whatever. Everyone already hates me, Elle. Mom, Angela, Liv, Marjorie, who wrote me up again for wearing a cocktail dress to work, even though she'd told me not to worry about changing. Stupid Marjorie. So, Elle, to you I say: Take a number, sister. I'm done apologizing for Friday night. She and Mom are probably getting manicures right now, laughing and enjoying each other as I stand here on Forge Bridge, the wind whistling through my hollow bones.

They're happier without me.

And I bite my nails anyway.

I close the clamshell compact, my thumb grazing the gold filigree design on the rim. Overlaid on a mint-and-peach floral design is a monogrammed "H."

H for hurtful.

"People with normal jobs don't get it," Mona said as I packed up my things to leave. I turned my face away from her, not wanting her to see the tears that threatened to spill onto my canvas bag. "If I had to count how many friends this job cost me over the years—not getting holidays off or weekends off or just being able to confide in anyone outside of here—we'd better put on a pot of coffee 'cause we'd be here all morning." Her laugh turned into a cough. "What am I saying, I never had that many friends to begin with, but you get the idea, Fargo."

The tears that I've been holding in the time it took me to leave the PD and drive to the bridge freeze on my lashes. I turn over the compact, looking at the tiny scratches that crosshatch its surface.

H for hopeless.

I check over my shoulder to make sure the vacant lot is still vacant. My Blazer waits, its windshield wipers paused in the middle of the window. I toss the compact. It feels like a cold stone leaving my hands. My heart constricts as I wait and listen for the plink of it diving into the water, but it's soundless.

H for Hazel.

My phone suddenly vibrating in my jacket pocket startles me.

It's Elle, or Tommy, I think. He usually texts about this time when he knows I've left work.

It's Kole. *I need to see you*, he says.

I inhale sharply. That one four-letter word is enough to do me in. *Need*. It's almost as if I am air or water to him, a force essential to his survival. He needs me, and yet, I narrow my eyes at the message, perhaps hating him a little, too, for being so distant. I know he's in the middle of a homicide investigation, but still . . . he doesn't take breaks?

It's been four days since I sat in on the interview and I've hardly heard from him. No updates on the whereabouts of Krejarek or the investigation of who murdered Sarah Dylan, the confidential informant who was working both sides of the law. I slipped out of the police department not long after the interview, when I was sure that Kole was preoccupied in the evidence room. It felt scandalous, like I was cutting out of work early, but my work was done for the night.

And besides, it had been below freezing. Perhaps it was my *up north* showing, but I couldn't let Sam walk all the way back to the duplex. He hadn't made it a mile when I slowed to a stop on the road next to him and rolled down the passenger-side window. "Can I give you a ride?" I asked.

He froze, stared at me with suspicion, his hands jammed into his pockets. My headlamps reflected in his eyes, dilating his pupils.

"Please, Sam," I urged. "It's too cold out here."

He looked over each shoulder as though to ensure it wasn't a setup. Then he opened the door and climbed in. I closed the window. It was as frigid and silent as a coffin for a moment. My vehicle wouldn't even be half thawed by the time we reached our destination.

I searched for what to say. There was no point in pretending I didn't know why he was out here. He'd seen me. We'd locked eyes even, for a second, when he was sprawled on the stone-cold sidewalk and I was inside the police department, protesting at the top of the stairs. I'd given myself away, but I wasn't his enemy. I wasn't Kole.

"Are you all right?" I asked. My voice shook.

Sam turned his wrists in his lap, examining the road rash. He shrugged.

"I'm sorry," I said.

Sam snorted. "For what? You didn't throw me out on my ass."

I sighed. My breath fogged my window. No, I hadn't thrown Sam out on his ass. But I'd encouraged Kole to bring him in, hadn't I? And I'd offered to transcribe in real time behind the scenes, so Kole could drill him for information concerning Sarah Dylan's murder. I'd been an accomplice.

We rounded a curve and the duplex crept into view with its sinking porch and siding that's seen better days, like the rest of Black Harbor. I watched Sam from the corner of my eye, and could tell he was chewing on the inside of his cheek, wanting to say something.

"Don't tell my dad, OK?" he said. He picked at the broken skin on his knuckles. "He's got enough problems as it is. I don't want him worrying about no cops busting down his door any minute."

I nodded. The less Old Will and Tommy knew about Sam's proximity to the investigation, the better. I wonder what would happen now if Kole were to find out that I live next door to his person of interest. He'd assume I was hiding something. And I am—the fact that my husband goes over there to drink and smoke cigars. Who knows if he might slap some drug charges on Tommy like Liv said he did to Pearl's boyfriend. In the eyes of the police department, me living there is a conflict of interest. I could lose my job. It would be disastrous for everyone.

I promised Sam I wouldn't tell.

Now, four days later, the wind rocks me back on my heels, rips at my hair. My phone vibrates with another text from Kole. *Hazel, please.*

I sigh and wonder if this is the part where he finds out where I live. If this is the part where he starts questioning me about the goings-on of the duplex and my husband's involvement with the neighbors.

I'm spinning tales; I know it. Nikolai Kole is not after me. *OK*, I send.

Are you free tonight? Beck's at 7?

Or earlier, I think. I don't have to dance around Tommy's shooting schedule. A sense of euphoria floods through my veins, a stark contrast to what I'd been feeling in the moments before Kole's text message. I *am* free. Tommy is a good four-hundred miles from here. Even if he were to find out about me meeting Kole tonight, he couldn't stop me if he wanted to.

I don't want to come off as eager, but the burning need to see him, touch him, just talk to him, makes me brave. *6*, I reply.

See you at 6, Podunk.

For the first time in nearly four days, I smile. Even though I'd be lying to myself if I didn't admit he scares me a little. But everyone lies.

• • •

There's a Diet Pepsi with a cherry on top waiting for me as I walk up to our table. Dressed in jeans and a T-shirt, Kole smiles and walks to meet me. God, he looks good, I think, even if a little worse for wear. I wonder how long it's been since he's slept.

I hold out my hand, prompting him to turn his over, so I can drop the quarter from last time into his palm. He smiles at me, a pair of perfect quotations framing the corners of his mouth, and I instantly feel bad for having felt bitter toward him earlier. "You kept it." He says it proudly, like it's more than a quarter. "You're up, though." He gives it back and presses my fingers closed over it. He's warm from having been inside.

"When did you get here?" I ask, hanging my jacket on the tall chair back.

He doesn't answer right away, and I realize he's dazed by my low-cut sweater. It's thin and hunter green. I picked it out while thrifting with Elle last fall, and never wore it until tonight. I paired it with a-thin silver chain that matches the V-neck and disappears down, down, down, lightly touching just above my belly button. Inappropriate attire or not for meeting someone out while my husband is across state lines casting lures and stabbing bait with hooks and probably drinking himself to unconsciousness, I won't be getting written up tonight.

Suck it, Marjorie.

Kole shakes himself from his trance, his eyes darting up to meet mine again. "Five minutes ago."

We sit. He tells me where he's been since we last saw each other. He returned to Pearl's complex Saturday morning and interviewed her neighbors, showing them a six-person lineup comprised of four known drug dealers, plus Sam, and Tyler Krejarek. Her neighbor from the building over acknowledged having seen Krejarek and Pearl meet under a bus stop a few times.

"Well, that's enough to go after him, isn't it?" I ask.

He shrugs. "Eyewitness accounts aren't always 100 percent accurate, but that identification coupled with recent events, yeah, we're on the hunt for him. Again."

"Why aren't they 100 percent accurate?" I ask. "Why even do interviews and neighborhood canvasses, then?"

He takes a drink and sets the sweating glass back down on the coaster. "Because people tend to see what they want to see. Sometimes their desire to contribute and help solve something overrides their memory of what they actually saw. Unfortunately, eyewitness reports are sometimes all we have to go on to get us at least looking in the right direction."

I like watching him speak, studying the way his mouth forms words. I like the mystery of wondering where some of them become ridged, if it happens on their way up his throat or when they roll off his tongue. I watch his neck as he speaks, imagine pressing my lips to his skin and sinking my teeth in, just barely, to elicit a gasp. That's all I want of him: to take his breath away.

Reaching from across the table, his thumb lightly caresses my hand. I lift my gaze to meet his, feeling color bloom in my cheeks, and check my peripheral vision for anyone I recognize. But, Beck's is pretty empty tonight, as always. A couple sits at the bar watching the basketball game on TV and two guys play darts in the back.

I lean with my elbows on the table, my hands forming a "v" to cup my chin. He smiles when he realizes how intently I'm watching him, the way his eyes routinely scan the bar, particularly the entrance, ever on the lookout for threats. "What?"

"It's just . . . crazy. All of this," I say. *And you're . . . indescribable*, I want to add. But that's not true. Everything is describable, even nothing. To label something as indescribable is a cop-out. Nikolai Kole, therefore, is my darling oblivion.

Ooh, that's good. Remember to write that down later.

"Welcome to Black Harbor, baby," says Kole. "You mean murder and mayhem weren't on the brochure?"

Baby. No one's ever called me that before. "Did you find Krejarek?" I ask.

His expression sobers, then, his eyes seeming to frost over like the window that fateful morning when Sam wrote his confession with Jordan McAllister's severed finger. "No. But we found the murder weapon," he says.

"You did?" The pitch of my voice shoots up, and I immediately quiet myself. "How long were you gonna hold out on me?" Although I say it as a joke, I realize I'm hurt by the fact that he chose to keep such a critical update from me. Friday night into the early morning hours of Saturday, as we pored over Pearl's message threads and captured the interview with Sam, it had felt, almost, like we were in this together. I'm a fool to have thought that, of course. He's the investigator here. I'm just a transcriber.

Instead of answering me with a day or a time, he leans toward me and lowers his voice. "Tell me something confidential," he says, and offers his pinky.

I hesitate, staring at it like it's a Rubik's Cube, and hook my little finger with his. A small smile tugs at the corner of my mouth as I consider this might be the start of a game, but his tone says otherwise. "Have you ever been on Forge Bridge?"

The question catches me like an ice pick in the chest. I narrow my eyes and shake my head as he half turns to extract a plastic baggie from his jacket's inside pocket. He sets it on the table between us, next to the quarter I laid flat. Curled like a dead insect is a corded bracelet with my name spelled in yellow and emerald beads. The one I gave to the river two springs ago.

I steel my expression, forcing my right eyebrow to remain level. "What is that?"

"I was hoping maybe you could tell me."

I force a laugh. "You think because it says 'Hazel' that it's mine? There've got to be a hundred Hazels in this city."

"It's actually considerably less than a hundred. But I agree. It doesn't mean it belongs to you. I just thought I'd ask—"

"I don't even understand why this thing with my name on it, apparently, and the murder weapon are being brought up in the same train of thought. I mean—"

"Because we found them in the same vicinity. That's all. We sent a dive team from the county and they came back with the kitchen knife that had been used to stab Pearl and this. I saw the name and it struck me. Hazel, listen to me."

Sam, listen. He's questioning me. I feel sick.

He reaches for my wrist as though to clamp me down and stop me from going anywhere, but I pull my arm away, knocking over my drink. Glass shatters on the floor. The bloodred cherry rolls over the shards. Instinctively, I look up to see who's staring. The couple at the bar has turned around, my mess suddenly more interesting than the basketball game. The bartender, clearly annoyed, hops off her perch on the garnishes cooler and disappears around the corner, I assume to get a mop. Under normal circumstances, I would stay and clean it up myself, but I swear the walls are closing in. I yank my jacket off the chair and run-walk past the air hockey table and out the doors.

I hadn't realized I was sweating until the chill freezes beads of perspiration to my face. My Blazer is a welcome getaway vehicle, parked close this time. I start toward it when Kole suddenly grabs my bicep.

"Hazel, what the fuck?"

"Don't *what the fuck* me," I argue. "What the hell, Nik? You go dark on me for, what, four or five days, lure me over here, and accuse me of—"

"Lure you over here?" He sounds as flabbergasted as he looks. "I didn't *lure* you anywhere. Jesus, I simply asked if you would meet me."

"I need to see you," I repeat, my voice laced with toxicity.

He sighs. His breath is a cloud of vapor. His jacket's crumpled under his arm and goosebumps dapple his skin. "Exactly. I needed to see you. Jesus Christ, next time I have something I think might be sensitive to ask you, I'll just text you or send it over BHPD messenger."

"It's not my bracelet, Nik!" I'm shouting. I don't know why I'm shouting. I half expect someone to yell at me from their bedroom window to shut up, but the reality is that it's not even seven o'clock and this is Black Harbor, where people are accustomed to sleeping through gunshots.

"OK." His shoulders fall. "I believe you, baby. I do."

There it is again: *baby*. My fear and anger melt away like ice next to a fire. I let him pull me to him, and with my face buried in the hollow of his neck, I wonder what other things of mine he wrested from their underwater graves.

"Will you stay with me?" he asks, separating just enough from me to hold my face in his hands and search my eyes. "I've missed you."

My throat tightens. I nod. I've missed him, too; felt his absence like a ringing silence.

He smiles softly, the faint quotation marks playing by his mouth again.

"I don't want to go back in there," I tell him.

"Come on. I'll take you somewhere."

• • •

We sit in the back seat of his car, my back to his chest, our fingers twining and untwining as we stare at the adumbration of Forge Bridge. Its onyx outline is barely visible overlaid on a canvas of espresso sky, though the light pollution from Milwaukee adds a milky glow to the horizon.

It was exhilarating, speeding down a stretch of empty road in a city where cops have their sights set on worse things than traffic violations. I held my breath as we careened down the hill past Krejarek's apartment and the dumpster that once entombed Jordan McAllister's body, and Kole parked here, in the vacant lot in front of Forge Bridge.

It was I who suggested the back seat. I wanted to feel him pressed to me. I feel safe with him, suspended in a weird state of calm, but every so often, my eyes flick to the rearview mirror, where in the not-too-far distance looms the thicket I once scrambled through. For a second, my mind slips into imagining the pallid, dark-haired corpse wandering out of the evergreens.

The radio plays softly, but I can barely hear it over my heart drumming in my ears. "Tell me something confidential?" I ask.

"Anything." He hooks his pinky around mine.

I stare out the windshield, at the pitch-black cutouts of trees on the other side of the riverbank, on the brink of talking myself out of the question I've wanted to know the answer to since I crossed out his name on the personnel roster. "Why were you suspended?"

I feel his chest sink as he exhales. "Something that involved Pearl, actually."

I hear an echo of Liv's voice: *You know he's fucking his CI, right?* "What happened?" The question is enough to wring my insides. Maybe I don't want to know. But it's too late, now.

"Sarah Dylan, alias Pearl," he explains, "is Investigator Dylan's daughter, though you probably put that together by now."

I had. "Is that why he was upstairs the other night?"

"Yes. He's banned from the premises, but I guess his daughter getting stabbed to death earned him a hall pass." We're facing each other now. I can feel the cold seeping in through the window at my back. Kole looks at me as though to challenge me. *Any further questions, Your Honor?* But I sit quietly. Even if he was fucking her at one time, what does it matter now? She is cold and dead on the medical examiner's table.

Unprovoked, he tells me more. "Jack Dylan and I used to be friends. Really good friends, believe it or not. He was my Field Training Officer, Jesus, sixteen years ago. Not everyone likes their FTO, but I got lucky. He taught me everything, from how to write parking citations to how to kick in a door. He was a great fucking cop, and he proved time and time again he'd go out on a limb for people he loved." He pauses like he's sifting through memories. "Sarah was an only child. A good kid, too. Phenomenal: straight-A student, MVP of her volleyball team. I used to watch her matches with Jack and his wife. But then, the summer she graduated, she hooked up with a guy named Cyrus Jacoby. Massive piece of shit and big-time heroin dealer. Dylan was pissed, but what could he do? So, about two years later—last July—when he received word from a reliable CI who said they'd witnessed Cyrus dealin', he jumped at the chance to throw his ass in the slammer. Three controlled purchases and a search warrant later, we had him. Mission accomplished."

"Did you find anything?" I ask.

"A record-breaking amount of heroin. He'd even been supplying guys in Chicago. We had more than enough to charge him with distribution, plus we'd used a CI to capture several of his sales on tape."

I adjust myself so I'm facing him. "So, you arrested Cyrus for delivery. And Sarah as party-to?"

"You're getting good at this, but no. When we entered the apartment after Crue busted in the door, Sarah came at us." He shakes his head. "She threw herself down the stairs with such reckless abandon, screaming, hitting. Dylan had no idea. He thought she was off at rehab. She was supposed to have been, anyway.

"Mattox and Hansen detained her in the kitchen. I went upstairs in pursuit of Cyrus. I kicked the bathroom door in and found him flushing heroin down the toilet. Baggies torn open everywhere, heroin all over the floor. He ignored my directives to stop and put his hands up, and then grabbed the top of the toilet tank to use it as a shield. Pretty inventive, actually. He rammed me out of the bathroom, out into the hall. We wrestled. Finally, Dylan was able to make it up the stairs and push him against the wall."

"940.203," I say, reciting the state statute for Battery to a Law Enforcement Officer. "That's a felony."

His eyes flicker in amusement. "It's so sexy when you talk statutes."

I blush. "Did you get a punch in afterward for good measure?"

"I would have liked to. But no, once Cyrus was detained, I went straight to searching, seeing how much I could rack him for. It wasn't a big place, just a one-bedroom. It was clean—of drugs, I mean, the place was a dump—except when I checked the closet where I found a music box. I knew it was Sarah's; there was even an inscription on the bottom from Dylan. I opened it and found about three ounces of heroin." He pauses to clear his throat. His mouth hangs open for a few seconds, as though the next words are reluctant to come out. Daring, I rest my hand on his and thread my fingers through. He squeezes gently. "I dumped the drugs from the music box into Cyrus's dresser. Then I put it back where I'd found it."

Holy shit. I feel my brows shoot up toward my hairline. "You tampered with evidence?"

With his mouth clamped shut now, Kole exhales. I study his profile as he stares out the window. He doesn't appear to be focusing on anything at all.

"I don't understand," I say. "How did anyone find out? I mean, I'm sure Cyrus argued, but—"

"Sarah confessed," he replies, still staring out the window. "She marched into the PD the morning after Cyrus was arrested and demanded to speak to the Chief. She swore the heroin was hers, that it had been taken from her music box. She thought, though, that her dad—Dylan—had done it."

"Because you were both upstairs?"

"That, and the fact that he had a stronger motive. She was his daughter."

"But, you had a motive, too?" Of course he did. He wouldn't have done what he did without one. Perhaps Kole was in love with Pearl after all. Or, perhaps he'd planned on using her as a CI all along. It would have made sense to save her, then.

"Yeah, I guess. Like I said, I knew Sarah *before*. She was better than this. I wanted Dylan to have his little girl back. Plus, Cyrus hadn't done himself any favors by ramming me into the wall with part of the toilet. So if he got slapped with an extra couple ounces of narcotics that he'd probably given to her anyway, what did I care?"

I believe him on that. More than once, I'd witnessed Kole's explosiveness when it came to payback, from punching the mirror in Krejarek's apartment to throwing Sam onto the sidewalk. And there were undoubtedly more instances that I hadn't seen. He didn't admit to ever being in love with Pearl, though, and I feel some relief at that. The tension in my muscles eases, and yet, it still doesn't add up. "So, you tampered with the evidence," I repeat, attempting to sort things out.

"Yes."

"But Dylan's the one who got fired."

"Right, well, forced to resign. We had separate interviews up in Internal Affairs. I told Schumer, the lieutenant up there, exactly what happened. That I'd discovered the heroin in the music box and moved it to the dresser. But when he interviewed Dylan, Dylan confessed to doing just that. He swore I had nothing to do with it. Honestly, either story checked out. It just came down to who Schumer hated more. And he'd had it in for Dylan since before I even started."

"Why?"

He shrugs. "Politics. And Dylan being the lead on a search warrant into his daughter's joint drug trafficking business was enough for him to smell something rank. Dylan was forced to either resign or do prison time, which, as you can imagine—for a cop who's spent thirty years putting away guys worse than Cyrus Jacoby—is suicide."

"So, Dylan resigned?"

"Yeah, but that was just the start of it. He was sued and irrevocably defamed. He had to move out of the county."

Irrevocably. I like that word. "And you were suspended?"

"I was on administrative leave, technically, while the internal investigation was ongoing. Six months off isn't as pretty as it sounds. You still get paid, but you can't make any OT. No leading search warrants, no buys. I even started missing the paperwork. For six months, I didn't know if I'd have a job to come back to, or any friends. For a while, I even thought I might have to go to prison. It was . . . one of the worst times of my life." He looks up at me, as though searching for judgment. I know because I've looked at Tommy the same way, before I started avoiding his gaze altogether.

"I wish I'd never gone into that room, now. It'll haunt me the rest of my career. You know, I've been a cop at Black Harbor PD for sixteen years? I worked my first decade on third-shift patrol. I've been tased, bit, beaten, I blew out my knee chasing a guy over a fence. When I was promoted to Investigations, it was because I scored the highest on the test. Within my first three months, I cracked a cold case of a woman who was decapitated in 1997. I wrote hundreds of search warrants, and I can't tell you how many doors I kicked down during SWAT operations. And yet, when I got selected for SIU, there were people saying I only got in because, well . . ." He trails off, thinking better than to complete that thought. "You know how rumors fly around that place. There were a few—Crue, Ox, Sully, Match at least—who were in my corner then, and others who would have loved nothing more than to see me demoted back to Patrol or worse, go the same way as Dylan. It's impossible to know what anyone really thinks."

"Because everybody lies?"

"Because everybody fucking lies." He looks poised to say something else, but doesn't. His chest rises and falls quicker than before. My eyes follow up the curve of his neck, looking for the faint, frantic beating of his pulse.

"What happened to Sarah?" I ask, finally. "How did she become . . . Pearl?"

He sighs. "She began going by Pearl soon after she started going with Jacoby. It's a street name for cocaine. And after everything went down, she called me up, wanting to work off her charges."

"She wanted to be your CI?"

"Correct. I was her last hope. So, I called up the DA's office and got clearance, and I talked it over with Dylan. No cop wants his daughter being an informant, but it's better than being locked up. Again, we thought if she could just get away from Jacoby, she might actually go to rehab and get clean. Dylan knew it was the only way out of the colossal mess she'd gotten herself into, so he agreed. I let her do a couple buys that led to a search warrant over at Knock Street and Warren. We scored ten ounces of cocaine at the Koken brothers' residence.

"After the arrests, the DA's office dropped her charges and I told Sarah she was off the hook. But she liked the thrill of it, I think—diming people out—and she said she had information on a big-time dealer named Buddha. We hit him next, and the rest is history. She quickly became my most reliable CI to date." The exhale that escapes him is one of exhaustion, like he's just run a marathon, or perhaps pushed a gargantuan weight off his chest.

"I tampered with the evidence," he says finally, as though to sum it all up. "And Dylan fell on the sword."

"That was his choice," I say.

"One that I shouldn't have let him make. I fucked up, Hazel. Trust me. I've had months to do nothing else but come to terms with this. My actions were what set all of this into motion. If I hadn't touched that music box, and then walked it over to a location where it had never been, Dylan and I never would have gotten called up to IA. He never would have been forced to resign. I never would have gotten this black mark on my record. And Sarah . . ." He hangs his head. For a second, I think he might cry.

A black plastic bag rolls through the lot, a white receipt sticking out of it like a tongue.

Slowly, I reach for his hand, pressing our palms together. My eyes zero in on my left ring finger, where there's not even a ghost of the ring I once wore. When he looks up at me, his gaze is more intense than I've ever known it to be, and suddenly, I want to explore every uncharted part of him—swim through the catastrophic channels of his mind, dive down to the quiet alcove of his heart, navigate until I have every fiber of Nikolai Kole's being figured out.

He smooths back a piece of my hair, tucking it behind my ear. I feel his lips on my neck, first. His kisses are hot, trailing from beneath my ear to my collarbone. My back arches as though I'm possessed, my head falling back as my nose, chin, and breasts point upward. Maybe I am a little. Possessed. What do you do with a demon inside of you?

You set it free.

Letting myself fall gently to lie across the leather, I pull him on top of me, feeling him pulsing against the inside of my thigh.

"When do you have to be home?" he asks when we pause for breath.

Home. I bet he would love it up there. We could lay a blanket on the ground and gaze up at the stars, our fingertips re-creating the constellations on each other's skin. We'd toast marshmallows over a bonfire and wake up smelling like smoke and dew. Even though I'm here in a vacant parking lot that overlooks the suicide bridge, I feel more at home now, in my soul, than I have for a very long time.

But I know he doesn't mean up north. He means the duplex, where I normally return to change and check in with Tommy before heading off to work. "I don't," I dare, and when he looks at me with questions in his eyes, I say, "He's on a trip."

"I see." His fingertips trace my collarbone, and he plants a kiss every inch, his mouth following the curve of my neck, my lips his final destination.

"One second." I reluctantly break away and check my phone, which has been in my jacket pocket this whole time. A text from Tommy, from a half hour ago. *I love you with my all heart hazej.*

I shoot a glance over my shoulder at Kole, who's looking down, occupying himself with peeling my shirt over my hip bones, and text: *I love you, too.* Tossing my phone on the front seat, I slide back into Kole. His hands move smoothly but firmly up the contours of my ribs, encircling my breasts.

"I just can't be late for work," I remind him before we get too far.

He lightly bites my earlobe and I'm thankful I'm sitting down. The sensation turns my legs to water. "Like Marjorie doesn't already hate you."

"This is true."

He moves his right hand, then, up my neck, fingers dancing over my chin. I open my mouth, and when he grazes my lips with his thumb, I bite down so lightly and suck.

"Fuck," he whispers.

• • •

If people can be places, then Nikolai Kole is Homer's Island of the Lotus-eaters. His sweat mingling with his cologne is a concoction that transports me somewhere off the Libyan coast, where the air is warm and saturated with sea salt. We kiss for two dizzying hours, and when we come up for air, it seems only two minutes have passed. My shirt clings to me; his is soaked through. My lips burn from being abraded by his stubble. When the frigid air touches them after I finally open the door, I'm brutally reminded that I'm still in Black Harbor.

"OK, seriously," I say through a laugh, "Good night." It's the fourth or fifth time I've said it, but each time, I let him reel me back in for another kiss.

"You don't mean that," he mumbles into my mouth.

I wish I didn't. Even now with fifteen minutes until the start of my shift, I'm tempted to call in. Rourke or Hayes, who took Hammersley's spot, would answer and neither of them would interrogate me if I told them I was having feminine problems. Which is absolutely true. Making out with someone who is not your husband in a parking lot is definitely a problem.

I break away to check the dashboard clock. Just as I thought, it's 9:45. "You're a bad influence," I tell him.

"Takes one to know one."

"Touché, motherfucker."

I slam the door, and a second later, before I can even take one step toward my vehicle, he calls for me to come by his window. I do and lean my head in to kiss him one last time.

"You're something else," he says.

"Takes one to know—" I freeze. Reflected in his mirror, a figure emerges from the copse at the edge of the riverbank. Fear paralyzes me. How many times have I come here, imagining the corpse I saw that morning climbing out of the water? But it isn't him. It's Krejarek. I recognize the maroon sweatshirt from his interview.

"Hazel, what is it?" Kole's voice is sharp. His vision darts forward, like a sniper searching for his target. But he's looking in the wrong direction.

My hand shakes uncontrollably as I point to the figure in the mirror. "He's—"

The whites of his eyes suddenly burn bright when he sees him. "Jesus Christ. Hazel, get out of here!" He reaches for his gun on the passenger seat and throws his door open. I jump back as he bolts out of his vehicle and within seconds, is halfway across the lot. "Go!" he yells over his shoulder.

I drop my keys on the way to my Blazer. Scooping them up off the ice, I wrench the door open and clamber inside as though I'm the one being chased. The windshield is frosted. I press my hand to the glass and smear a window for myself. It's eerily silent. I brace myself for the crack of a gunshot that doesn't come. Both Kole and Krejarek are gone.

I think of the scene that Kole brought to life—of Sarah Dylan lying on her living room floor, bruised and stabbed, her insides pulled out like a jack-o'-lantern—and I wondered if that's what would become of him. Because Krejarek didn't happen upon us by chance. The last bead of sweat that hasn't evaporated from my skin trickles down my spine as the night begs the question: Who can toss a nine-year-old boy in a dumpster, then murder a double-crosser like Pearl, and evade arrest, only to track down the one cop who hired her to get buys on him and take him down?

The Candy Man can.

15.

LATER

It's past midnight and I've heard nothing from Kole, despite the burst of texts I sent him as a welfare check. I know better than to send too many, though. He could be in the throes of a manhunt, or—a vise squeezes my stomach—dead.

That's why, when an alert revealing a report marked urgent appears in the upper left corner of my screen, I close out of the auto theft report I'm typing and open the queue.

My heart skips.

It isn't Kole.

It's Investigator Rowe.

My mouth is suddenly dryer than dry, like I've just swallowed a mason jar's worth of cotton balls. *Fuck, fuck, fuck.* Someone is dead. Rowe's presence proves it.

Cringing as though I'm about to step on a bear trap instead of the transcription pedal, I begin the report. The three seconds of static that precede him seem deafening. If Kole's dead, I don't want to hear it. I don't want to hear it. I don't want to hear it. I realize I'm shaking my head back and forth like a glitching animatronic when Rowe's voice cuts through the white noise.

"Hello, Transcriber. This is a supplemental report regarding a suspicious death investigation. I'm sorry for the, uh, last minute-*ness* of this report, but, uh, I've been instructed by the DA's office that it is urgent and therefore must be received by them Thursday morning. I apologize if this requires any staying late on your part. Without further ado, here is the narrative.

"On Wednesday, comma, January 27, comma, at approximately 2215 hours, comma, I, comma, Investigator Rowe, comma, was activated by Sergeant Lewison as part of the Major Crimes Division, period. I reported to the area of Forge Bridge, comma, where I was met by several Black Harbor Police Department personnel, period."

10:15 p.m.? I step on the left panel to rewind the track and listen to the first paragraph of the narrative again. The image of the digital 9:45 on Kole's dashboard clock is branded on my brain. Why would Kole wait so long to contact anyone? Surely it hadn't taken him a half hour to track down Krejarek.

I wonder if he'd been without his phone. I'd seen him grab his gun, but I couldn't be sure about anything else. Even if it wasn't in his pocket, Kole wasn't one to let his phone stray too far. It would explain, though, why he's been radio silent for so long.

I press on the right side of the pedal again, to see if Rowe will answer my questions.

"I entered the thicket, comma, and approximately thirty yards in, comma, I was met by Investigator Kole, comma, Investigator Riley, comma, Sergeant Rourke, comma, and Sergeant Lewison, period. They stepped aside, comma, to reveal the body of who I knew from previous investigations to be Tyler Krejarek, comma, alias quote-unquote, 'Candy Man,' period."

Shock slams into me like a bullet. Suddenly, I'm standing outside again, seeing Krejarek's reflection in the side mirror of Kole's SUV. He was alive when he slithered back into the copse, black-beaded eyes gleaming like a snake in its den, drawing Kole to him like a rabbit. What had occurred in those violent moments afterward?

"Krejarek was lying in a position so that his shoulders were on shore, comma, and his legs were in the water, period. It should be noted that Investigator Kole informed me that he had removed the body from the water in an attempt to rescue him, comma, however, comma, he stopped when he realized Krejarek was already deceased, period. Next paragraph."

For as detailed as these reports are, they lack so much. *What did Kole look like when you saw him*, I want to ask. *Was he hurt? Did he look as mortified as he had the night he walked the scene of Sarah Dylan's murder?*

But, Rowe resumes.

"Upon first glance, comma, it was egregiously clear that Tyler Krejarek was indeed deceased, period. His skin was ashen, comma, and his entrails had been ripped from his body through a large incision, period. Due to the amount of tearing, comma, the wound appeared to have been made with a jackknife or similar weapon, period. Additionally, comma, due to the fact that Krejarek's body was not at all bloated, comma, ME Winthorp confirmed my speculation that his submersion into the river was postmortem, period. Next paragraph.

"Other injuries to Krejarek include multiple hash marks on his palms and between his fingers"—like Pearl's, I think, when she tried desperately to fend off her attacker—"and bruising on his neck, comma, to indicate probable strangulation, period."

Also like Pearl. She'd been strangled first, and when that didn't do the job, she was stabbed, *thirteen fucking times* as I remember Kole putting it. How had he known the exact number? A shiver runs through me so violently that my fingers punch the wrong keys. I pause and hold down "Delete."

Take a breath.

Step back on the pedal.

Images scatter in my mind. They seem random at first, but when they begin to assemble—the bruises on Pearl's neck, the stab wounds all over her body, the kitchen knife Kole mentioned earlier when he surprised me with my abandoned bracelet, the cruel laceration across Krejarek's torso—they all make a pretty clear story.

No. It can't be.

So I keep listening—to the soft static of the recording that sounds like someone breathing behind me. Keep typing—my finger taps crescendoing like footsteps gaining ground. Just keep going.

"Inside Krejarek's left pants pocket was a receipt from the Main Street Pharmacy, comma, the time stamp on which was 2049 hours, period. There were no prescriptions on his person, comma, however, period. Next paragraph."

Pearl's pill case had been dumped out on her bed. Everything taken. I envision Kole walking through her dismantled apartment, the soles of his shoes crunching on the broken glass of picture frames she'd knocked off the wall, as he took long, measured strides down the hall to her bedroom. It wasn't the first time he'd been in there, after all. He'd been there at least once before, when he discovered the heroin in Pearl's music box and relocated it to Cyrus Jacoby's top dresser drawer.

I listen to the last paragraph again. 2049 hours. At 8:49 p..m., I was with Kole. That might have been about the time he let me fasten his handcuffs around his wrists and do whatever I wanted with him. I kissed him first, my lips plush against his, then harder, like I was drowning and he was air. I traced every contour of his body with just my fingertips, except when I went to undo his zipper, he stopped me with two whispered words: "Not here."

Had he meant not here, or *not now*, I wonder. He may have been anticipating Krejarek's emergence from the trees. After all, he had been the one to suggest we go to the vacant lot in front of Forge Bridge.

Rowe concludes his report with, "Investigation ongoing," and says he will review it first thing in the morning.

I read it over once, my eyes catching on every mention of Investigator Kole, and it all suddenly becomes *egregiously clear*, as Rowe would put it. Everything contained in this report explains why Kole let Krejarek be released.

He knew they would cross paths again.

I look to the sworn personnel roster on my left, where Kole's name hides behind a pen strike, crude like the wound that ended Krejarek, and I can't help but think of the knife that was pulled out of the river—the same one that was dragged across Sarah Dylan's throat. He'd confessed to tampering with evidence once. Who's to say he wouldn't do it again if it meant a chance to hunt down the Candy Man?

16.

FRIDAY

It's close to nine o'clock when Tommy and I arrive at Figaro's—a small Italian restaurant at the tail end of an otherwise empty strip mall. My boots crunch on salt crystals as we make our way through the packed parking lot toward the one source of illumination, like moths to a porch light. Tommy squeezes my hand and my heart skips—not in a good way. "Good turnout," he says, noting all of the vehicles.

I'd hoped Tommy would have forgotten about my invitation to Hammersley's retirement party. I'd mentioned it over a week ago, before he left for the Boundary Waters and before I would have had any real reservations about putting him and Kole in the same room. But Tommy never forgets an occasion for free beer, and I haven't spoken to Kole since he chased after Krejarek into the woods. Maybe he won't even be here. The possibility of him being absent gives me some relief, and yet . . . I can't deny the fact that I want to see him. That I've spent the last two days in a wrestling match with my own mind, struggling between worrying over him or looking for other clues that point to him as the murderer.

"How do you know this guy again?" Tommy asks. He returned from his and Cam's fishing trip this afternoon. Plenty of time to have shaved his beard, yet it protrudes an inch or more from his cheeks and chin. His jacket reeks of cigarette smoke. He must have worn it inside his parents' house. That's the thing I hate most about cigarette smoke, it clings to you like a second skin.

"He was a sergeant on the night shift." I switch gears quickly from Kole to Hammersley. "He just retired last week."

"I see. Well, he sure has a lot of friends."

I nod as we approach the double doors, entering into a pocket of warmth and intoxicating pizza smells. My stomach growls to remind me how hungry I am. I'm so entrenched in my own investigations that it isn't uncommon for me to forget to eat these days.

The place is larger inside than one would expect from looking at the exterior, and filled with people. There's a collective buzz like atoms all bumping around a nucleus. "Hazel!"

I see a hand first, then a cinnamon-colored head bobbing toward us. "Oh, hey, Liv."

Her cheeks are rosy like she just sprinted a mile to get here. Her neck is blotchy. I wonder how much she's had to drink already. The one time I went out with her and Mona, she sucked down three old-fashioneds like a professional.

"Did you find the place OK? I know you're not from here." She touches her hand to her denim chest and giggles as though the funniest thing has just happened. It hasn't.

She's right. I am not from Black Harbor. I will never, in a million years, say that I am from Black Harbor, even if I'm eighty years old and still existing here. Shit, what a miserable thought. "Yes," I say, biting my tongue. "Um, this is Tommy—"

"Hello," says Tommy. He reaches out to shake her hand that she's let go limp.

"You are so cute!" she exclaims as though meeting a kindergartner or a puppy, and I fight the urge to slap her. She cradles his hand with her other one, locking him in. "I'm a friend of your wife's. I work in the Records Department."

It sounds as though she's put extra enunciation on the word *wife*. She throws a sidelong glance at me. "So, Hazel, Mona tells me—"

I can just make out the top of Kole's backward hat as he walks in. My breath hitches. I want to call him over, but I know better, and so does he. He wades through bodies, making his way to the far corner of the restaurant, where I expect the SIU crew must be huddled. He catches my eye for a fraction of a second, flashing a smile so faint I might have imagined it.

There's something on his cheek, though. A scratch? I can't see from this far away.

"Earth to Hazel." Liv waves a hand in front of my face. I'm almost knocked out by the scent of cherry blossom hand lotion. I snap to and she cackles. "Sorry, there are just so many people here," I say. It's not a lie. The restaurant is teeming with what has to be a hundred sworn personnel and their significant others, most of whom I've never laid eyes on with the exception of Crue and Kole, Rowe, Rourke, and Marjorie, who audaciously wiggles her fingers at me, standing next to a guy in a Canadian tuxedo who must be her husband. What's with all the denim tonight? Apparently I missed the memo.

Mona's not here. When I asked if she'd be coming, she began an analogy of work life being one bubble and personal life being another. "It's not like a Venn diagram," she explained. "Work life. Personal life. No mixing." She gesticulated, then, as though she were putting one unruly child in one chair, and an equally unruly child in another, and warning them not to instigate anything.

"But you went out for drinks with me," I reminded her.

"That's different, Fargo. I was showing you around. It was pretty much an extension of your training."

"Ah." I wondered, then, if Mona's friendliness toward me has only ever been obligatory, but then refused to let my brain go there. We don't see each other for more than a few hours a week when our schedules overlap on Thursday and Friday mornings. It really doesn't matter.

At the bar, Rourke is being handed a plastic cup of beer. I should go say hello. I start to suggest it when suddenly, a meaty arm is thrown over my shoulders. I see the blurred tattoo on Hammersley's forearm.

"Hazel! Glad you made it!"

"Hey!" I one-arm hug him back.

He reaches out to shake Tommy's hand. "Helluva chick you got here, boy. Smart as a whip, too. She comes back with questions on arrests that give us all a run for our money."

I blush. Tommy smiles at me as though I've just earned top marks on my report card. He's wearing the same canvas jacket he always wears. I wish he would have chosen something less . . . smelly. It reeks of gunpowder and there's a stain near the breast pocket that looks like ketchup but I know it's blood. Deer, rabbit, quail, salmon, who knows.

Tossing her hair back, Liv moves closer to Hammersley and places her hand on his bicep. "Money? You are retiring from the PD, right?" She laughs loud enough to be heard over the buzz.

I leave the two of them to their merriment, Tommy tagging along like a lost duckling as we head to the bar. Even though I don't particularly like the taste of beer, I'm glad for something to hold on to.

Crossing to the far corner of the restaurant proves to be a more arduous process than I thought, as I'm constantly stopped by people who want to formally introduce themselves. It's an odd sensation, knowing someone for their voice rather than the way they look. I recognize Investigator Riley from the photo on her desk. She has a strong handshake and bright white teeth that look like they could go from smiling to snarling in 0.2 seconds.

I smile discreetly at Kole as I finally make it to the back, my eyes scanning him for clues. As I suspected, there are rake marks across his cheek. If I could undress him, I bet I'd find more. I'm dying to know what happened in that thicket. What he saw. Why he waited so long to call for backup, and why he refrained from contacting me afterward.

I recognize Match and Crue, and a compact, muscular guy who must be Mattox—Ox. There are others I don't recognize who introduce themselves as Jeff, Danny, and Ryan. I mentally pair their last names with their firsts: McDermid, Hansen, and Tolliver. Match and Crue shake my hand, naming themselves Jeremy and Milo, respectively, and I see that Match really does resemble a matchstick—tall, thin, wiry hair. Kole shakes my hand, a nice touch. "Nik," he says.

"Hazel." I bite my bottom lip to keep from smiling. "This is Tommy . . . my husband." I hope they don't notice the grimace behind my eyes when I force out the last two words.

They all nod hello. There are women, too, who are Crue's and McDermid's wives. Crue's wife looks like a runner. A pretty dark-haired woman rejoins the group, handing Mattox a beer. I wait and watch the crowd, but no one ever comes up to stand beside Kole. My nerves settle somewhat.

"Well, Hazel, you do a bang-up job knocking out our reports," says Crue. He looks so different from when I saw him last week. Less on edge. Almost friendly.

I feel myself shrinking as everyone mumbles in unison. Tolliver even raises his cup.

"You shoulda seen Milo," says Mattox, "all hunched over his keyboard hunt 'n' peck method. Plus he can't spell worth a damn—"

I smile along with them, picturing it, and remember what Kole said about some investigators typing their own reports when Beverly died. Or *trying to*, in Crue's case. Not everyone has endless hours sunk into honing their typing skills like me. Some people, those affiliated with the Black Harbor Police Department, at least, have bigger fish to fry. Catching Candy Man, for one.

Crue's laughter pulls me from my daze. "Oh, come on, I wasn't that bad," he says.

"Spell *hallucinogen*," Kole suggests.

Crue's mouth pulls into a tight line and the others laugh. "You see what I have to deal with?" he says just to me.

I shrug. "Spelling really isn't a reflection of intelligence. It's just memorization."

"I like this girl," Crue says, and I feel like I've just won an award.

I love standing here. Although I've only just met most of them, I feel like we could be friends, if only I were free of Tommy, and what an awful thought that is. I watch as Kole feigns interest in Tommy's fishing stories and the ones about him and Cam attempting to drink the locals under the table. I feel his eyes dart to me, and when Tommy excuses himself to refill his beer, Kole slides over.

"Did you have to come dressed like that?" he says under his breath. I instinctively look down at my ripped blue jeans and gray V-neck under the faux leather jacket I always wear whenever I'd rather not look like a bipedal sleeping bag. He picks up with me so effortlessly, as though he hadn't ignored my last string of messages. God, he smells good. Just one inhale of him is enough to jump-start every nerve ending in my body.

I look over at the bar, where Tommy has been sucked into playing bartender, refilling plastic cups, laughing, being Mr. Congenial. My stomach twists. He has no idea I'm fifteen feet away, whispering dirty nothings to a detective who only pretended to make my acquaintance for the first time. We've gotten to know each other quite well over the past two weeks, actually.

"You drive me crazy, you know that?" Kole says out of earshot, and I wish I could grab him by his belt loops right here, tease him as I would at Beck's or somewhere people would pay no mind. Or at the lot, even, where Candy Man made his final encore.

"What happened the other night?" I need to know. Give me something, anything, that will stop the gory slideshow in my head. What I should be asking instead is: *Why did you lie? Why did you wait until 10:15 to call dispatch?*

"So, Hazel"—Crue pipes up—" what the hell is someone with actual talent doing in Black Harbor?"

I don't know if typing—regurgitating their words—is talent, but I'll bite. In the minutes that Tommy's gone, I take the liberty to pretend that I did not come with him—or anyone—but that I simply showed up and met my new coworkers on my own accord. They ask me the usual questions: where I'm from, why I'm here. It's unanimously agreed upon that if they weren't in law enforcement, none of them would be in Black Harbor.

The fact that Kole is the only one truly from here surprises me. "There are some nice areas," Kole defends. "Like along the lake and out toward the interstate." And just like that, the hushed conversation between me and him is swept away, like a wave retreating from the shore.

I remember what Mona said about the police department being in the rotten nucleus of the city, the bad stuff all concentrated in the center and spreading outward. The toxicity is pretty well dispersed by the time it reaches the lake. I've noticed it, too. In the summers, I run past neighborhoods that look as though they could belong to any wholesome city: cute little houses with rosebushes out front, kids playing in the yards. There's one street toward the lake that's all cobblestones, even.

I used to hope that if Tommy and I had to stay for a while, we could look for a place over there.

"I think of it like pockets," I say, and they look at me inquisitively. "There's not really a good or a bad side of town; more like good or bad neighborhoods just scattered here and there."

Crue points to me. "Yes, that's a perfect analogy."

The conversation shifts, then, and Mattox says to McDermid so everyone can hear: "I still can't believe we got Nik to come out. Can you?"

McDermid smiles tight-lipped.

"What now?" says Kole. His face turns red; he knows they're about to roast him.

"Kole's a goddamn hermit," Crue says as he leans my way. "This is probably the first function he's gone to in . . . ten years?"

"Ten years?" says Kole. "What's-his-name's off-probation party at Sangria's."

"Yeah, Sangria's closed forever ago," Match states matter-of-factly.

"See, this is why I don't come out with you lot. 'Cause every ten years or whatever you gotta make shitty comments about me never coming out." He knows he's stirring them up. I can see it in his smile. I feel happy and a bit in awe, watching him interact with his friends. He makes talking to people look so easy.

"So we give you shit once every decade," says Tolliver, "but how about us putting up with your shit every day in the office? You know he switched all of McDermid's pictures on his desk to—what's that calendar called—"

"Firemen and cute animals," Kole offers.

"Well, what about when WPD came by for that sting operation and he'd Velcroed all my shit to my desk—mouse, stapler, coffee cup," says Mattox.

"Don't leave your shit unattended." Kole shrugs.

These are the friends I wish I could have, I admit to myself. I survey the women next to Crue, McDermid, and Mattox, and I'm bubbling with envy. They probably go to events like this all the time, unashamed and free. They can go to sleep unafraid that everything could end by the time they wake. And, if something bad ever happened on the street or during a search warrant, they wouldn't be the last to know. Kole wavers a bit in his stance and dares to graze my pinky finger. His touch sends a current through me. If my husband weren't in the same room, I know the question he'd be asking: *Wanna get out of here?*

Yes. A thousand times, *yes.*

The conversation shifts, then, to darker matters: the cross-referenced murders of Jordan McAllister, Sarah Dylan, and Tyler Krejarek.

"Insane" is the word Mattox uses to describe the series of events, to which everyone agrees. I watch Kole to see what's going on behind his eyes, but there's nothing to betray he knows any more than anyone standing here. Goddamn, he's good.

Mattox's girlfriend looks genuinely concerned, a hair-thin wrinkle of worry stitched across her forehead. "That poor little boy."

"Well, you found Krejarek first the other night, Nik," says Hansen. "How did you even know he'd be there?"

"I didn't," says Kole. I watch him intently, searching for the tics that give someone away in interviews—nervous sweating, shifting gaze, mindless scratching—but he exhibits none of these.

"You just hang out in that lot occasionally, or what?"

A hush falls. It's so subtle, so imperceptible, that if you weren't anticipating something of its nature, you wouldn't notice it. It makes the hair on the back of my neck stand on end, though. I'm suddenly self-conscious of my cheeks reddening. It feels so hot in here. All these bodies.

"Yeah, I do sometimes." Kole's voice has an edge that I've never heard before. It's both scintillating and frightening. "What's it to you?"

Hansen looks taken aback. Crue steps in. "That's enough."

From the corner of my eye, I see Tommy returning. He's not holding a beer anymore, and I know what that means. He's ready to go. I search the walls for a clock, my eyes finally landing on one above the restrooms. Ten minutes to midnight.

A finger pokes my side. Trying not to visibly cringe, I turn to Tommy. His eyebrows are raised. "We should go," he mouths.

I look around again. The place is no less packed than when we arrived. "Why?" I ask. My sheer audacity is enough to slam my mouth shut. I know exactly why.

"You know the rule."

My jaw clenches. The rule. *Nothing good happens after midnight*. It's what he always says whenever 12 a.m. rolls around and we're not in company of his choosing. If we were out with Cam or Old Will, we could be out until the sun comes up.

"You a pumpkin or something?" Mattox jokes, looking right at me.

I try to hide my embarrassment. Of course they heard it; they're detectives. I avoid Kole's gaze at all costs. I don't want him to see how broken I am.

"Aw, come on," says Hansen. "Stay a while. This party's just gettin' started."

"How long do these go for?" I ask, attempting to lighten the atmosphere.

"Shit." Hansen looks to Mattox. "Sometimes 'til 7 a.m."

"Who's gonna shut us down," says Mattox. "The cops?"

Tommy laughs, but it isn't genuine. "I have an obligation in the morning," he says as though that is enough to adjourn the conversation. His obligation is probably sleeping in and then wandering over to Old Will's. He hadn't mentioned anything else.

"I—" I start to protest. *I don't want to go.* But my words drift off my tongue like fresh snowflakes taken by the wind.

"Aw, man, no worries," says Mattox. "We can give her a ride home." He looks to his girlfriend, who nods.

I smile, suddenly hopeful. But, the way Tommy looks at me stops my heart. Perhaps he saw the pinky graze between me and Kole. Or he heard me laugh, a genuine laugh like I haven't laughed in months—maybe longer. Whatever it was, his look has the power to make my knees almost buckle as I start walking toward the exit. When I chance a glance at Kole, I see that he's gone.

17.

SATURDAY

"You embarrassed me," Tommy says as we pull out of the parking lot two minutes past midnight.

I scrunch my forehead, my right brow raised half an inch above the left one. I wonder what he saw. Or what he knows.

"You don't accept rides home from other men, Hazel. Do you even think about how that kind of behavior makes me look?"

Staring at the glowing dashes on the road, I feel myself harden. They blur into one connected line, reeling us back into the duplex. An uncomfortable thought steals over me and I consider the hypothesis that there is no free will. We will return to the duplex—him to crack open a beer and me to wrestle with a blank Word document—because our DNA and history of behavioral patterns has already mapped out our destiny. I'll avoid Tommy until the tension fades, an ember smothered by ashes, or until he drinks enough to forget what we're fighting about. *Write what you know.* What if most people only live what they know, too?

I'll continue living my cold, mediocre life unless I do something to break the pattern. I stare at the wheel as though calculating my success of seizing control of it and executing a Y-turn. My fingertips tap on my lap, typing out the words *free will, free will, free will*, over and over again.

Just sitting in the passenger seat next to him is suffocating. "He has a girlfriend, Tommy. She was right there." Of all the things to be mad about, I can't believe he's upset about Mattox offering me a ride. Honestly, it's a bit of a relief. Mattox, my red herring.

Tommy chuckles facetiously. "Yeah, for tonight. What happens when he ditches her and thinks you're available 'cause you accepted a ride home? You're so naive, Hazel, it's honestly comical."

I say nothing the rest of the trip back. My jaw is clenched too tightly to speak anyway. *It's not home*, I think, and I hold on to that truth like a bitter pill dissolving on my tongue.

• • •

Morning. I stare at my reflection in the cloudy, beveled glass mirror as I rub foundation into the violaceous crescents beneath my eyes. My cheekbones look more pronounced than usual, sharp. I look and feel harder, more wood than person, like one of Dad's sculptures. Wood doesn't feel it when you carve into it.

Tommy's absence puts me at ease. His *obligation* turned out to be hunting rabbits with one of his coworkers. He left at the ass crack of dawn. Half awake, I smelled the gunpowder that's become part of the fabric of his shooting polos, felt his whiskers scratch my forehead when he kissed me goodbye, as though he hadn't been a complete asshole hours before. I can't decide if it makes matters better or worse that he hadn't even been intoxicated. At least he's nicer when he's drunk.

On the pedestal sink, my phone vibrates. I check Kole's response to my last message when I'd just texted him *Hey* upon waking up and shuffling down to the kitchen to brew a pot of coffee, as if I hadn't just ghosted him for hours. My coffee sits steaming on the windowsill, now, fogging the glass.

Hey, he texts back.

I need to see you, I try out, knowing its effect when he's sent it to me.

He's silent for a few minutes. Maybe he's bent about me leaving prematurely last night. Or maybe I just caught him as he was getting in the shower. Or maybe he's at the breakfast table with his wife. Just because Pearl wasn't his wife doesn't mean he doesn't have one.

I brush smoke on my eyelids as I wait for a response.

Now? he asks.

I check the time. It's quarter after nine. *10*, I say, and then add: *I'll text you the address.*

OK. Is everything OK?

Yes.

• • •

The man at the front desk has a sore on his forehead that looks like a bullet hole. I try not to stare at it as he studies my driver's license. He swipes my $100 bill with the special marker and holds it up to the wavering fluorescent light. Christmas money from Dad. He'd no doubt expected me to spend it at a bookstore. It never would have occurred to him that I would be exchanging it for a room at a scuzbucket hotel.

He hands me back my license and twenty dollars change. "Room 304," he says.

A woman who could be his wife walks behind him with a stack of white towels. She looks me up and down like Liv or Angela would do. *She knows*, I think. I'm sure she's pegged me as either a hooker or a runaway, and she's not really wrong about either. Although runaways are typically younger.

I climb the three flights of stairs, my boot treads leaving little grids of snow on the ugly carpet. Room 304 is at the end of the hall, next to a window overlooking a Dairy Queen.

The room is what I expected: nondescript, with a color palette inspired by a pasta box. The bedspread is a muted green and gold, and the walls are sweet potato orange. The carpet is so red it stings my eyes. There's a flat screen on the Formica dresser, a table with an office chair and a lamp in the corner. I drop my bag on the bed and check my phone.

I hold my breath as I open Tommy's message, and let it out when I see it's a photo of him holding a dead rabbit upside down by the legs. I cringe, hating myself. Hating him. I should act like I'm still mad at him—which I am—to free myself of having to converse back and forth all day. But in the end, being mad gets me nothing. He will just get home sooner, then, to show me he's minding his p's and q's. He'll never apologize, because Tommy is never wrong. He's like his mother that way.

Nice! I send.

I switch to Kole's message. *Address?*

I copy and paste the address from my GPS app and text it to him. And then, to drive home the fact that there is no turning back now, I strip out of my clothes and toss my jeans and sweater on the chair by the window. Then, I sit on the edge of the bed in just my buttercream yellow bra and panties, my hand pressed down on the mattress between my thighs, and snap a picture. Send.

Oh God, I hope I've sent it to the right person. It isn't entirely unthinkable for a woman to send her husband a sexy photo, and yet, I've never sent one to Tommy. He would either think something is up, or race to get back. Neither of those end in my favor.

Kole's response is immediate. *Jesus Christ.* He blows up my phone with three more short messages. *10 minutes. Stay right there. Don't get dressed.*

I bite my lip to try to keep from smiling. The excitement of seeing Kole suddenly snuffs out the guilt I feel over betraying Tommy. What was once a series of stabbing pains in my stomach has morphed into butterflies, and the shiver that felt like the tip of a knife dragging down my back has dispersed to making everything—from the translucent hairs on my neck and arms to even my nipples—stand on end.

Room 304, I respond. I set my phone down on the bedspread beside me and look around. It's so still here, I doubt there's anyone else at all on this floor. From outside, I can hear the gentle shushing of highway traffic. I could drive to the interstate and be swept up in its current and carried home. It's a calming thought, never having to look Tommy in the eyes again after this, but I know it's just a fantasy. What does one typically do while waiting for the catalyst to end her marriage? I should have brought a book. Scooting to the middle of the mattress, I fall back on the pillows and reach for the remote, thankfully finding a show about botched plastic surgeries.

No matter what Kole's performance is—good or bad—my marriage is over. There's no going back after this.

Kissing him would have been forgivable . . . with time.

If I ever told him I love him—that could be chocked up to confusion.

But this. This is the coup de grâce.

I feel electric; my mind buzzes with possibility. The sensation falls away as quickly as it came, replaced with doubt. What if it hurts? Although it isn't the first time I've considered it, but here it is, creeping into my thoughts at exactly the wrong moment, whispering for me to pack up my things and bolt.

There's no turning back, I remind myself. If it hurts, I have to fight through it. I've done it hundreds of times with Tommy, I can endure it once with Kole. I can't let him know how broken I am.

I check my phone. Nothing.

My stomach churns and I suddenly wonder if I've terribly misjudged him. He didn't bring a woman to the party last night, but she might have been at home or working. He could be like Mona, not wanting to mix his professional life and personal life.

There's a knock at the door.

My heart throws itself against my rib cage. What if it's Tommy? He could be on to me and tracked me here. The photo he sent could have been of another time hunting rabbits.

I walk softly to the door, and, taking in a deep breath, slowly press down on the handle. Trepidation courses through me. It would be so easy to click the door back into place and slide the dead bolt like I've done countless times at the duplex. Whether it's Tommy or Kole on the other side, if he doesn't see me, I was never here, stripped down to just my bra and panties in this grimy hotel room.

I think of the eighty dollars I paid to the man with the scab on his forehead. I could have put it toward my new laptop, or a few good pairs of jeans. Or rather, I could have gone to Elle's and my favorite thrift store and gotten a whole new wardrobe.

It's that thought—quantifying the things I traded to be in this position—that causes me to rebel against my own fear. I pull the door open about three inches, as far as the chain will allow. A mix of relief and excitement floods my veins. Kole stands in the hall in a plaid button-down and jeans, a different backward cap than he'd worn last night. Melted snowdrops glisten like gems on his shoulders. His eyes move from my face to my bare feet, and back up. His mouth falls open. "Holy shit, you're perfect," he whispers as I slide the chain off the door. He steps inside and, in one fluid motion, hoists me up against the wall. His hands are cold against my skin. I cover his mouth with mine, breathing in every molecule of him. He tastes like mint.

I pull off his hat and toss it somewhere in the room. He carries me to the bed and lowers me to the mattress. We stay like this for a minute, him leaning over me with my legs locked around his torso. He moves to lie beside me, then, and propped up on his elbow, his other hand touches my cheek with just two fingers, moving them down my neck, finally tracing my collarbone and the space between my breasts. My chest rises as I arch my back. I have never wanted to be naked so badly, to feel his skin pressed to mine and watch him drink in every inch of me. I tug at his sleet-dampened shirt to pull it from his jeans, and work my way from his chest to his navel, undoing every button. His hands might be freezing, but the rest of him is hot.

I see him for the first time without his shirt. Diagonal lines of his ribs converge toward a light grid that's cut into his abs. His chest is defined like someone who does his fair share of push-ups. I can see his heart beating beneath his skin, the black anchor pulsing. I dare to touch him, pressing my hand to the middle of his chest as though to leave a handprint, and then exploring farther down. He exhales, ab muscles contracting like I'm ice and he's fire. I grab his waistband and undo the metal button, the zipper. He doesn't stop me this time. I let my fingers graze the bulge in his navy boxer briefs, and he looks for a second like he might pass out. "Hold on, baby," he says. He begins to slide off the bed, pausing to kiss my rib cage and pinching one corner of my panties. He pulls them down enough to expose my hip bone, which he kisses before lightly biting it. "Take these off," he says.

I close my eyes and obey his gentle command. It's exhilarating and frightening to know I would follow any directive he gave in this moment.

He shackles me with one hand. I never noticed how long his fingers are, how powerful, until he closes them over both of my wrists. I glance upward, my gaze following the corded veins traveling from his bicep through his forearm. I don't think I could escape him even if I wanted to.

Not that I want to.

He pulls me to the edge and lowers his head between my legs. Every cell in my body awakens at his tongue's caress. I gasp and bite my lip to keep from crying out. *Oh fuck, oh fuck, oh fuck, oh*—Pleasure erupts within me and I'm too overtaken by it to be afraid the moment before he comes up off his knees and plunges inside.

A breathy moan escapes me from deep, deep down. I turn and sink my teeth into my bicep, my muscles pulled tight as I grip his forearms. He moves back and forth, thrusting in and out.

It doesn't hurt. In fact, it feels . . . incredible.

"Fuck," I say, because I want to, and because it feels right to say it. He smiles, his eyes flitting to lock on mine. I feel his thumbs press to my throat, and suddenly my moan is cut off. Fear swells inside me, carbonates my blood. I can't breathe.

I stare at him intently, desperately, silently begging to know what he's doing. He isn't smiling anymore. He's concentrated. I feel beads of sweat form on my skin beneath where his hand encircles my neck like a collar. I open my mouth but no sound comes out.

I am dizzy without the sickness. Floating. The edges of my vision bleed to black. He presses with expert hands, like choking is as natural a part of sex as kissing.

Like he's done this before. On the trail or on a living room floor. What had he said the night that Pearl died? That strangling someone is harder than it looks.

He makes it look easy.

Finally, he releases me. His grip slackens around my neck, and with his fingertips, he touches all the bones in my sternum as though counting them, his hands moving separately clockwise and counter-clockwise to encircle my breasts. I am blissfully aware of every erotic sensation. This has to be better than drugs, even.

After, he collapses on top of me and I feel safe under his weight. I kiss his shoulder, tasting the salt on his skin. I lock my limbs around him tight, clinging to him as though I've been shipwrecked.

Still entangled, he rolls to his side, turning me with him. He stares at me, into me, and tucks a piece of hair behind my ear. He moves his hand down, then, his fingertips swirling invisible designs on my shoulder, like finger painting. I've never looked so deeply into someone—deep enough to count the flecks of silver in his eyes, to map and memorize every faint line and crosshatch in his skin, to study the chevron-shaped scar on his cheek—and I wonder if this is what being with someone is meant to feel like.

"God, you're so beautiful," he says.

I smile down at the mattress, moving my right hand to settle on the dip of his waist. He kisses me and I kiss him back, and we stay like this for a while, the lotus-eaters, with neither care nor concept of time. Later, we lie naked beneath starched sheets watching daytime reality TV, and I realize there has never been anything more divine. He holds his hand up and I slide my fingers in the spaces between his, in and out.

"Tell me something confidential," I say. I feel intoxicated, still, from lovemaking. If that's what that was.

He sighs, and a smile plays on his lips. "I would have found you even without the address."

I quirk my brow. Has he been watching me? Could he have put a GPS tracker on my vehicle? "What do you mean?"

"That pic you sent? I'd know this decor from anywhere. We've done . . . shit, I don't know how many search warrants here."

"Ew." Suddenly, my skin itches. "For what? Drugs?"

"And the occasional wanted person. Some sex trafficking." Sensing my discomfort, he wraps me up in his arms. "Relax, I never came across any bedbugs. Here. Can't say the same for the hotel across the street."

I shiver, as though to shake off any imaginary insects. My hair follicles tickle now. "You owe me another one, now. Tell me something else."

He laughs. "What do you want to know?"

"Do you ever take this off?" Facing him again, I touch his necklace. The chain slips between my fingers like water, though the anchor has some weight to it. Tiny words are etched into the crescent. I squint to read them: *Vincit omnia veritas.*

"No. To be honest, I forget I'm wearing it most of the time."

A muscle in his jaw twitches. A lie?

"Your turn," he says.

My gaze falls to my bag on the chair, the very presence of which says being here with him, in this room, is temporary. Every moment with him is stolen. I feel suddenly compelled to tell him I love him. To tell him that I plan to leave Tommy and Black Harbor, and that he should come with me. But I can't. Not right now. "I hate you," I say.

Lying with my cheek pressed to his chest, I can feel him smile, hear his heartbeat quicken. In the background, the interstate shushes. He kisses my forehead. "I hate you more."

18.

SUNDAY

Four words. Just tell him and it will be over.

I'm cheating on you.

Simple, yet impossible.

How do you shatter someone's world, I wonder, as I watch our distorted reflections in the coffee decanter. From behind, his hands move up my sides, squeezing my breasts. His beard makes the back of my neck itch. I stare through the glass decanter, at the tar-colored pool inside it, wishing I'd never come back. Wishing that instead of getting dressed and letting Kole's hand slip away from mine in the hotel parking lot yesterday, I'd asked him to leave with me. He might have said yes. Who knows where we'd be right now. We would be together, and that's all that matters.

It's been twenty-four hours since I first had sex with someone else. Not just anyone. Nikolai Kole. His name, alone, is enough to make me feel punch-drunk. I could have stayed in that room forever. Ironically, I'd felt safe. Completely invisible. No one would ever have suspected Hazel Greenlee to be inside the hotel with the cracked, sun-faded siding, the sidewalk confettied with spent cigarette butts, fucking the detective who was the last person to see both Krejark and Pearl alive.

I thought I would feel worse about fucking him. Guiltier. But to be brutally honest, I felt worse about it before than after. Perhaps because before, I had a chance to turn back. I had both morals and selfish desires to grapple with. But now, what's done is done. There's no point in beating myself up about it. It seems that everyone was right about me all along—my mother, my mother-in-law, Elle, whom I still haven't heard from; they all sensed what I'm capable of.

I looked up the Latin words engraved on the anchor: *truth conquers all things*. And I wonder how Kole came to wear it. Had the necklace been given to him, or had he chosen it for himself? Perhaps he'd merely happened upon it as fortuitously as he had my bracelet. If only I could heed its advice.

Tommy pushes me into the dining room. *I don't want to. I don't want to. I don't want to.*

Just say the words, Hazel, and you won't have to.

It's over, Tommy. I'm cheating on you.

But I can't bring myself to say them.

I let him steer me into the bathroom. He tugs at my jeans, a nonverbal cue for me to take them off.

This morning, Kole had undone the buttons with his teeth. I've come to love the way he undresses me, like I'm a gift he can't wait to unwrap.

We got coffee at Minerva's. I've been coming there lately to write. It's more inviting to creativity than the duplex. I learned that the frizzy gray-haired waitress is Minerva herself, who has seen the best and worst of Black Harbor. To clarify, *I* got coffee. "What are you, five?" I asked as Minerva brought Kole's hot chocolate to our table.

"You should talk," he said, and he looked directly at the napkin I'd been drawing on with a pen.

I swiped my finger in the dollop of whipped cream floating at the top of his steaming mug and dabbed it on his lips. He smiled and let me kiss it off. I allowed myself, then, a moment to reflect how we must look to a passerby: a couple happy and in love, enjoying a lazy Sunday morning. What the passerby wouldn't have noticed in the seconds that followed were my eyes darting left and right, to check if anyone had seen.

Sometimes, I want people to see. It would have to be over, then. No more hiding. No more lying.

"What are you working on?" he asked, craning his neck to see and knowing I wouldn't let him. I'd already been here for hours when he walked in with a dusting of snow on his shoulders, ordered, and sat down as though meeting me here was entirely serendipitous.

I closed my laptop screen. "It's confidential."

He didn't smile. Not that damn crooked quirk of his mouth I've come to anticipate. Rather, he held on me, his gaze steady as though calling my bluff. And then: "If it's anything like those texts you've been sending . . ."

There it was. The smile I wanted.

I knew what texts he was referring to, the ones where we play out specific scenarios—being back in Krejarek's apartment or in a hot tub under the stars at a cabin far, far away—and describe in detail what we would do to each other. I put my creative writing degree to good use in those messages. Tens of thousands of dollars in debt were worth it to turn a man on with just words. There's some pride to be taken from that.

As embarrassing as his praise was, I felt illuminated from within; happy and lucky to have someone like him. I grinned.

"That's my girl."

He asked me to find him a book.

"For what?" I asked.

"The sergeants' test is coming up."

"You're going to leave SIU?" I felt selfish for not wanting him to promote out of the Special Investigations Unit. No more plainclothes adventures undercover. He'd be back in uniform, commanding second- or third-shift patrol, most likely.

He shrugged. "I'm guaranteed another six months. I might get a year extension, but after that, I'm out. I don't want to go back to GIU, investigating car thefts and bad checks."

"Lucky for you, I used to buy textbooks every day at my old job."

"I know." His eyes glinted. He gave me his credit card information and his address. *813 Carnegie Circle.* "Tell you what, you score me a good deal, and I'll take you away for a night. We can even have a pizza delivered."

"Keep speaking my language, Detective."

Now back at the duplex, I peel myself out of my jeans for Tommy, my ankles catching on the bottoms. He turns on the water and takes off his work polo. His jeans fall to the floor to form a puddle, leg holes plainly visible for him to step back into when he's done.

It takes everything in me to battle my own will and step into the shower. My eyes lock on to the dried soap scum on the sides of the tub, my mind seizing hold of how to eradicate it in the future, trying to focus on that instead of the pain that flares when he shoves two fingers between my legs.

He leans into me, his fingers mashing, not gentle. His breath in my ear is deafening.

Earlier, upon leaving Minerva's, Kole parked his vehicle in the vacant lot in front of Forge Bridge, where Krejarek had been murdered just four days ago. While I kissed him, my eyes kept darting to the mirrors, to see if he would come stumbling out, his guts dragging on the frozen ground behind him. Kole noticed and took my head in his hands. He pressed his forehead to mine. "It's OK," he whispered. "There's no one there."

We didn't stay long. Just long enough to get a fix. We are two addicts, knowing that what we do is bad for us, but always just needing one more. One more time. One more minute. One more false forever.

At least, that's how it is for me. *I'll quit tomorrow*, I lie to myself.

Now, tears well in my eyes, hotter than the lukewarm water that pelts my skin. I can't do this anymore.

Just say the words.

He's trying to force it in, but it won't go. I can feel him softening as he pushes against the back of my leg, grazes the bottom curve of my butt. His hands slide from my sides. I can feel him give up.

"I'm sorry," I say, but I mumble it so quietly I don't think he can hear me. I can barely hear me. What am I even sorry for? For having sex with Nikolai Kole twice in two days, or just sorry that Tommy's caught in the middle of it? Perhaps I'm sorry that his life with me isn't what he thought it would be.

Normally, this is when he pulls back the vinyl shower liner to step out. I'll finish up, scrubbing my skin raw and washing the tears from my face while the chill seeps in. But the shower liner remains in place. And Tommy is still in here with me, even as the water starts to turn cold. Goosebumps erupt on my flesh. I can feel my hair, wet and clinging to my back, being moved aside to expose my neck. His fingertip pokes me. I wince, feeling a sharp sting. "How the hell did you get all these bruises?" he asks.

19.

MONDAY

I told Tommy I got the bruises from a machine at the gym. "The squatting machine where the pads press down on you. I guess I used too much weight." The more detailed a lie, the better. Kole taught me that.

I couldn't tell if he bought it. He just stared, then nodded slowly. His gaze flitted somewhere off to the side before landing back on me. "Just be careful, OK? Less weight next time."

"I'm sorry," I said. For lying.

He didn't say anything, just stepped out of the shower and the cold blast hit me as I knew it would. A shock at first and then, nothing. Numbness.

I didn't sleep when I got home from work this morning. Instead, I went to Minerva's. I'm here now, watching the snow fall from the coffee shop window. *Write what you know.*

A professor told me that, once, in college. I've heard it other places since, but he was the first one to say it. The editor I interned for used to combat me on it all the time. Perhaps I should be glad that my manuscript never made it out of his slush pile. Or slush room, rather. Whereas most editors have a slush pile, he'd had an entire room devoted to dust-covered, deteriorating manuscripts into which we interns would venture when he struck a lull with his handful of clients—an event that became more common the longer I stuck around. By my last semester, I was reading and providing detailed reports on two manuscripts per week, and after I graduated, I'd let him send me ten a month. He paid me only in empty promises, but when I finally worked up the nerve to send him my manuscript, he didn't even have the decency to read it.

I think of it sometimes, entombed in that dusty attic room, its pages discolored by the bit of sun that leaks in through the window. It's not much different from the things I cast to the bottom of the river. No one will ever find it.

Except Kole found my bracelet.

When I saw it on the table Wednesday night, lying like a waterlogged insect in that plastic bag, I felt the color drain from my face. He had a point. How many Hazels are there in Black Harbor? I'm sure a quick search of the database gave him the answer. Whether or not he believes me about it not being mine, he hasn't brought it up again.

Write what you know. The document is all that and then some. It's an outpouring of every emotion I've felt in the past couple of weeks, full of truths and fears I didn't even know I had inside me until Kole extracted them. Yesterday afternoon, I laid against his chest, my legs bent, twining my fingers with his. We learned more about each other by telling two truths for every lie. His favorite color is blue, like my eyes. "No one named Hazel has a right to have eyes this blue," he said. Ecstasy flooded my veins, then, when he pressed his lips to the valley between my collarbones. The way he felt, every inch of him rock hard, from his chest to his abs and farther down.

I savor the memory.

The same professor once asked everyone in class to answer the question: Why do you write? A boy in my class replied *because the world is more beautiful as a lie.* I thought he was full of shit at the time, trying too hard to be artistic, but now, I think he wasn't. The proof is in these pages, where I allow myself to get lost in a dream where Kole could be mine.

I scroll through my Word document. I'm 23,000 words in, now. There's something here. For the first time since shelving my last manuscript, I see a glimmer of potential, like when you spot a foil wrapper in a pile of leaves or a tiny diamond buried in the river's silt. I sift through the words, mentally highlighting the passages that can be reshaped, sculpted into something more. The process reminds me of the wooden sculptures in my dad's yard, the blocky trunks that he carves away at, each slice with the chain saw planned and impactful, until he reveals the wolf or owl hiding in the wood. There is the same truth in writing, beginning with a block of words and carving away at them, reshaping them until you find what it is you meant to say all along.

I miss my dad. Confiding this secret to myself feels like a stitch ripping in my heart. I miss the shared looks and all the words we don't have to say because we think so alike. I miss watching him work, the sawdust that sprinkles his pushed-up flannel sleeves like snow, the fragrant scent of basswood and black walnut. An ember of hope warms me and I allow myself to dream: If this manuscript goes anywhere, if it's publishable, maybe I wouldn't have to miss him anymore. I could go home, and just write. I've accepted the fact that there's no work for me up there, but writing—I could do that—and I'd no longer be racked with the guilt of leaving him like Mom and Elle did.

Write what you know.

I know about being left, of not being enough for even my own mother, an agony that's almost imperceptible most of the time, but hits me some mornings upon waking, crushing my bones, and all I want to do is pull the covers over me like a wave and sink back into oblivion.

I know about longing for somewhere or someone who no longer

exists as they were. There's a Welsh word for that: *hiraeth*. It's a word I feel deeply. I feel it down to my marrow, this persistent ache, every morning I awake in this coal-blackened city.

The people of Black Harbor feel it, too. I can see it in their eyes as I realize that what I've often mistaken for fear is actually disbelief of what their home has become, a longing for Black Harbor to return to the way things used to be, when banks weren't vape shops and when Forge Bridge was meant to be crossed, when it really was known as the *city on the lake*, not the *small city with big-city crime*.

My fingers dance over the keyboard—swirling, reaching, tapping—feeling the words come together in a song I'm starting to like as I chronicle the deaths of Tyler Krejarek and Sarah Dylan. My thoughts are interrupted by a sudden prickling sensation, like a termite gnawing at my brain stem.

Kole is the common denominator.

He was the last person to be in contact with Sarah Dylan before she died, and the one who chased down Krejarek. I'd seen him with my own eyes. He would have motive to kill both of them—resentment, revenge—and the resources to do it. Slowly, as if commanded by invisible marionette strings, my fingers lift from the keyboard. I sit, still, with the sudden sensation of being watched. But the reflection in my computer screen reveals no one, just a plastic bag trapped in a tree across the street.

• • •

I stand the shovel up against the side of the duplex after hacking snow and ice off the porch again. Tommy's car is here, but I know he isn't home. He'd texted earlier to tell me he was going to the range with Cam after work.

I step on the newspaper like it's a welcome mat, and turn the key in first one lock, then fumble for the one that unlocks both dead bolts.

Inside, it feels hollow. My footsteps echo.

The chair on which Tommy's tactical bag normally sits is empty.

My stomach growls as I hang my jacket and stand my boots by the register. It feels colder in the kitchen, like when you enter a walk-in beer cooler at a gas station. A cursory search, however, shows that the windows are shut. I close my hand around the freezing door handle of the fridge and crack it open to look inside. The milk expired two days ago; it's probably fine. A few triangles of thin-crust pepperoni pizza are petrified on a plate, the tips curled up like the corner of a rug. On the shelf below is a pair of defeathered mourning doves in a plastic bag, and to the left a venison steak that's starting to regrow its fur. Holding my breath, I toss the meat into the garbage and pour myself a bowl of cereal.

I take my dinner to the couch and turn on the TV. Despite my stomach's protests, I have no taste for anything. My mind races like a pinball as I retrace the thinking that led me to Kole being a killer.

Despite the distraction of the TV, I don't want to believe it, and yet . . . it's possible. What had he told me once—that the simplest answer is usually the answer? In that case, Kole killed both Pearl and Krejarek. And he's using Sam to draw eyes away from himself. Sam's mistake was confessing. He could have left Krejarek's apartment after dragging Jordan McAllister out to the dumpster and no one would have been able to put him there that morning. He'd been over to Krejarek's multiple times before; his DNA would have been expected to be on things inside the residence. Instead, he'd been honest. He hadn't lied, and now, question after question, he was being made to dig his own grave.

My cereal tastes like sand. I look at my phone. Nothing from anyone. I don't know if I'm relieved or lonely. A bit of both, perhaps.

Skimming the thread between Kole and me, I compose a new message. *How's it going?*

His response comes a minute later. *Good! She's cooperating.* About an hour before I left the coffee shop, he texted to tell me he was off to work a scene regarding a woman who stabbed her boyfriend in the neck.

She confess?

Yep. Said she was sick of his shit.

So she stabbed him?

With a letter opener.

Cutthroat.

Pun intended?

Perhaps my blood should turn cold at the fact that I'm corresponding with a murderer, but it doesn't. I am detached, I think, echoing the words of the therapist. Unfeeling—Tommy's words. Worthless—mine. But if I can figure out someone like Nikolai Kole, maybe I have more worth than I thought. I want to know. I want to delve deep into the shadowy recesses of his mind and examine every hidden memory.

Gotta love Black Harbor, he texts.

The city that never sleeps . . . Because everyone's too busy killing one another.

So true.

I found your textbook by the way, I tell him. *You should have it in a few days.*

You're amazing! I owe you a pizza.

I send him a smile.

He's quiet for a while, now. I imagine they're conducting a search of the residence, photographing the scene and collecting the letter opener as evidence, among other things. The reports will begin trickling in over the next few hours. Strange how typing accounts of a gruesome attempted homicide is something I look forward to. Because I'll get to hear him. The subtle dips and serrated edges of his voice. Because even if he did kill Pearl and Krejarek, they weren't good people. And I love him. I love him, I love him, I love him. It's the first time I've admitted it to myself. Albeit silently.

My mere two hours of sleep this morning has caught up with me. My eyelids feel heavy, like fingertips pressing on them, pulling them down over my eyes like the shades I keep closed every night in the Transcribing office.

I walk upstairs, setting an alarm for 8:30. An hour nap will hopefully recharge me before I have to get ready for work. Upon entering the bedroom, I startle, just short of turning on the light. Tommy is indeed home—and has been all this time. His body is a mound beneath the blankets. The image makes me think of a freshly dug grave I'm about to go lie beside.

Perhaps I should return to the couch downstairs.

No. If he wakes, I want him to know I was here. That at least for tonight, I'm playing the good wife.

I wonder if he feels OK. I hold my breath for a few seconds to listen for his. It comes in long inhales and exhales. The drunken slumber. Using the flashlight on my phone, I creep to the dresser to change. I strip, goosebumps erupting on my naked skin. The hairs on the back of my neck stand on end, as I get the uncomfortable feeling that I'm being watched. Standing in just a sports bra and leggings, I turn. He's still asleep.

I pull a long-sleeve over my head and keep my socks on, then climb softly into bed.

The mattress groans as he rolls toward me. Facing the window, I stay still, even when his hand slides under my shirt. His fingers drag across my ribs. I cringe, praying he doesn't want to have sex. I'm not ready for the searing pain. I just want to sleep for an hour. His hand explores me like a mole, blindly searching my body. His fingernails feel short and torn. *Scritch, scritch, scratch.* One of them digs at me. I twitch and he does it again. *Scritch, scritch, scratch.*

Is he testing to see if I'm in the mood? Because I'm not. I inch away, but his arm drapes over me. He pulls me to him. He reeks of weed, I realize. And sweat. He must have been over at Old Will's earlier. I envision him slugging a last beer and stumbling from Will's door to ours, then dragging his ass up the stairs and collapsing into bed.

I swallow a lump of anger. I wish I'd have stayed on the couch. I should just get out. I can shower and get dressed and sit in the municipal lot until my shift. With the heat on in my Blazer, it'll be warmer than inside the duplex anyway. Maybe Kole will even be done with his investigation and we can sit in his car together.

His hand flattens across my abdomen, grazing the steel ball bearing of my belly button ring as it travels down. *Scritch, scritch, scratch.*

My ears perk up at the sound of the locks clicking downstairs.

Someone's here.

Muffled through the floor, I hear the sounds of my husband's heavy boots walk into the dining room. The chair scrapes across the floor. He drops his tactical bag onto it.

I freeze. Look down at the arm draped over me like a snake. And scream.

The sound is shrill enough to shatter the windows. Within seconds, Tommy's silhouette is in the doorway, brandishing a gun. There's shouting, but I can't make out the words. I wrest myself away from the intruder and fall off the bed, then scamper to the corner of the room. My back up against the dresser, I cower with my head buried behind my forearms and my knees.

The light turns on.

Peeking through my fingers, I see Tommy holding Sam at gunpoint. Sam looks like a rabbit caught in a snare. He puts his hands up, interlacing his fingers behind his head. "I don't know where I am!" He sobs. "Help me, I just wanted to get home and sleep. I don't know where I am!"

Tommy lowers the gun. "Sam," he says, and then he repeats it louder. "Sam. Calm down. You're OK."

"Where am I?" Sam cries.

"Are you hurt, Hazel?" Tommy calls to me from the doorway.

I can't move. I'm frozen with fear. I feel like the weight of his arm is still on me.

"Hazel!" Tommy yells.

"Yes!" I yell back. "I mean, no. I'm not hurt. Just, Jesus, what the hell, Sam?"

"Don't kill me!" Sam pleads. He falls forward as if in prayer.

"Sam, you're safe," Tommy tells him. He holsters his gun. I hear it click into place. "See? We're gonna get you home. Come on." He touches Sam on the back, gentle, like he's coaxing a child, and I feel so grateful to him at this moment.

I watch as Sam uncrumples himself and follows Tommy out of the bedroom. My skin burns where he scratched me. When I hear the door shut and I'm certain no one is left in this side of the house, I stand and lift my shirt. A series of pink hashmarks emboss my abdomen. They're already fading, so that come morning, I'll be convinced the entire incident was a dream.

Or a nightmare.

The sound repeats in my mind, as though his fingernail is etching the surface of my brain. *Scritch, scritch, scratch*. Not so much scratching, though. Digging. He was looking for something.

20.

WEDNESDAY

After Tommy returned Sam to Old Will's—it was all just a misunderstanding, of course, an *accident*—another walk-through of the kitchen showed that the door to the basement was ajar. So he'd come from underneath. I shuddered, thinking of him high out of his mind, slinking up the stairs. It didn't appear he'd taken anything. He just thought he was in his own place.

It might have been true. It might not. I've narrowed down the conclusions to two: either that Sam was high out of his mind, or that he mistook my kindness for weakness when I drove him home the other night. Tommy was right. I can be so naive.

I washed the sheets before I went to work, making Tommy stand watch while I went to the basement and tossed them in the washing machine. "You didn't know he was here?" he asked me.

"Not until I went upstairs. I thought he was you."

"But you knew I was at the range."

"I thought you'd come home, 'cause you didn't feel well or something."

We've rehashed the conversation a dozen times since. I can hear the doubt in his voice every time he asks, tweaking his questions just a little bit each time. He thinks I invited Sam into our bed. He won't admit it, but I know that's what he's thinking. As infuriating as it is for him to presume I couldn't do better than a degenerate like Sam, it puts him off the trail of Kole. Perhaps this is one of those infamous blessings in disguise.

Speaking of, I haven't told Kole and don't plan to. He would become enraged. Maybe even violent. And I don't need Sam's blood on my hands.

Tommy's car is parked along the curb when I return to the duplex. It's twilight, the sky an ugly bruise with a halo of yellow hovering along the horizon. I park in the driveway after having spent the last several hours at Minerva's and walk up the stairs. At my feet, newspaper pages flip frantically, like a flag waving for my attention. As I should have done months ago, I grab hold of it and break it out of the ice. I bring it inside with me, planning to toss it in the recycling bin by the pantry. Most of the ink on the front page is erased, but the date remains, although faded. April 16.

I feel a twinge of shame for letting a piece of trash sit on the porch for so long. I turn it over, about to finally discard it, when a familiar face catches my eye. It's a photo of a police officer. He's midthirties, maybe, with dark hair, gray eyes. His bone structure is a little more rigid, his jaw a little squarer, but it's the same one my fingertips have memorized. The caption beneath the photo reads: Investigator Kole.

My breath catches. A shiver grips my spine as my eyes flick to the headline: *Forge Bridge Claims Another as Cop Commits Suicide.*

I feel like I've just swallowed an ice chunk and it's melting at the bottom of my stomach. I toss the newspaper as though it's on fire, and it lands on the countertop. My eyes still trained on the picture, every detail flashes through my mind, like a movie gone off the track. Crossing out his name, Mona's voice echoing, "You can forget about him, kid." All the times he's crept into my office, when I am alone and there is no one to see him.

I start to feel sick again, as I consider the possibility that the man I know as Nikolai Kole is someone else entirely. Everybody lies. Had I simply believed who he was because he told me?

But then, there was Hammersley, who knew him when he invited him to his party. And Kole had been there at Figaro's, among others who knew him well enough to joke with him.

I filter through possible scenarios, arriving at the simplest explanation. Nikolai Kole had a brother. He'd been telling the truth when he mentioned him during our game of two truths and a lie at Krejarek's apartment.

Allowing myself a long, calming exhale, I re-approach the article.

> On April 14, Investigator Evan Kole is suspected to have taken his own life by jumping from the Forge Bridge at approximately 10 p.m.

April 14. I had last gone to the bridge around that time, before my nine-month hiatus, until the interview triggered my return. I look at the photo again, my focus slipping to allow his features to distort, for his skin to pale and his eyes to become cloudy like fish eggs, and I know, beyond a reasonable doubt, that I have seen him before. He is the corpse I witnessed floating faceup that frigid spring morning. The one who sent me running into the trees, away from the cops as they arrived on the scene.

My head spinning, I read what I can manage from the blurred, eroded type. *Investigator Kole served as a member of SWAT and an investigator for the BHPD Special Investigations Unit. A source says he had been suffering from depression and PTSD due to his involvement in a shooting last year. He is survived by a brother, who is also a sworn officer of the BHPD.*

Jesus Christ.

It's surreal staring at what looks like Nik's face—but isn't. The man in the photo is dead, now, and has been for nearly a year. I think of all the times Kole and I parked in the lot, overlooking the bridge that took his brother.

My hands shake as I set the wet newspaper at the bottom of the recycling bin, turning it over so I don't have to look at it anymore. This side of the duplex is empty. I can feel it. I hear Tommy's laughter through the paper-thin wall.

I set my phone on the windowsill as I step naked into the shower. The cold that seeps through the cracks is like a hand gripping mine that doesn't want to let go. Under the showerhead I am thankful for the rushing water drowning out the noise in my head and washing the salt from my face. The residue of my tears lifts from my skin, sliding down the curves of my body and eventually into the drain.

I don't hear Tommy return to our side of the duplex until he's already in the bathroom. I jump when the doorknob punches the wall.

"Hazel, are you in there?" he calls.

"Yes," I answer. My voice sounds tinny, shrill.

"Didn't you get my messages?"

I can tell by the slurring of his words that he must have run to the corner store to get more beer.

"I texted you like five times . . ."

I can't understand him over the noise of the shower. "Just a minute," I say. The water's turned cold already. I shut it off and wring my hair out. When I reach for the towel on the wall rack, I graze Tommy's shoulder. His brows are knit, and to my horror, he has my phone in his hand.

"What is this?" he asks, and I've no doubt he's opened the message thread between Kole and me.

"Tommy—"

His eyes are blurry, his nose red. I can't tell if it's a side effect of drinking or of the conversation he's just read. Oh God, which one has he read?

He tears his eyes from the phone just to glare at me. "Hazel, what the fuck?" His voice cracks on the last syllable. He sounds strangely sober.

"I'm sorry, I—"

"You're fucking him, aren't you? I knew there was somethin' goin' on. Even at that party, that lady pulled me aside and told me to watch out for you two."

"Wait, she what?" Although the water droplets on my skin start to freeze, my blood suddenly turns hot with rage. He must mean Liv.

"It's true, isn't it?" I've never seen him so angry. He grips the phone so tightly his fist shakes.

I'm shivering, stark naked.

"Answer me, Hazel."

"Yes, Tommy! I had sex with him, OK? Is that what you want to hear?"

He looks like he's just been shot. "You . . . what?" He grabs at his chest, and in this moment, I realize I am watching his heart break before my eyes. "How many times?" He cries out, then, as if asking causes him physical agony.

"Once." The lie burns as it leaves my lips.

"When?" When I don't answer, he repeats it louder.

"Last week," I say. "When you were—" Where had he been? At the range? Fishing? Hunting? "—weren't here," I finish. Because you're never here, Tommy. You're never fucking here.

He's quiet as he reads through the text messages. I let him, because short of wresting the phone from him, there's nothing I can do. "Tommy, don't."

"I'll do whatever I want. I pay for this goddamn phone."

I step out of the shower and rip the towel from the rack, wrapping myself up in it tight. It's a joint checking account. We both pay for it. But there's no point in setting him straight.

"Seriously, Hazel," he calls after me as I run up the stairs to get my clothes. "What are you, like some kind of prostitute? How much does he pay you, huh?"

I throw on the first clothes I find—black leggings, a sports bra, and a sweatshirt—and grab my duffel bag from the bed. I empty what I can from my drawers into it: pants, T-shirts, socks. Blood rushes to my head as I run to the closet and shove my feet into a pair of shoes. I don't have much time. I've got to get out of here.

He's never been this angry before.

He'll kill you, I tell myself. *He will literally kill you. Get out. Just get the hell out.*

With my things in tow, I head toward the stairs, but Tommy's already at the top of the landing, blocking my escape. He clutches my phone in his hand like a grenade. His face is a concave thing, all his features collapsed in. Trails of mucus run into his beard. I've never seen a more pitiful creature.

"Hazel, why?" he wails. "How could you do this to me? I loved you with all my heart—"

"Don't say that." My words are sharp, a warning. Freezing water drips from the ends of my hair.

"Say what? That I love you?"

"That you love me with all your heart. You only ever say it when you're obliterated." My voice is harsher than I mean it to be, but there's no sense holding back now. Not after everything I've done to get to this point. I watch with sick, morbid fascination as my words cut him, watch how his eyes twitch like a pair of tiny beating hearts. Tiny beating hearts, like the ones I've watched him cut from grouses' chests, little meaty things shattered by shot. I archive the visual for my manuscript.

His mother is right. I am a monster.

"Hazel, how could you do this to me?"

"Give me my phone, please."

He shoves it down into his back pocket.

"I have to go," I say louder now. "Give me my phone." I don't care if Old Will or Sam hear. Let them.

Tommy takes a wider stance at the top of the stairs.

The only way out is down.

I move to shoulder past him, and he grabs my wrist, twists it behind my back. Pain shoots up my arm. "Let me go!" I shout. "Or I'll call the cops and you can kiss your stupid guns goodbye." My voice cracks a high-pitched yelp on the last syllable. I hope he doesn't notice that my bravery is now oozing out of me, like a tire that just rolled over a nail.

To my immense relief and shock, his grip loosens. I'm so tightly wound that when he lets go, I fall forward, one knee hitting the landing, and the other missing the first stair so I tumble all the way down. The edge of each stair bites into my back; my elbow connects with the railing once, twice, three times before I land on the hardwood floor, my face slamming into the register. Tommy comes careening down the stairs, horror screwing up his face.

"Hazel—"

"Don't," I warn. I push myself up onto my palms. There's a smear of blood on the register that would explain the film of red filling my vision. The room spins.

"Hazel, please don't leave me." His voice is almost a whisper.

Write what you know. I will know, now, how a man's face can crumple like a can being crushed by a fist, and how his eyes instantly become dim, like a house with the lights shut off. I'll know the power of words, especially when I choose to say nothing at all.

This is the moment when victims become villains. I stand and reestablish my balance. I will not fall to my knees anymore. I will not bend or break. I am done cowering in corners. Instead, I'll marvel at my ability to destroy someone's universe with the simple act of leaving it.

21.

THURSDAY

Everyone writes about the calm before a storm. But no one writes about the calm afterward, the deafening silence made up of emptiness and ruin, of sediments settling; the gravity of the realization that you've demolished the future you had in front of you, and chances of a better one are ground into molecules finer than dust.

I dream I'm home. I'm in my bed cocooned in flannel sheets, my head nestled on a pillow whose memory foam still molds to the shape of my head, even after all this time. The air smells sweet like maple, smoky like bacon. I shift, and the fabric of the pillowcase stings my raw face. My eyes burn behind closed lids, and I sink back into what might be a memory.

Tommy twisting my arm behind my back. I fell down the stairs and hit my head on the register. That was all real. It had happened, and just last night, I think. The reel plays in my mind, choppy like the scenes have all been stitched back together. I struggle to remember what happened after all that.

Perhaps because what happened next was so humiliating, I've already erased it from my mental Rolodex.

I'd driven to Kole's house, having memorized his address from when I ordered his textbook. There was nothing to distinguish it as a police officer's house—no blue light on the porch or in the front yard; in Black Harbor, something like that's just an invitation for a brick to be thrown through the window. The porch was framed in by wooden spindles, and dark shutters bookended the windows. I couldn't tell what color they were in the nighttime. Forest green, perhaps, or black. The windows glowed amber. He was still awake.

My heart pounding, I ran up the sidewalk and knocked on the door. As I waited, I glanced to my left, reading a monogrammed "K" on the lid of the metal mailbox. I heard footsteps as someone approached the door. My stomach twisted into knots as the doorknob clicked. Waiting for him to emerge, I suddenly became very aware of the frigid air freezing the back of my neck, my wet hair turned to icicles.

I was almost as nervous as when he'd shown up at the seedy hotel. Jesus, had it not even been a week ago? I'd managed a lot of destruction in such a short amount of time.

The door opened and a woman stood, looking like a portrait. She was auburn-haired with pale skin and freckles; her brown eyes widened when she took me in. I studied her, too. She looked like she'd just returned from dinner, wearing a black knee-length dress. Tiny gold hoops hung from her earlobes. Her neck was plain, but her hands were adorned with simple rings, including a wedding band.

If dictionaries had pictures instead of literal definitions, hers would have been next to the word *discombobulated*. "Nik," she called over her shoulder.

I peered around her to catch a glimpse of him wearing a blue button-down and jeans, his tie undone. His approach was silent; he wasn't wearing any shoes. Panic flashed across his face, then molded into pity, and when the woman turned to him, he furrowed his brows as if he'd never seen me before.

I ran. Down the sidewalk and across the street. I hurled myself into my Blazer and drove off before anyone could stop me. I drove for what seemed like forever, traversing the same interstate Tommy and I had taken just over a month ago on our way back from Christmas up north.

The house was unlocked as I knew it would be when I stumbled in after midnight. Dad was asleep. Reuben, his seven-year-old German shepherd, followed as I dragged my duffel bag across the floor and crawled into my own bed.

And here I am.

Home. It isn't a dream at all. I reach beneath the pillows for my phone to check the time, and remember that I left it in Black Harbor. *Along with my dignity.*

My head throbs. My mouth feels like cotton. I pause at the edge of the bed, waiting for a wave of nausea to pass. I hurt from my skin to the marrow of my bones. The floor's cold beneath my feet when I finally stand. I check under the bed for a pair of old slippers and put them on. The bathroom's just across the hall. I almost don't recognize my reflection in the mirror. My eyes are puffy and red. There's dried blood on my forehead. Everything about me sags downward. My mouth looks like a capsized parenthesis, my eyes a pair of sad apostrophes. I wet a washcloth and cleanse the blood from my face. Luckily, it isn't a deep wound. I brush my teeth and drink water straight from the faucet. The coolness of it clears my head some.

When I come out, Dad's on the couch holding a plate of bacon and eggs. Reuben sits at his feet.

I half wave, knowing full well that I look like a disaster.

Dad offers a close-mouthed smile. Dimples that match mine press themselves into his cheeks. "There's breakfast in the kitchen if you want it. Coffee."

I try to give the same smile back, and wander to the kitchen and fix myself a plate. Pour a cup of coffee. Dad doesn't drink it. He keeps the coffeepot around only for when Elle and I come to visit; though Elle doesn't come very often. Just Christmas, usually, and maybe once or twice more throughout the year. She's closer with Mom.

I can't say I'm much better anymore, though. Since moving away to Black Harbor, I've been home only a handful of times.

I set my plate on the armrest, coffee cup on the end table. We sit with an empty cushion between us, staring up at the TV that's playing *Gunsmoke*, but not really watching it. After several minutes, Dad clears his throat. "A guy's got some fence posts he wants to sell me. I was gonna check 'em out this morning yet, if you wanna come."

Everyone within at least a fifty-mile radius knows about my dad's wood carvings. He doesn't advertise any more than putting a sign out at the end of the drive, and yet he's always getting phone calls for commissions or someone wanting him to take old wood or railroad ties or tree trunks off their hands. I nod. It feels good to not be pressured to explain myself, and perhaps that's why I decide to tell him everything as we drive twenty miles farther north to see a guy about some fence posts. Well, not quite everything. I tell him about the fight between me and Tommy. He asks about the cut on my forehead and I say I fell down the stairs, cringing at how I know it sounds. But it's the truth.

"He didn't push me," I clarify. "He had me by the wrist and when he let me go, I lost my balance. And I fell." My voice falters at that last bit.

"That isn't right, Hazel. He shouldn't be putting his hands on you."

"He doesn't hit me."

Dad clenches his jaw, his hands tightening on the steering wheel as he stares through specks of precipitation on the windshield. I hold my hands up to the vents, absorbing the heat.

"I deserved it, Dad." My shoulders shake as I start to cry.

He pulls the truck off to the side of the road, and I concentrate on the words that stream from the radio as Dwight Yoakam sings about guitars and Cadillacs. He sits patiently, letting me cry, and finally, I admit my greatest sin, the one that will cast me into the same pool as my mother. "I left him."

"You must have had good reason."

I let his words flow through me, filtering through the fissures of my mind. The answer is there. It's been there for a long time, bobbing at the surface. I just stamped it down again and again, trying to hide it. "Do you ever feel like you're in the wrong story?" I ask.

There's a break in the music. Poor reception. The whine of the windshield wipers count the seconds that pass. Dad scratches his chin and I realize I'm holding my breath, waiting for his response. "No," he says, finally. "But," his gaze shifts to me, his eyes taking in my cuts and bruises, the hollow thing I've become, "why don't you just write a better one?"

• • •

Elle lives in a quiet complex just outside Milwaukee. Hers is a beige building in a neighborhood of buildings that all look the same, with a circular window at the peak and a balcony off the second-story master bedroom. The trees in the courtyard are strung with little white bulbs that glow like fireflies in the twilight.

It seems like forever since I've walked this cobblestone path to her door. I feel like a lost kid who's been returned home to her mother, and I can't help but hang my head as I ring the doorbell.

It's Saturday, now. I spent three days at home, mostly in the shed writing while Dad carved wood spirits and foxes into fence posts. The sound of his chain saw provided white noise, a perfect companion to my chaotic thoughts. I emailed Elle in that time, too. I laid it all out, or the big stuff, at least. I apologized for my recent behavior and told her I left Tommy. She invited me to stay with her, and that was when I broke into tears.

Now, on the outside looking in, I'm transported back to the other night when I came face-to-face with the woman whose husband I've been sleeping with. But, the door swings inward, and there is Elle in gray jogger pants and a T-shirt, her hair wrapped in a towel. Her cheeks are blotchy from having just stepped out of the shower, and without makeup, she looks more like the Elliot I remember, who we'd always thought to be a boy with soft features, and at six, I knew nothing of the bruises on her back or the meaning of the three-letter word that had been carved into her skin during recess.

My eyes water. "Elle. I'm sorry—"

She holds her arms out to me. I drop my bag on the porch and embrace her.

"I'm such an asshole," I say.

Elle laughs. "You are. But. So am I."

Afterward in the kitchen, I sit at the island as she pours us each a glass of wine. I look around. The strangest thing about the pictures in Elle's place is that they hold no concept of time. There's an old photo of our parents at an outdoor concert, she and Kinney DJ'ing a baseball game; a photo I recognize as being taken at her engagement party of her, Garrett, Kinney, and me all toasting with champagne.

There's only one photo from our childhood. We're sitting on a bale of hay in a wagon, near-silhouettes against the orange October sky. I'm dressed as a jack-o'-lantern, sitting on the lap of a child wearing a Batman mask, Elliot's hands closed tight around my puffy waist. I wonder how long she knew she'd been born in the wrong body. How many years had she kept that secret to herself, before researching hormones and gender confirmation surgery?

All I know is she enrolled in college as Elliot, and graduated as Elle.

"I really am sorry, Elle," I say. A typed email apology isn't enough. She needs to hear it from me. "About leaving your party that night. I know how important this is to you."

Elle sighs. "We still had a good time, didn't we? And I bashed you pretty good over the air. I'm sorry about that. That was really . . . juvenile."

"I deserved it."

"You really didn't, though."

"I'm not a good person, Elle. Or at least, I haven't been. I've done some pretty messed-up stuff."

Elle snorts into her wine. "Sis, try me."

And that's how Elle gets me to tell her everything, from Sam's confession in the frost to me and Kole searching Krejarek's apartment for the satchel. She listens with rapt attention as I narrate Pearl's brutal murder to be followed by Krejarek's. When I get to the fight between me and Tommy—

"Wait. Pause," Elle says. "How did Tommy get into your phone? Did you have the messages showing up on the lock screen? 'Cause you can turn that off, you know. I do all the time. I don't need my coworkers seeing any cutesy messages between me and Garrett."

"He knew the passcode."

"You never changed it?"

I wince. "I thought if I changed it, he would notice, and then he'd get suspicious as to why I changed it in the first place."

"Isn't that better than him opening up a sexting string?"

"Hindsight's 20/20. I now know to change my passcode next time I embark on a marriage-ruining affair." Potentially life-ruining, actually. How could I go back to work? I may have to permanently crash on Elle's couch. I've now arrived at the part about me showing up at Kole's doorstep.

"You saw her?" Elle asks, wide-eyed. "Did she know who you were?"

"I don't know. I took off as soon as she opened the door."

"Did he go after you? Kole?"

I shake my head. *Don't you dare cry.* "I haven't heard from him. He can't really contact me even if he wants to." I hope he wants to, though. I hope not hearing from me is killing him. After being phoneless for three—going on four—days, now, I'm seriously considering never owning one again. I feel invisible without it. Free.

"I'm sure he wants to," Elle says, echoing my wish.

I take a sip of my wine. Elle drinks the last of hers and pours another, topping mine off again. She tells me I can stay with her as long as I want.

"What about your lease?" I ask.

She waves dismissively. "It's through May. I asked my manager about possibly subletting it and he said that would be fine. If you're the subletter . . ."

I nod, considering it. We're a few days into February, now. Three months of staying with Elle would buy me enough time to find a new job and get far away from Black Harbor. Hopefully back up north. Writers can write from anywhere, I've learned.

It's hard to imagine everything that's unraveled in only three weeks' time. I first heard Kole's voice on January 17, and followed him up the stairs early the next morning to put a face with it. That chiseled, criminally attractive, stupid face with the circumflex scar. Auroral eyes that could pierce flesh and bone. Lips that lied. I fell irrevocably in love with him somewhere in there. Falling out of it felt like waking up from a hangover.

I ask Elle about the wedding and what she needs done, yet. We make plans to work on wedding favors tomorrow night.

"So, what's the verdict?" I ask. "Can I still be your maid of honor, or have I been replaced?"

"The job is still yours if you want it," Elle says. "I mean, it doesn't pay well, but the perks are pretty good, I hear. Free room and board."

"Complimentary wine," I add, raising my glass.

"There's plenty more where that came from, too. The vineyard gave me a whole year membership to wine-of-the-month club for booking my wedding there."

"Damn. I can't believe Kinney's not putting more of a dent in it." I notice, for the first time since sitting here, her fully stocked wine rack.

Elle sighs. "He was, but . . . Seattle called."

"Huh?"

"He got a job on *Wake Up, Seattle*. As a host."

I frown. "Like on TV?"

"Yeah." She takes a deep breath, touches the rim of her wineglass to her lips.

"Well . . . he always said he was too beautiful for radio. No offense."

Elle's shoulders shake as I watch her laughter turn into tears. Panic wells within me. She's never cried in front of me before. I bite my lip. "Do you have ice cream?"

"It's low-fat," she moans.

"We'll add marshmallows." I've got her by the arm, now, and I'm already leading her to the couch. "Do you have *Bridget Jones's Diary*?"

• • •

"I hate him so much," Elle says as she digs her spoon into the ice cream carton.

"Who?" I ask. "Hugh Grant?" It's the part in the movie where Bridget's just found the chick.

"No, Chad." She can't say the name of her new coworker without rolling her eyes. "God, he's such a douche."

"Everyone named Chad is," I reason, and I tell her about the time when, in one of my creative writing workshops, we all crucified the writer for naming their protagonist Chad.

Elle wrinkles her nose.

Kinney's never been quiet about the fact that he aspired to be on TV, but apparently, he'd kept the entire interview process top secret until he announced last week over the air that it was his last show. That was the first Elle had heard anything about it. Maybe that was her karma, getting blindsided in front of the whole metropolitan area.

"I think he just didn't want me to suffer." The way she says it, with a note of reluctant acceptance, tells me she's been mulling it over for a while, now.

"But in the end—"

"I feel totally betrayed. Not just because Kinney kept it from me, but because management obviously knew about it and no one told me. I wasn't even included in the interviews of my new coworker. Don't you think I should be there to see if there's any chemistry?"

She had a point. What undoubtedly made *The Elle & Kinney Show* such a success was the constant bickering and banter between Elle and Kinney. She's scared for the future of her show. Her career. I can hear it in her voice, and I daresay that over the past couple of months, I've gotten pretty good at reading voices.

"You're right. Elle and Chad doesn't exactly have the same ring to it as Elle and Kinney." A thought suddenly occurs to me. "What's his last name?"

"Vandervelzen. Ugh." She falls back against the couch, mushing a throw pillow into her face.

I can't help but laugh. "The *Elle & Vandervelzen* show. The *Elle & Chad* show."

Elle groans from behind the pillow.

"Well, maybe he'll tank and you can use that as leverage to be included in the next round of interviews."

She shrugs. I'm sure she's already considered that. Whoever they hire, though, we both know they'll be no Todd Kinney.

"Well, where do we go from here?" I ask.

Elle clinks her spoon against the ice cream container. "To the store. I can't take this low-fat trash anymore."

22.

SUNDAY

I return to work Sunday night. It feels weird being back here, like I'm in a lucid dream. I creep through the Records area, my heart hammering as I near the Transcribing office, half expecting Kole to be sitting in Mona's chair as he's done before.

The office is dark and empty. I unlock it and exhale. I set my tote bag on the counter next to the printer and draw the blinds closed. I don't want to see anyone or anything tonight. I just want to type some reports and go back to Elle's where it's safe.

There's a newspaper that's a few days old near Mona's portal. I read the headline: *Uninhabitable for Humans.* There's a picture of the blue apartments. A sign in the window states "Condemned."

I separate the blinds and peer out. There's a void across the roundabout where the apartments once stood. The lone streetlamp illuminates an empty lot, glinting on splinters of glass left in its wake. I don't know how to feel about it. At least I don't have to look at them and be reminded of my adventures with Kole, when I wandered up the stairs and discovered a lethal cache in the wall.

I log in to E-scribe and discover a slew of messages, most of them from Kole.

THURSDAY

From: Kole, Nikolai
To: Greenlee, Hazel
Sent: 7:02 a.m.

Can we talk?

THURSDAY

From: Kole, Nikolai
To: Greenlee, Hazel
Sent: 8:14 a.m.

You're not answering your phone. Are you OK?

THURSDAY

From: Kole, Nikolai
To: Greenlee, Hazel
Sent: 12:07 p.m.

Hazel, I just want to talk to you. If you're at work and you're reading these, please answer your phone.

THURSDAY

From: Kole, Nikolai
To: Greenlee, Hazel
Sent: 1:52 p.m.

Are you OK?

FRIDAY

From: Kole, Nikolai

To: Greenlee, Hazel

Sent: 7:34 a.m.

Just let me know you're fine and I'll stop bothering you.

FRIDAY

From: Kole, Nikolai

To: Greenlee, Hazel

Sent: 11:20 a.m.

I stopped in at your office. Mona says you called in sick last night. I'm worried about you.

FRIDAY

From: Kole, Nikolai

To: Greenlee, Hazel

Sent: 1:45 p.m.

I know you're probably not getting these, but just in case you happen to see them, I'll wait for you at Beck's tonight from 7 on.

I wonder if he'd really gone to Beck's. I imagine him sitting alone at the high-top table by the Pac-Man machine, with two diet sodas perspiring in front of him. I hope he'd been miserable. I hope he'd been haunted by the image of my face over and over and over again, the way it had been when I'd looked upon the woman opening the door. I hope he'd been worried about me, and that every second of my silence had been like a new knife wound.

I close the blinds so no one can see in, and busy myself with the backlog of PO Holds and CIB Hits that Mona didn't get to, plus a handful of fresh arrests. When midnight rolls around, I switch to dictation. Transcribing is therapy. My fingers dance quickly and effortlessly as I listen to Investigator Rumele's burglary investigation, a DOA by Rowe and a supplement for the same case by Riley, a search warrant by Sergeant McDermid where four children were found sleeping on a pile of tires in a decrepit drug house.

After every report, I think about responding to Kole's messages. I could ease his suffering with a simple *Hey*, but my silence is the only power I have. Once I give it up, it's gone.

I run on autopilot, clicking down the list without even reading who the author is. The queue is endless. His voice jars me from my trance.

"Hello, Transcriber, this is Investigator Nikolai Kole, payroll number 6186, calling in a supplemental report." He lists the case numbers to cross-reference. "No victims, no witnesses. Please just add the name Cyrus Jacoby as mentioned. Thanks."

Apparently, he and Crue had paid Cyrus Jacoby a visit in prison while I've been gone. The report itself is brief. Jacoby claimed he hadn't overheard or orchestrated anything in regard to Sarah Dylan's death, and that was it. I punch my initials at the bottom of the paragraph and open up a new message in Onyx. *Investigator Kole, your report is ready for your review.*

Wishing for him to suddenly appear in the doorway and simultaneously hoping I never lay eyes on him again is a constant and exhausting war that I fight all through the night. I check obsessively for a reply, but it remains blank.

• • •

"He isn't gonna leave her. They never do." A woman's voice stops me in my tracks as I walk through Records. Liv sits at her desk with a stack of tickets in front of her. She's here two hours early.

"Excuse me?" I pause with the coffee decanter in hand. I'd been on my way to rinse it out in the women's bathroom.

"Nikolai Kole. I saw you two at Minerva's. Talking, holding hands." She shakes her head in a manner of *tsk tsk*. "You might want to be more careful who you cozy up to, especially in public. I know you think differently coming from a small town, but Black Harbor really isn't that big of a city."

I shrug, even though I feel a little like I'm upstairs being interrogated.

"You can do whatever you want. I just feel bad for your husband. And even you, to some extent." The way she says "you" is twisted more like "yew." She sighs and when I think she's gone back to processing tickets, she resumes her monologue. "It's always the woman who gives up everything, and in the end, the man never has the balls to leave."

I look at Liv in the gray, barely morning light. She is what, forty? Faint vertical creases stitch across her forehead. She looks tired and unamused to be here.

"You know he probably killed that woman, right? Or at least, knew someone who could get the job done for him."

The familiar screw in my gut twists. I know it. But I don't want to believe it. Even now when he and I—whatever we had—is clearly over. "She was a CI," I say, as though that fact, alone, is grounds for a suspicious death. I have no idea how much Liv knows about the investigation. She could be baiting me to divulge confidential information. After the two write-ups she got me, I don't trust her as far as I can throw her.

"Exactly." She laughs a shrill, cruel note. "You think it's pure coincidence that the CI who's been sleeping with a cop suddenly shows up murdered? And by the way, he's living with someone else and might have reason to want her gone? *And* by the way, he was allegedly *there* the night it happened? OK."

I don't know where she learned it, but I know the last part to be true. Kole had even admitted to going over to Pearl's that night. He'd taken out her garbage for her. And then what? Surely he hadn't just gone over there for that. "He's not a murderer." I clench the plastic handle of the coffeepot so tightly, I imagine the whole glass decanter shattering.

Liv snorts. "And I used to believe my ex wasn't doing lines of coke in the bathroom." There's a sharp, definitive clicking sound, then, as she resumes punching her pile of tickets.

• • •

The absence of Krejarek's apartment building feels like a page torn from a book. I drive slowly around the curve of the roundabout, my eyes picking up glints of glass ground into the gravel that's been pressed unnaturally flat. The descent to the parking lot looks more severe than I remember it being when I stood there with Kole as he explained the way into Krejarek's apartment. The dumpster that served as Jordan McAllister's aboveground grave is gone, too.

In a second, I am past it, the vacant lot shrinking in my rearview mirror. My stomach twists as I close in on the duplex. I have to get some things: more work clothes, for one, and my charging cable for my laptop. Maybe some books, if Tommy hasn't burned everything by now.

I ease off the gas as I approach, allowing myself an opportunity to check for Tommy's car. The only vehicle on the property is Sam's rusted brown pickup. I park at the curb and set my jaw as I walk up the stairs and try my key. The door swings inward. I'm not really surprised. I don't know what would have hurt Tommy more about having the locks changed: having to admit to Old Will that he and I are on the outs, or coughing up the cash to get the job done.

Inside, the silence is thick, like when you put a cup to your ear and press it to the door. The tunneling quiet draws me in, and I find myself staring into the barrel of the 9mm. It lies on its side on the dining room table, next to a sticky cereal bowl. On the third chair, as always, sits Tommy's tactical bag.

I keep moving, past the table and into the kitchen. I tense up, clenching my fists so hard my knuckles turn white as I sidle past the gun, making myself as small as possible as though it could spontaneously go off at any given second. I've never been scared of it before, but now . . .

The stairs creak and I wince. I train my eyes forward, not turning to look at the gallery wall made up of pictures of people I don't know anymore. The bed is unmade and disheveled, and the pillows look like pale, belly-up pill bugs. I grab a laundry basket from the bathroom, dumping out the dirty clothes, and begin to empty the rest of my dresser into it. I toss my bras into the basket, squishing them down with my running shoes and a pair of black heels. From a ceramic leaf-shaped dish on my dresser, I slide a bracelet onto my wrist and shove two necklaces into my pocket that I vow to untangle later. It feels like I'm burgling my own belongings.

Hauling the basket down one step at a time, I jump to the sound of his voice.

"Find everything you need?"

The basket falls from my hands, toppling down the last few steps. Clothes and books and shoes are strewn about the stairs and down to the hardwood floor. Clutching my chest, I look into the living room, where Tommy sits on the sagging couch. "I didn't—" Shit. A cold sweat breaks out on my neck.

In front of the window with the hoary light illuminating the beige shades, he's mostly a silhouette.

"Jesus, Tommy, you scared me." He must have taken the day off from work. He knew I had to come back sooner or later. I feel like unsuspecting prey that's just wandered dumbly into one of his traps.

"I read through all your conversations," he says.

The statement makes me nauseous, even though I knew he would do just that. I feel less violated than guilty. I'd never meant to hurt Tommy with those messages. Some of the worst ones flash through my mind.

He tosses what I assume is my old cell phone on the ottoman like a bone. "You know, it wasn't the raunchiness that hurt me the most, Hazel. It was the . . . playfulness. If I didn't know it was you behind those messages, I would've assumed it was someone else, someone fun."

You don't know me, then. I squeeze my eyes shut and a burning tear escapes, sliding down my cheek. Tommy doesn't know me. He never cared to get to know me for what I wanted, or what I needed. It's always been about him. I grit my teeth so hard it feels like they could break.

"Why can't you ever be like that with me?" he asks. "You don't even like sex. But, you seem to fake it well enough with him."

I cross my arms over my chest, stare holes into the clothes strewn about the floor. I want so badly to pick them up, but I'm afraid that if I move, he'll take it as a cue to get up off the couch. I don't want him to come any closer.

"What's wrong with you, Hazel? Huh?" My heart tears at the sound of his voice cracking. "You're my wife. The woman I chose to spend the rest of my life with. And this is how you behave?"

I sink down to the bottom step, crumpling like I did when I came home from work that first day with the reprimand about my attire. Apparently, this is my default position for when I've fucked up. "I'm sorry," I cry, and my face is wet with tears.

As I feared, he rises from the couch. He's dressed for work in a light-green polo and jeans. Apparently, trapping one's wife is as nonchalant as a routine dental appointment. You don't even have to take the day off for it.

"He doesn't even want you," he says, looming over me now. His voice steadies, hardens. He sniffs, and drags his forearm across his nose. "He'd have had you by now if he did. You came off really naive, Hazel. He took advantage of you."

I say nothing and fix my eyes on his scuffed steel-toed boots. The strings are frayed at the ends. The top eyelet is missing on the left one, and there's a dark stripe across the toes that could be animal blood.

"I just don't understand how you can pretend for all these years that sex is so ungodly painful and then—"

"It doesn't hurt with him," I say, but my voice is too quiet to be heard in the ringing silence. It's true. It doesn't hurt. For the first time in years, I've felt like more than an empty husk, a whole person. I should have known the feeling couldn't last. I don't deserve it.

"It's all in your head, you know that, right?" says Tommy.

I draw in a breath to try to steady my nerves, but it has the opposite effect. My whole body starts to shake.

"Psychosomatic." He's repeated it to me so often in the past year, I wager it's become his favorite word. He loves to remind me that I am the problem. He first heard it from the mouth of the marriage counselor, and therefore credits it as the word of God. We went to three consecutive sessions, but stopped going once they weren't free anymore. Tommy had gotten what he'd wanted out of it, anyway: confirmation that I was crazy.

The counselor had said the sexual pain was psychosomatic, but that wasn't all she'd said. Tommy had heard only the pieces he'd wanted. *Something hurt her or scared her, at some point, and you didn't give her time to heal. Now, she puts her guard up every time you touch her because she's afraid of the pain. It's her body's involuntary reaction.*

"I still want you, Hazel. I still love you, even though you betrayed me." He kneels in front of me, reaches for my hand. His fingers are chapped. His skin feels like sandpaper. "You can come back home. Nobody has to know. I'll let you make it up to me."

I look away, my gaze fixed again on the bloodstain on his boot. Rising, he tips my chin up, and presses his lips to mine, shoving his tongue into my mouth. I hate every second of it.

"I just need to . . . go . . . for a while," I whisper once I manage to pull away. I try to gather my things and stuff them back into the basket.

Tommy sighs. "Here, let me help you."

We both crawl on our knees, reaching for things that have fallen out and putting them back in. He grabs my black heel that toppled end over end into the kitchen, and a book that slid up against the rug in the living room. I watch him from the corner of my eye and shove three pairs of folded socks into the basket. It's almost all picked up, now. I reach for my college dictionary that leans against the register. My blood is still smeared across the vent. "Thanks," I say quietly, and I feel my armor soften, like a bruise.

Tommy's already risen. He nods, then unzips his jeans and pisses all over my things. "You'll never leave Black Harbor," he says.

23.

LATER

From: Kole, Nikolai
To: Greenlee, Hazel
Sent: 7:55 a.m.

So it's back to "Investigator Kole" now?

From: Greenlee, Hazel
To: Kole, Nikolai
Sent: 10:11 p.m.

I guess so.

24.

TUESDAY

From: Kole, Nikolai

To: Greenlee, Hazel

Sent: 7:47 a.m.

Will you please talk to me?

From: Greenlee, Hazel

To: Kole, Nikolai

Sent: 10:08 p.m.

We are talking.

25.

WEDNESDAY

From: Kole, Nikolai
To: Greenlee, Hazel
Sent: 8:16 a.m.

Not like this. I can't say what I need to say. You know these can get flagged.

I've stared so hard at Kole's last message that the type starts to blur. My lip quivers. I want to see him more than I want anything in the world, even if it's just to punch him in the teeth. I take a deep breath, and open the window to reply.

From: Greenlee, Hazel
To: Kole, Nikolai
Sent: 10:34 p.m.

FUCK OFF.

26.

THURSDAY

There aren't any new messages from Kole when I log into the portal. A string in my heart pulls tight. Perhaps the "fuck off" had been a little harsh.

It's too late to take it back. And I'd meant it when I sent it.

The night has been quiet so far; I can tell by the handful of arrests I pulled out of the drawer: Disorderly Conduct, CIB Hit, CIB Hit. There are two juvenile apprehensions for criminal trespassing: two sixteen-year-olds who set off fireworks in a backyard. I process the three arrests, leaving the apprehensions for later.

The dictation queue is as empty as I've ever seen it, with only an hour and thirteen minutes' worth of audio. Depending on the complexity of the reports, it will take only half the night to complete them all. The longest of them is by Investigator Riley. Jumper, I bet.

Suddenly, a report appears above the others in the queue, a red exclamation point in its left margin. There's neither an author nor a complaint number. Could it be toxicology results for Jordan McAllister, I wonder. Who called those in? Curious, I click to open it.

The first thirteen seconds are static.

But when he begins, I would know that voice from anywhere, with its smooth dips and rough edges, the depth that envelops me, makes me believe it's just the two of us alone in the dark.

"Hi, Hazel. It's Nik." He sighs. "I've already started over like seven times. I'm much better at this when I'm dictating an investigation, but, there's no template for this kind of thing, so here goes. I miss you. I miss everything that you could possibly miss about anyone and more. I miss talking to you, listening to you. I miss looking at you, for Christ's sakes, the way you bite your lip when you're thinking about something really carefully, which, let's be honest, you think about everything really carefully. The way you cross your legs right over left, never left over right. I even miss that terrifying eyebrow that quirks up whenever I've said or done something asinine. I'm sure it's up right now, actually." He pauses. "I know you're upset with me, but if you can just do one thing for me, just let me know you're safe, period. Jesus Christ. No period. Ah, I'm not rewinding it, so you'll just have to listen to my stupid mistakes."

I smile.

"I hope that made you smile, at least. You're usually entertained by any display of my ineptness. Good word, right? I may have consulted a thesaurus."

I rest my head against my hands, my fingers coming together like a blade in the center of my face, thumbs hooking gently beneath my jaw, as I listen intently.

"I just . . . I need to explain some things to you. And it'd be better if we could meet in person. Just tell me where and when and I'll be there. You don't owe me anything, and if you never want to speak to me again, I understand. This is the last time I'll contact you, and then I'll fuck off, like you wanted. Anyway . . . thanks."

I listen to it again. And again.

I can't bring myself to delete it, because once it's gone, it's gone. I step on the left pedal, rewinding it, and then press down on the right pedal to replay. ". . . I know you're upset with me, but if you can just do one thing—"

The blinds aren't all the way closed. I stare out their narrow spaces at the void where Krejarek's apartment building stood not so long ago. It's just a flat lot, now. There aren't any news vans or reporters waiting to sink their teeth into a story about Candy Man and the dead kid in the dumpster. It's like everything's been erased, as effectively as Sam's confession on the glass.

Write what you know is shit advice. Because life isn't like it's portrayed in books. Most of us aren't heroes of our own story. We're not villains, either. Worse, we're ancillary characters of our own lives, who stand by and watch it crumble with zero power to change what happens on the next page. Catharsis doesn't exist in the real world, and the only people being swept off their feet are those who dive into the cold, cruel waters of Forge River. We make connections to cope with the pain of living, and that's it, because some people wander into your life for no reason at all but to ruin it.

Liv's warning echoes in my mind: *He isn't gonna leave her. They never do.*

It's time to say goodbye to foolish dreams. Lifting my foot from the pedal, I silence Kole's voice for the last time, and click "Delete."

27.

FRIDAY

Looking down at the water is like staring into a drum of oil. I watch as the light rainfall creates disappearing dimples in its smooth obsidian surface. My Blazer waits in the lot a hundred feet behind me, the lone witness to my final tribute.

The wind makes my eyes water. I edge toward the middle, carefully setting one foot in front of the other. The rails are encased with ice. My thin gloves stick if I leave my hand in one place for too long.

As always, my eyes scan the water for bodies. If there are any today, they're caught in the eternal merry-go-round beneath the surface, the wicked undercurrent that pulls and sucks and keeps forever.

I close my eyes and I can see the silhouettes of the clouds through my eyelids. They're bold and obumbrating, moving quickly across the sky, their bellies punctured by the tops of evergreens. I feel the mist freezing to my face, forming crystals on my lips and icicles in my nose, and then with my eyes open again, I reach into my bag and extract what I came to leave behind.

The manuscript is two hundred loose pages—well, 197. It's

everything I know. It's being left and leaving. It's the sour smell of beer bottles on the countertop and gunpowder pushed beneath fingernails. It's dendrites beneath a cold corpse's skin and waves crashing against the half-sunk pier. It's black plastic bags floating by like tumbleweed, ghosts in an asphalt graveyard.

It's all true.

But then there are the parts about the lotus-eaters. Kisses like heroin, caresses that electrify. Pinky promises and confidential confessions.

Lies.

With one gloved hand stuck to the railing, I hold my arm out over the water and shake the pages free like 197 white flags. They collide into one another as they descend, eventually floating on top of the water like sheets of ice.

I'm free of it now. I deleted the file from my computer. But this is the only way to truly cleanse myself of my own story. The one I lived to write. The one that will no longer unravel me. Besides, a manuscript won't get me out of Black Harbor, but tenacity and a tank of gas will.

Thunder growls overhead. The bridge vibrates. The river whispers my name. *Hazel.*

It wants me to jump.

I hear my pulse in my eardrums. All the blood rushes to my head, leaving my toes and fingertips frozen. I force myself to keep going, one foot in front of the other.

Hazel.

I glance down through the slats at the pages floating on the water. My crashing into them would be almost poetic, giving literal meaning to drowning in one's thoughts. I would dive headfirst, an exclamation point careening through the pages.

Hazel.

I pause. How did they all do it, I wonder. Evan Kole and the man who left his scratch-off ticket, and all the ones before and after. Did they stand on the railing or climb over it and jump from the edge of the railroad ties?

The bridge begins to shake like a series of footsteps are hurrying this way. I bend my knees to steady myself and hug the railing. A wintry gust rips at my fingers, feels like a blowtorch against my face.

"Hazel!"

I only catch a flash of blond hair when, suddenly, I'm yanked backward. I scream, believing that I've fallen, and when I realize I'm being hoisted over his shoulder and brought back the way I came, I pound my fists into his back. Upside down and intensely aware of the abyss peeking through the slats, I cry.

• • •

We sit in stunned silence for a long time. Maybe fifteen minutes. He asks if I was going to jump.

"No."

From the back seat, I watch him watch me. I refused to sit up front. His voice is more rough around the edges than usual. "So you think I'm a murderer." We lock eyes in the rearview mirror and I feel like a cold knife is being dragged down my spine.

"What?" It comes out more like a gasp.

Kole unfolds a piece of paper I didn't know he had, then, and reads: *"I envisioned Krejarek lying half on the shore, his entrails torn from him like a jack-o'-lantern, and I thought of the spark in Kole's eyes, so ephemeral you could miss it, as he chased after him into the thicket. Moments before he would murder him. Just five days after the murder of Sarah Dylan."* He looks up. "You were at least gonna change names, I hope."

Panic floods through me. I go to grab the handle, but he presses the automatic locks. I pull up on the manual one, and he presses the automatic command again. Click. "We can play this game all day," he says.

I can't look at him anymore. I squeeze my elbows in, tuck my feet beneath the seat, trying to shrink into oblivion. The page must have stuck to the bridge. I sigh. There's no arguing or lying my way out of this one. I've incriminated Kole as much as myself with my own writing.

"You really think I killed Pearl and Krejarek?" He shakes his head. "You are something else, you know that—"

"Everybody lies." I recite his own words back to him. The ones he's drilled into my brain.

He looks perplexed and a little amused. "What are you getting at, Hazel?"

I muster the courage to argue with him. If he's going to kill me, he'll kill me. At least I won't have to endure Black Harbor anymore. "You've got motives."

He raises his arm and bends his fingers back and forth as though summoning an imaginary server to his table. "Let's hear 'em."

"You were screwing Sarah Dylan."

"OK, I've heard that one before. Not true, by the way, but what would that have to do with me murdering her and Krejarek?"

"You found out about them," I say. "That they were sharing pills and she was double-crossing you. She wanted you to come over that night. I saw the text messages, remember? She was begging you to. You went over to her place after you left me at Beck's and you killed her. Then you pretended to be surprised."

Kole seems to chew on this for a moment. Then, his mouth quirks up in a wicked smile. "What else you got?"

Anger boils my blood. I hate the way he's looking at me. I hate him. "You ran after Krejarek."

"Correct."

"At 9:45."

"Was that the time?"

"You know it was."

"What's your point?"

"Why did you wait thirty minutes to call it in?"

He laughs. "Is that seriously what triggered this?"

My face burns. "Rowe's report said he received a call at 2215 hours. That's 10:15 p.m., Nik."

"I understand military time, but thank you."

"You're such an ass—"

"I was waiting for you."

"What?"

He sighs. His hands are at ten and two on the steering wheel. I notice his knuckles are cracked and I can't tell if it's from the cold or from getting into a brawl. "I wanted to make sure you were punched in at the police department. So you'd have an alibi. If I called right away, someone going to the scene would likely have seen you driving from this direction, and I didn't figure you'd want to be mixed up in all this. Not that you weren't, but, the less people who know, the better."

"What do you mean?" I manage, and what he says next chills me to the bone, as though I really had jumped into the river after my pages.

"I know where you live."

The words slam into me. I realize I've been waiting with bated breath a long time for him to say them, for him to find out. Dread paralyzes me.

"You gave Sam a ride home that night, after the interview."

My throat is so dry it's difficult to swallow.

Kole looks amused, but he doesn't smile. "This is my city," he says. "You think I don't have eyes everywhere? It's just incredible to me that you never thought to tell me you lived six inches away from a person of interest. A person—mind you—who confessed to dragging a dead child to a dumpster, and who snapped his finger off to write you a little message. You've been lying to protect him all this time and I can't figure out why. That is, I couldn't. Until a few nights ago when I set up surveillance and watched your husband stumble back and forth from door to door."

I feel myself sinking in the seat. Tears burn hot, collecting in the corners of my eyes. "Please don't." I begin to cry. If Tommy gets interrogated by the police and he has any of Old Will's weed on him, he'll lose the ability to legally own a firearm and probably his job. I want to leave his life, not ruin it. It isn't like I never loved him, after all. I did, once.

Thinking back to the night of the interview, I remember Kole throwing Sam out onto the sidewalk. He'd been savage with him, and it wasn't the only time I'd witnessed that side of him. "The bruises," I start. "On Krejarek and Pearl. They were strangled."

"Yes." He sounds exhausted, like a suspect who's been drilled all night in an interview room. "Just say it, Hazel."

"I had bruises on me, after we slept together."

In the rearview mirror, I see a set of creases appear between his brows. His eyes slope downward, like a pair of quotation marks. It's the first time he's looked sincere since we've been sitting here. Whatever armor he had on has fallen away. "You did? Hazel, I'm so sorry. I didn't mean—"

"You choked me."

"I thought you liked it. It was just sex. I didn't mean—"

Just sex. My breath hitches and I set my jaw. Tommy was right. I am a fool.

"Hazel, come on." He turns around and reaches for me, but I pull away.

"It wasn't *just sex* to me, Nik." I can't believe I'm arguing with him about this. I can't believe I'm fighting with him, period. Days ago, everything was a dream. Perhaps that's all it was. Raindrops patter harder against the glass. A different day, we would be fucking.

"That's not what I meant." He tips his head back, closes his eyes in frustration.

"It's what you said."

"I didn't mean it that way."

"Don't say what you don't mean, then. Words matter."

"You know, Hazel, you're right. Words are the only thing that matter to you, obviously." He waves the ruined piece of paper and slaps it on the dash. "What was I, huh? An experiment? A behind-the-scenes pass for your novel?"

His statement strikes a chord. I glance at my own reflection in the mirror. My hair is matted to my face. The dark strands make it look as if long-fingered hands are clawing at me, dragging me back to the bridge. He's right. I used him. I inserted myself into his life, as much as he inserted himself into mine, for a chance at uncovering a story. A story that's bleeding out into the river, now.

I look at Kole. He's staring at something to his left—the raindrops collecting at the bottom of the window, perhaps. There are rake marks on his neck from me. They're red and raised already. I wonder how he will explain them to her.

"Who is she?" I ask. I have to know.

"She isn't my wife, if that's what you're thinking." He talks to the windshield.

My mind clouds again. I feel like I'm treading water in Lake Michigan, and the waves are tossing me from pier to pier. "She isn't?"

I peer past him as I wait for his answer, listening to the raindrops dance on the windshield, freckling the glass like clear apostrophes. Beyond them, Forge Bridge lies like a predator in the haze.

He takes a deep breath. "She's my sister-in-law. *Former* sister-in-law."

His admission is a double-edged sword. On one edge, the fact that she isn't his wife is a relief, while on the other rests the fact that, of the two of us, I am the only coldhearted cheater.

"There was a memorial dinner, honoring fallen police officers. They made a plaque for Evan. She asked if I would take her."

"As her date?"

"As her friend."

He doesn't sound wholly convincing.

I think back to how he'd looked that night. His tie hung loose about his neck, first few buttons of his shirt undone, barefoot. She'd been barefoot, too, like she was poised to stay a while. I avoid his gaze in the mirror, homing in on a thumbprint on the leather headrest of the front passenger seat. It's probably mine. Or hers. It's astonishing how uninhibited I feel when I know I've got nothing to lose. "So, do you fuck her in parking lots, too, or is that just reserved for me?"

He turns his head to look out his window. He looks like he's about to laugh, as though I've just said the most ridiculous thing. But then the pain begins to surface, gripping his features and pulling them down. "I wanted to chase after you," he says, finally.

I can still see his face, dumbstruck, as he let me run into the dark. "Why didn't you?"

"Because I didn't know how you would take it . . . this conversation. I called and you didn't answer. I must have texted you a hundred times."

"He had my phone."

"Oh."

Part of me wishes I could read those text messages. I'm sure Tommy did. If I just knew what they said, this conversation could be over already. And yet, I don't want it to be. There's something calming about just sitting here with him, in this quiet bubble, especially now that I'm less sure that he killed anyone.

"You know, I saw you there, that morning."

At first, I have no idea what he's talking about, but then, the memory comes to me like a body floating up to the surface of the water. He fixes me with frost-colored eyes, and my blood turns icy cold as I remember fragments of that morning: sheer terror coursing through me as I ran through the thicket, away from the corpse in the river and the police SUV cruising into the abandoned lot, my entire body suddenly paralyzed with trepidation, and then my calves burning as I'd raced up the rain-slicked slope. I'd caught a glimpse of two officers exiting the vehicle, one of them pursuing me as I'd sprinted and tumbled through the trees and thorns.

The final puzzle piece fits into place.

"I chased you." Kole confirms the details of my memory. His voice is coarse. I have to strain to hear him over the rain and the pounding of my heart. "But then, I heard them identify Evan over the radio and I just froze." He looks away from me, out the window again. His Adam's apple bobs in his throat. "I ran back to the riverbank and I saw . . . it was him. I fell to my knees and . . ."

I remember him. All this time I've wondered why he turned back. Now, I know.

"What were you doing there that morning?"

Silence. My jaw feels wired shut.

"Hazel."

I draw a deep, ragged breath and let it out. Still nothing.

"You know what? It doesn't matter. I drove myself crazy wondering why someone would have been at the bridge then, and I promised I wouldn't wonder anymore. It doesn't matter." And then, he breaks into tears. His shoulders shake and he covers his face with his hand. "When I saw you on the bridge just now, it broke me. I know how much pain Evan was in when he jumped, and I couldn't stand the thought of you feeling anything close to that. Because of me."

"Not just because of you," I mumble, but my voice is so quiet I might as well have not said anything at all. I wish more than anything I could cry, so I wouldn't look like an emotionless sociopath in the back seat. "How long have you known?" I ask.

"Since the second I saw you. You were hiding in the observation room, holding your shoes." His gaze returns to me, challenging me to deny his statement.

Our brief history unfolds in my mind. That was why he'd come down the following night. He wanted to see if I was who he thought I was, that the woman behind the mirror hadn't just been a figment of his imagination. "Why didn't you say anything?"

"Because I didn't want to scare you off. I wanted to be sure, and then when your bracelet was recovered. . . ." He sighs. "I thought you might be able to give me answers to Evan's death. Like, if you'd seen anything suspicious or unusual that morning, or any other time you might have been there."

"I'm sorry," I say, and I mean it. "I didn't see anything."

Silence.

"Is that how you knew to find me here?" I ask.

He nods. "I drove here that night. I even fell asleep. I thought maybe you'd come here. I was really worried about you."

The rain is falling harder now. I kneel on the floor between the seats and press my hand to his cheek. His skin is hot. He brings his hand up to cover mine. I lean so that our foreheads touch. "Come back here," I whisper. "Please."

When he's at last beside me, I bury my face in the hollow where his shoulder meets his chest. I breathe him in, filling my world with his scent that I've missed so much. Then, rising, I press my lips to his. His energy feels different, though. We are yin and yang, his letting go against my desperately hanging on. *Don't let me drown, Nik. I will never forgive you. I will walk right back to that bridge.*

"Do you love her?" I have to know. My cheek rests against his chest again. I can hear him swallow and I know he's staring out the windshield.

"She's family."

"Answer the question."

"I don't know how."

"It's simple. All you have to do is say yes or no." I can wait all day. I have nowhere to be, and no one to get back to. The realization is incredibly freeing, if not laced with loneliness. I'm not good at being alone. At least, I don't think I am. I haven't not been in a relationship since I was sixteen. The sad truth is, I'm afraid. And perhaps the even sadder truth is that this is exactly where I want to be. With him. I find his hand and slip my fingers between his. He lets me, but he doesn't squeeze back. I didn't come here to be placated. I was fine out there, on the bridge.

When remains silent, I go for the lancing blow. "She doesn't want you. She wants him."

He rakes his other hand through his hair. "I don't know what to do, Hazel. It keeps me up at night. I haven't slept more than two hours since—"

"Leave her." Even the rain pauses for these two words.

He huffs like I've just said the most ridiculous thing in the world. "It's not that simple."

"Sometimes it is."

He shakes his head. "Leave her like Evan did? I just . . . She came to me because she had no one else. She moved here for him. She has no family in Black Harbor."

"Sounds like a good reason for her to leave and go back to them."

"You're being really cold, you know that?"

"I'm being logical." My eyes rest on his necklace. I can bet that his brother or his brother's widow gave it to him; that his brother, the bloated corpse I met belly-up here in this very location, is the anchor keeping him in this hell. I stare at the ornament as though to set it on fire—or better yet, to rip it from his neck and throw it in the river, where it would lay in a graveyard of muck and all of my surrendered nothings. *Vincit omnia veritas.*

Does he even believe it, I wonder—that the truth conquers all things. Or does he simply enjoy the bitter irony of it? He wears truth on his chest, yet cloaks himself in lies.

Our conversation moves like a stream of consciousness: thoughts divided and connected by ellipses until I give it a hard stop. "I'm leaving." The decision has just become clear to me.

"Right now?" He touches my arm as though to dissuade me from getting out of the car this very second.

"I'm leaving Black Harbor," I clarify.

His eyes widen. In a sick way, I like seeing the torture in them. It's well deserved.

"Where will you go? Home?"

"Maybe. Or maybe Chicago," I tell him. There, I'd at least have an opportunity to hit the reset button. I could find a job as a writer—a copywriter or a journalist, perhaps—get my foot in the door.

"That's not too far," he reasons.

"Or New York."

"New York?"

"Or Florida or California; someplace warm."

"I'd miss you."

Good. I feel my resolve hardening again.

"Don't feel like you have to leave because of me," he says.

I squint at him like he is the stupidest organism on the planet. "You're exactly why I have to leave."

"I won't bother you, Hazel. I won't come by anymore. Just, please, stay."

The thought is enough to worsen my grief. Spending nights on end alone in the Transcribing office, with no hope of seeing him at four in the morning or whenever he decides to show up, is misery-invoking.

"I can't stay," I tell him. I tell myself.

"Why not?"

"Because, a year from now, where are we? What are we doing?"

Kole shrugs. "Here. This."

This. The word is a hot knife hissing as it slices through my flesh. *This* is lying, cheating, stealing moments with each other away from those to whom we made promises. The thought of it going on for another year—and that he would not only allow it but perpetuate it—makes me sick. And here? I can't stay in Black Harbor for the rest of my life; I can't die here.

"What's wrong?" he asks when he sees the tears brimming in my eyes. He presses his palm to my cheek—it's cool like the underside of a pillow—and wipes away the tears that roll off my lashes. I turn my head down and to the right, my chin touching my collarbone.

"I can't—" The words catch in my throat. "I can't stay here, Nik." I raise my gaze, now, to meet him. I can feel my eyes searing into his. We stare hard for a moment, engaged in a silent wrestling match.

"Hazel—"

I slide across the seat and pull back on the door handle. "Hazel, come on, don't go like this. What, what did I say?"

"You said *this*, Nik. That we'd be doing *this* for another year. I can't do this for another second." Finally, I push my thumbnail into the unlock button on my fob. I get out of his vehicle, but when I reach to open my driver's-side door, he's already between me and it.

"I didn't mean we'd be doing this exactly. I meant we'd be together, you and me. I don't want to fight with you, Hazel. *This* isn't what I want to be doing. But *here*? Yes, here, in Black Harbor. You know I can't just throw away sixteen years of my career, right? I can't jump from one job to another like you."

I don't even feel the rain anymore. The anger that heats my blood warms my skin to the point that I listen for raindrops hissing, like water dripping onto a stove burner. "I don't jump from job to job."

"Oh please. You were at that bookstore for what, a year and a half? And now that you've been at the police department for a month, you're already making plans to get the hell outta Dodge."

I feel like Sam or Krejarek sitting across from Kole in the interview room, or like myself when I argue with Tommy. He's right and I'm wrong, and there's no point in wasting my breath. My throat feels tight. Any words I want to say are stuck.

"You think everything has a connection and it doesn't. There are dead ends and sometimes you just gotta turn around and try again. Because sometimes life sucks. And work. And people. But you can't let it take you down. You can't just leave all the time. Because, guess what? You'll keep walking into these same situations somewhere else. It's not Black Harbor that's the problem, Hazel. It's you."

The last ten words feel like a kick to the kidneys. "I'm the problem." I repeat it softly like an epiphany.

"No, I said—"

"I know what you said." I should have known he would eventually use my own stories against me. It's what he does, logging people's pasts to build a case against them. I wish, now, that he'd never been allowed back at the police department. I wish he'd been forced to resign along with Dylan. I wish that the act of crossing out his name had barred him from ever crossing paths with me again. I'd escaped him once, here, when he'd chased me through the copse. I could do so again.

"Hazel, please, stop." He cups my elbow.

I wrest my arm from him. "Don't ever touch me again."

Still holding me, he asks, "Do you mean that?"

My eyes search his face. The curved shadows beneath his eyes are deeper, hollower. The caret-shaped scar is so faint it's almost invisible in this light. I was wrong about that scar, the circumflex given to things that don't belong. Nikolai Kole belongs here in Black Harbor, where kids are thrown away like yesterday's trash and where heroin needles cozy up to the curtilage. Where cops tamper with investigations and where people like me don't last. "Yes," I answer.

He lets me go. I feel the distance immediately, like a glacier suddenly wedged between us. We might as well be worlds apart.

I open the door and climb in. True to his word, he doesn't try to stop me, though I wish he would. I slam the door and turn the key. In a matter of seconds, Nikolai Kole is nothing more than a shrinking figure in my rearview mirror. I watch as Forge Bridge swallows him up.

28.

MONDAY

I think of sitting in a lawn chair on a frozen lake, breathing in the stannic smell of fish and blood, watching as people in ushanka-hats and Carhartt overalls slowly drilled into the ice with an auger. That's what hearing his voice over my headset feels like, now. Last night was the first I heard from Kole since I'd left him at the bridge just over a week ago. A brief, three-minute report detailing the toxicology results for Jordan McAllister. As suspected, the nine-year-old died in the early morning hours of January 15, after overdosing on oxycodone hydrochloride.

The results for Anya Brown are still pending.

Pearl's and Krejarek's deaths remain under investigation. Even if Krejarek murdered Pearl, the fact remains that whoever killed Krejarek is still lurking in our midst. Sometimes it feels like the whole city is holding its breath, waiting for another body to turn up so there are more clues to piece together. One will. I have no doubt. It's Black Harbor, after all.

Springs creak. The mattress sinks, and me with it, as Elle sits on the edge of the daybed I crawled into eight hours ago. She was at her kitchen island, drinking coffee and pinning wedding ideas on her iPad, when I hung my jacket by the door. "You couldn't do it, could you," she said without looking up.

It referred to finally going into the duplex and collecting the rest of my things: my clothes, my books, my phone. Basically whatever I haven't tossed off the bridge at this point. And dropping off the divorce papers I'd filed for last Friday. All it cost me was $200. I always assumed it'd be more than that. But there are no lawyers involved. I won't be fighting Tommy for anything. I don't want his guns or hunting knives or fishing gear. He can even keep all the furniture. Most of it came from his parents' shed or the side of the road, anyway.

With or without Kole, I'm leaving Black Harbor. The statement I'd made on impulse when we argued in the empty lot has become my promise to myself.

"No," I said as I have nearly every morning for the past week or so that I've driven out to the duplex and choked before even making it to the front porch. Most times I didn't get out of my vehicle or even stop, because Kole's black SUV was always there, parked along the curb or a few houses down the block. And now that I've noticed him, I can't miss him. I wonder how many times he's sat outside while I've been sleeping, or writing, or having sex with my husband and I had no idea.

What do you want? I wanted so desperately to ask him. To pull up alongside him or even better, get into his vehicle and the two of us sit in the back seat. I would demand to know why he was in my territory, and he would confess that he missed me and that he loved me and beg me to stay with him.

I'd run that fantasy in my mind so many times it was like a favorite movie being played on a loop. I knew all the lines by heart. And yet, it would never be more than that. Because every time I saw his vehicle, I was too paralyzed to get out of mine, too paralyzed to even take my foot off the gas pedal. I just kept driving as though traveling four miles out of my way was a necessary detour from the police department to Elle's place. And so every morning I crawled into the daybed in Elle's spare room, as empty-handed as when I'd left.

I yawn and breathe Elle in. She smells like Mom used to: Lavender Lace, that was the name of the perfume. I remember, because it was the last thing about her to leave. I took her pillowcase and covered my pillow with it so I could dream of her, and when all the fragrance had dissipated from its threads, I burned it.

I force one eye open. Elle is wearing a floral silk robe. Her hair is pinned up, the ends darkened from soaking in bathwater. Her toes, nails painted minty blue, curl into the plush carpet. "I could do it, if you want."

It takes a moment to register that she's picked up where our conversation drifted off this morning. That she's volunteering to go to the duplex for me and get my things.

"Thanks. That's really nice of you. But, I think it's something I need to take care of on my own."

She nods like she'd expected that response.

The truth is, I would love for Elle to take care of it for me. It would mean that the last time I'd run out of there was the last time I ever had to set foot in that sinking, worm-colored eyesore. That I wouldn't have to smell the stale beer from the empty cans piled on the cupboard, or see the loaded guns daring me to make a wrong move. I wouldn't have to see the blood on the register where I'd smashed my head. I wouldn't have to march up the stairs ever again.

But in two whole years of residing there, Elle had never witnessed my squalid state of living. I'd be damned if she would, now.

She doesn't know that it's fear of Kole, not Tommy, that keeps me from going inside. I'd told her about the time he was there, waiting for me. I haven't told her, however, that Kole is watching the place. She would ask questions. Questions that I can't answer.

I sit up and rub the sleep from my eyes. I imagine my hair is a halo of frizz and I don't care.

"You're too good for him," she says.

I bite my bottom lip as though to stop it from pulling into a frown. Plump tears well in my eyes and slip down my cheeks. "Which one?" I ask.

"Either one."

"Thanks, Elle."

She reaches over and dabs my tears away with her sleeve. "It's gonna be OK, Hazel." She scoots closer to me so that she can stroke my hair. "Sometimes you just have to cry until you can't cry anymore. And then cry some more."

"Is that what you did when you ended things with Max?" It's been years since I've spoken the name of Elle's ex-fiancé. I've never investigated the situation more than asking the shocked "But why?" when it happened. I wonder how many times she had to answer that question, and how many different answers she tried out before settling on the whole "cookie-cutter" logic.

Elle straightens her legs out in front of her, leans back, her elbows sinking into the mattress. "Yeah. I did. And I went through a lot more ice cream than you have by now, so you've got some catching up to do."

"You didn't break up with him because he was too perfect."

"That part is true . . . up until the point he just couldn't accept me. He looked at me differently after I told him." She sighs. "He felt I betrayed him. And I did. I lied. I lied about who I was. But I was just protecting myself. I'd had so many—" She pauses, her eyes glistening as she gazes up at the ceiling. Her chin quivers. "I should have told him sooner, Hazel. I do wish that. I should have told him before I ever said,

'Yes' to marrying him." She smiles ruefully. "I guess I let myself get swept away in a fantasy."

"It's not hard to do," I admit. I knew all along Nikolai Kole was a fantasy, a dream, a character I might as well have simply created out of sandalwood, sage, and coal-blackened air. And yet, I let myself fall in love with him. I allowed myself to believe that he was real and that a future with him was, too.

Elle pulls her knees into her chest.

"What did Garrett say . . . when you told him?"

"OK." She looks at me, her cheeks naturally rosy, eyes sparkling. "That's all he said. And that one word . . . it really did make everything OK. Suddenly, all the pain I'd gone through with past relationships was worth it. I had to walk through those fires to get to where I am today. To get here, less than three months from my wedding to the most amazing, genuine soul on the planet." She places her hand over mine, her thumb moving back and forth in a caress. "And you had to walk through your own fires, too. You're already on the other side, Hazel, I can see it. You just have to pick yourself back up, now, and keep moving forward."

She's right. I see myself on the other side of Forge Bridge, squinting through orange flames, seeing Kole and knowing I can never go back to him. I will miss him. But what I'll miss most is how I'd been with him: brave and brazen, even though many of those instances had been peppered with incredible stupidity.

"I'm sorry, Elle," I say.

Elle laughs and cradles me to her. "For what?"

"For just being a judgmental asshole. For being . . . jealous of you." I take a deep breath. I can't even begin to count up all the instances I've judged Elle for this being her second engagement. At least she called off the first one before finding someone else. She acts so confident, it's easy to forget what she's been through. And I'm sure I don't even know the half of it. If I did, it would probably break my heart. "You always have your shit together. And I'm a royal mess."

She hugs me tighter. "Hazel, to be human is to be a royal mess, right?"

"That sounded profound," I manage through sniffle.

"I've been taking notes during our coffee klatches."

I sit up and wipe my tears away. Elle is smarter than she gives herself credit for. "Does anyone even know at work?"

"Just Kinney."

"You know, it's nothing to be ashamed of, Elle. Maybe you should tell people. Trust me, secrets—"

"—secrets are no fun," she finishes, and lifts a teardrop off my eyelashes. I pause. The phrase hits me like déjà vu. I've heard those words before. Or seen them. The memory surfaces of me sitting in the Transcribing office with Kole, pouring over Pearl's bloodied cell phone. Tiny white letters on a black screen. "Secrets, secrets hurt someone," I whisper.

I took a picture of the conversation that night. It's on my phone.

"Hazel." Elle touches my arm. "Are you OK?"

I turn to her. Two parallel lines form between her brows.

"I have to go." I tear the blankets off and I'm out the door, grappling with my keys before she can stop me. "Secrets, secrets." My breath issues from my mouth like smoke. I throw myself into the front seat of my Blazer and yank the gearshift in reverse. I know where I've heard that warning before, and if there's any connection, it means Pearl hadn't been texting Krejarek for oxys.

She'd been texting Sam.

29.

LATER

My heart is still hammering after the thirty-two-minute drive from Elle's apartment to the duplex. I park in the empty spot where Tommy's car usually sits. He'll be getting back from work soon. I have fifteen minutes at most to get my things and get out. I just hope I can find that damn phone—and that Tommy hasn't destroyed it.

I'll text the photos of Pearl and Sam's conversation to Kole and be done with it. At least then, I'll have done everything I could to help solve the case, and I can wash my hands of Black Harbor and its victims.

Of course, he's already here.

Just seeing his vehicle makes my muscles stiffen. I don't want to get out. But I have to. I think of Jordan McAllister blue and ravaged by rigor mortis, lying atop soiled Chinese food containers and diapers. I think of Anya Brown, whose parents found her catatonic on her bedroom floor. I think of Sarah Dylan desperately pressing a towel to her throat to stop the blood from gushing, staining her skin and soaking into the carpet. If there's anything I can do to point police in the right direction of who put them there, I have to do it.

But there's something else I need to do first. I glance at my reflection in the rearview mirror. Jesus, I look like hell. *Couldn't have grabbed some concealer or mascara on your way out, Hazel?* Whatever. This is me, naked and raw and real, and he doesn't have to like me.

I march toward Kole's black SUV parked along the curb. My boots splash in the puddles of snowmelt that fill the pockmarks and craters of the asphalt. It's atypically warm for February—has been for the past couple of days. Even the porch of the duplex seems to have sunk lower from the ground thawing.

I tap Kole's window. I can barely see him through the tint. He stares beyond me, eyes on the duplex. *Tap, tap, tap.* Again.

The glass slides down beneath my knuckle. He's wearing the same backward cap he wore when he met me at the hotel, the one I tore off his head and tossed aside when he picked me up and brought me to the bed. How things have changed in just two weeks. Imploded, more like. He looks like he hasn't shaved for a few days. Amid the blond, flecks of silver glint like shrapnel. Damn, he looks good.

"Don't think I haven't seen you," I tell him.

"Don't think I care," he says without even tilting his chin toward me.

At my sides, my hands form into fists. "Well, you can go on and get outta here."

His mouth twitches slightly. "This isn't up north, Hazel. You can't just tell me to go on and git."

"There's nothing here for you. If you're after Tommy—"

"I'm good enough to fuck. I'm good enough to drag through the dirt in a goddamn manuscript." Finally, he tears his gaze away from the duplex to drill into me. "But I'm not good enough for you to tell me that you live next to the guy who ripped off a dead kid's finger? The same guy, mind you, who had a connection to Candy Man, who was selling oxys to my dead CI? That's cold, Hazel. Even for you. Now you can tell me to leave. You can tell me to go jump off the bridge or eat lead or whatever you want me to—"

I wince. Did a door just slam? I turn around, but there's no one on the porch. The duplex and everything around it looks as still as an oil painting.

"—but I've got a job to do. There's something going on between these walls"—he points his first and second finger at each of the front doors—"and I'm gonna sit here and watch until I see what it is." He looks at the clock on his dash. His voice is lower than it was a few seconds before. "You've got about nine minutes until your husband gets home."

I fight the urge to kick his fender. He's right. I have less than ten minutes to get my shit and get gone. "You leave first." I don't have time for games. But the more I stand here and talk to him—even if we're arguing—the more chance there is of us coming to a resolution. Of one of us saying I'm sorry.

"I was just on my way to pick up Riley for an autopsy anyway," he says.

The mention of another woman stings. I know she's his colleague and yet, he hadn't been too hesitant to start something with me, the transcriber downstairs. Although, I'd been the one to start it, hadn't I? Volunteering myself to sneak into Krejarek's apartment and find the satchel. But he'd kissed me. And I hadn't stopped him. Well, I had once, but I'd gone right back in. None of it matters anymore. I'm leaving.

"Don't care," I say, and stalk off toward the duplex. My ears prick at the sound of his tires shushing over the asphalt. I don't need to look to know that he's gone. I can feel it. His absence is palpable. The silence of it descends so heavily upon me, it presses me down on the disintegrating stairs so they creak beneath my weight. It feels like I'm sinking with it, the walls bowing, the roof concaving until the whole thing folds inward and devours me like a pearl in a clamshell.

My key still works to get in. The door opening sounds like the whine of a wounded animal. Wide-eyed, I leer from corner to corner, checking to see if Tommy's waiting for me again. The couch in the living room is empty. The TV is shut off, the remote on the cheap end table. Three empty beer bottles sit on the floor like bowling pins.

My footsteps echo off the plaster walls. The place feels vacant, even though his tactical backpack sits on the chair. The table's clear for once, I notice—guns and outdoor magazines stacked neatly in the middle like a centerpiece. I leave the packet of divorce papers there, already hating myself for the expression I imagine on his face the moment he walks in and sees them.

My phone isn't there. I walk through the kitchen. The floor creaks loudly beneath me as though warning of an intruder. There are dirty cereal bowls by the sink, a pizza box sprinkled with Parmesan crumbs, more beer bottles lining the counter. No phone.

I think back to our last encounter, when he surprised me. He'd tossed my phone on the ottoman. I cut through the hall between the stairs and the living room, passing the blood-spattered register, and find it there, lying faceup where Tommy left it. It would be like him to torture himself with its presence. I press the home button. Dead. I plug it in in the kitchen while I tread upstairs to grab the last of my things. Books, clothes, shoes. I stuff everything I can into a basket—silently apologizing for now having taken two of two laundry baskets—and head down the stairs. I leave the gallery wall untouched. There isn't a single photo I want. I wish they weren't there—happy faces watching, judging as I take what's mine.

My phone turns on again. It's up to 8 percent battery life. Enough to text Kole the photos and block him from my contacts. I shove it in the side pocket of my leggings and, as I do, I notice Tommy's hunting knife in the sink. I stop, and stare at it. A collage of images scatters through my mind: rows of smallmouth bass filleted like Tyler Krejarek had been at the edge of the river; Tommy's hands holding a rabbit by its feet, its throat cut like Sarah Dylan's had been; the stripe of blood across his boot when he told me I would never leave Black Harbor.

Alive. That's the word he'd omitted.

I have to get out of here. Now.

Shifting the basket onto my hip, I open the door with one hand. A book topples out, hitting the floor with a loud *thwack*! I leave it. On the porch, now, I check my surroundings. The driveway is still empty. Tommy isn't back yet, though what I wouldn't give to jump into the back seat of Kole's SUV and urge him to step on the gas. But I'd had to chase him away, too.

Something shatters.

It might as well be the crack of a gunshot. I jolt so hard that more books spill from the basket. Glancing down, I see the clay shards of a flowerpot. A mess of long-dead leaves, dried-up soil, and crushed cigarette butts lie amid the debris. I bend down and retrieve one of the white-and-tan stubs. Pinching it between my thumb and index finger, I hold it close to my face and read the print just below the filter: *Newport*.

I turn my head ever so slightly to look at Old Will's window. The shades are drawn. There's no one there, yet. If Will heard the pot break, either he or Sam will be out in a few seconds. I spring to my feet and start down the porch, realizing when I get to my Blazer that I forgot the keys on the table.

"No."

I pat my pocket and feel the reassuring shape of my phone. My ears pull back to the sound of a lock being clicked back, and I bolt. Across the street. Down the hill to the running trail. The ground sucks at my soles like it's made of leeches. The muck squelches with each step I manage, kicking up wet leaves in my wake. A root pops up and nearly trips me. I leap over it and land in a frigid puddle. The water is at least shin-deep.

I look up toward the top of the hill, half expecting to see a silhouette. But there's no one. Realizing the smoked Newport is still in my hand, I take out my phone and snap a photo. Before I can talk myself out of it, I text it to Kole.

I catch my breath as I watch the blue bar crawl to the edge of the screen. Sent.

He texts back immediately. *Where are you?*

I send him a second photo, this time of the reflections in the flooded trail, at the upside-down trees with their branches stretching down instead of up, the clouds above swirling like nimbus plumes. The way the path disappears reminds me of the piers that vanish into Lake Michigan. It's as though all possible ways out of Black Harbor result in a dead end.

Duplex, I text. *Across the street.*

Rain starts to fall. I wonder if I should try to sneak back into the duplex to grab my keys and drive off. Or if I should continue to the police department and get a ride. I know I'll come out behind Forge Bridge. It isn't far.

Ripples form in the pool at my feet, distorting the reflections of the trees, making them fracture and come back together. I'll have to head back.

I feel his text like a pulse. *Run.*

I stand still, like a deer that suspects it's in a hunter's crosshairs. I quell my breathing. My eyes scan right to left. The clearing is vacant, and then I see something move in the water. I veer closer to observe, when suddenly, my feet lift off the ground and I'm thrown face-first into the pool. My teeth bite into the earth. I taste blood first, then feel a searing pain in my ribs. I start to turn over and a force above me pushes my head back down. My cheekbone hits the edge of submerged asphalt, sending a rocket of pain through my skull. I could drown, I think, terrified. What's got me, a dog?

Underwater, crushed in my fist, my phone rings. Kole must be calling me. I fight to get up, to accept the call so he can at least hear the sounds of my struggle, when the phone is ripped from my hand. The motion pulls my head out of the water, long enough that I can gather enough air to scream. I scream until I feel light-headed, and when I've expelled the last bit of breath from my lungs, my vision dims to black. The last sensory perception I have is the musty smell of wet and rotting leaves before I'm dragged off the trail.

• • •

I wake moments later to a familiar scratching noise. It's like a fingernail scraping inside my ear. *Scritch, scritch, scratch.*

All the afternoons I've woken up feeling as though I've been hit by a train are nothing in comparison to the way I feel now. I feel as though I've been struck by a meteor and plowed six hundred feet underground with the weight of the earth crushing my skull. I must have vomited while I was out, because the pungent reek of it prompts me to do so again. I can only dry heave.

Something tugs at my leggings. Oh God.

A capsule of dread opens inside of me. *This is what Mona warned you about, Hazel. Stay off the trail. You never fucking listen.*

The tugging stops and there it is again. *Scritch, scritch, scratch.* I inhale sharply, painfully, and force myself to partially sit up. I see dark, scraggly hair and even darker eyes, and I'm suddenly jolted by a shock of recognition.

"Sam?" My voice sounds as though I've eaten a handful of dirt. I probably have. I give him a quick once-over. His clothes are mottled and wet. He looks worse since the last time I saw him, when Kole tossed him out of the police department, like a corpse that's started decomposing into the earth, and here I came along and interrupted him.

Scritch, scritch, scratch. He scratches himself so vigorously, scraping what's left of his blunted fingernails up and down his forearms, digging into the back of his neck as though trying to gouge out an unwanted implant.

His eyes widen at the sound of his name. Darting from left to right, they finally rest on me.

I try to move, but the sharp pain in my side forces me to stay put, lying like a wounded animal off the beaten path. My eyes search the leaves for my phone. Blind hands feeling the earth, hoping to connect with its smooth glass surface.

His hands are streaked with blood, I notice, when he waggles my phone in front of me. Horror grips me even harder.

"Sam, why?"

He starts to sing. At first, it just sounds like mad mumblings, but after a few words, I discern a melody that prickles my flesh. ". . . and make a groovy lemon pie, the Candy Man . . ." He snickers. "The Candy Man can!"

I gasp, suddenly paralyzed by my imagined nightmares: the corpses of all the children who overdosed, licking the powder off their blue lips like sugar. Sarah Dylan dragging a finger through the blood on her neck and painting a crimson smile over her colorless mouth. Tyler Krejarek sitting up on the riverbank, stuffing his intestines back in. "You're not Candy Man—"

He rolls his eyes. "No. She was."

"She?"

He hikes up the sleeve of his grungy sweatshirt to reveal a tattoo of a cartoonish clamshell and pearl. It matches the style of the one I'd glimpsed on his wrist a few weeks ago, which I see, now, is a blue piece of candy.

"Pearl?" I ask.

He grins, flashing yellowed canines. And then, with a grimace, he starts to mutter. "Get her before she gets you. Get her before she gets you. She screwed me over. She screwed me over hard, she didn't have to do that." He slaps his face, leaving a soiled handprint, then he pushes his fingers into his hair and yells. The veins in his neck pop. When he looks at me again, his eyes are red. "Women are wicked, aren't they? You should know. I loved her, I really did, that's why I gave them to her because she said she needed 'em. I didn't know she was selling to Tyler and he was givin' 'em to that kid and I dragged him out to the dumpster and now here we all are."

I see him as I saw him that morning, when he came up to the Transcribing window with Jordan McAllister's severed finger, and I realize he did it all on purpose. He wanted to establish himself as a victim, being coerced by Krejarek. He wanted to follow the case as closely as possible. It worked.

"She was a secret agent. Working for that detective. I couldn't find the wire, but she had a wire. I wasn't even selling 'em to her." He *pfts*. "I *gave* 'em to her to help her out. Stole 'em from my old man and then when I'd see how much horrible pain he'd be in and he'd be out of pills . . ." He starts to sob like he did in the interview room, before Kole tossed him out on his ass.

Sarah Dylan. My fingers twitch with the memory of typing Kole's report. The pills poured out onto the bed. The ragged black sweatshirt on the floor. The smears of blood on the walls and soaking into the carpet where she was found. I can still see the text message thread between Pearl and who we thought then was Krejarek. *Got any blues?* she'd asked.

It was Sam, after all. The blue candy emoji she'd had in lieu of his name in her phone matches the tattoo on his wrist. He'd stolen oxys from Old Will's medicine cabinet and given them to Pearl—Candy Man. She'd double-crossed Kole pretty good.

And Sam, apparently.

"Get her before she gets you." He squints, trying to see through his tears. "Get her before she gets you. She was gonna sell me out. She sold out her old man. Why not me?" He advances toward me.

"I'm not her, Sam! You know me!"

"I know you've been fuckin' that same cop. You got the wire now and you're gonna get me." He pulls a knife from behind his back.

I scream, but no sound comes out. He's cut off my air, squeezing his sinewy hand around my windpipe. My feet slide in the mud as I fight to put inches between me and him. I wonder how I'll be found. Someone walking their dog will find me, probably, and I'll be swabbed for DNA and zipped into a body bag by Riley the Reaper. I wonder if anyone will know to tell Kole about me, or if he'll have to find out on his own. And after, like a month from now when my body's been folded into a neat little box, I wonder if Elle will keep photos of me on her walls. I wonder if the memory of me will keep Kole awake at night, haunt him as I have all this time since he ran after me on the bridge.

I catch a flash of the knife gripped in his hand and my leg flares with the sensation of flesh tearing. I cry out.

He yanks my clothes. Rips my shirt. I don't even feel the cold anymore, just the sharp edge of the blade as he tells it which way to slice. The freezing cold water envelops me, numbs me, as he drags me in. All those times I stood on Forge Bridge, wondering what dying feels like. Now I know.

Fighting to breathe, I plunge my hand into the freezing water, searching blindly beneath the leaves until I grip a loose piece of broken asphalt. I pick it up and smash it as hard as I can into his eye socket. He stumbles backward and I seize the opportunity to hurl myself to my feet, gasping as my own ribs feel like they're stabbing through my abdomen. I run as fast as I can to where the trees begin to clear, where I know the trail wends its way to Forge Bridge.

Sam's close behind me. Even injured I'm faster than he is, though my vision's beginning to eclipse again. But not before I see the bridge. My black beacon. If I can just make it out of the trees, someone will see me.

I hope.

My lungs and calves burning, the gash in my leg sucking in the frigid air, and rain pelting my face like translucent bullets, I push myself as fast as I can muster. The last bit of my energy propels me into the clearing and into the lot where I've parked so many times.

The railroad ties are beneath my feet before I realize it. I slip, and cling to the railing. Beneath me, the river roils. His footsteps send vibrations through my bones. Sam's caught up to me. He smiles like he's just won a race.

I start seeing spots, like acid eating through a photograph. I don't want my murderer to be the last thing I see. On the other side of the bridge, where I've never made it, there's a small spruce tree. I stare at it through a curtain of rain and wait for it all to end: the pain, the fear, the guilt at disappointing everyone I've ever cared about, when suddenly, I'm jarred by a crack so loud it sounds like the world is splintering.

I know the sound of a gunshot.

Four more pop off in quick succession. My ears ring.

I watch in shock as Sam's body dances, suddenly riddled with bullet holes. He stumbles one way, then looks as though he's going to fall on top of me. I hold my arms out to stop him. He scratches at me, his eyes wild, pleading. A scream tears through my throat as I rouse the last bit of my strength to push him over the railing. His body plunges into the water like an exclamation point.

I hear footsteps running onto the bridge then, and before I fade out of consciousness, the voice that was the beginning and end of everything.

30.
SATURDAY

The wedding party disperses like florets blown from a dandelion and I am left standing alone, on a warm June night, beneath a canopy of small lighted globes on the vineyards's patio. They drape from rustic posts, their bulbs clear, low-hanging fruits. Each glass capsule is filled with beads of condensation that look like stars. I touch a manicured hand to my cheek to wipe away the kiss Elle planted a moment ago and observe my nails as I have probably a dozen times since getting them done. Simple, elegant French tips. I won't keep up with them, but going to the salon with her and Mom was, surprisingly, a pleasant experience. Maybe I could do it once or twice a year.

A rhythm bounces out of the reception hall as someone opens the door. I feel the music pulse against the soles of my feet. The drinks are flowing. It's only a matter of time until Elle and Kinney perform their crowd-favorite "Summer Nights" duet.

I think back to just four months ago, when I awoke in the hospital to Detective Amarillo showing a photograph. Once I saw the face in the water, I couldn't unsee it. He was more still than the pool itself, camouflaged amid tall grass and tree branches, poised like a snake ready to strike.

"Did you take this photo?" Amarillo asked. He had severe cheekbones and pitch-black hair. I didn't know him. The badge over his heart identified him as being from a neighboring jurisdiction. It would have been a conflict of interest for a Black Harbor investigator to lead their own officer-involved shooting case.

"Yes," I replied, holding the printout of the image I'd sent to Kole seconds before the attack. Zoomed in to a small section of the photo, among the crosshatching of branches distorted by the water's reflection, Sam's face was visible.

"You know this photo probably saved your life, right? That and Investigator Riley's impeccable aim."

He wasn't wrong about that. I saw the photos where Sam had been dealt three entry wounds to the chest, and one final hole in his forehead. So, it had been the two of them—Riley and Kole—just as I'd thought in those moments when everything had been fractured and fading. I couldn't be sure what had been real and what had been figments of my imagination. I remembered, though, the arrhythmic sounds of footsteps pounding on the railroad ties and the feeling of weightlessness when Kole picked me up.

"He told me he stole the pills from his dad," I said.

Detective Amarillo nodded.

"He just gave them to her? Why?"

"People do crazy shit for love." He laughed when I asked if he'd stitch that onto a pillow for me. "Kole was close to having the whole thing figured out," he added. "He knew Tyler Krejarek had supplied the oxys to that kid, but he didn't know his own CI was the source."

I thought back to the conversation we found in Pearl's phone the night her body was discovered. *Got any blues?* When Kole and I assumed she'd been asking Krejarek for pills, she'd really been asking Sam. He'd stolen the oxycodone from his dad, packaged them in a Newport cigarette box, and given them to her. She'd turned around and sold the pills to Krejarek, who gave them to Jordan McAllister. What she hadn't sold to Krejarek, she'd sold to Anya Brown, who overdosed two days later.

"So Candy Man had, in fact, been Candy Woman."

I spent six days in the hospital, after. My mom flew in from Phoenix and my dad drove from up north. Elle was there most days, and Tommy stopped by just to drop off the signed divorce papers. He didn't beg me to come back, and it was probably the first time in our marriage I truly respected him.

Some days I'm convinced it had all been a dream. That everyone—Kole, Riley, Sam, Old Will, Pearl, Krejarek, Liv, Mona, even Tommy—were nothing more than fictional characters. That I had lied to myself, perhaps just to escape the mundanity of my life, written a novel in my head that no one would ever read. The scar is evidence that it was all real, though. It runs from my thigh to the bend of my knee, raised to resemble a wire, like the kind Sam had been looking for when he attacked me in the woods. I shiver, thinking about all the times I'd spent alone with just a wall between me and Sam, not knowing his plans. The night he'd stolen into my bed, pretending to be too high to function. When I closed my eyes, I saw his bodiless Cheshire cat smile, like when he'd sit in the glow of the television, and I recognized, now, his amusement at being always one step ahead of me.

I feel weightless again as the breeze swims through the patio, catching the gossamer-light fabric of my mint dress, and carrying with it the scent of flowers and something else, sandalwood and sage? I'm taken back to a night less than six months ago, when I breathed him in for the first time as we stared through the blinds at a row of apartments that don't exist anymore.

"Hey."

My breath hitches at the sound of his voice. The globes above me still like suspended raindrops and the warm wind pauses. Even the music subsides to create a pocket of silence. I turn to see Nikolai Kole standing in front of an ivy-covered wall. In his arms is a kraft-paper box with a yellow ribbon securing its lid. Looking closer, I see that the ribbon is actually caution tape.

"Your sister let me in," he says, answering a question I never asked.

I look him up and down, from his polished black shoes to his navy-blue uniform. Three winged chevron patches adorn each sleeve. A gold badge is fastened over his heart, his nameplate above his right breast pocket. "Sergeant Kole," I read. "So you passed your promotional test."

He shrugs. For the first time since I've known him, he's completely clean-shaven. His mouth offers an ephemeral peek of that off-kilter smile. "Did you ever doubt me?"

There are so many words I want to say, but all the ones I've rehearsed collide like butterflies in my chest, beating torn and fragile wings against one another. I want to touch him to make sure he's real. Instead, I cross my arms. "The gift table's inside."

He glances down at the package he's holding. "It's for you, actually. Sorry, I . . . um . . . didn't have any ribbon. Or gift wrap. It's not really a gift, I guess. It's yours—"

Unless it's my dignity back, I don't want it. "Word on the street is you were on leave again. Because of the shooting and all."

He looks embarrassed. I wonder how many times it's been brought up by now. "What version did you hear?"

"All of 'em. So, Riley the Reaper reigns again."

He laughs. "That should be a headline."

"You know, your track record's not much cleaner."

"Sshhh." The mischievous sparkle in his eyes reminds me of old times. "I like to fly under the radar." He takes a step closer and, instantly, I detect fissures in my tough outer shell. I feel lighter as pieces of it fall away. Like the bridge shedding its exoskeleton. All those times it could have killed me and in the end, it helped save me.

"Well, you're doing a shit job of it." I smile.

He does, too, but his expression sobers almost instantly. "You left."

I nod. I returned for a handful of shifts after I was cleared to go back to work, but I couldn't sit by that window. Every time the printer hummed or someone was in the lot scraping their windshield, I swore Sam would be standing there, watching me. And then there was Kole. I knew when he returned to work, I would inevitably send him a message and jump into blissful purgatory with him again. We're both junkies and each other's fixes. I would waste away in Black Harbor forever with him.

"I went home," I say.

"Good for you."

The words feel like screws tightening. I wish he would say something else, ask me to stay. But he knows better. And yet, when I look at him, he has a genuine soft smile again. That hurts even more.

"Thanks," I say quietly. He doesn't ask what I'm doing in the meantime, and there's no point in telling him that Elle helped me get a freelance job writing advertisements for 95.9, which in turn led to other work, like more advertisements, blogs, articles, you name it. It seems I've found a way to keep pretty busy while living at the northern edge of civilization. And, since getting a new cohost—Chad didn't last long—her show's ratings are almost back up to where they were in the *Elle & Kinney* days.

There's no point in telling him about my divorce, either. I'd only just turned in the paperwork at the courthouse when word of it spread like wildfire around the PD. I think Liv has a permanent smirk on her face now.

"So did she go back home or what?" I ask. I received word of his situation in the same fashion. Mona still texts me updates with occasional gossip.

He shifts his stance, swaying slightly. He holds the package with one arm, now, and tucks his left hand into his pocket. "Yeah, she did."

"Why?"

"Why wouldn't she? I came clean about everything. First time in my life I've ever done that. She didn't take it too well." He sighs so heavily his shoulders rise and fall. Then, he looks down as though remembering the package in his hands and reoffers it to me.

I take it, eyeing him as I tug at one end of the caution tape. The knot comes undone and the ribbon falls away. He steps on it so it doesn't blow across the vineyard. I remove the lid, sliding it beneath the bottom of the box. Inside is a stack of rippled pages. The ink is smeared and blotched, each letter accompanied by its own ghost. And yet, the type is mostly legible. I read a line I've read a hundred times: *I stare at a row of blue apartments across the street. They're almost lost to a beryl-colored sky . . .*

Tears well in my eyes. "How did you get this?" Now that I have my manuscript back, I'm reluctant to ever let it go again.

"I went back to the bridge that day, after you left. Some of the pages had clung to the bridge, others were in the water or scattered on the bank. I think I got most of them. I figured . . . you know, you might want them. Eventually. I didn't read it. I didn't feel like that would be right—"

"Thank you."

I throw my arms around him. I can lose myself just for a moment with him again, imagining that we are the only two people on earth, lying to ourselves that fate has rewritten it in the stars for us to be together.

I feel the palm of his hand press against my back. "You're welcome."

I step back and hug the rescued manuscript to my chest. I look past him, my eyes following the neat rows of verdant vines until they disappear. The apology that happens next has been a long time coming. "I'm sorry," I say. "I was out of my mind, I think, when I convinced myself that you were behind the murders of Pearl and Krejarek."

Kole shrugs. "Black Harbor will do that to you. And, to be honest, you had a pretty compelling argument. I would have looked into me, too."

"I was so sure that it was Krejarek I saw coming off the trail that night."

"I was, too. Now you know why eyewitness accounts aren't the most reliable. We see what we want to see."

"And we don't see what we don't want to see."

"Exactly."

"So Sam jumped Krejarek on his way back from the pharmacy?"

Kole nods. "A junkie's gonna get his fix, whatever it takes. He'd already killed Krejarek and stolen his pills by the time he emerged into the lot."

Sam had seen Kole and me together. And that's how he'd come to the conclusion that I was Kole's new informant. My heart rate quickens when my memory unearths images from that night. Or perhaps it has something to do with the space lessening between us right now.

"After we found you, we raided his place. We found his father's prescription bottles of oxycodone, some weed, and Sam's cell phone, which, when I downloaded it the next day, it corroborated everything including his relationship with Pearl. Her music box being in his room was the coup de grâce."

"Music box? The one that Dylan found the heroin in?"

"The same one. Sam must have taken it the night he killed her. Something to remember her by, I suppose." He shakes his head. "My own CI was a murderer. She dealt the pills that killed Jordan McAllister and Anya Brown. Who knows how many other close calls there were." His shoulders fall, guilt visibly weighing on him.

"Sam said he loved her," I say, validating Kole's story.

"He did. It's what killed him in the end, too. Pearl was a two-timing dealer. She wanted to make sure we nailed Krejarek for the delivery, which goes back to why she texted me about him hiding his stash in the walls. I have to admit, sixteen years in law enforcement and I've never been played like that before. If Sam hadn't cracked, I don't know that we'd have ever figured it out. I really thought he was just . . . messed up."

"So did I," I admit. "Was Krejarek in love with Pearl, too?"

"He was more in love with the Candy Man legend she created. He was pretty pleased with the fact that we thought it was him. At the end of the day, he was just a cockroach sharing his prescription pills with minors, and whenever he ran out and was afraid his friends would stop coming around, he'd buy off the real Candy Man. Or trade with her. He had enough other shit."

I think back to finding the satchel in the wall and Kole dumping all of its contents into the sink. There had been everything from sleeping pills to narcotics, pipes, tobacco papers, and more. Everything except the oxycodone, which had been found in a Newport cigarette box beneath the couch cushion.

A sudden breeze brings a chill. I hug both arms around myself again, my fingertips touching my rib cage. Kole touches my hand, slowly guiding it away from me, twining his fingers with mine.

"Tell me something confidential," I whisper.

"Anything?" He stands still for a moment. I can see the setting sun in his eyes, and with his silhouette rimmed in gold, I see how fearlessly he's been made, sculpted by the city that almost decimated me. "I hate you, and I'm going to miss you terribly."

A tear falls from my lashes. I smile. "Hate you more."

Not too far away, the door opens and music spills out of the reception hall. My cousin Liza calls out my name. They're cutting the cake soon.

I wave to her and look at Kole. Exhale.

"Well, you know how it ends, now," he says after a moment. His voice has that subtle serrated edge again that I fell in love with. "You should finish it."

How it ends. He's right. This is how it ends. Where he and I end, for now. We are two halves of a sentence, split by a set of em dashes. It's been written on his face all along. The circumflex scar on his cheek that I'd once convinced myself was a symbol of his not belonging in Black Harbor, I know, now, is really a mark of his not belonging with me.

Linking my littlest finger with his, I promise: "I will."

ACKNOWLEDGMENTS

Writing often gets a reputation for being a lonely endeavor. But it really isn't. Because if it were, books wouldn't have acknowledgments filled with all the people who helped make them happen.

The first of these instrumental people for *Hello, Transcriber* is my literary agent and fellow Barnes & Noble veteran, Sharon Pelletier. Sharon, your thoughtfulness and commitment to every word on every page is beyond anything I could have hoped for. Thank you for trusting me and talking me off the proverbial ledge more times than I've kept count.

Without Sharon, I never would have been connected with my fantastic editor, Leslie Gelbman; her assistant, Lisa Bonvissuto; Joe Brosnan; Kayla Janis; and the entire team at St. Martin's Publishing Group/Minotaur Books. Leslie, your surefootedness, encouragement, and vote of confidence are invaluable. I love our phone conversations.

To all the bibliophiles, bookstagrammers, booksellers, book clubbers, book lenders, and book reviewers—thank you. Without your love of books, there would be no publishing industry. This includes my BN friends from over the years, especially Kevin, Amy, and Tim: ever since

I started shelving books in 2011, it's been my dream to one day see my own in the *Discover New Writers* bay. Thank you for your encouragement, your enthusiasm, and for helping me make it happen. Of course, my BN experience wouldn't have been the same without my BFFF, Becca. You are the second breakfast to my elevenses.

To all of my family and friends who always believed I would get here, even when I wasn't so sure. Mom, Dad, Grandma, my sisters: April, Elizabeth, Lily, and especially Miranda, who responds to novel-length text messages with no shortage of gifs and great ideas. And to H, for being my partner in wine and true crime, and for living across the woods that inspired Hazel's creepy running trail.

Among friends are early readers of this novel: Nicole Sharon-Schultz, Alaxandra Rutella, and my longtime critique partner, Alissa Stormont. I appreciate your honesty, your input, and your time. To my fellow Savages: for being the first to call me "writer"; and to every author who penned a thoughtful quote: Thank you for taking time away from your own books to read mine. I hope I'm called upon someday to return the favor.

What writer would be complete without her writer's group? Allied Authors of Wisconsin, you guys are the best. A special thank-you to David Michael Williams, for inviting me and for having the uncanny ability to pinpoint when I should have ended a chapter two sentences sooner.

This story wouldn't exist at all if not for my police family. Some years ago, you welcomed me into your world. Thank you for your service.

My trusty pugs, Griswold and Muffins, you are the best companions anyone could ever ask for—even when you snore like diesel engines. Thanks for doing the 5 a.m. wake-up call with me.

Lastly, to Hanns. For all the *tell me something confidentials*, pinky promises, and helping me connect the dots. I love you more than words.

Turn the page for a sneak peek at
Hannah Morrissey's new novel

Available Fall 2022

Copyright © 2022 by Hannah Morrissey

1

MORGAN

The key was a blackened talisman, tucked into her leather cuff. She'd gotten in the habit of keeping it there since it had become the only tangible thing she owned when, three months ago, her entire life was reduced to ash and ruin. The fire department had already come and gone by the time she arrived, her boots crunching on caramelized glass and stepping over hissing metal. Everything was wet and charred—mannequins with their faces melted in, the once larger-than-life Mylar tree shriveled to a root—which meant that whoever had left the key had watched and waited, like a tiger stalking its prey. But Morgan knew better. Only humans tortured their food before eating it.

A red balloon floated in the sulfurous haze, tethered to a small, coffin-shaped box set on a step of the smoldering staircase. A simple note scratched on the back of an envelope revealed it was for her: *My Ruin: All roads lead back to home.*

A puff of vapor escaped her lips—a silent scream, perhaps, at the omen from beyond the grave. The only person who would have used that moniker was dead. The last image Morgan had of her aunt Bern was of her lying faceup with her skull shattered on the concrete, mouth open to catch snowflakes. It was one of few childhood memories she hadn't overwritten. Rather, she kept it sequestered in a safe place so she could recall it at will, the way normal people preserved memories of their wedding day or the moment their first child was born.

Now, standing on the Reynoldses' back porch, she turned her wrist and pressed her thumb to the key, tempted to free it from its holster. The iron stung. The key would not fit, she determined, as she considered the aperture in the ornate metal plate.

All roads lead back to home.

This was not her home. If the sea glass–colored mansion at the top of the bluff hadn't tipped her off on her drive in, then the twelve-foot-tall Gothic gate that swung inward to grant her entrance to the estate made damn sure she knew she wasn't on her side of the tracks anymore. This was Reynolds country, she'd thought, following the cobblestone path that wended past topiaries draped in white lights and a pair of concrete tigers, their faces frozen in midroar and thick necks wrapped in festive, Fair Isle scarves. Then, she'd parked her salty little Honda Civic next to a newly waxed Land Rover and felt more than a little inadequate.

The Reynolds family was enshrouded in wealth, status, and mystery, and Black Harbor's entire eroding shoreline belonged to them. What remained of it, anyway. Over the past decade or more, Lake Michigan had eaten away the limestone as effectively as the city's grim atmosphere gnawed on people's morals. If they'd had morals to begin with. In her thirty-one years on this planet—most of them spent here in this frozen purgatory—Morgan had learned that some people were born purely and inherently evil. And Black Harbor was their breeding ground.

Morgan surveyed the snow-covered estate. Giant red bulbs hung from evergreen boughs, and three wreaths decorated the middle tier of a stone fountain. A lone lamppost wore a gold velvet bow and to her left, fairy lights twinkled as they wove through the crosshatched trellis that would work well for group photos. It was creeping up on two o'clock. The golden hour would be here soon, when the sun was low and its amber hues came alive to brush its subjects' skin tones with a warm glow. She raised her camera, snapped a test shot, and returned her attention to the door. Her worries melted away. It was just her and the keyhole. She felt the autofocus lock into place and took a photo. She could add it to her collection—the one she'd started since inheriting the key—of all the doors and their corresponding keyholes into which it didn't fit.

Not terribly unlike herself.

Pierced and gangly with a death stare that could intimidate a bull, Morgan didn't really fit anywhere, either.

Except The Ruins. She'd fit there. And then it all burned down.

Morgan considered the keyhole again and sucked in a breath. This wasn't home and yet, was it so wrong that she wished it was? That her childhood had been spent here, running free through an orchard and pushing siblings on a front porch swing; not curled up on the floor, left to lick her wounds like a dog and pray her door remained closed until morning.

A gust of wind came and pulled tears from her eyes. She repositioned her gear bag slung on her shoulder and, turning her back to the wind, slid the key out of her cuff. It didn't hurt to try. With the key pinched between her thumb and forefinger, she reached forward, when the door fell away. The woman who appeared behind it was so beautiful it hurt, Morgan thought, as she took in her verdant eyes and the short layers of russet hair that framed her face. She looked surprised, and Morgan suspected she hadn't anticipated someone who looked like her—dressed all in black, with a pierced septum and two studs in her bottom lip, skin pale as the Ghost of Christmas Past—to be standing on her doorstep.

"Oh!" she exclaimed. "You must be the photographer! Morgan, right?" She shifted the chubby-cheeked toddler she was holding to her other hip. It stared at Morgan in that unapologetic way that babies do. Morgan estimated 1.2 seconds before the drool on its lip froze into a "spitcicle."

She nodded and slid her key back into her cuff. Later.

"I'm Cora." The woman smiled, showing teeth brighter than fresh-fallen snow. Her lips were painted holly red, the same shade as her knit, short-sleeved sweater. Goose bumps stippled her arms. "And this is Charlie. We were just about to get Mamó some ginger ale, weren't we, Charlie?" Her voice pitched and fell. How easily some people could slip in and out of baby talk, Morgan mused, and she wondered, was *Mamó* some type of nickname for Mom? Grandma? Just like *Omi, Oma, Nana, Yamma,* and the cringey-beyond-all-get-out *Glamma*?

When Cora leaned over to grab a six-pack of cans resting atop a resin storage chest, Morgan stopped her. "I'll get them."

"Thank you," Cora said, speaking like an adult again. "Come in, please. My mom will be so excited that you're here. You're her gift," she added with a quick glance over her shoulder.

Morgan scrunched her brows. A gift? She'd never been anyone's gift before, and yet, perhaps that was how the people who'd paid her aunt had looked at her—a guilty little pleasure they'd never tell a soul about. Her throat felt dry. She licked her lips, tempted to suck down one of those ginger ales. Being back here had that effect on her. One breath of Black Harbor was potent enough to turn her devil-may-care armor brittle. She imagined watching it disintegrate and fall away like fish scales, leaving her raw and exposed while she served herself on a silver platter to the black widow of Black Harbor: Mrs. Eleanor Reynolds, whose husband, Clive, vanished twenty years ago. Eleanor was the obvious suspect, and according to the court of public opinion, she was guilty as sin. The eleven-million-dollar life insurance policy she'd taken out on Clive just weeks before his death had been, for all intents and purposes, her hand hammering the nail in his coffin. And he'd had an affair. Which meant he'd pounded the final nail in himself.

Morgan's ears pricked at the sound of the door closing behind her. Noting that Cora wore only Fair Isle stockings, she heel-toed her combat boots off in a mudroom she doubted had ever seen a speck of mud. Plus, it was larger than the space she'd recently moved back into at her parents' house. She set the ginger ale on a bench to straighten the tops of her stockings, making them even, and hung her jacket on an empty hook. Her glasses fogged.

"Mom," Cora called. Her voice carried through the kitchen, rose, and dissipated somewhere between the hardwood floors and the cathedral ceiling. "Morgan is here!"

Following cautiously in Cora's wake, Morgan set the cans of ginger ale on a granite countertop and waited. A current swam through the great room, fragrant with cloves and thyme and buttery croissants. It smelled of roast beef, too, and seasoned potatoes. The countertop boasted a trove of mini mince pies and single-serve sherry trifles. Adjusting her camera settings, Morgan took a few photos to show her mom the spread. Up until six months ago, when the highway construction shut it down, Lynette's Linzers—her mother's bakery—had been a beloved staple of Black Harbor, serving homemade cookies, tarts, and biscuits on the daily. Now, it was simply one of dozens of vacant storefronts.

Over the home's surround-sound system, a slow piano melody melted into a chorus of accordion, flute, and bagpipes. As the song picked up, Morgan recognized it as "Fairytale of New York," by the Pogues, and smiled.

Where was everyone, she wondered. Cora had gone and disappeared with Charlie down a corridor, and aside from someone who was clearly a caterer coming to check the oven, there wasn't a soul in sight. Had she gotten the time wrong? No, the email had stated two o'clock. She'd read it again this morning to be sure.

In a mansion this massive, there were a million places people could be hiding.

Morgan looked to her right and surveyed what appeared to be the living room. Overstuffed gray couches that could have swallowed her parents' dinky little sofa formed an L-shape around a glass coffee table. In the corner, between the stone fireplace and a large picture window, stood a tree that had to be fourteen feet tall. Its branches dripped with faux crystalline icicles; expensive-looking ornaments nestled in its boughs, and a glass Swarovski star twinkled at the top. Jesus, had they jacked this tree from Tiffany's?

Her gaze traveling upward and across the ceiling, Morgan noticed a lofted upstairs where all the bedrooms must be. Beneath it, in the wide hall down which Cora had previously vanished, floated a radiant, white-haired woman. She wore an emerald top cinched with a leather corset and flowy sleeves; her smile and socks matched Cora's.

"Uh, hello," said Morgan. "I'm . . . um . . . the photographer?" Her voice trembled. The sight of Eleanor Reynolds, here, in the flesh, had left her dumb.

"Morgan, what a delight." Eleanor beamed, revealing eyeteeth that were sharp, stark white, and perhaps a centimeter too long. Spreading her arms, she welcomed Morgan into a straitjacket hug.

"You must be Eleanor," Morgan said.

"The devil herself." Eleanor raised her hands as though holding up praise.

Eleanor's acknowledgment of her less than savory reputation put Morgan at ease. "Your home is stunning, by the way." Her eyes roamed the four-seasons room and the English-inspired kitchen with marble backsplash. A Prussian-blue china cabinet fit snug in a shallow alcove, holding stemware that undoubtedly cost more than Morgan's entire education. And yet, on the counter beside it was a red rotary telephone. It looked out of place here where everything was modern and cool-toned. Not to mention, who even had a landline anymore?

"Oh, thank you, darling."

"Mom was an interior designer for many years," chimed Cora, who had reappeared, sans Charlie. "A home stager. She even designed sets for Hallmark."

Eleanor rolled her eyes at Cora's praise; nevertheless, she grabbed her daughter's arm and gave an affectionate squeeze. "Puff pieces, dear, honestly. I should have done something important with my career. Cora is a child psychologist."

Morgan lifted her chin as though she cared. She couldn't tell if Eleanor and Cora were displaying genuine admiration for each other, or putting on a show.

"Help yourself, won't you, Morgan?" said Eleanor. "They're setting up food in the dining room. There's wine, beer, cocktails, coffee . . ."

"Nog," suggested Cora.

"Yes, nog," Eleanor repeated. "Make yourself at home, really."

Morgan smiled politely. She'd never heard anyone abbreviate "eggnog" before. The slang made these characters slightly more human. But then, she'd never been told to make herself at home while on the job, either. She was used to shooting cocktail parties and corporate events that took place in warehouses and banquet halls. Never someone's home, and certainly never in a murderess's mansion.

A gentleman between Cora and Eleanor's age swept in. Morgan watched as his hand grazed Eleanor's waist. Eleanor twirled gracefully, turning her body toward his. "Don, darling, this is Morgan, my *gift*. She's our photographer for the evening."

"Oh." Don looked impressed. He had a sophisticated, salt-and-pepper aesthetic. If Morgan had to guess, she'd put him at twenty years younger than Eleanor. *Damn lady, get it,* she applauded silently.

"Pleasure," he said, and offered his hand for her to shake.

The second Morgan offered her hand in return, jingle bells tinkled from down the hall.

The front door opened and Reynolds friends and family members filtered in, all toting decorated sacks and gifts wrapped in kraft paper and twine—ironically rustic. Morgan watched them with shameless fascination. They looked like they'd just stepped off the set of a photo shoot, so cozy in their chunky knit sweaters, moms and daughters wearing matching suede boots, gentlemen in flannel shirts that had never seen the elements for which they were intended. A little blond boy wore a marbled cardigan with elbow patches. Crouching, Morgan snapped several photos as he ran off with his cousins.

There had to be forty people once everyone arrived. Kids crawled beneath tables and thundered up and down the staircase. The clamor of conversation drowned out the Celtic Christmas music. The women clinked their wineglasses. Men guffawed and sipped dark beer. Morgan captured a photo of a freckled girl wearing angel wings and a tinsel halo eating a powdered cookie.

"You know you can eat the food, too. You don't just have to photograph it."

Morgan stood and turned to find the source of the suggestion. A man sat on the sofa, legs casually crossed, clutching a bourbon neat. He looked to be about her age. Early to mid-thirties? There was something about his eyes. Dark like his drink, and salient, they made her feel as though he was looking through her, not at her. She swallowed. What did he see, she wondered. Did her interior—dark and damaged beyond redemption—match her exterior? She hoped it did; enough, at least, so he would stay away. And yet, a quiet voice in her head pleaded for the opposite. Perhaps it was the way he stared through her, or the winsome smile that tugged at the corners of his mouth.

But, she was here on business. "Thanks. I might get a plate later. I was actually eying up the seven-layer bars."

"Want me to get you one?" The man shifted as though to get up. The natural light streaming in from the window subtly illuminated his face so she could see a shallow cleft in his chin, like a thumbprint.

"No, no, I'm good. Thanks, though."

"A drink then?"

She shook her head.

"You think this is one of those fairy places where if you eat the food or drink the wine, you'll have to stay forever?"

"Something like that." You didn't spend your childhood in Black Harbor avoiding cracks in the sidewalk only to be welcomed into the proverbial mansion and eat the food. "I don't drink on the job," she added.

"Because your pictures will be out of focus?" He lifted the glass to his lips. The corner of his mouth ticked upward.

Morgan nodded. "It's a risk I'm not willing to take."

Nor was it a risk she could afford. When she left Chicago with only the key and the clothes on her back, she'd used everything in her bank account to buy a one-way bus ticket to Black Harbor and a professional photographer starter kit—camera body, two lenses, off-camera flash, extra battery pack, the whole shebang. With the rest of her money, she'd purchased the only car her skimpy budget allowed. But, she was debt-free. Not everyone could say that.

"How 'bout after, then?"

Morgan tilted her head, sizing him up. "Anyone ever tell you you're a little forward?"

He laughed, the comment sliding off him like oil on a feather.

Searching for a distraction, Morgan turned and observed the photographs on the mantel, locking on to a portrait of a young Reynolds family. Judging by the scrunchies in the two girls' hair and Clive's color-block vest, it looked to have been taken in the early '90s. There was no denying that Clive was old-Hollywood handsome. He and Eleanor made an attractive couple. The frame was a touch out of line with the others. She nudged it forward, making it straight, when her hopeful suitor came up behind her. He stood close enough that she could feel the heat coming off his skin like she was sitting in front of a crackling fire; smell the sharp, evocative scent of his cologne: bourbon and black ice and a little bit of char. It was as though he'd simply selected them from a catalog and had them bottled into a quintessential male fragrance.

"Scary that that was twenty-five years ago."

Morgan did the mental math. "So, 1995?"

He pointed to Eleanor in the photo. "I can tell the decade by the height of my mom's hair. It was a sight to see in the eighties."

"I bet." Morgan pointed to one of the girls. She was nine or ten maybe. "Cora?"

He nodded, then drew her attention to the younger, fox-faced girl with golden hair, and a raven-haired boy who might have been thirteen. "Carlisle and David," he said, packaging them together. "It's a joke in our family, that David doesn't love anyone but himself. He loves Carlisle, though, 'cause she's his mini-me. They don't look alike, but trust me, inside they're made of the same stuff."

Morgan studied each of them in turn. They had the same stare. The way their eyes bored into the camera, it was almost as if they were challenging it. Daring it to call them out for something and yet not caring if it did.

"And who's this?" She pointed to a wild-eyed boy leaning over Clive's shoulder. He was wearing a striped T-shirt and a bulky Power Rangers wristwatch.

"The boy with the very unfortunate bowl cut, you mean?" He offered his hand for her to shake. "Bennett Reynolds."

"Morgan Mori," she said, though he already knew. He'd been the one to email her about the job.

"When do you get off the clock, Morgan Mori?"

She bit her lip. She could do this. "You tell me, boss. Though I believe the arrangement was for eight."

A wicked glint flashed behind Bennett's eyes. "Eight o'clock," he repeated. "You'll need a drink by then, trust me."

"Is that a bet?"

"It's a promise."

It was through Morgan's 50mm lens that she came face-to-face with each of the Reynolds clan. She led them out to the trellis, staging groups about four feet in front of it to capture the soft bokeh of the lights strung between the cedar boughs. She photographed Cora and her little family, adding in

Eleanor and Don, Carlisle, David, and Bennett, who stood at the edge of the frame, still holding his drink.

Carlisle was gorgeous in jewel tones, wearing a teal sweater dress belted at the waist and black tights. She looked like a snow angel come to life, her long golden ringlets cascading down her back. Morgan couldn't help but wonder if it was a wig. Everyone wore them these days, didn't they? David, on the other hand, was her antithesis, and that made him her complement. They were yin and yang together, light and shadow, dove and raven. When everyone else had dispersed, they posed to re-create an old photo from their childhood: Carlisle crossed her eyes and pretended to pick her nose while David looked on in animated disgust. Afterward, they huddled around Morgan's camera to see the photo appear on the LCD display.

"That's it, that's our Christmas card!" Carlisle laughed. They left Morgan to finish up before the sun went down, and later, when everyone was gathered inside by the fireplace, sleigh bells sounded.

Of course they got a freakin' Santa Claus, Morgan thought, as the children's eyes widened in excitement. They tumbled over one another as they ran down the hall, sliding in their socks when Santa Claus burst through the door with a festive "Ho, ho, ho!"

He was a convincing Santa—albeit nontraditional in a red patchwork robe trimmed with Celtic knots. A green beret with a shamrock perched atop his head. Toting a sack full of presents, he ambled in and plunked into the high-backed chair Cora had previously occupied. Then, he withdrew a pair of half-moon spectacles from an inside pocket and read the names off his list. Every single child received a present, which was damn impressive, considering how many kids there were.

Afterward, the kids took turns sitting on his lap and telling him what they wished for under the Christmas tree. Morgan captured every interaction, and when the last child had spoken, Santa gestured to her, bending his white-gloved finger. "And you, young lady. What do you want for Christmas?"

"Oh." Morgan gave him a dismissive wave.

"Come on, now." He patted his knee.

Morgan looked around. The chaos had quieted. The lights had dimmed. It had to be eight o'clock or close to it. She looked around, searching for someone to save her, but caught only Bennett's gaze. He sat at the end of the couch, a reflection of the firelight dancing in his green eyes. Morgan stared back, her brow raised, and lowered herself onto Santa's lap.

She bit her lip and prayed he didn't touch her.

"What's your name, young lady?"

"Morgan."

"Morgan." He sounded it out one syllable at a time. "What a lovely name."

"Thanks, I didn't choose it."

Santa chuckled. "What would you like for Christmas, Morgan?"

Sarcastic responses raced through her mind. A puppy? An Easy-Bake Oven? One of those fancy power lift recliners so her grandpa could hold on to a shred of his dignity instead of getting hopelessly stuck in the La-Z-Boy every night? That last one wasn't sarcastic. "A Butterfinger," she said.

Santa's eyes twinkled. "A Butterfinger?"

"King-sized."

"That depends. Have you been naughty or nice?"

Morgan froze. A shiver started at the base of her skull and trickled down her spine. It might have been the question itself, or the fact that his asking it made something pulse against the underside of her thigh.

Now finished and packed up for the night, and having said her goodbyes to the Reynolds family, Morgan stood on the porch where she'd stood hours earlier, contemplating the keyhole. She slid the key out of her cuff, and this time, as she approached the door, she heard a voice in the dark. "Looks like you're off the clock, Morgan Mori."

Tracy Koeper | Hungry Heart Photography

HANNAH MORRISSEY earned her bachelor of arts degree from the University of Wisconsin–Madison. She grew up on a farm in a small northern town and now lives with her husband and two pugs. *Hello, Transcriber* is her debut novel, inspired by her work as a police transcriber.